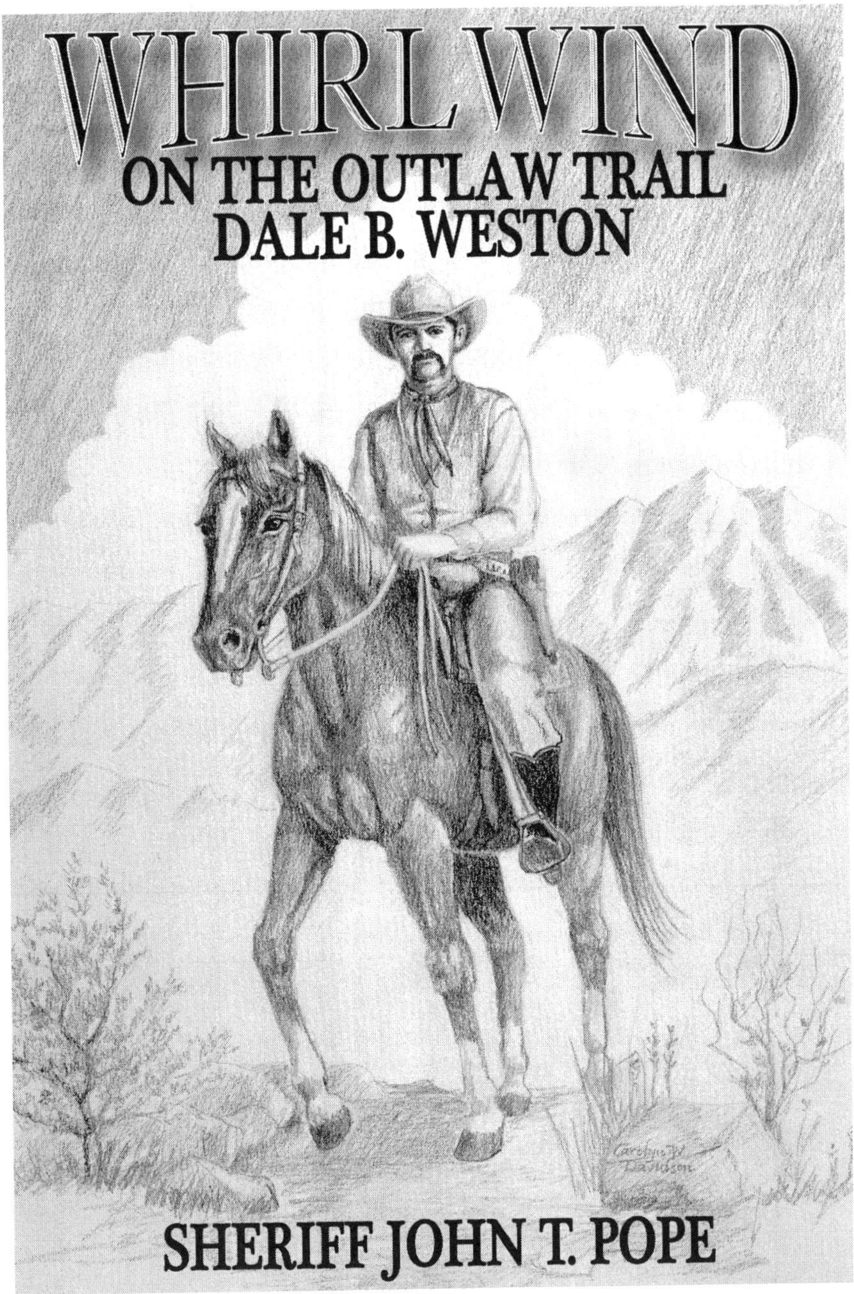

authorHOUSE®

AuthorHouse™
1663 Liberty Drive
Bloomington, IN 47403
www.authorhouse.com
Phone: 1-800-839-8640

First published by AuthorHouse 09/24/2011

ISBN: 978-1-4670-3611-5 (sc)
ISBN: 978-1-4670-3610-8 (hc)
ISBN: 978-1-4670-3609-2 (ebk)

Library of Congress Control Number: 2011916593

Printed in the United States of America

This book is printed on acid-free paper.

FORWARD

By June Marie W. Saxton

In July of 2010, my dad, Dale B. Weston, read my manuscript, *Into the Second Springtime* out loud to us as we traveled to Driggs, Idaho, for my daughter's softball tournament. We all loved to hear Dad read, and his laughter was always hearty. His encouragements for my writing were unsurpassed.

"I sure wish you'd write about Sheriff John T. Pope, Junie. That would be a story that everyone would want to read, and the neat thing is it would all be true!"

I conceded the fact that his story needed to be told, alright, and I had done a lot of research on this colorful character. He was a great, great uncle of my dad's, and an amazing person to learn about. Still, I was hesitant, worried about pairing historical facts into a story that could be read and enjoyed as a novel. "I don't know if it's in me to do all the research, and I don't feel like I'm sharp enough on the western, cowboy, old-fashioned lingo to do it."

"I could help you, maybe."

A brilliant idea! Dad *was* a cowboy, born seventy-five years too late. He walked the walk and talked the talk already! "Why don't you write this book, Dad?"

Laughter.

"No, I'm serious! You write this—get all the details down, and I can help you make it into a book. I can help edit and organize, you just write. I'll work with the publishers, take on that headache."

The car was quiet for a split second, but I could hear the cogs turning in my Dad's sharp mind. "Well maybe I will, then."

And the possibilities of such a project got us both excited. We chattered like magpies about this new inspiration for several miles. I was writing *Pirate Moon*, and was busy scheduling book signings for *Into the*

Second Springtime, but I told Dad that I could get really serious about our project just after Christmas.

"That'll give me time to write anyway."

So that's how this book came into Dad's mind. He took a trip to Vernal, Utah, not long after, and visited Red Creek, Brown's Park, Jarvie's Crossing, and traveled Six Mile Canyon from Vernal to Price. He was hot on the research trail, and he began filling notebooks. He was excited about it and called to read to me often, sharing with me.

"It's wonderful, Dad, but slow down a little bit. Nobody said you had to write this book all in a month!"

He laughed, but his enthusiasm didn't permit him to slow down a bit. The harvest season was filled with research and writing, and he was eager for me to catch up with my work. "I wonder how many type written pages this would be so far."

I was eager to type up his handwritten chapters to soothe his curiosities, but I was busy with work, Tahnee's basketball practices and games, shuffling sons in and out of the mission field, preparing for the holidays, and finishing my book signings. Poor father received too many excuses from me.

He took his first notebook to his sister, Anita Weston, in Garden City, Utah, and she set to work at her computer. Soon Dad knew how many pages of manuscript a whole handwritten notebook would equal. He was very excited. My Aunt Anita continued to type, or should I say, translate his penmanship. This saved me hours and hours of time. She typed the words precisely as Dad had written them, and then I would get the files from her and begin editing, careful not to overdo it, for my father really was a gifted storyteller, and his writing reflected his speech patterns. As I read, it sounded like he was sitting on a stool, spinning a story, just as it fell from his lips. I didn't want to over edit anything! I wanted my Dad's book to be his, and sound like him.

Dad was mostly finished with his story in about January, but he worried about a few details, and he kept wondering exactly how to end the book.

"Dad, the beauty of this whole thing is, we can change whatever you want changed, and it's easy to do."

He kept working at it—kept studying histories and adding colorful episodes here and there.

He went to Providence, Utah, to talk to his other sister, Carolyn W. Davidson, about illustrations and artwork for his book. He sat with me and perused her art blog, finding paintings and sketches that she already had done that would work for his story. We made a list of them. He was very eager to couple his writing with her artwork.

On March 24, I had a good conversation with Dad on the phone. He had written the prologue to the book, and he was immensely satisfied with it. "I just felt like these things needed to be added." He read the chapter to me, and I was tickled with his work as well. I agreed. The book would not have been complete without the added information.

"It's great Dad, and I am so proud of you!"

Dad laughed, as pleased by my encouragements as I had been of his. "I can't wait to see this done, but I don't know what to call yet it."

"I'm working on it fast and furious, and I bet the title will come to you."

"I wish I could just visit with John T. Pope and ask him, for sure, about some of this stuff."

As we talked, I noticed the rich timbre of my Dad's voice growing weaker. He'd had a cold, and I feared he'd stressed his voice with so much reading, but I so enjoyed our hour long conversation.

We got a phone call from my mother just after midnight. My Dad wasn't doing well, couldn't seem to get his wind. My husband and I raced to their home in Cokeville and helped him to the car. He didn't want to go to the hospital, but he really couldn't breathe, and so he was going . . .

Dad died just as we pulled up the hospital doors in Montpelier. He didn't want to go the hospital, and believe me; he didn't have to, apparently. Now . . . none of us were expecting or wanting that outcome, but as I stood over my Dad's body an hour later, weeping, I said, "Dad, I will finish this book for you! But you are going to have to help me! I guess you can go meet John T. Pope now, and clarify every question you had. I will change anything you want me to change, but you are going to have to let me know."

Oh the agony that accompanied those grey days—I kept chastising myself for putting my book project before Dad's. It hurt me in so many ways, and yet, I could not have had enough time to get it published anyway, even if I had gotten to it immediately. It's a process that takes time, but oh! Was I ever thankful that Dad had felt so inspired to hurry!

It was tough tackling the manuscript. It was so painful for me and my emotions were very raw, but after seven weeks or so, I felt very compelled to get it done, to live up to my word and keep my promises to Dad. I dove in. It was bittersweet, knowing he was gone, but still having his words. As I got lost in Dad's stories, it felt again like he was sitting on a stool in the corner, just talking away.

As I read, I would cry, "Dad, you're a genius!" He had so skillfully made history come alive! His book was better than a history, and more than a novel. It was a perfect pairing of the two—and it lived because it was in story form, and yet the information was wonderful! And best of all, it was a testament to my Dad's own testimony. His convictions, his beliefs, and his pride in his lineage and country were unmistakable. I had never before read such a rootin', tootin', cowboy shootin' book that uplifted me.

One day, just as I was about three or four chapters from the end of the book, I found a word that didn't make any sense to me. I decided to check the word against Dad's handwritten manuscript, and as I found the word, it was circled, and an arrow was drawn along the sentence, to the margin, and Dad's arrow continued up the margin to the top of the page. It said, "Insert Idaho." The word Idaho didn't make any sense, so I began rifling through his thick notebooks, hoping to find something. I did—in one of the other notebooks, toward the back, stuck in a section of blank pages, was a whole chapter! That was like winning the lottery—a whole chapter more of my Dad's precious words, what a treasure.

I started typing from my Dad's manuscript, and I was laughing at his humor. I laughed until tears streaked down my cheeks, and then I realized that my Dad was laughing with me, tickled that I was so invested in his story. His spirit stayed with me for the rest of that day, enlightening my mind, helping me make corrections. The title was given to me, and a few precious paragraphs were added. His wishes concerning the dedication page were made known.

I knelt in prayer, pouring my gratitude out to the Lord for His tender mercies, in allowing my Dad to complete his work. I was grateful for my family heritage and for Dad's preservation of this part of our history! I have had a few spiritual experiences in my life, but I must say that working on this book with my Dad has been the crowning pinnacle of them all.

So people often ask me which of my books is my own favorite, and I now answer, *Whirlwind on the Outlaw Trail*, which is not my book at all, but is the summation of tales spun by the greatest storyteller I have ever been permitted to know, my dad, Dale B. Weston. Enjoy!

Editor's Acknowledgements

I'd like to thank Shannyn S. Davis for the cover design. The boots and spurs that act as background on the book's cover were the author's, and so sentimental meaning is attached. Carolyn W. Davidson provided inspiring artwork and illustrations, and I appreciated the opportunity to work with her on this project. Thanks to Anita Weston for all of her work, transcribing the manuscripts, one notebook at a time.

Due to Dale's untimely death, not all works were cited, and I do not know if any quotes were directly taken from other sources. My apologies go to any contributing, unrecognized sources. I do know that Dad gleaned information and knowledge from the following list.

The Last Cowboy Sheriff, by Lora Sannes. (This is an unpublished history of John T. Pope to a granddaughter.)

Badges and Badmen, by Kerry Boren

The Outlaw Trail Journal

Silver Stars and Jail Bars, by Doris Karren Burton

The Outlaw Trail: a History of Butch Cassidy and his Wild Bunch, by Charles Kelly, Ann Meadows, and Dan Buck

Queen Ann Basset, Alias Etta Place, by Doris Karren Burton

Oral histories and lore of the Pope family, passed to the author from his grandfather, Royal Robert Pope, his uncle, Arden Pope, and his mother, Marie Pope Weston.

About the Artist

Carolyn Weston Davidson

Carolyn W. Davidson spent her childhood years on a cattle ranch in the Bear Lake Valley of northern Utah. She loved horses and riding.

Carolyn and her husband Ted make their home in Cache Valley, where they raised five sons. Each year they grow a big garden, and enjoy visits from kids and grandchildren. When there's work to be done, Carolyn is the first person to show up, but she's the last person to show off. Carolyn has always been actively engaged in the scouting program, and has received the prestigious Silver Beaver Award.

Carolyn's background in western artwork comes from a lifetime of living in the valleys of the Rocky Mountains, and a reverence for her western heritage. She captures the spirit of cowboys and horses, the innocence of children, majestic beauty of landscapes, animals, and nature, painting them all with respect for the diversities of creation. Carolyn is skilled in different mediums of artwork; oil, acrylic, pencil, ink, pastels, and watercolor.

Davidson's artwork is showcased on her artist's webpage at www.sagewaststudios.com.

She is a master calligrapher and she sells cards, prints, and original paintings.

For the Two of You . . .

This book is dedicated to my mother,
Marie Pope Weston.
She had me young and we grew up together.
No son has ever been prouder.

This book is also dedicated to my wife,
Pamela Porter Weston.
She's just as beautiful to me as she ever was!
I married the best.

Chapter One

Gunfire!

THE YEAR 1896 SHERIFF John T. Pope of Uintah County, Utah, rode alone on the trail of Butch Cassidy and his Wild Bunch. He made a pretty picture on his favorite horse, Old Shorty. As he sat the horse, he was straight and tall with shoulders thrown back. He wore a wide brimmed beaver hat pulled down low in front, and mule-eared, high heeled riding boots stuck closely in the stirrups. John modeled a black shirt tucked into jeans, pant legs tucked into boots, and a wide belt full of 44-40's.

His holster containing the colt's peacemaker was of his own design, cut low down by the trigger guard, with a safety loop that kept the gun in place. It could be swept up by the thumb during a quick draw which he had practiced every day since the time he was sixteen years old.

John's saddle was a form fitter with a longer tree than most saddles of the time. It was high backed and had high, wide swells. The saddle was custom ordered and made for him. The horn leaned a bit forward, compared with most form fitting saddles. It was worn and dark from the oil it had received, and had wide, long skirting. Saddlebags hung behind the cantle, and a slicker was rolled up and tied neatly on top. He was single rigged with a Winchester 44-40 rifle hanging in front of the saddle on the right side, and tied to the cinch ring at the bottom of the scabbard.

The saddle squeaked a bit as he rode along, and the spurs could be heard as a little more of a rattle than a jingle.

Old Shorty was a big horse. He wore number two shoes. His weight was about fourteen hundred pounds. He was out of a thoroughbred mare and a Percheron stud. Pope was positive this fourteen year old should have been retired, but John had broken him in as a colt, and they really made a good pair. The horse's hooves made little noise in the dust unless he hit a rock and then it could be heard from a ways away. Horse shoes on stone rang loudly.

Old Shorty was a pacer. He naturally took this gait and could keep it up all day long. A good traveling horse can walk about six miles per hour. Old Shorty paced about eight to ten miles per hour. He seemed in no hurry and didn't really labor to keep it up. Many times over the last eight years he had nearly killed travelling companions while trying to keep up with him. Other horses usually had to trot or lope to catch up.

As a colt Old Shorty was a roan, but he matured into a pretty, dark sorrel with a white strip in his face and four stockings. As he got older he kept getting more white hair. Now Old Shorty was giving the Wild Bunch fits because they were trying to distance themselves on their best horses and were getting outdone.

Sheriff Pope prided himself on being fair. He finally had a writ and warrant for Butch Cassidy, a man that he had treated with friendship—until now. He was going to serve the writ, but he heard Butch bragging, saying that he wouldn't go back to jail. He said he'd do whatever it took to remain a free man.

A few days earlier the outlaws had ridden west of Vernal, to the bar by the Strip, ready to party. Sheriff Pope sent a man out with the message that he had the writ for Butch's arrest and was coming that very morning to serve it. Pope warned, "If you want to have it out, okay."

When Sheriff Pope rode up to the bar that morning and went in the front door, he carried a sawed off shot gun in hand and was expecting a shoot out, or no telling what. Two men sat at the table with a bottle between them. The room was smoky and dirty. The bartender leaned on the bar, eyes bloodshot, empty beer bottles were everywhere. Somebody's shirt was crumpled on the floor in front of the bar, soiled with blood.

Sheriff Pope motioned with the shotgun, demanding, "You boys get over here!" They both jumped up and came around. "Who are you and why are you here?" The men were quick to spill names and conjure up excuses as to what business brought them to town. John T. had been informed that the outlaws had a lookout positioned to see if he *would* come, giving them a forty-five minute head start.

One of the young cowboys told the sheriff that the betting was about three to one that he wouldn't show up. The bartender said, "You better go home son, there are a dozen gunmen in that bunch and any one could take you."

Now, three hours later, Pope could tell by the tracks that he was catching up. This wasn't his first rodeo. He'd been up the creek and over the mountain—in fact the outlaw gunman had offered a reward of fifteen hundred dollars to anyone who could kill Pope. John had even heard rumors of a higher amount—that of four thousand dollars—as the price for his head.

Every instinct told him that they would try to ambush him. He was talking out loud to his horse. Sheriff Pope couldn't seem to bring himself to fear. The trail led to the rim of the canyon. He pulled up on the rim, looking at the trail going down to the bottom and then east along the White River. Willows grew along the bottom. Open sand seemed to reach up for several rods, extending for about a block. The rest of the canyon was full of green creosote bush.

"Shorty, old boy, what do you think? Should we follow through there, and take a chance of getting bushwhacked, or go around and cut tracks on the other side? If we do, we lose our advantage. They gain precious miles and time."

Shorty's ear twitched a response and John nodded. "Knowing Butch, I don't think he'll try it until I'm closer."

John considered his options for several moments, and then bowed his head. "Heavenly Father, you know I didn't try for this job. I didn't want it, but we've got to live here and it's time we have law and order. Please help me. Keep me safe for my wife and family's sake and my mother's sake as well, in the name of Jesus Christ, amen."

John challenged the canyon, and nudging Shorty, they descended. When they hit the bottom, the air was still, being protected from the wind. Mosquitoes came, and botflies. A horsefly bit Shorty in the nose. He jerked his head a bit each time.

Studying the tracks along the canyon bottom, Pope could see the horses he was following were struggling in the soft sand. Old Shorty, with a dislike for the bugs, actually picked up a bit, pacing along in the sand, and was even rocking the saddle with the increased gait. Pope's eyes were watching the white-grey rocks along the edge of the canyon, and then they would sweep ahead again. Botflies caused his horse to jerk again. He looked down and saw two big horseflies with their heads down and their tails up. John leaned down to kill the pests.

Bang! Bang! The shots rang as one rackety noise. Pain registered in the calf of John's leg. He felt his faithful old horse lurch, stumble, and go down. He managed to jerk his rifle free and get his feet out of the stirrups as his loyal companion fell. He was able to roll off and lay behind the horse, quickly crawling closer behind Shorty for cover. John T.'s leg was throbbing with a deep hurt. He knew he was hit but he told himself, "It's a long way from my heart." He looked down and wiggled his toes. The bone wasn't broken.

With his pocket knife he cut a stalk of greasewood so he could raise the saddle blanket a little, and propped it up. He could then see the rocks under it without being seen. He got the rifle into position and lay quiet, listening. All was quiet accept for the frogs along the river and the loud raspy rattle of flying grasshoppers. Normal nature sounds were returning now the shooting had stopped.

The sun began torturing. John turned his head, looking for his hat. It lay by his feet. It took a while, trying to slide it up with the toe of his good leg a few inches. Several minutes passed in a struggle to get his hat. He finally got his hands on it. He brushed dirt and sand off and bent the crown back up, shaping it with the crease; just the way he liked it. He saw the bullet holes in the back of the crown, and out the front near the top. Looking at the brim he noticed the hole that lined with the other holes in the center of the brim.

He realized in a flash that reaching down to slap a horsefly from Old Shorty's shoulder caused the outlaws' bullets to miss. In that second he remembered his prayer for safety. In his mind he formed the words, "Thank you, Father. You were doing your job, and now I'll try to do mine."

He had a lump in his throat when he thought of Old Shorty. Death was the only activity in which this faithful mount had ever let him down! His dad, Robert Pope, had been an instrument in starting the Percheron Association of Bear Lake. They had imported a large stud to try to put some size and quality into horses of the area for work or draft, as well as to handle deep snow and mountains, and Old Shorty had been the product of such breeding.

John continued to watch the rocks and mountains. He had picked a spot he thought would be used by ambushers, a long chunk of white cliff had fallen from above and stopped nearly at the bottom. He suspected this to be their position and started looking for the place they would have left their horses. He could see a couple of easy places in the willows that could have been used.

He knew at least two shots, and maybe three, had been fired. He knew at least two men, maybe three, were watching his dead horse and wondering if they had scored or not. They were within seventy-five to one hundred yards of him.

The members of the Wild Bunch fancied themselves good shots. They had confidence in their partners' shooting skills as well. They would congratulate each other for a job well done, but John T. knew with the sun beating down, these outlaws would be feeling terribly hung over from the big three-day spree, no breakfast, and being forced to run from a spot lawman just didn't go.

The young sheriff had patience to wait. He had learned from Indians in a lifetime of dealings with the red men, and cowboys, and his family. His mother was Sarah LeDuc Pope. She was as straight up the back as her boys. Sarah was gentle enough in her own way, but she didn't put up with nonsense. As he thought of her, he found himself grinning. She was the daughter of a French Canadian fur trapper and trader. She knew fur, and could grade, judge, and price it. She tanned pelts beautifully, and they could last through hot months till they could be shipped or sold. She spoke several dialects of the Sioux Indian language, and she could sign and communicate with them all. During those early years, his mother's trading added greatly to their living.

Brigham Young called her to train to be a midwife. She learned, and by now she had delivered more than four hundred babies without losing a mother or babe. John's thoughts turned to his own life. He made three hundred dollars a year as sheriff. His mother charged only five dollars to deliver a baby. For that fee, she would stay and help with work for a week or so. Families usually paid her in kind—a couple of hundred pounds of flour, or a lamb or some other commodity worth five dollars because money was really scarce.

Time was passing, and he heard nothing more from the outlaws; no rustling, no movement. He kept his eyes on the rocks, and he began thinking of all kinds of things. He was sheriff of an area that had been an outlaw hideout for many years. This was a sanctuary from the law. It was located on the Outlaw Trail, extending from Canada to Mexico. In this immediate locality, south of the San Rafael Swell, and through the "Hole in the Rock" to John D. Lee's Ferry on the Colorado River, south across outlaw flats, Hanksville, across the Dirty Devil was Robbers' Roost. Behind him, where he started his chase this morning, was the Strip with its red light districts, shanty town, and bootleggers selling their whiskey to Indians from Ouray and Uintah Indians Reservations, and soldiers from the fort, cowboys, miners, and others. The Strip was famed for sinning and riotous pleasure. From the Strip, the outlaw trail led south and west into Nine Mile Canyon. Indian ruins were evident the canyon's full length, running along the great rock walls to Price.

From the direction Butch had taken this morning, John T. couldn't tell whether they would veer to Brown's Hole, synonymously called Brown's Park, or if they would head into Colorado. It looked a little like they'd cut for Rifle, Colorado.

Wham! Another bullet slammed into his horse. That jerked Pope out of his reverie and made his heart race and little. The outlaws were running out of patience. He could see a hat raised over the rock on a stick. A few minutes later another shot slapped home. Pope could hear their voices a bit, but he couldn't see them.

A couple of minutes later, two men came into sight. They held rifles ready and began coming toward him. Pope cocked the rifle. A third man showed behind the rock. He had laid his rifle out on the rock and stood watching. Immediately, John drew his bead on the last man's head and slowly squeezed the trigger. The head disappeared behind the rock. The two men who were coming down were caught away from cover. John's second shot took the man on the right as two more shells hit his horse. John T.'s third shot killed the third man as he dove for cover. The air stilled before he dared move. He reached around, pulled three shells from his belt and loaded the rifle again. What to do now?

Keeping his bad leg straight, using his rifle and the dead horse, he managed to get to his feet. Then, he hobbled up to the rock and made sure of this guy. He was dead, and Pope's bullet, had taken him squarely between the eyes, leaving him unrecognizable. Both eyes were bulging out of the sockets, and the top and back of his head was gone.

Pope took the man's gun belt, twin 45 colts, with four and a half inch barrels, and went through his pockets one by one. In one pocket he found three twenty dollar gold pieces, a nickel and two dimes. No clue yet of his name. Grabbing the gun belt and extra rifle, he started back down the hill. About half way to the next dead outlaw, he stopped and was sick for a while with dry heaves—due to the shock of the day, the loss of his horse, his own injuries, and the corpse's awful gore.

As soon as Pope turned the next outlaw over, he knew him, Ed Swain, a known killer and bad man. Hobbling closer, Pope recognized Dude Jolly; these were two of Cassidy's gunmen. Pope pulled their gun belts off and went through their pockets. Dude must have won some in a card game. In his front pocket he had a small leather poke—a leather bag with a draw string, it carried one hundred and sixty dollars in bills and coins. Ed wasn't so flush with about thirty-five cents, but he had a brand new 1886 model Winchester rifle in 45-90. He had probably been spending his cash. The sheriff left their pocket knives.

Pope went in search of the place they left the horses and picked up a club for a crutch as he moved forward. About fifteen minutes later, he found them staked out on grass. He bridled a coupled bay gelding, and leading the other two, he went back. The horses got a whiff of blood. He couldn't get them very close. What to do? The sun was setting.

He knew with great effort he could put a coat over the horses' heads, blinding them so he could lift a man on, tie him belly down over the saddles. But these were limp and dead weight. John T's leg was hurting, and he didn't want their blood all over himself. That made up his mind. Besides, he only had three horses. He didn't want to walk and lead, so instead, he put rifles in scabbards, and hung pistols on saddle horns, tying them with saddle strings.

He piled rocks over and around the dead man behind the rock. He did the same for the others, hobbling back and forth with rocks until they were buried shallow, but rock would make it hard for predators to get at the bodies. A horny toad blinked from the pile.

John removed his hat and bowed his head. "Heavenly Father, Thou didst deliver my enemies into my hand. I thank thee. Now because I'm hungry and wounded, and it's dark, I have decided to save the county the expense of burying them. Help their families if they have any. Do the best for their souls that you can. Please forgive any ignorance, in the name of Jesus Christ, amen."

He refused to leave without his own saddle so he un-cinched and put a lariat on the saddle horn. This little bay backed up and balked before he loosed it much. Old Shorty was laying on the cinches and stirrup. Finally he pulled it loose by going forward. John T. then changed saddles, leaving that one. He put saddlebags over the seat and tied them also. He tied up the extra rifle. He nearly bawled as he left Old Shorty and started home. "Goodbye old mate."

The little bay seemed awful small. He had a running walk, but his trot was way too rough for John's sore leg. It seemed like he had been riding all night before he came in sight of the lights in Vernal. He circled around and came up on his mother's house, to the corral and barn. He opened the gate and let all the horses file in, unsaddling them as each one came through the gate. He climbed on a stack of hay and pitched enough hay to last the night.

Finally John walked up to the porch door, stepped inside, and knocked on the inside door. There was no response so he opened the door and stepped in. He struck a match and lighted a lamp on the table. Carrying the lamp, he went to his mother's room.

"Mother?"

About the third time he spoke, she answered and got right up, pulling on her gown as she came into the kitchen. She was a great doctor; endowed with healing intuitions and willing to be guided by the spirit. She treated gunshot wounds, set broken bones, and pulled teeth. John needed his leg fixed, and something to eat, but he mostly needed his mother. She brought in the little wash tub and set it by a chair. The water in the reservoir on the stove was still warm. Sarah carried a couple of pans full to the tub and tried to help him out of his boot, but the bloody stocking was stuck to the inside of it. She soaked the blood-stuck sock until it came loose, and then found his father's bootjack. John took off his spurs, and with encouragement, finally pulled the boot off as well. The leg was swollen, red and ugly.

Sarah's brows rose, but she maintained calm and gentle discipline, never allowing challenges to betray her confidence in fixing them. At all times she refused hysterics—knowing the harm of fear. She spoke in soft gentle tones, eyes smiling at her son. "When was the last time you had anything to eat?"

Sarah fixed breakfast while John soaked the wound, rinsing it with her medicine. He told her about being ambushed and losing Old Shorty. He left out the part about settling accounts with his assassins. He didn't bother to tell anyone in fact. (A short time later Old Shorty, a saddle, and two graves were found by Randy Jones who was like a loud speaker telling everyone.)

"John, do you know who I sympathize with in the Bible?" John shrugged, not knowing where the conversation was going. Sarah's voice was quiet, but she continued, "David's mother—what fear must have gripped her heart as her boy faced the Philistine army." The room was quiet except for the sound of eggs frying on the stove. "But in her heart I'll bet she knew that her son was raised up to conquer Goliath and those like him. He was foreordained to do the deed. But I bet David's mother hurt for him just the same. Every once in awhile the world needs a David."

The tender words rang home, drawing tears to John's eyes. He didn't say anything, but surely it was true—he was facing corruption on a lawless frontier. "Did the Philistines hide behind trees and rocks Mother? Were they back-shooters?"

"No, they hid behind a giant."

"I reckon that's what I'm up against, alright."

After breakfast, a bath, and skilled bandaging, John went to bed and didn't wake up 'til eleven o'clock the next day. When he did stir, his mother, Sarah LeDuc Pope, helped him out to his chair again to bandage his leg. She poured whisky on both sides of the wound.

"Didn't that hurt?" Sarah studied her son's face.

"No."

She smiled and waited. Suddenly it did burn, and badly! Dr. Pope put on a new clean bandage. She handed him his socks, all freshly laundered, and his pants as well. Sarah found an old pair of ankle high lace-up shoes of his dad's to wear until he healed. Now he was cleaned up and was nearly normal. He would dare go home to a concerned, beautiful wife, and throw his hat in, at least.

Charlotte Ann Stock Pope was a woman with one of the hardest jobs in the world . . . she was the wife of John T. Pope. To be wife to the lawman would be a worry, but this good looking, fearless hunk thought he could out draw, out shoot, outride, and win over the most feared, hunted outlaws in America. Not only was he sheriff with a price on his head by the lawless element, he was the first lawman to be brave enough to ride into Brown's Hole alone. If that wasn't enough, he filed on a homestead on Red Creek, right in the middle of the Hole. When he rode away she never knew when she would see him again—whether he was chasing outlaws or improving his homesteads, prospecting, hunting, or what.

It was hard for her to hold her emotions in check. She had a young family to tend. She also had a big garden that she had to weed and water, as well as two cows to milk. Charlotte got angry and turned the old sow and little pigs out so she didn't have that chore, and the chickens had the run of the yard.

Charlotte was hanging clothes on the line when she saw John come around the corner of the house. She squealed and ran to him, throwing both arms around his neck. She hung on to him and sobbed a few minutes. All of a sudden she pushed back, and looked at his handsome, innocent, smiling face, she asked, "Where have you been? What have you done to you leg?"

John pulled her close before she could say thing else, and kissed her, tenderly at first, and then hungrily. She struggled against that for a minute and then surrendered and responded in kind. She found herself in his arms as he carried her to the bedroom for a good and proper hello.

When John and Charlotte came out of the bedroom, they were talking and laughing. It was alright. The kids came home and ran to their dad, and it was at least an hour of roughhousing with children that worshiped their father. The scurry of chores and supper, and mundane evening tasks lasted until the lanterns were doused and the sun was soundly sleeping.

Moon gleamed through the window. Charlotte sighed and rolled on to her side. "So how many men did you kill this time?"

"I didn't say that I had killed them."

"You can fool a lot of people, John T. Pope, but you can't fool me. Anybody that even made a remark about Old Shorty would have been in trouble. How many?"

John hedged, but realized how many graves would be found and answered, "A couple more—in self defense." Surely nobody needed to know that one of the graves held two outlaws.

As an eight year old boy, he and his friend, Edwards, watched as a war party of Bear Hunter Indians ran two men, both neighbors, out of the mouth of Smithfield Canyon where they were hauling wood and logs. They were making a run for the settlement. First their team was killed. These men took refuge behind the load but were soon shot so full of arrows they looked like human pin cushions. As these boys crouched in sagebrush, they watched as Indians stripped off their clothes and scalped and mutilated the naked bodies. After the Indians had their way with the men, John's father and other men came to help. The Indians retreated and were chased a ways. While they chased, John T. and his friend ran down to the victims, thus seeing they were mutilated. Eyes had been poked out, genitals cut off, hands severed, legs and feet off. He learned in this manner the Indians crippled these men so they couldn't make it to the happy hunting ground.

Charlotte knew that this incident in young John T.'s life had indelibly marked him. It set him on this path. That winter Captain Connors of California Volunteers and the greatest lawman ever, Porter Rockwell, fought the bloodiest battle ever fought west of the Mississippi River, measuring by the lives that were lost. After the Battle of Bear River, the wounded and frozen were hauled over to Franklin where they were doctored and bandaged up. The dead soldiers were loaded in covered wagon boxes, loaded on sleighs, and they started for Salt Lake City. That night they stopped in Smithfield. Young John went out and coaxed the guard to let him see inside one of the covered wagons. Reluctantly, he was shown dead soldiers, frozen in grotesque positions, piled on top of each other.

Young Pope asked, "What are they gonna do with their stuff?"

The guard didn't know.

John said, "We could really use that soldier's pistol. He's not going to use it anymore."

The guard looked around, then stepped up on the sleigh tongue and reached in, unsnapped the holster, and pulled the pistol out, handed it to John T. and said, "Don't tell anybody. Hold this under your coat."

So Charlotte's husband John T. had carried a gun from a young age! When she married John in 1879 in Fish Haven, Idaho, her bishop had interviewed them extensively. Upon learning he had killed men before, the bishop became alarmed. At that time, Charlotte heard John say he had killed five men. The bishop threw a huge fit and preached a long sermon to them, himself being ignorant to the reasons surrounding the killings. John was then angry enough to kill a Mormon bishop. After that incident, John T. would never tell a soul of killing or about the shootouts in his life. Charlotte knew all of this before she married him. She just wished she could stop this way of life before she lost her mind, or his life.

They owned a small farm in Vernal with a corral, outbuildings mostly, small log barn, chicken coop, pig pen, a good water right, and a two-holer outhouse, fifty yards or so on the way to the barn. Charlotte had a comfortable house. It was a two room log house to start with. John T, his dad, and brothers, working together, hauled the logs for her house as well as their own homes. Now he had bought lumber and hired a couple of neighbors to build a front porch and pantry, plus two more rooms on the back. She had a well and pump on the front porch.

They had taken a wagon to Price two years ago and hauled a whole load of stoves back with them. When they moved here four years earlier, all she ever heard the area called was Ashley. Now most people called it Vernal.

Charlotte knew she was better off than most women. Maybe she just wanted John home all the time. Probably she saw how other women looked at him and that they would be glad to trade places with her. She knew this, and she loved him, and liked him, but he annoyed the hell out of her when he'd stay around for more than a few days.

The first thing he put on in the morning was his hat. After his pants, that big pistol was next. He wore it continually, even to church. In the winter, or cold weather, he'd put on his coat, then the pistol on the outside, ready to hand.

When they were first married, before the kids came, she used to ride with him. Sometimes they would just ride along the foothills above Fish Haven to get a chicken or two for supper or Sunday dinner. The first time a sage grouse flew up he grabbed his pistol and killed the chicken. It happened so fast, she hadn't had time to have things register in her mind.

Her horse had shied back, and she had fallen off. Then two more had flown up, and he shot them both in two shots. No question, her husband was the fastest and best shot in Bear Lake. Charlotte's thoughts tuned to the fact that they hadn't done anything like that for a long time. Maybe and probably she was a woman about to lose her mind.

John's leg was bruised and sore but healing fast. That morning, he was up early, had a breakfast of eggs, warmed up ranch potatoes, and his usual three or four cups of coffee. As usual when he was home, they said the blessing on the food and made a plea for safety and blessings for all.

He had milked and done chores before breakfast which was also normal when he was home. Before he left the house, he stepped up behind her. She was busy with her hands in the dish pan. He put a hand on each of her shoulders, bent down and kissed her on the cheek, and thanked her for a good breakfast and great night. He continued to hold her shoulders so she couldn't turn. Then he kissed her cheek again, sliding the affections to her neck, below her ear, and the back of her neck. She was feeling a swelling of passion building when he let go and walked from the kitchen, leaving her once again with a confusion of thoughts teetering between annoyance and a rush of romantic love.

He didn't say where he was going. But when she stepped outside to throw the dishwater out, she saw him walking toward the canal with a shovel. Relief went through her. He'd be here a while at least. She watched as he took a cut out in the canal and started the garden irrigation stream down the town ditch, and then returned to his work. He stayed that morning and irrigated the garden and weeded while waiting for the water to soak down the rows.

The potato patch looked good—not many weeds because John's brothers Rock and Marcellus had been over to cultivate them several times, pulling the cultivator up and down the acre of potatoes. This killed the weeds in between the plants as well as hilled fresh dirt around the base of the potatoes, getting rid of most of the weeds.

There were lots of squirrels in the pasture next to the garden. John noticed they had been helping themselves, so he ran the water out onto the pasture. The water moved slowly, but as it moved it filled up squirrel holes, forcing the squirrels to come to the surface to get air and find another place. As they did so, they were immediately dispatched with the colt .44. Each time John killed one, he practiced the draw. Charlotte watched from the window, actually enjoying the show. Her husband's practiced skill drew goose bumps to the surface of her flesh.

People in Vernal knew Sheriff Pope was home, and gunshots were normal and a comfort for many people of the area who had lived there before the Popes began putting Vernal off limits to the outlaws. The Pope Family worked together. They were a hard headed, stiff backed bunch. They weren't big men. John T. was about five foot, ten inches, and weighed about one hundred sixty to one hundred eighty pounds, depending on how regular his meals were, but the family didn't take any pushing around.

That afternoon he gathered up the guns and saddle bags and things that had been taken from the recently departed outlaws, and locked them in the jail. He went through saddle bags and still didn't find a clue to the identity of the one man. He looked the 45.90 over and decided to try it one day. He knew Butch carried one. If he could get a box of ammo from the post that would really be good. The Gatling Guns had fired 45.90 ammo.

John rode the little bay horse back toward home, then rode around to see what his brothers were doing. He found them unloading a big load of alfalfa in Rock's barn with a Jackson fork. His dad was pulling the whip cart with old Jack and Rowdy. Marcellus climbed out of the barn after the last of the load was stacked. Rock was the Jackson Fork man. Marcellus' eyes and nose were running from hay fever. They were all glad to see him, and they stood and talked for thirty minutes or so.

John's brothers and father were his deputies when he was out of town or needed help. They were all glad to hear that Cassidy had decided to run rather than shoot it out. None of his family thought anybody could out draw or out shoot John T., but they were really concerned because he was outnumbered. Some of the men he was after were back shooters and murderers.

Chapter Two

Earning a Reputation

IF THE POPES WEREN'T here trying to get each other's hay stacked and enough food grown for the whole family then one of them would have ridden with him with no fear at all for themselves. As John rode back toward home, he was thinking of this.

He remembered the time when his dad and brothers had jailed Matt Warner, Bill Wall, and LeRoy Colman, and defended them and the jail from the townspeople who would have lynched them. They were on the one hand, and on the other was Butch Cassidy, the notorious leader of the Wild Bunch, who wanted to get them free. The Pope's had sent a man to Brown's Park to get John from his ranch on Red Creek.

Chuck Atwood came loping up to the house yelling, "There's hell to pay in Ashley Valley. There's gonna be war! Shots have been fired. Wake up and saddle up. You are needed bad!"

Chuck was excited and jabbering about everything. He said the river was too high. Pope saddled Old Shorty and had no worries of the river when riding him. He gave a couple of dollars to Chuck and asked him to stay on and irrigate a patch of his alfalfa, as well as finish the fence around it to keep out the neighbors' stock.

Since Chuck's horse was all in, he couldn't have kept up to Old Shorty anyway. Then Pope mounted up and paced off to an adventure that would test his reputation. John rode to the river.

The ferry man was still on his side of the river. He hadn't dared take it back across. He said he came close to capsizing Chuck when he ferried him over. The river had raised at least a foot since then.

"The old river is crazy," he said.

John turned Old Shorty and rode up river watching water and the other bank. The ferryman followed.

"You aint gonna try to do what it looks like you're thinking, are you? Tell me you won't try! It's impossible. It'll wash you to California, but you'll be drowned. Please don't!"

Pope dismounted, undid the throat latch on the bridle, and then slipped the headstall over Shorty's ears, dropping it down a ways. He waited 'til Shorty spit out the bit. Then he slipped the bit behind his chin and replaced the headstall and did the throat latch back up. Shorty now had a bridle without the bit. He tied the reins around the small of his neck. Then, he unbuckled his belt and hung it on the saddle horn and tied it in place. Pope finally turned to face the ferry operator.

"I can do this safely. The Shoshone Indian boys I used to play with in Randolph showed me how to cross Bear River when it was high and flooding. Horses are all good swimmers. The thing that gets most men in trouble is, they ride into deep water while sitting up, holding onto the bridle reins to control their mount. If they try to correct his direction or whatever, it puts pressure on the bit, dipping the horse's nose under. It can panic even the gentlest old saddle horse. Once panic sets in anything can happen . . . sometimes panic kills both horse and rider. The other trick is to judge the river, riding upstream for enough of a ways so that you come out on the other side where your horse can walk out. Bog in mud, or get stuck where banks are too steep to climb is another bad mistake. Indian boys all know this—just us stupid whites that have more education than intelligence that don't know how to cross a river."

Pope turned around, and took hold of the rigging. He kissed to Old Shorty, and he walked into the river. In a few short steps they were swimming. Another short way and they were being swept downstream fast. When they were in between the large swells and waves, they were out of sight of shore, but when they were carried up on a swell they were visible to watchers on the shore. John T. thought for a couple of minutes he had misjudged his river because they were being swept down fast. They then came up on a swell, and he saw they were close. Bless Old Shorty! He was a powerful swimmer, and they soon started to walk out on the bottom. They walked up to the ferry cabin.

While John bridled his horse, the two men who were waiting for the ferry on that side ran up. "Man that was exciting! I never knew anybody could cross when it was high like this."

The other chimed in, "Mister, we thought you wuz a gonner! I guess if you can cross, there's no need for us to sit here and wait for the ferry to come back. We'll just swim her."

Pope sat down on the porch steps and asked, "Would you help me, please, to pull my boots off?"

The man stepped around and straddled Pope's leg. Bending down, he got a good grip on the boot just below the spur. Pope put his other foot against the man's butt and pushed. The boot gradually slid off. It took his sock part way with it, so Pope pulled the sock off, wringing a bunch of water out of it. The man dumped about a glass full of water out of the boot. Then they repeated the process on the other leg. The other fellow handed him a towel that was hanging outside the door by a wash basin. John dried his feet and hands and dried his boots as good as he could. As he pulled his boots on, he looked at the fellows and thanked them. And then he said, "Unless you know how your horses handle in the water very well and have had experience, I would wait for the ferry."

He buckled his artillery around his middle. One man saw the badge fastened to the belt. He asked, "Are you a federal marshal or something?"

"I'm John T. Pope, sheriff of Uintah County."

Pope swung stiffly into the saddle and started the long, wet ride up Crouse Canyon and over the mountain. As the sun went down, he gave Shorty his head and said, "Take me home," and he did.

Pope dozed most of the way. He rode past the jail. No lights shone out. There were no lights at his house, but his mother had a light on, and so he stepped down and went in and knocked lightly. His mother answered the door immediately.

"Oh I'm glad you're back! Your brothers and dad have had a job!"

"I heard. I just got in from the Hole. You were the only one in town with lights."

"Oh, there's a Wilkes family down near Myton. Their little boy's horse ran away with him. He wound up with a broken arm and some bad cuts. They hauled him clear over here because they didn't trust the post doctor. I got his arm set and splinted, cleaned up the cuts, gave him a bunch of stitches, and they took him back home. They just left a few minutes ago. They woke me about two o'clock. I started some water to heat for tea, so sit up and I'll fix us a bite of breakfast."

John tipped the chair back on two legs and visited with his mother. He knew he was home. As he was leaving, he put his arms around her and told her he loved her.

Pope knew members of Cassidy's gang were around town, watching the jail. There had been at least six attempts to kill him since the reward was offered for his death. So far he had been protected by divine help. As he walked to his horse, he pulled the sawed off shotgun from the roll behind his saddle, leaned against the saddle, and reached up with his left hand and took his hat off. He bowed his head for a few seconds, forming words with his thoughts. He tanked God for helping him across the Green River, and for home, and for these people he loved. He asked to be guided in what to do, and asked for protection. He led Old Shorty around the house to the corral, unsaddled and fed him. The town ditch ran through a corner of the corral so he always had a drink.

About four horses were tied at a rail across the street in front of the store. He recognized two as belonging to neighbors in the Hole, and sometime members of the Wild Bunch. It was too early for the store to be open unless the Wild Bunch wanted it open. So he concluded they were watching the jail from the side window.

No matter which way he approached the jail from, somebody could get a shot at him. On inspiration, he slipped across the street quickly, pulling slip knots loose on two horses. He started for the jail, walking between their horses. It took a ways to get them to walk to his side instead of behind him, but a bit of prodding in the belly with the shotgun and a jerk or two on the bits convinced them nicely. As he reached the incline up to the jail, he saw his deputized family members had dragged some logs up and made a low barricade around the jail. His dad, Robert Pope, sat in a chair in front of the door with a rifle across his knees. John turned the horses loose, vaulted over the logs, and stepped on the boardwalk. His dad stood up with a big calloused hand reaching out for a shake.

"Let's get inside before somebody shoots us. You ought to stay out of sight! I don't want to lose my only dad."

"If anybody tries to hurt my boys or my family, they've got to come over me to do it." They stepped inside. Marcellus had his stocking feet up on the desk and was slouched way down in the chair, head back, mouth open, sound asleep. Rock was asleep on the only cot in the room.

"Sleeping on the job, I see."

Both brothers came up, and there was about five minutes of happy banter and laughing. Someone yelled from the cell, "Shut up out there!

They wouldn't let us sleep last night, now you're starting this infernal noise already this morning. It's still dark back here, so let us sleep."

The men started a fire and pulled a large sack of salt pork down from a nail. Somebody sliced up meat. They dug four or five spuds out of a sack and washed them off a bit and sliced a big old cast iron fry pan full of spuds to fry with a chopped onion, a bunch of salt and pepper, and a big dipper of grease from the pork they had been eating. The other pan had the pork and they visited noisily while cooking breakfast for the prisoners as well as themselves. Another handful of new coffee grounds went in with the old and the big black pot was filled with water.

"Think that'll be strong enough for ya?" Marcellus asked.

"I don't know, but it'll be hot and bitter enough."

John T. asked, "Why was it so noisy around here last night? Did somebody have a bottle or something?"

"Most of the men in town got drunk last night. Yesterday afternoon, a couple of our dear neighbors stopped by the jail to see how we were getting by. They were afraid we'd let Butch's gang have them since Butch's bunch had been prowling around the night before with a lot of shots fired. It's a good thing we hauled these logs up. We stayed low and the only casualty was one of their own horses. The fine citizens of this fair city informed us that they would come for the prisoners last night and take care of the problem before they escaped. Dad said it didn't sound like they had much faith in us. They thought if superman Sheriff Pope was here, we might hold out, but we had no chance against Cassidy's Wild Bunch."

"When it got dark last night, Dad slipped out and brought Dick and all us boys. We snuck in, and we could hear the party going on down town. It got really noisy while they built up their courage to come get the prisoners."

"We put our lamps out and went outside and spread along the stockade, sat down with our backs against it, and listened to them come. The prisoners had been coaxing for their guns and Rock said if we couldn't stop them, he'd hand the guns to them. They were shaken."

"The men had four or five lamps and a few horses with ropes. They were really gonna do it. There must have been thirty big, brave, drunken men. The leaders stopped just out of the barricade and yelled, 'Popes!' Then again, only louder, it sounded like Jerry Sandcaster."

Rock nodded his head, eager to join in the telling. "Marcellus said, 'What do you want?' in a conversational quiet voice, and suddenly the noise stopped—you could hear a pin drop. 'We'll take your prisoners,' Jerry said. Again, Marcellus answered quietly, 'When Matt Warner came to town to get help for those wounded men after the shootout, there wasn't one man jack of you that would go help at all. Well, we got back with the wounded men, Dick Staunton, David Milton, and Ike Staunton *without* your help! Before Warner and Wall were disarmed and locked up, none of you wanted any truck with them either. Now they are disarmed and locked up. You've got more gall than a pack of coyotes.'"

Rock continued, with a particular sparkle in his eye, "Wilford Hansen yelled from the back of the mob, 'Out of the way, Pope! Maybe we won't string you up with them.' Marcellus snarled in a loud voice this time, 'I'll kill the first man that tries to cross this wall!'At that time five more men pushed the weapons over the wall and cocked them."

John T. grinned at his brother, raising his brows with interest. "And?"

"Dad said, 'We got buckshot loaded in these shotguns. It's nice you brought lamps so we can see where to blow holes in this mob.'" Rock paused to chuckle. "The mob started backing up slowly. Somebody said, 'Looks like an army.' Another said, 'I'll bet the sheriff's back.'"

Marcellus chimed in, parroting the nighttime conversation, "I don't want 'em to shoot that buckshot my way."

"And a real squeaky voice stated, 'Hell, a lot of men could be killed kinda quick around here if they open up with those shotguns.'" Robert mimicked, trumping the tale with a merry laugh while thumping two of his sons on their shoulders.

The spuds and meat were done. They dished up for breakfast. John T. said, "I already had breakfast. I'll drink another cup though." They only had three plates in the jail, so Popes ate, scoured the plates off, and then fed the prisoners. Everyone but Robert, Rock, and Marcellus had gone home after the mob broke up, while still under the cover of darkness.

After breakfast they put a pot of beans and salt pork on the stove. They sliced an onion in with it and added a bunch of pepper—bachelor cooking for sure, cowboy staples.

The sheriff said, "I want to be filled in more about what's going on, but, I worked long and hard yesterday on my place. I came seventy miles, swam across the high and wicked river and rode all night. I'm going to sleep."

He borrowed a coat from the rack and a blanket off the cot. "It is way too hot in here with that fire." He ducked out the door, keeping his form bent low. He turned the corner of the jail and sat down where the shadows from the morning sun were still long. He spent a couple of minutes on hands and knees throwing rocks out of the way and smoothing the ground. He spread the blanket and unbuckled his pistol. He began to work those boots off again. They were mostly dry. The leather was starting to curl and crack. He rolled the coat and used it for a pillow. John undid his Levis a bit for comfort. He went to sleep holding his pistol.

When he woke, the sun was cooking him. He arose, picked up everything and slipped inside.

"Have you been saving the pork grease? I need to oil my boots. They were soaked in the river yesterday."

Marcellus found him a quart of grease, a rag, and a cup. John's dad took one boot and he took the other. They tore the rag in two and poured the cup full. Each would soak a corner of their rag and work it on his boot. The warm bacon grease soaked into the leather, turning it dark and softening up it up until it almost felt stretchy.

Robert said, "It will be water proof for a while anyway."

John T. took paper and pen back to the cells to get sworn statements from the prisoners and the whole story from Marcellus. This took the afternoon.

May 7, 1896, a gun battle had taken place above Dry Fork, high in the Uinta Mountains. E. B. Coleman had been up there hunting a gold mine and had found a rich silver and gold float. Now he was back trying to find the source it was coming from. He needed to stake a claim.

Pope knew, as most of the people in the area knew, of the Rhoades Mine. It was the source of gold for the early minting of gold in Salt Lake City, when money was so scarce that Chief Walker, keeper of the sacred yellow iron, had given the gold to Brigham Young and the LDS church. Brigham Young had introduced Rhoades to Walker, and the wily chief agreed to let Rhoades get one pack horse load at a time. This Rhoades did, hauling it to Salt Lake City.

Several others were killed by Indians getting too close or nosey about it. The reservation was right there. There were sacred burial grounds as well as the yellow metal to protect. The Wild Bunch had all done their share of riding and looking, and everyone seemed to be a prospector.

Now E. B. Coleman claimed to be working with Judge John W. Burton of Salt Lake City, that he had come to locate their claim. Pope felt they were probably both working for a mining company in Alta, Utah, and that they would deny this to keep clear of the murder charge on their engineer.

When Coleman and his companion, Bob Swift, took their mining utensils into the mountains, three men had been watching and thought they would follow closely so if they found any thing, they could file on it themselves. These men were David Milton, an Ike and Dick Staunton. They were well known and liked. They had been in on a few deals with the Wild Bunch, but were mostly fun loving and going straight of late. So they followed the prospectors into the mountains closely. When Coleman and Swift camped at night, Milton and the Staunton's would camp close by. So day by day they traveled around without going where they planned to stake their claim. Coleman finally walked into their camp to see what could be done. Dave Milton had a grudge against Coleman.

Milton said, "You robbed my father of a mine in Deadwood, South Dakota, years ago."

Coleman said he might be able to settle the score by cutting him in as a partner in the new mine. When that failed, they said he could buy them off with paying them a large sum of money—blackmail. Coleman's partner, Swift, stayed in camp while Coleman went to town to borrow money. He borrowed one hundred dollars from a storekeeper in Vernal, but couldn't raise the three hundred dollars they wanted.

Stepping into the saloon he met Matt Warner and William Wall, gamblers and gunmen. He offered Matt one hundred dollars to move his camp in the Uinta Mountains to Matt's Diamond Mountain Ranch for the winter. Matt accepted the deal, and Wall went along for the ride. Coleman wanted to scare his tormentors and blackmailers away. With known gunmen, they rode out of town and kept at it 'til morning.

When they were riding into camp, Warner didn't notice Coleman had faded way back. Suddenly a shot rang out, killing Matt's horse. Matt jerked his rifle from the boot and jumped behind an aspen and started shooting. He shot into the tent a few shots, hitting David Milton while he still lay in bed. Dick Staunton came running to see what the fuss was about, and was shot down before he knew what was happening.

Ike Staunton had stepped out first to relieve himself. Seeing horses and riders coming in, he thought the Indians were protecting the gold again. He grabbed a gun and shot the first shot, hoping to scare them and give the others warning. Now, he was wounded by Matt's first shots, but he leaned against an aspen and shot back. Wall and Warner shot 44-40's but Ike shot a big bore 45-110 caliber single shot, shooting five hundred grain bullets.

Matt had taken refuge behind a fifteen inch thick aspen. He had to stand sideways to keep out of sight. Ike began to shoot the tree in the same place, thinking that the big bullets would bore through soon. The second shot made the bark bulge on Matt's side of the tree, and he was starting to sweat, but a shot from Wall cut Ike across the bridge of his nose, filling his eyes with tears and blood, he couldn't see to shoot.

Matt stepped out, ready to shoot, when Swift came out of the other tent. Matt snapped a shot, cutting Swift's hat brim clear across, letting it flop down and dangle.

Swift yelled as loud as he could, "Don't shoot!"

Matt yelled back, "Then you get your hands up!"

"I've got 'em up as high as I can."

"Well, tear those tents down. Let's see who else is hiding around here?"

When the tent came down, it revealed David Milton and Dick Staunton. Staunton was shot in a couple of places and was bleeding badly. David Milton was hit in the shoulder and ranged down the spine.

"My God, Dave, if I'd known it was you, I never would have shot! I'm sorry man," Matt cried.

"I don't blame you Matt, it isn't your fault. It was damnable, dirty, double crossing Coleman I blame! He went to town after money and look what he brought back."

Matt Warner took charge, sending Wall to town for a doctor and help while Warner did his best for the wounded men. He also told Coleman and Swift that they would stay and help or they would stay and never help anyone again. They stayed.

Wall got to Vernal with a lathered, winded, horse and couldn't get anyone to go back with him—no doctors and certainly no citizens of this fair city seemed to want to go help.

As Sheriff Pope thought of this and his family, his heart swelled with love and pride the way they had come through in his absence! When no one else would go help, his brother Marcellus Pope, acting as sheriff in his absence, hooked up old Bell and Good Eye to a light wagon with a wood rack. He pitched in several forks full of hay, picked up some blankets, and five gallons of whiskey and bandages. Old Bell and Good Eye was a good traveling pair of thoroughbreds. They were also a great buggy team. They went back up Dry Fork to the scene of the affair on Diamond Mountain. Marcellus picked up the gruesome load and hurried the load as smoothly as possible, but a high wheeled wagon has a dead axel. In other words, there are no springs or give, so the wounded men were bounced and jostled along over hours of torture on the way back to Vernal.

Dick Staunton died that night, and David Milton the next morning. Ike Staunton was in critical condition for about a week. They had to amputate his leg. He finally began to recover and survived the ordeal.

On the arrival in Vernal, word spread like wildfire and the townspeople were enraged. Warner and Wall thought a court of law would not convict them since they only finished the fight started by the others. Coleman was scared to death. Marcellus pointed out that to run was useless so he suggested the jail. He said he'd protect them until a trial could be held. Marcellus recruited his family's help and they drug up the logs and supplies for a siege, if necessary, and built the barricade. His family had broken up the mob and now things could settle down a bit.

John T. said, "I'll hold the jail tonight and let everyone get back to their families."

"Now son—I'd feel better if you had someone here with you. I'll send Dick back to help." Robert's mouth set into a stubborn line so John was obliged to agree.

Dick and John T. didn't light a lamp after supper. They just sat around and visited until John fell asleep in the chair with his head on his arm on the desk. When John awoke later that night, cramped and stiff, Dick was snoring loudly from the cot, and someone from the cells in back was running competition with him.

Pope stepped outside and looked around. Clouds were moving in and he could only see a few stars. The breeze seemed to be colder. In just a minute he stepped back through the door and took the coat from the peg, and then he stepped out and closed the door quietly, took off his gun belt and put the coat on, then replaced the gun belt.

He was looking over a quiet and completely dark settlement in Uintah Basin. He listened to a dog bark on the other side of town and a couple of owls were talking to each other. A coyote howled a high, long howl and the chorus of dogs tried to howl back. They sounded more like wolves than coyotes. Pope laughed out loud at their attempts to communicate to their smaller, wild cousins. He thought that must be what he was to these people. There was a difference between him and everybody else. John felt that he was a wild, fellow citizen, hard to be understood by them, and that's why he stood apart from the pack.

He remembered the time his dad was called by Charles C. Rich, Mormon Apostle and leader of the settlement of Bear Lake, to go with Randolph Stewart, east to the Bear River Valley and choose a place for another Mormon Community to be settled. After riding a couple of days, they chose a place between Big Creek and Otter Creek which promised to be a good place to settle.

Robert and Randolph raced their horses to see what the town should be called. Randolph won the race. Then the Robert Pope family received a call from the Lord to settle Randolph. (Calls were received like young men in the church receive mission calls today.)

Charles C. Rich had learned it was hard to get people to stay in Bear Lake area. They would stay through the first winter and as soon as snow melted enough to get through the canyons in the spring, they would pack up and move again. So these families were called for seven years.

Young John T. moved to Randolph to live. He remembered the giant sagebrush. It seamed like he grubbed sage brush with a grub hoe for a whole year. He'd chop and haul it to cook fires and to clear garden spots and fields.

They couldn't survey the town because of the sage. They chained it off, measuring the lots with chains by hand. His father worked with other men, long hours, hauling logs out of canyons west of town. They soon had cabins up and wells dug. Pioneering these towns was back-breaking, hard work. Log cabins were raised with dirt roofs. A diversion dam was built in Big Creek and a canal was plowed north to town using plows, and scrapers, and manpower. Otter Creek was diverted and some grain planted. John's dad, Robert, continued to haul logs until he had built a trading post and store.

The Indians watched the progress. Small groups stopped to watch. Several just hung around and begged. Toward fall a huge tribe of Shoshones came single file, looking as they went by. They talked long with Sarah and about thirty came back the next day with fur and pelts to trade. Townspeople brought the horses and livestock in close for the night. Armed guards kept watch.

Now Robert Pope took his best team, loaded a large bale of furs and pelts and with rifle in hand took them south to Evanston, Wyoming. He bought trade goods and stuff for the store. The items brought in moved so quickly that again, he had to go to Evanston for more freight. Again John and his mother had to look after the work.

Indians came with more fur. John suddenly found himself surrounded by Indian boys. He was a warrior because he had a gun. They wanted John to hunt with them. His mother, Sarah LeDuc, interpreted and said they wanted to see John T. shoot. She said it was all right to go for a ways with them to show them how he could. Young John led Old Apple to the hitch rail in front of the store and stepped up, then vaulted on bareback, and rode out with them.

He was nine years old, and could hit a target most of the time with a rest. He rode down toward the river. There were large natural meadows where Big Creek spread out on the bottoms and watered a quite a large area. Hay had grown tall here, but was ripe and getting dry, and some was lying down.

A jack rabbit jumped and ran a ways, stopping about a hundred and twenty yards away, and sat up. The Indian boys wanted John to shoot, so he slid off, sat down, held the gun in both hands over his knees, and squeezed off a shot. The bullet hit at the rabbit's feet, causing him to jump high, spin and kick crazily, then run away hard. That old black powder caused a big cloud. Those Shoshone friends were laughing and they all crowded around to see John reload that cylinder with black power, round ball, and primer on the nipple. That was the start of a friendship. John T. was the white warrior.

They say a man is a product of his environment and experience. If that's so, maybe it explains Sheriff Pope. He was very complex. He was taught to pray at a young age by his mother. He had witnessed answers to her prayers many times, so he continued to pray as well. He craved the big, rough country.

That spring in Randolph, Utah, he was ten years old. A letter came from a friend to his folks. A former neighbor in St. Charles, and his friend, had trapped muskrats all winter in Mud Lake, north of Bear Lake. They had a few coyotes, a bobcat pelt, about twenty wild mink, and a few prime ermine as well as hundreds of muskrats. They wished to sell them, but couldn't get away to haul them over the mountains to Randolph. They hoped Popes were interested and would come buy the fur. John T. said he could take a wagon to get them. His folks, being really busy as well, talked it over and finally sent a ten-year-old boy and his big pistol, a freight wagon, and a length of rope to tie the load with. He had his bed roll and tarp and a well broke team. His mother sewed the money with which to pay for the fur in a handkerchief and stitched it inside his coat pocket so he couldn't lose it. It took him three days to make the trip. John T. Pope never felt like a boy after that!

The still of the night was interrupted by a soft chuckle. Sheriff Pope realized he was laughing at his memories. Pope compared the boy of his youth to the neighbor's kid who was just ten or twelve, and John would bet anything he couldn't even harness a horse, and the sad comparison made him chuckle again. "Hell, this modern age is making kids soft."

He was thinking of the old two track road from Randolph, as it wound up Otter Creek, nearly to Twin Peaks, over the mountain, to the head of Laketown Canyon, the Old South Mill Canyon, then down a draw to the northwest, into Round Valley, north to a crossing on the Big Spring Creek. There were no bridges so he had to drive through the Swan Creek, and Fish Haven Creek. There were no bridges or improvements at all. He could see it in his mind, how it looked before it was settled. Virgin land is always wild and dangerous.

Maybe instead of being like the coyote to the bigger dogs, maybe he was more like a bigger wolf to them. His mind was busy with his thoughts when he noticed a light had come on in the home of a widow lady. She had been selling donuts and bread from home, and was such a hit with the Wild Bunch, and bachelors, and the mail carrier. She set some tables up and folks could get a meal and some hot coffee.

John T. looked at the sky, solidly overcast now. He had no timepiece. He decided to get some breakfast for everyone in the jail. He vaulted over the barricade and met a pretty stiff west wind, but he sauntered along the middle of the street and into Mona's Donut Shop. She was in the kitchen mixing bread.

"Good morning, Sheriff. You are up early, aint ya?"

"I don't know. What time is it?"

"I've got just past four. I think that's as close as anybody knows. I wind my watch every night before I go to bed. The mailman comes in from Duchesne every day. He sets his watch by mine. What can I do for you Sheriff?"

"Just finish your mixing job, and then we can get me a cup of coffee. And, we'll figure it out from there. Save some of that dough. I just thought of scones. Man, a couple of scones with a bit of honey or just sugar. That sounds good."

"Step in here and get yerself a cup of coffee. It's been boiling for a while. I've got my hands in this dough."

He stepped into the kitchen and spotted a whole tray of donuts already done, with sugar sprinkled on them. "I can see one thing we'll have to have up in that jail, a whole sack of those sugar donuts."

John got his cup and went back in the other room to a table. In a few minutes the early-rising baker came in with a plate and a jar of plum jelly. "Sugar or plum jelly, these are your choices," Mona offered.

"I haven't been to the trough too regular lately, so it sure sounds good to me. What have you got that I could take over to Dick and the prisoners at the jail, besides donuts?

"Wonder if they would eat pancakes, a couple of eggs apiece and a jar of plum jelly?"

"They'd be tickled to death. They're tired of sow belly and beans."

"I've got a basket in there you can carry it in, if you'll bring it back."

"I'll do that all right."

"I'll fix it for them while you eat."

She brought out a couple of hot scones as big as the plate—and after John downed them and about five cups of coffee, he paid for it all and took the basket with a dish towel over it and strode out the door. It was still dark and blowing, and starting to snow, so he hurried to the jail.

Pope stepped out and got an armful of wood, and started a fire. He set the pot on, lit a couple of lamps and then took the plates of pancakes and eggs back to the prisoners before they got cold. "Coffee will be hot in a minute." After Dick and John finished all they could of the donuts, the rest went to the prisoners and they nearly foundered.

After breakfast and dishes were done, John took pen and paper to Dick and had him write a report to the circuit judge to inquire what to do with the prisoners. On his way to mail the letter, the sheriff returned Mona's basket and relayed a hearty thanks from the others.

While visiting over a cup of coffee with a group of men in the warm shop, Teddy Longhurst offered his assistance in any way, so Pope said, "You could stay and have guard duty in the jail tonight with me if you want."

"I'd be glad to do it."

So John T. said, "Go tell Dick he can go home to his family if he wants, and I'll be up there in a while after I get enough of Mona's good coffee."

There was six inches of wet, heavy snow and it was still coming down. John knew the mountains were being dumped on. The rivers were already high, high, high. As John walked toward the jail he heard a loud bang. Teddy came stumbling out of the jail, and seeing John T. said, "I'm not feeling good. I can't stay after all!" Longhurst dashed past him, leaving tracks in the snow. As John entered the jail, he heard noisy, bellowing laughter. He walked back to see the prisoners, rolling on the floor, holding their sides. The donut sack was busted, and a rifle was lying on the floor.

"What did I miss?"

The prisoners reported that after Dick left, Teddy took the rifle, put it over his shoulder like a marching tin soldier, and was walking a beat every few minutes. He'd come in, walk in front of the cell doors, turn and go out. When he came the last time, Wall reached out and poked a finger in his ribs like a gun barrel while Matt exploded the paper sack. It went off loud. Teddy jumped, dropped the rifle, and ran out. The prisoners laughed about it all night and rehearsed the incident for several days to come. Even Coleman thought it was funny. John T. listened while picking up the rifle and sack. He remembered the stricken look on Teddy's face as he passed him outside, and John, too, took a fit of laughter which started the prisoners howling again.

A few days later a little group of officials arrived so the prisoners were given a hearing, and bound over to District Court to be held without bail, as these outsiders considered the case to be cold blooded murder.

"Cold blooded murder," Matt Warner howled, disbelieving of the whole, senseless situation. "I only thought I was helping some fellows out, and I was shot at! It's terrible! The whole debacle was a mass of confusion, and senseless, but it was *not* cold blooded murder! Those men were my friends."

A date was set for trial a few days later, but when the date arrived, the regular judge was ill so a substitute was sent in his place. When court convened, the council for the defense asked for a change of venue, saying, "With the bias and lynch mobs in evidence, it would be impossible for the prisoners to get a fair trial here." So the change was granted and the sheriff was ordered to take them to Ogden for trial.

The pressure from Wild Bunch seemed to be a lot less because now they were waiting for the move to get them free and away from the bastion of a jail. As the pressure eased off, Pope was able to spend some time with his family which was so precious for him.

Charlotte Ann told him he was really a long way behind with his homework (love life). He agreed, but in a couple of days he found himself wondering how he could be so far behind and then catch up so fast. John knew that the things that happened while he was away were gone forever—and he missed out on too many milestones of a growing family.

Dang! He vowed he was going to spend more time with his family. He didn't want to miss out on the very best that life offers.

As he was in jail next afternoon, he watched Butch Cassidy ride up and dismount, vault over the log protection, and stick his head in the door.

"How about a cup of coffee? It smells purty good."

"Sit down." John T. poured a couple of hot, steaming cups of boiling coffee. Pope knew it was strong, had a couple of day's grounds in it.

"I thought you good Mormons didn't drink coffee," Butch teased.

Now John T. Pope knew Butch had been raised a Mormon himself, and smiled with the jostling. "It's a frontier staple, and if we all drank out of the creeks and rivers as we traveled around, we'd be dead of dysentery!"

Butch nodded with a chuckle. "If I've gotta boil my water, I'm puttin' coffee in it too. Your alfalfa looks darn good in Red Creek."

"I don't know when I'm gonna get time to put it up. Why don't you take a scythe back when you go? Since its starting to blossom, put it up to save it."

"Ah," the outlaw grinned. "I never got the knack of a scythe. I'm a poor mower. You better hire some of the loafers around here to go do it for you. Whew! That coffee is bitter as hell, Pope. You better change the grounds once in a while."

"We got sugar and milk if it's too strong for the likes of you."

Cassidy laughed at that, and stood up, taking the hot pad, and poured them a couple more cups. "Can I talk to your prisoners?"

"Sure can, but you'll have to take off your *decorations*."

"I forgot they wuz there. I guess I'm just that used to them." Butch unbuckled his gun belt and hung it over the back of a chair, and John picked up his own shotgun and followed Butch back to the cell, listening to their conversation.

Matt Warner was glad to see his friend, and they trusted Pope, so it was an interesting conversation. Butch told Warner he'd get him free one way or the other.

"Maybe it's better to stand trial, serve my time, and clear my name. They can't give me too much time for what I've done. But I could *really* use a lawyer."

"If we don't get you free on the way to trial, I'll get you a lawyer. I'll hire Douglas Preston from Rock Springs, but you aint there yet, Matt." Cassidy winked at his friend. "We'll be ready and keep an eye on what's going on. Okay?"

"Sure."

"Can I get you anything?"

"No, Pope feeds us what he eats. We've never had it so good or so easy."

As Butch buckled his gun around his waist, Pope said, "I don't have a warrant out for you Butch. So as far as I'm concerned, you have earned amnesty. You can get a ranch, marry a gal, raise a family, or whatever you take a notion to do. But if you do some of the things you indicated to Matt that you are willing to do, well then I'll have writs and circulars coming for me to arrest you, just as sure as God made little green apples."

"Little green apples," Butch repeated, showing his rapt attention.

"When I have a warrant for you, I'll come and serve it! I'll give you notice somehow ahead of time, if I can, because you're a likeable guy, and I'd like to have you as a friend."

Butch walked outside, vaulted the log barricade and reached out, taking the bridle reins, but before mounting, he looked back at Pope and said, "If you try to arrest me, I'll kill you, John Pope."

So there it was.

A couple of days later Colonel Randlett, who was stationed at Ft. Duchesne, rode up to the jail, was invited in, and visited for a few minutes. "Sheriff, you need to know that the Wild Bunch is over at Myton and Nine Mile—and they are just waiting for a chance to shoot you and take the prisoners away. They've got men watching all the trails. I'm offering you a hundred troops to escort you and those prisoners to Price. Then you can catch the train."

Pope thanked him very much and said, "I'll let you know. I've been waiting for the water to go down in the crossings, and just deciding what to do."

John got a letter from Judge Thomas. He told Pope to deputize one hundred men as an armed escort to help transport the prisoners. The judge expressed his regrets for granting the change of venue and placing Pope in such danger. The judge realized Pope would be in a tight spot now, taking the men to Ogden, carrying out his orders.

John T. smiled when he read that one. "Uh huh. I'd have the lynch mob deputized and give them another chance to carry out their black ideas! That won't work." With spinning thoughts and a constant prayer for inspiration, the sheriff wisely engineered another plan.

Sheriff Pope took the prisoners out of jail about eleven o'clock that night. Warner was in great spirits when he saw no soldiers or deputies to escort them.

Sheriff Pope handcuffed Matt Warner and William Wall to their saddle horns. Coleman was an older man, and not in good shape, so Pope let him ride a gentle horse with free hands. About an hour later they were climbing the Uinta Mountains, in a round about way that continued to lead higher, and Matt Warner realized, all of a sudden, that Pope had pulled one over on his friends! The Wild Bunch would be waiting to free him on the road to Price while he was riding north! He really ripped off an oath of swear words, yelling, until Pope said, "You've got a filthy mouth, Matt. I hope you're not as rotten inside as your mouth makes you sound."

Sheriff Pope took them over the high Uinta Mountains on an old military road he knew. About seven o'clock he stopped for a few minutes for a bathroom break. They watered the horses. They were already in Lone Tree, Wyoming. Then, he handcuffed the men to the saddle horns again and hit the Old Oregon and Mormon Trail west of Ft. Bridger. They followed the Oregon Trail alongside the deep set ruts, and then along the muddy creek, near railroad tracks to Carter, Wyoming, where they were able to buy dinner in a café.

Carter was a main shipping point for cattle from Montana and Idaho. Between the coming of the railroad in the 1860's and the extension of the Oregon Short Line in the late 80's, the hands in Carter shipped more cattle than Dodge City or Abilene at their heyday best.

Pope bought the meal and tickets to Ogden, Utah. He sent a telegram to the police in Ogden to meet him and give him the assistance needed to get the prisoners to jail in Ogden. They climbed off the train in Ogden at seven-thirty that evening. Two officers met them, and they had a stage coach to ride the last way.

He signed over the prisoners, and in visiting with authorities there, he briefly explained what he had done. "I just don't know how long the outlaws will stay on the road to Price waiting to take these prisoners away from me!" They all got a good laugh. Because of Butch Cassidy's and Matt Warner's reputations, extra guards were put on around the clock, no matter how funny it was.

A short time later, the guards read a note from Butch Cassidy to Matt Warner saying the Wild Bunch was camped close by, and if he wanted out, they would take him out if they had to take the jail down one rock at a time to do it. They then took the note to Matt. Matt sent a note back saying he'd stand trial for his crime and serve time. He was tired of living as an outlaw, but he could sure use that lawyer. His note was taken back by the messenger who delivered it in the first place.

Douglas Preston was a very gifted criminal lawyer and had worked for the Wild Bunch on several occasions. He knew of their occupations and reputation so his fee was high. He was hired by Butch and Sundance, but to get the money to pay for his fee, they would need a pretty penny. They talked it over and decided on the Montpelier Bank, in southeastern Idaho. It was fairly close—only a two-day ride, and it had enough money on hand to pay the fees and a little for their time. So Elza Lay, Bob Meeks, and Butch Cassidy rode north to pull a robbery that would be talked about in Bear Lake for many years to come.

The money was netted in a bold, broad daylight robbery of the Bank of Montpelier. Butch Cassidy and his men rode out of town on a walk, like unhurried cowboys of the area. A portion went to pay Douglas Preston to defend Matt Warner and Bill Wall. Even with Lawyer Preston's aid, because of the outlaws' reputations and long list of crimes, they were sentenced to five years in jail. Matt Warner was later released, after serving two and a half years, for good behavior. Coleman wasn't sentenced, and after the trial he left the state and never returned.

It had taken quite a lot of Pope's spending money to feed the prisoners during their stay in jail and when John got back to Vernal his deputies had three more locked up to care for while awaiting trial. He sent a letter to the county with a long itemized list of expenses incurred from feeding and caring for prisoners. His request was ignored so he kept sending it in. The county probate judge and Board of County Commissioners refused to reimburse him. The county was small, and not real flush itself, and not really sure of ways of doing things yet as this was a first experience for all.

Pope made a big wage of three hundred a year, which wasn't a fat sum at all, considering his time—that most valuable resource which was spent away from his family. The day came to hold court again. So Pope went to the judge personally with the request that funds be appropriated and set aside for the care of the prisoners. The judge on the bench was annoyed at having this come up so often. He acted like he had a special grievance towards Pope, personally. He not only refused the request, but directed a stream of insulting abuse, and the worst kind of gutter swearing at the sheriff. Pope never batted an eye. He looked the judge in the eye, picked up his petitions, and retreated.

Next morning, John picked up his basket of breakfast at Mona's Donut Shop for the jail. Stepping out in the street, he met the judge coming for his breakfast. John set the basket down against the building. He reached up and grabbed the judge's nose. The end stuck out between Pope's thumb and index finger. The judge made high pitched squeals as he clasped onto Pope's hand and wrist with both his hands, and squatted down, turning his head away as Pope twisted the skin off his nose. Blood began oozing in drops. Then pushing away, Pope pulled his pointed toed boots away from the judge's posterior several times, giving him a good, old-fashioned butt kicking. Pope picked up the basket and went on, unaware that quite a number of citizens had been watching.

Shortly after court convened that morning, a number of men with Levis tucked into high topped boots, with high riding heels, carried a long pole up the walk to the open door of the courtroom where they deposited it outside the door. They then proceeded into the room with a long rope coiled like a snake on one man's arm. They walked up to the judge's bench. The judge looked up at these rugged cowboys standing on both sides of him.

"Sit down, gentlemen, and I'll hear your case in a few minutes," the judge blustered with as much dignity as he could muster.

"Damn right you'll hear our case now," said Bill McCaslin, spokesman for this uninvited delegation.

"Sit down and take your turn," the irate judge ordered.

"We'll take a turn with this rope around your neck if you don't pay the sheriff all he's got coming to him for taking care of the prisoners! We'll just drag you out and hang you to the top of that pole we just toted up here!" Upon so saying, men standing closest to the judge grabbed him by the muscles that extend on either side of the neck in a hard grip. The judge noisily and hastily reconsidered. He took up the sheriff's account and ordered it paid in full.

Before leaving the courtroom, Bill McCaslin said, "Don't you try anything against the sheriff for decorating your nose this morning either or we'll find you and finish this job. You know, the show Sheriff Pope put on this morning was worth all it cost you anyway!"

There was whispering in the court for a few minutes after they left, with people trying to find out what had happened. Many a laugh was enjoyed for many years as this story was told. For years afterward people would say, "Don't do this or that or I'll have to twist your nose."

The accomplishment of fooling the townspeople *and* the Wild Bunch, and delivering the prisoners safely to Ogden brought Pope some notice and acclaim. Until this point, the Wild Bunch couldn't have known the kind of man they faced. Now Pope had his warrants for Butch and others for armed robbery of the Montpelier Bank. Butch had had his warning that he would serve it.

Many of his bunch said, "Who the hell does this lucky, dimwitted sheriff think he is? We've never seen any of his graveyards."

Butch had once stopped by John's ranch on Red Creek for a cup of coffee and found him friendly, but fearless. Sheriff knew of Cassidy's reputation and didn't seem awed by it. For that reason, warning bells were edging into the back of Butch's reason, making him careful and cautious. Now Butch and his bunch knew of one of his graveyards—and the friends of theirs who lay under the rocks in the bottom of the canyon. More warning bells began sounding in Cassidy's head because Sheriff

Pope didn't notch his guns or even tell anyone about it. Butch knew in his heart he was playing a game of roulette with a curly wolf. If Butch Cassidy had known of John T.'s skill with a gun, or the many times he had used it, he could have saved grief for himself and his Wild Bunch.

Chapter Three

Kid Pope Earns his Spurs

Sheriff Pope learned to track from his Indian friends in Randolph, Utah. As a boy he had gone with them many times as they taught him how to stay on the track of one horse when the road was full of tracks. When he was nearly fifteen years old, a circular came by mail and was put up in the Pope store. *"Help wanted! Who knows the trail to Oregon? Driving two thousand Texas Long Horns from the Pecos River of Texas"* Wow, that seemed a good idea. John knew a man could ride distances like this. It was called riding the grub line. At night riders stopped at ranches or camps. The homesteads would feed them, put them up for the night, and try for news.

So, young John T. rode off to Texas with saddle, horse, and pistol, of course. He met the trail herd after nineteen days' travel, already underway, deep in south Texas. At that time, in 1874, the fast draw was quite new, but Texas was where it became famous. On this drive, there were two or three who thought they were really good gunmen. One older fellow had been a Texas Ranger for awhile. He was good to John and a friendship developed.

As they were traveling in North Texas, a large rattle snake bit the ranger's horse on the front leg. The horse shied back, but he had a lot of hair on his fetlocks, and the snake's fangs were stuck in the hair. As the horse came back, he saw the snake coming, too. He panicked, taking another backward lunge. This time, he threw himself down where he floundered and kicked a few times until he got his feet under him, and he began running and kicking.

At first John thought perhaps his friend had gotten himself free, and then he saw he had a foot stuck in the stirrup. His first thought was to get a rope on the horse, but in a flash he realized even if he got a rope on this fear-crazed bronco, his friend would be killed with the kicking, fighting horse on a rope. The next thought was to kill the bronco, and before he even stopped to think, he tried to see the best place to put his bullet. The next second he heard the report of his pistol, and the crazed animal dropped on his belly and slid a little ways. Pope rode up and shot the snake's head off. He jumped off and ran to the aid of the ranger whose foot was on a bad angle. He couldn't get loose without help.

By the time Pope got his foot loose, and was checking for broken bones, seven cowboys had come to help. They undid the cinch and drug the saddle out from under a very dead saddle horse. Two of the men studied the damage done by Pope's pistol. Both looked with new respect at a recently turned fifteen year old, John T. Pope, who had expertly placed a bullet two inches below a running, kicking horse's ear, right through the brain. The other shot had taken the head off the deadly serpent.

The ranger had to ride the chuck wagon for about a week, while all his bruises and a badly sprained ankle and wrenched leg healed up. But he began each day to work with "the kid" as he nick named him, "on a fast draw." No teacher ever had a more willing student. Over the next three months he acquired and built his rig. The ranger got in his roll and brought out the 44-40 which shot metallic cartridges. Pope was already a dead shot and extremely fast. So the God of the Universe, who knew, understood, and loved the free spirit of this kid, was preparing and sharpening the tool he would use in an outlaw infested wilderness to make it a safe and blessed place to raise families.

Pope was valuable to the drive as a drover, but because he knew the trail through Wyoming and Idaho, he took them over the Sublet cutoff on the North Oregon Trail where there was more water, and which saved many miles. They camped on Sublet Creek about a mile south of the confluence of the Smith Fork River on the Bear River. A large camp of Indians was camped along the Smith Fork.

Before going into camp, Pope rode to see if any of his friends were there, but as he got near enough to see, he realize they were Bannocks, and not his beloved Shoshone. As they were having chuck that night, he told Mr. Shurley to put on extra night herders and a few guards on the horse herd.

"What for?"

"Because those Indians are Bannocks."

"Are they on the war path or something?"

"I don't think so, but they'll steal anything that's loose and if it isn't loose, they'll kick it loose."

Mr. Shurley was skeptical.

John said, "I lived in the next valley, just to the west of here, in a Mormon settlement. The Mormons tried to be peaceful and get along with the Indians. A large group of Bannocks came one day under Chief Pocatello. Charles C. Rich was the colonizer and leader. Pocatello came demanding a cow, so Rich mounted up and rode over where they were guarding the cattle. Charles C. Rich said, 'All right, you can have any cow here but that one; and that one belongs to a widow lady. That's her only cow.' So that's the cow Pocatello wanted. No other beef would do. 'You'll have to pick another.'"

"Pocatello got sullen and said, 'I have many braves.'"

"Charles Rich was six feet, six inches tall in his stockings. He lost his temper, crawled off his horse and told Pocatello to get down. 'We'll decide in combat, just the two of us.'"

"Suddenly Chief Pocatello said. 'This other cow will do.'"

Some of the drovers laughed at the story. Mr. Shurley seemed slightly put out, probably the mention of the Mormons. It caused men to bristle sometimes, which was curious to John in the first place. Anyway, Kid Pope and a Mexican boy were assigned the duties of night herd. So they roped up fresh horses from the remuda. These Texas longhorns were wild cattle and at night when they couldn't see too well, they easily became scared of the dark, especially if they heard something unfamiliar. So the night herders would ride around the bedded cattle slowly, and sing to them, or at least talk in a gentle way so they knew where the riders were and wouldn't scare suddenly.

Late that night Kid Pope heard some loud popping noises. It sounded like buffalo robes or heavy blankets being shaken and popped like a whip. That did it! The cattle left the camp on a dead run. Horns were rattling and the hooves sounded like thunder. A heavy cloud of dust was coming 'til it was hard to breathe or see.

Pope offered a prayer and began trying to work to one side of this mob. He barely cleared the bunch in time to keep from being swept into the river. He loped south a ways and found where he could cross. If he hadn't cleared when he did, he would have been trampled into the bottom of the river. He tried to turn and stop them and had no luck.

When daylight came next morning, he spotted the Mexican boy still alive and coming a long. The cattle were still trying to stampede but they were walking with tongues out, froth dripping from their mouths. But they were determined, like a band of wild, animal outlaws, they were determined.

The Mexican boy's horse couldn't make more than a walk. Pope's could at least trot so he drew in front of a big brindle bull who was leading the pack. He would hold up till he was quite close, then the old bull would put that eight-foot horn-span down and charge. He was given out, so he couldn't make much speed either; so when he'd charge to take Kid Pope, he'd only trot and Pope would begin to lead him around. Gradually, he would stop chasing him, so he'd slow up, get closer again and the process would be repeated until at last they were going back the way they had come. They got the cattle turned way up on Lake Ridge where you could see into the Bear Lake Valley. The cattle had stampeded for about twelve to fifteen miles. Other cattle had gone in different directions, so all cowboys were out hunting and gathering the herd. The Mexican boy and Kid Pope had the biggest group.

After taking them to the bottom of the mountain they were on, they stopped on water and then bedded down. The Kid slipped off bridles and let the horses graze a while, gave them water, then staked them out. He and the Mexican then lay down and slept. They didn't have a bite of food for about three days.

Finally a man from camp found them. He brought coffee, sow belly, and sour dough bread. That was the best meal the Kid had ever had and he thanked deity for it. It was five or six days before they were ready to go. They had lost a bunch of cattle in the rivers, and they lost others they just couldn't find.

Kid Pope said, "I'll bet Pocatello got enough hides and meat to last a long time out of that raid." Seven hundred head had been lost.

After a great experience with a Texas trail drive, Pope was finally paid one hundred and twenty dollars for staying on to the John Day River in Oregon. He shook hands with these friends for the last time and then rode away, going home by crossing mighty rivers and riding east. He came though a part of Montana, seeing sites and country never before experienced by him or his family.

He came upon a man walking alone in Idaho. He stopped to see what his trouble had been and to offer help.

This guy brought his rifle to bear on Pope and said, "Yes, you can help. Leave your horse and your outfit."

Pope raised his hands, but the right hand swept the pistol up quickly and smoothly, and John never told of killing this escaped prisoner. However, a posse from Montana tracked him to a rock covered grave. John's family had only been told of a man trying to rob him.

When he rode back through Bear Lake, he found his family working on their new farms in Garden City. The seven year mission in Randolph was up. They had been so busy with the store and family, they had failed to build a ranch, and they wanted land for their boys, and room to grow.

John T. was the third son in Robert and Sarah's family. His oldest brother was Charles Holmes, ten years older than John. Next he had a sister who had died at two years of age while still in Minnesota. Robert Alexander was next, just three years older than John. Rob married a Garden City girl and stayed behind when the family migrated to Ashley Valley. George Eugene was two years younger than John. Richard Henry (Dick) was four years younger. William Franklin lived to eighteen years of age and died. Adeline married Ed J. Longhurst who went with the family to Ashley Valley. Sarah Adell married Nathan Charles Hunting. She was twelve years younger. Marcellus Barnum was fourteen years younger, and Rock Marcus seventeen years younger, being the caboose on Robert and Sarah's winding family train.

In the Bear Lake Valley, the family could raise apples, pears, plums, raspberries, corn, and wheat. Many more garden things and survival food could be raised in Garden City, than in Randolph or Woodruff, which seemed to be the coldest two places on earth. John gave his dad the biggest half of the money he'd earned on his drover adventures for the family.

After helping a few weeks with this back breaking pioneer job of building, clearing, planting, digging the canal from Swan Creek, digging wells, digging a cellar, and building granaries, this free spirit rode off again to look at his old home in Randolph. He thought he would visit the place the stampede had happened, between Sage and Cokeville, Wyoming. Maybe he could find some of the cattle.

However, he rode into a busy bustling ranch, Beckwith and Quinn Company. A wagon train was encamped on the river. Nearby they were trying to obtain fresh teams, and many had brought wagons up to the blacksmith shop for repairs. A well-muscled, colored blacksmith was trying to do everything he could for them. He was a former slave. John learned later that he was known for his skill as a blacksmith.

Several hundred broken oxen grazed in a large irrigated field. Also, about a hundred head of work horses grazed in an adjacent pasture. As the wagon trains reached this point on their journey, they needed to find fresh teams, so A. C. Beckwith brought these animals and provided this service. However, he always demanded boot—no straight trades. So Beckwith made money, and pioneers got fresh teams which sped them on their way. John, too, found many of the teams they received were traded from earlier wagon trains, but the rest refreshed them, and they were able to do again.

Probably fifty teams were at work on the ranch, hauling cedar posts off the Crawford Mountains east of Randolph, and hauling building logs and poles from the mountains east of Sublet. Others were hauling supplies from Evanston. A commissary building full of supplies had been built for hired men as well as for selling to travelers on the trail.

A diversion dam on Bear River was under construction. Men were hauling rock from the hills south of the dam site. A large cook tent was up with a Chinese cook, cooking long, hot hours every day for men who were bachelors. They killed a beef nearly everyday and cut meat for the cook. One man spent his time breaking horses.

Another crew was building a canal and diversion dam on Twin Creeks. Stoic Indians stood around and watched. Carpenters were working on log houses and huge barns. The lure of this carnival of activity stopped John for awhile. He was hired on the spot and became a teamster, hauling supplies from Evanston.

A large herd of cattle had come in from Texas and branded with the shield brand. John was amazed to find the ranch claimed all the land from Bear River to Rawlins, making it one of the biggest ranches in Wyoming. His experience working on the BQ later was a help for him to understand, as so many of the rustlers in Brown's Hole had rustled BQ cattle, and tried to cover the brand with something to hide the old brand. However, the big shield high on the left rib was obvious to a man familiar with the brand. The BQ had many herds of sheep as well. The sheep were also branded with a BQ.

As a lawman in the Hole later on, when he saw cattle with the shield brand, if these people were good folks trying to go straight, he never mentioned them; however if they were still outlaws, he had evidence to convict them of cattle rustling crimes.

The Kid freighted supplies for several months. He also packed supplies to cowboys herding cattle in the Big Horn Basin. The BQ established a range right in the Basin. They had three thousand cows with twenty cowboys looking out for them. It took two men to pack twenty-two head of pack mules each morning and unpack and hobble them at night. It took about twenty to twenty-five days to make the round trip, depending on weather and other troubles that fell.

John drew his wages and went home for a visit and to see what was going on. He stayed around Garden City for a few months in 1877. He rode his horse away again to see what the life of a miner was like. He worked first for the Dry Canyon Mining Co. He worked a short time for them, then went to work in a little mine in the hills west of Stockton, Tooele County, Utah, when the price of metals dropped so low the mine had to shut down which put a lot of men out of work.

Pope rode to his uncle's place. Charles LeDuc was the owner of a cattle and horse ranch at Soldier Canyon, about three miles southwest of Stockton, Utah. There was a migration of about a hundred men leaving for somewhere else. Not one of them would walk if they could find a horse. Uncle Charles hired the Kid to do chores and guard the horses. LeDuc had a fine bunch of horses broken to ride or work. He kept them in the barn at night so the kid rolled his bed out in the tack room so he could hear if anybody tried to steal a horse.

He had a colt out in the pasture broke to lead, but not to ride or work yet. Later that night Charles walked out and couldn't see the colt. He ran to the barn and told his nephew. So John ran for the other end of the pasture, thinking if he was going to steal him, that's where he would take him out. As he neared the end of the pasture, there was a gunshot. The flash of the gun was still visible when Pope's 44-40 blazed back after that smooth, subconscious draw, which was now an automatic reaction. As soon as the gun went off, John side stepped so if somebody shot at his flash, he wouldn't be hit. However, the only reaction was the colt, running past him toward the barn. So he ran back himself.

He met Uncle Charles coming up. "John! Are you alright?"

"I am fine."

"My heart nearly gave out on me as I heard the shots!"

They retreated to the barn where they visited for an hour or so. Charles went in the house to bed. After a long time, the Kid went to sleep. Next morning, John awoke to the approach of Uncle Charles LeDuc, whose first words were these, "Well . . . that horse thief won't be stealing any more horses." So the Pope family had news of the first documented, for sure, killing by their teenage son and brother.

After the disposing of this horse thief, Uncle Charles sent word to the marshal in Stockton. He rode out and looked everything over and asked a lot of questions. He cleared John of any blame in the affair. John was hired as a deputy for a short time, as people were being robbed of their horses, right and left. He worked about a week and became extremely mad at the marshal for letting a mob lynch an Indian who had stolen a horse. John rode away from that incident, exercising all the restraint he could muster to refrain from killing the law man. He vowed if he were ever the law, he'd try to be fair. He'd protect people under his jurisdiction whether they were black, white, red, or whatever! Everyone should have the freedom to live and do what they wanted as long as it didn't hurt anyone else. John despised the yellow cowardice, lawless injustice!

So once again, he turned his horse east and rode for home. He rode through Ogden where he bought a new outfit—boots, shirt, Levis, and a new beaver hat. He looked at himself in the mirror. Wow, he could go to church, or a dance, or anywhere . . . if he wiped a little cream on his face so a cat might lick off the peach fuzz that was starting to grow up there. John grinned, rubbing a hand along his chin to check his progress. He walked into a café and ordered roast beef. It came with mashed potatoes, brown gravy, and several cups of coffee. It cost fifteen cents, but he felt like a man, and ready for his ride over the mountain.

He rode up Ogden Canyon to Huntsville and stopped at a ranch for the night. He left early next morning, rode a ways up Monte Cristo, then cut north over into Blacksmith Fork, out to the north a ways, the trail turned east past Strawberry and Saddle Creeks, and then down Cottonwood Creek into Round Valley. He rode north to Cook's Ranch then a ways east toward the gap and north over the hill to Hodges' Ranch, and on north about four miles. He was surprised that he had made the trip from Huntsville in about ten hours. Everyone was glad to have him home, so they were up visiting until a late hour.

Uncle Charles LeDuc's letter had just beaten him by a few hours, so his mother Sarah asked him to tell about the shooting. She was wondering if she had let her boy have way too much freedom at too young an age.

John T. said, "I would have been a bit hard to stop. I've never done anything I'd be ashamed to tell you about. I was working for Uncle Charles, sleeping in his barn to keep out-of-work, homesick miners from stealing his horses. Somebody tried to steal a colt, and as I went to investigate, they shot at me in the dark. I shot back, and I didn't miss."

"What about being a lawman for awhile?"

"I didn't find being a lawman any different from what I've done all my life. When we see somebody stealing, or killing, or bullying, we just naturally take a hand to level the field a bit, so we have justice and fairness. You don't have to wear a tin badge for that."

There were further questions from brothers about mining and from sisters about Tooele and Ogden, what the Great Salt Lake was like, and about Uncle Charles' ranch and so forth. John finally got to sleep. He took his bedroll to the barn and forked up a bit of hay and slept out there. Next morning he awoke as his dad came to milk, and his bothers started the chores and got ready for the day.

Chapter Four

Free Spirit

FOUR TEAMS WERE STANDING in their harnesses eating oats when the Pope's went in to a breakfast of strawberries and cream, coffee, baking powder biscuits and gravy. The strawberries were really tasty, almost too sour, but grown in this high colder climate, they just naturally had more taste. Robert Pope and four of John's brothers hooked up to wagons and went south. He asked his mother what to do. She said there were a million jobs to do before winter, and to take his choice, but she sure wished he would stay closer for awhile. He looked around a bit and realized he didn't even know which ground they owned. He saddled his horse, thinking of the rifle he had taken from the robber in northern Idaho, and the twenty dollars that went along with it. He added that sum to the hundred and some dollars in his pocket, and thought he'd look around. Maybe he could find a team and rig so he could help out and be more of an advantage on the ranch.

He rode south and saw where his father and brothers had gone up Hodges Canyon. As he rode past Hodges Ranch, he saw quite a few men working there. There were lots of teams; four men were following teams, hanging on handles of plows, plowing grain stubble.

On the beach ridge as he rode by quite close, the man on the lead plow hollered "Whoa!" The team stopped very quickly and began chewing the bits and nodding their heads. The man said, "Mornin' to ya. These horses need a break for a minute anyway. I do. Where ya headed?"

"I'm kind of looking to buy a team. I didn't know just where to start. Any ideas?"

"No, old Nat is buying, not selling. You might try Ira Nebeker. He's got a big old horse ranch up in Laketown." Pope knew of Ira, so he thanked the fellow and rode on south. Pope knew Ira was bishop of the Laketown Ward. He had broken the horses for the pony express. John laughed out loud as he remembered the way he did it. They bought the best colts, three to five years old, unbroken. They were almost exclusively out of the army remount station, all thoroughbreds. Ira broke them to lead and rode them only once. He had them gentled enough to saddle up. That's all. So when the pony rider got on, the horse would usually run away with him. It was all they could do to guide the animal a little, and by the time he had slowed to a lope or a walk, ten minutes or so was already behind them. No Indians could catch them.

"I wish I could find some colts like that," John called to a darting meadow lark.

As he neared the south end of the lake, he saw that Rendezvous Beach was occupied by a large group of Indians. Tents and tipis were pitched for three-quarters of a mile. Pope estimated about six or seven hundred Indians were camped. Pope made sure his pistol was ready and rode by the camp, warily passing around them on the south side, then following the road. When he came to the Big Spring Creek, he was surprised to find a new plank bridge. When the road turned south to Laketown, Pope stayed on, east along the beach ridge, crossed Falula Creek and then rode the remaining three-quarters of a mile up to the Nebeker house.

A very pretty gal, about sixteen or so, with blonde hair and blue eyes, opened the door. "Hi."

"Hello, I'm looking for Ira."

"I sure hope you have good luck finding him. You are a stranger to me. I'm Becky Nebeker."

"I'm John T. Pope. My folks are starting a ranch in Garden City."

"You're one of the Pope boys huh? Seems like there are a lot of you Pope's."

"Oh?"

"Rob is quite a dancer."

"Oh?"

"But darn him! He went off and got married so he's out of circulation now, but George is really good looking."

"Yes." John felt the fuzz on his upper lip twitch at the female assessments of his brothers.

"You have a brother named Dick, I think. He's younger than me, but I'm impressed."

John felt a smile give way again. "And then there's me," he fished.

"You look like a bad rustler or something."

"I'm definitely the black sheep of the bunch all right."

"Well, you're good looking enough, but if you'd shave, get a haircut, and come to the dance a week from this Saturday night, I'll save a dance or two for you. The dance is held in the top of the livery barn in Laketown. You better leave your gun off, too."

John had taken his hat off when she came to the door, and he had been backing slowly to his horse throughout this uncomfortable encounter. She had been following. John put his hat on, and stepped back on his horse.

John asked, "Is Ira your dad?"

"Yes, what did you think?"

"I don't know what to think, but I wish you would give me a clue about where I might find him."

"If I were looking, I'd ride over to that corral, and if he's not out there, ask the chore boy which way he went. I don't think he's looking for anybody to work for him right now though. He's pretty filled up."

Reaching up, John tipped his hat a little, said "Thanks," and he rode to the corral where he'd certainly feel more comfortable.

An Indian boy, about seventeen years old, was leading colts to water, one by one. John knew by the first look that these colts had only been tied up a few days and were just learning to lead. This kid was pretty handy and was working with them quietly and gently. He wore a beaver hat with a feather stuck in the band. He had on faded jeans tucked into deep, scalloped boots with spurs, and a leather vest over a bright red cotton shirt.

John said, "Nice colts."

The boy looked up, but went on about his business without saying anything. John saw the boy lead out his old Shorty colt.

"What's that colt out of?

The Indian finally looked at him and said in perfect English. "Why?"

"I like him. Maybe I can buy him."

The Indian led the colt to a little gate, opened it, led the colt through, and started leading him on north along the corral. "You follow me, and I'll show you."

When they came to a small stud corral, they were greeted with a squeal, and a big dapple gray Percheron stud, weighing about sixteen hundred pounds, came trotting along the fence, arching his thick neck and making stud talk. John looked him over. He was tall, almost built like a thoroughbred, but broad across the rump, with good legs, and feet. John was thinking that since his dad had imported that first Percheron stud, the breed was really popular the whole valley over.

Next he was shown the colt's mother, a light bay thoroughbred mare.

"What's your name?" John asked the boy.

"Dick Nebeker, but folks just call me Indian Dick, and I don't mind if you do."

Indian Dick showed John a bunch of two-year old cross colts in a pasture across Duck Creek, west of the house. He rode back around the house to go take a look at these colts. As John rode by, Becky stepped back out of the house, asking if he'd found her father.

"No, but I talked to one of you dark-complexioned brothers."

She looked like she'd been slapped, and then she said, "For your information, an Indian squaw of the Shoshone tribe gave dad two little boys several years ago. He raised them like they were his own. So they are not my *real* bothers." John was caught off guard by her reaction, and he couldn't help laughing. She whirled and flounced back to the house.

Later that afternoon, Ira rode into the yard in a wagon loaded with sand. The horses were lathered and winded. Their muscles were shaking and they looked all in. Ira got down, holding the lines. He unhooked an outside tug and hooked the chain on the breeching, on a hook for that purpose, then stepped behind the horse, undid the inside tug, and hung it up. He unhooked the other horse's inside tug, then stepping on across, he unhooked the outside tug and hung it, all the time keeping the lines so he could control the horses. Ira then took the halter rope down, which had been half-hitched on the hame, throwing the lines out away from him. He took the close line, reaching out about three feet, and then folded it back about three times. After Ira folded the line together, he pushed it through the large bottom ring on the hame, pulled it through, and put the fold over the top of the hame and tugged it down.

John T. had the other line up, and was already undoing the neck yoke when Ira stepped around front. So John T. let the neck yoke down and unchecked the lines, being sure to leave the ring the lines run through in one line as he checked the end on the inside of the hame.

"I'm Bishop Nebeker."

"I'm John Pope." They shook hands.

"Garden City?"

"Yeah, my family is living in Garden City. I've been working off for awhile."

The bishop said, "A fellow had a run away with this team yesterday down to South Eden, busted up an outfit pretty bad. I took a gentle team and another man down this morning, and fired that guy. I hooked these runaways up and they were scared to death and ready to run again, so I loaded a load of sand and took them down in the sand on the lake shore to see how much devil they had. I've dammed near killed them. There's no run left now, but once they run away, you can't trust them anymore."

John T. studied the horses. "Do you want to sell them?"

"Yes, but I couldn't sell a couple of runaways to you. If somebody got hurt or something, I wouldn't like it on my conscience."

"I'm not very well heeled, but we've got more men than teams and horses to work in Garden City. So if you'll put a price on them, the harnesses and wagon, maybe I could swing it. I'm probably going to have to ride away anyway, but try it."

Ira's eyes squinted with thought. "I'd take a hundred fifty for the whole rig."

"Now I saw a colt that Dick was working with this morning, a colt you just weaned and are breaking to lead, a pretty little dark sorrel with four stockings. I'd like to try that cross."

"I'd have to have at least twenty bucks for him."

Pope got in his pocket and counted his money, a hundred and fifty-five. He put five of it back in his pocket. John grinned as he counted the bills out to Ira, paying for the rig and horses, and then pulled the 38-55 rifle that he'd taken off the outlaw in Idaho. "A ranch like this with sheep herders and everybody could surely use a rifle like this one. I'll trade the rifle for the colt."

Ira took the rifle and looked it all over. "This looks pretty new . . ."

"It aint shot but three or four shells, but I figure I need the colt more than the rifle."

So Ira invited Pope to spend the night while he decided on the trade.

That night during supper and the next morning at breakfast, Becky chiefly ignored him for which he was glad. The next morning the team was gaunt, but still alive, and acted all right when they hooked them up. Dick Nebeker led the colt out and tied him to the back of the rig, then got a shovel and rode down on the lakeshore to unload the sand.

Pope kissed to his team, and they stepped right out, and he was back in Garden City by noon. He was really proud of the colt, and the team, too. If they would continue to act this way, he could be an asset to his folks and the place. He drove up in front of the house and tied up to the hitch rail, and then went in and had dinner. The family came out to see his rig; team tied to the rail, and saddle and colt tied behind.

John unhooked his team and led them in the barn and unharnessed and unsaddled, and fed and watered them. He worked on the box on the wagon. He pulled it to an out-of-the-way place and unloaded the box. He then loosened the bolts, which held the reach and back axel, then slid the back axel backwards about four feet, and retied them. He was ready now to haul logs or wood. He'd need a chain to bind his load and another axe or saw. So he walked uptown to the Satterthwaite Store.

After carefully looking over what selection they had, he bought an axe, single bit for a dollar and a quarter. Walking home, he found some wire and tied it on the front standard so it wouldn't get lost. He didn't know if his dad had an extra chain or if he would have to try to borrow one.

The Pope men came home with four loads of logs, and carefully unloaded them in the back of the corral. They were covered with soot and sweat. Everybody got busy with chores. John milked one of the cows and showed off his addition to their horse herd. Everyone was happy to have another team, but nobody was going to drive runaways but him.

Next day, the Popes left out with five teams. John brought up the rear. They went up Hodges Canyon, then up Left Hand Fork, then past a pretty spring to Richardson Flat. John was dumfounded. A fire had come through the area a few years earlier, killing a beautiful stand of timber which extended for several miles from Richardson Flat to Cheney Creek, and G Bow on clear to Slide Out. The fire killed the trees and burned the smaller limbs, but the logs were intact. The blackened outside actually treated and protected.

Many of the houses, barns and outbuildings in Hodges Ranch and Garden City were constructed with these logs. When they loaded their loads, they fixed a drag for John's team to keep the logs from pushing them into a runaway down the steep places. They sat down and held the load really good. John was proud of them. He hauled logs with his dad and brothers five days in a row. The fifth day's haul went into the church tithing yard. As the Popes had already hauled awhile, and Robert said they wanted for sure to give the Lord His tenth.

On Sunday, John went to church. There was a woman in town that the kids all called Old Lady Miriar. She said John looked really bad with his gun buckled on at church, but she was glad he came anyway, as if her opinion could matter one iota to John.

A Benson girl and a Brooker gal were giving him the eye. Also, two black-eyed Kimball gals showed interest. John decided to invest in a haircut and razor, but his brother Dick offered to do him for free. John thought he might cut his throat with the razor. After the hair cut, he looked in the glass and could see all the cat steps and ridges. He thought he was nearly scalped, so much had come off. He looked at Dick and saw his younger brother's anxious expression and said, "Thank you. It'll do."

Dick broke into a grin, he was so happy. "Well, maybe I'll try it again. I thought you might be mad. I've never cut hair before."

John never answered.

The next morning four teams left out for Swan Creek to help the Cook family dig their spuds. They threw some planks on the wagons for a floor. John knew they would be sacking and hauling potatoes to a cellar. One team would pull the digger which was nothing but a hand plow, but instead of a plow, it was a flat plate which dug under the ground as it went under the potatoes, tilling them to the surface. Most were left on top, but some had to be scuffed out with boots. The front of the plate dug deep, but it sloped up to the rear. The man on the digger handles had to adjust the depth and angle by pushing down or pulling up on the handles. It was work, and Robert and John's brothers were busy digging, but John turned his team up to the west, up across the canal, and across Sage Brush Flat. He was going to get a load of aspen firewood.

On the south edge of the flat a big grove of aspen had died and many were down. He went into the middle of a big bunch, and tied his team solid. Then he started loading the trees. He didn't trim them, just carried them to the wagon and stacked them on the standards. In about an hour, he was loaded and bound on. The pioneer binder was done by throwing the chain over the load and hooking the hook in the link, then putting a strong pole through the chain, then going around with it in a circular motion. As the chain twisted, it became really tight. The end of the pole was fastened tight so it couldn't loosen up.

So John got a big load home in time for dinner. He tended the horses. After dinner he cut wood, and by night had the wood box full, and most of the shed was full and stacked. Five days of this and the family started to feel good about the coming winter. When John had gone to Sagebrush Flat the first day, he'd noticed how thick the chickens were along the canal. Also, while loading wood, the coyotes seemed to be yelling for him. It sounded like a whole bunch talking to each other.

"Mother, do we have anything to treat traps with?" John had about ten double long spring traps, and twenty or so single spring rat traps. Sarah LeDuc ordered wax at the store. As a French Canadian fur trapper's daughter, she definitely knew the business.

John hauled a couple of loads to the tithing yard, then went up a little higher into a grove of live aspen and cut and hauled a couple of loads of those. They were heavy. He trimmed and lifted them on, a lot of work, and a heavy load for his team to hold back on the steep places, but they behaved beautifully. The green aspen was used for posts and fence poles and also by spring it was dry enough to burn.

The third trip he went a little farther north. He worked into a different bunch of aspen. He tied the team. He still didn't trust them to stand. He undid the axe off the standard, and then stepped out a few steps, sizing up the tree when he caught sight of movement out of the corner of his eye.

Looking back, he saw a coyote running all out with a black wolf after him, and about ten feet back a big white wolf was also in pursuit. They came from the north out of Broad Hollow. They were running up the open ridge between Broad Hollow and Sage Flat. Thinking a shot might scare his team he bent low and ran a ways to meet them. When they were about a hundred yards from him, the lead wolf caught up and in a single move sent the coyote about twenty feet in the air, doing back flips. The white wolf was looking up, trying to stop, when Pope's bullet hit him in the throat.

The black wolf caught the coyote and was turning with its prize held high when the 44-40 bullet caught him on the point of the shoulder, rolling him back down the hill a few feet. They would all be valuable unless they had ripped the coyote up too much. He was going to try to trap some anyway because he was about broke.

John only cut about six trees which made a floor on the wagon and gave room for his fur to ride on top. John T. was excited. It was fun to shoot again, and now he would have the scent he needed so he could catch more coyotes. When he reached the wolves, he was amazed at their size and weight. They were the big old buffalo wolves like he had seen following the herd through Wyoming. Pope held the lines in one hand while loading the fur. It was a terrible job to lift the wolves on, but he finally got it done. The coyote was easy by comparison. He stole a halter rope from a work horse and tied them in place.

He went home, and while passing the store, Gus Sprouse hollered at him, so he stopped. Gus came out to look, and seeing the huge wolves, yelled for everyone to come see what John Pope had. There were about twenty people in the close area. They all came to see wolves. The gathering was amazed at their size and the cruel, wicked look of the slanted eyes and fangs. Before John could skin the wolves about every house in town had a few of their family members go take a look at the big, menacing animals.

Sarah sent John to the lake to cut four birch poles, crooked on one end. She showed him how to make large stretchers out of poles for the wolf pelts. After they were on the stretchers, she pushed handfuls of dry grass into the legs, and even all over, so it would all dry, no skin to touch other skin. John saved all the urine he could for scent for trapping coyotes.

Bear Lake and Bear River in those early years were about as isolated as Ashley Valley. Most white men in the area, though, were Mormon settlers. But those early years were always uneasy because of Indians. The Utes who came each year were mostly tame and beggars, but there were Bronco Utes as well as Shoshone.

Chief Washakie loved Bear Lake. When his people camped on the south of Bear Lake, they varied in number, but between six, ten, or even eleven thousand Indians, sometimes for a short period. People all had to be in the square at night, but next morning they could go out to irrigate crops and so on. While the Indians were near Bear Lake, they had hunting parties out in every canyon and on every mountain for miles. As a result, elk were extinct. Deer were very scarce, and it was rare to see even a track. Rabbits and sage chickens, ducks and geese were abundant. Also grass livestock did great. So a man was more likely to run into a bear or predator than game of any size.

For the last week, Robert and the boys were hauling hay. They had eight loads of wild grass hay hauled from Mud Lake. It took three days to make a round trip: cut hay with the scythe, load the hay racks with pitch forks, and haul it back home. They could never keep enough hay on hand. The one advantage of Ashley Valley, although it could get cold and nasty, pasture could usually be found year around. Bear Lake on the other hand had snow all winter, sometimes over the fences.

One morning one of the neighbors rode up and asked if anyone had seen his milk cows. Robert said, "We always give our milk cows a bit of grain at milking time so they always are on hand come time to milk." Everyone in town turned the cows in the streets after milking. They had a choice of roaming the lakeshore or any place not fenced. There was more ground unfenced than otherwise. Sometimes cows strayed quite a ways.

Robert offered John's service as a tracker. So John went with L. Cook back to his corral. John studied the tracks and memorized them. They rode out slowly. John followed the tracks south through town.

Cook said, "I'll bet you're just guessing. The road is packed with tracks." John rode ahead about twenty feet and climbed off his horse, showing a track to Cook.

"This is one of your cow's tracks, right?"

"It could be."

"It's the one I've been following from your corral."

So they rode ahead. The cows took the road up Hodges Canyon. The canyon was quite packed with tracks from ranch cows. He kept watching to make sure the cows didn't leave the road at the forks. They did leave the main traveled trail, going up the North Fork. There was water all the way. The cattle went from water to some grassy meadows. They wandered a lot, but continued on west until they topped the divide into South Sink. About a mile or so, they found a herd of twenty-five cows and calves lying in the grass a few yards from the timber. L. Cook said he was amazed anyone could track so good and so fast.

"It's just a few miles from here, over the divide, to your ranch in Meadowville. You want to push them that way?"

"No, back to Garden City, if you'll help me."

They quietly rode around the cows. With gentle nudging, the cows realized what was expected of them. They walked along quietly so there might still be a little milk for the family. They had strayed about fourteen miles, and must travel back the full distance, arriving home in time for a late lunch or early supper.

John rode up to the store to check on the wax. It was in. They had snares with the hardware which let the loop tighten, but once tight, it couldn't come loose which choked a fighting animal to death quickly. They were two cents apiece, so he took twenty-five. These would be much better than the snares the Indians had shown him how to make and set.

That night John made a fire under the large soap pot. It was generally used for making lye soap. John added a couple buckets of water. He kept feeding the fire until it was hot enough, and then added the wax until it was liquid. He dipped all his traps, stakes, chains, and wires. Next, he treated the new snares as well, putting the film of wax on the metal. This made the metal scent invisible. Without treating the traps, he'd catch no coyotes, for they were wilier than that.

Another rule to be followed was to never touch a trap with a bare hand, or the animal would smell the trapper and shy away. For this purpose, a smart trapper always wore leather gloves and moccasins. The rat traps were mostly set underwater, so they needed no wax.

Next morning John hooked his team, loaded his gear, and left on a new adventure. He was painstakingly careful with his sets. He dug a hole the right depth and size for his traps. He used dry grass and sage brush leaves which were very fragrant once stripped from the brush. This soft, cushy material went under the pan of his traps, and by putting dry aspen leaves on top, it kept material from leaking down which might interfere when the trap went off. He covered the whole thing with dry dust. His stakes, chains, and traps were all buried and completely invisible. The sagebrush, or trees, or whatever he used as a back for the set, was then sprinkled with the animal scent, or urine. These sets were chosen strategically along the trail and ran wherever John saw tracks.

It was after dark when John unhooked and finally got to eat that night, and he was even later to bed, but he arose in the morning, just like the sun, and used his team once again to run his trap line. The snares were all blind sets, no scent, but set in runs in brushy places along the rough. Pope had five in snares, and three in his sets. He was very careful in resetting. With eight coyotes in one day he thought maybe he was making better wages than cowboys, but time would tell.

Coming down Long Ridge, and almost back to Hodges Canyon, he ran into a huge flock of sage hens. It looked like the whole hill was covered with them as they were walking out of his way. Taking both lines in his left hand, he drew his pistol and shot one's head off. The horses jumped and fussed a bit, but didn't run, so he emptied the old colt. The horses didn't seem bothered after the first shot. He killed about a dozen because they had many mouths to feed, and Pope's loved sage hens. He tossed them in with the fur, kissed to the team and . . . nothing.

"Get up."

Still nothing.

"Get up! Haw!"

No response.

"Hey! Get up now!" John hollered at them. Finally he slapped them with the lines to get them started. Shooting that close to them had made them deaf as posts! It was several days before his team had their hearing back.

Two weeks into trapping and it snowed. Pope had to pull his traps and call it a season. He had about fifty-five coyotes, and two wolf pelts. "The stockmen will rest a bit easier, now, I'll wager." His mother was working with the pelts a bit as they came off the stretchers, adding greatly to the value of the fur. John T. then went to the lake and sloughs below town and set out a long trap line for muskrats and mink. He set many snares in runs and shallow places.

After a couple of weeks of rat trapping, he had about two hundred muskrats and six mink. He then moved all his traps to the Meadowville bottoms and Big Spring Creek area, where he hit a bonanza. He brought in forty or fifty a day. And other members of his family had to step in to help stretch the hides. Much time was spent in travel, and it was hard work. He pulled his traps a week before Christmas. The carcasses of all these trapped animals went into the pig pen. Those pigs ate bones and all, and really floundered on them, plumping up nicely. When the pelts were baled, he had six hundred muskrats, one mountain lion caught in a snare, two bob cats, and about twenty-two mink—-at least two wagon loads of fur to ship.

Sarah LeDuc had written to her furrier in New York. Because of so many wild furs in the Morgan and Ogden areas, and this large consignment, they would send a man out to check and buy the fur in Evanston, as well as on west. He would be in Evanston on the Fifth of January. They loaded John's wood rack on a set of his dad's sleighs, and spent a day getting bows on and covering it. His dad had a good covered buckboard which they loaded on another set of sleighs. It took two days to load everything. Seven or eight beef hides and some sheep pelts were loaded on the bottom of John's load. The Garden City store keeper told Robert he would gladly knock off thirty dollars from Pope's store bill for a couple of loads back to him. So he gave Robert a signed check on the Beckwith Bank for goods from Beckwith and Louder Co. in Evanston.

The storekeeper told John, "Just fill in the amount at pick up time," and included his list.

This would be a seventy mile trip, one way in winter. It was not a job for most teenage kids. John packed two sacks of oats for his horses. He would leave after the holidays.

Chapter Five

Christmas Blessings and New Year Bounty

On Christmas Eve, a big dance in Fish Haven promised a crowd. John's brothers and one sister wanted to go. Sarah told John she would feel better about the kids if he were along to see to them. So he had to take a bath, shave, and have a haircut, but he was careful not to let Dick do it. He dug out his best clothes and took everybody in the buggy. It was nine miles, and so they took blankets, and John wore mittens and a sheepskin coat. When they arrived at the dance, he left the team tied to the hitch rail, and left his coat and mittens in the buggy.

The dance was toasty. There were pot bellied stoves on both sides of the room that were cranking out heat. A piano and a fiddle were providing toe tapping music. Lots of older people were sitting on chairs along the side. Several of the men stopped to shake hands with him and introduced themselves. John realized he didn't fit with the young set, yet he didn't fit with the older folks either. A lot of people seemed to be looking at him and whispering to each other. He guessed they were looking at the hardware he carried. But if he left it off, he'd feel naked. He was just himself, and nobody asked him to leave.

He started looking all the girls over, dancing or not. One gal was dancing with a shorter kid and didn't seem very happy about it. Between dances she turned to go and he caught her, and then danced with her again.

As they went by John, she happened to see him watching. She smiled and John was smitten. When the dance ended, she again tried to escape. Her partner caught up and grabbed her arm, pulling her back around.

John heard him say, "Where ya going?"

John reached out, took him by the arm, turning him half around. "She promised this dance to me, bud."

The girl beamed and a touch of pink colored her cheeks. She took John's arm and turned away from her tormentor, saying, "Thanks."

"It's all my pleasure—what is your name?"

"Charlotte Ann Stock." She flushed again, and John thought her blushing was most bewitching.

"Shall I call you Ann or Charlotte, or what?"

"Either one."

John grinned, for surely she had a preference! "But what do your folks call you?"

"Usually just . . . Charlotte, unless I'm in trouble, and then it's the whole handle: Charlotte Ann Stock!"

"Okay, Charlotte. I'm John T. Pope."

"I know. I've been eager to meet you, John. I didn't think you would ever ask me to dance, and then you stepped up and saved me from that clod-hopping creep."

John laughed out loud.

"What's so funny?

"I'm bashful and scared of pretty gals like you, and I didn't have the nerve to start up a conversation or nothin', but you made it easy for me. Besides, you are easy to talk to and such a good dancer. You've been keeping out from under my own *clod-hopping* feet."

John danced the rest of the night with Charlotte Ann Stock. She liked it. So did he. The old folks on the side noticed and wagged their tongues for sport.

"I've got a couple of brothers and a sister with me or I'd try to take you home."

"I came with my folks," but she introduced John to them before they left the dance. John felt like a young bull in the springtime—happy to indulge in green pastures, for oh! He was twitterpated for sure.

Christmas was really nice. The Pope kids all got an orange shipped from Florida and wrapped so it wouldn't freeze between Evanston, and the store. There was also a bit of candy. Dinner was lip-smacking with ham, potatoes, gravy, corn, and squash from the cellar. Bread pudding and cake had also been prepared. There was a family prayer and lots of visiting. John almost put on the entertainment, answering questions about trail drives, freighting, packing, and about the bighorns, Texas, mining, and trapping. Brothers and sisters tried to tease him about Charlotte, so Sarah and Robert wanted to know about the dance. He was glad to walk outside and cool off.

Waves could be heard lapping on the beach and a bunch of geese set up a lot of honking, talking goose talk along the shore. A cow bawled north of the settlement. Some sounds were peculiar to Bear Lake, and some were familiar and found every place in the west. Garden City was called Poverty Flat the first years until the ditch was finished. With water available, large gardens were planted; trees and orchards were also planted. The water and fertile soil combined to bring beautiful yields. Nice frame homes were replacing crude cabins.

Pioneers grew what they needed to eat. Their stock provided leather for shoes and harnesses, as well as meat, milk, eggs, butter, cheese, and wool to spin homespun clothing. The mountains contained timber, log wood for houses, barns, fences, fuel for heating and cooking. The mountains also provided pasture and water—water for irrigation and stock water.

In Mormon settlements like this, settlers stayed in the community for protection against the Indians. One man filed on a homestead, and then everyone got lots, and fields which had to be fenced. Water was filed on and was the private property of first person to file as long as it could be put to beneficial use. When they didn't use it beneficially, then later filers could gain ownership. This was called the Prior Appropriation Law.

Settlers also filed on the grass which was a renewable resource. Sometimes the amount of stock a rancher would run depended on his water rights. At this early period, already boundaries of people's grazing ground and numbers of stock he could run were known. Cattle and stock associations began to bring law and order to the settlements, limiting people's ability to grow and expand because most of the so-called public land was claimed by those ranchers who first filed on water and grass.

Pope leaned against the corral, watching his colt eat, wondering at the things that were happening around them so fast. How could they find the place they wanted? Cooks had two nice ranches, one at Swan Creek and one in Meadowville. Most of the land south of town was Nat Hodges', clear to the gap on the south of Bear Lake. He came with money and bought out Bisbing's and Gibbon's homesteads and who all else's, John didn't know. Hodges had bought and imported twelve hundred sheep and over a hundred cows. He kept quite a number of hired men. Several settlers in Garden City worked at *The Ranch*, as it was called.

So Pope's had a couple of nice homes and fields. They turned about thirty cattle loose to graze the hills. They kept about sixty sheep, but coyotes were so bad they had to be kept close. The crafty coyote would always pick the biggest, fattest, and best lambs. A wily coyote was always a good judge. John's trapping should help.

He thought of the coming trip to Evanston. It could be dangerous. They had to go over the mountain. There would be a lot of snow. Hopefully, the mailman would have a sleigh road John could follow. He decided to pray for good weather.

He stepped in the barn and gave his team a coffee can of oats apiece. He worked his horses every day so they would be hard and full of grain. Next day, he hooked up and took his wagon, just running gears, no rack on it, and rode north along the lake. About a mile north there was a point that reached out into the lake a ways. Cattails and tullies grew high along one side. John could hear geese talk coming from beyond the screen of flags. He hadn't tasted a goose for a long time and wondered if a New Year's goose would help. He nosed his team into some trees, tied up, and went hunting.

John T. bent low and worked up close, finally crawling in the snow a ways. When he was as close as possible, he stood up and made a fluid, smooth draw, but the geese didn't fly. They were under cover of another row of flags across a pond of open water. Many were lying with heads under their wings. Several had heads up as sentinels. He stood with legs spread a bit sideways of them.

In one place there was a cluster. He decided to shoot one in the middle and hope for more than one for his shot. So he cut loose then, in a roll, his shots went so fast it was one roll of sound. Pope concentrated on each shot, and he dropped a goose with each shot for the last five. Hundreds of geese flew, honking noisily. John got home with eight Canadian geese.

Then came one of the worst jobs of John's life—picking geese, but his mother was too resourceful to waste a thing. All the down was saved carefully. Pillows were sewn and stuffed with fluffy, delightful down feathers, but during the picking process it got in John's nose and itched. Lice crawled up his ears. His hands were too messy to do anything about it, and Dick and Adeline looked even more miserable than he felt! Torches were lit to singe the hair and pin feathers of the picked geese, then the family cleaned them.

"The geese must be clean," Sarah clucked, dropping them in cold water. John thought it was fun hunting them, and shooting was good practice, but one goose would be plenty to have to clean! He felt errant to have shot so many. The whole kitchen had goose down decorating it. It was a typical pioneer experience, except most people used a shotgun. To John it was practice to keep ready for any trouble that might come his way.

"I can't stand the smell, Mother!" Dick sputtered; blowing floating bits of down from his nostrils, then he jerked his collar over his nose.

"Think of new pillows, Richard, and smile, for we are lucky that John is such a good shot!"

On the day of the trip, the family ate breakfast really early. John and his dad had two hours behind them when it got light. They were in Laketown when the sun came up. They stopped at the bottom of the canyon and unhooked, slipped the bridles off, hung them on the hames, then led the horses to water. Both teams drank deep of the water which ran down the city ditch out of old Laketown Canyon or Mill Canyon. They then poured a gallon of oats in each feed bag and hung them over the horses' ears, and let the horses eat their grain for about fifteen minutes or so. They hooked back up and drove up the canyon.

The road went up to the Forks; there most woodcutters left the way to Randolph, going right, so the road faded at that point. However, there was a sleigh road on up and over. A sleigh road is simply the tracks made in the snow by a team pulling a sleigh. As the storms continue to come, the team steps in the same place they did when they went over it the last time. A good winter team could follow the road and never step off, even after it had stormed and blew till a man couldn't see it at all. Up on the mountain, if a horse stepped off the road, he went into four or five feet of snow. So if a horse made a mistake, he jumped back up to get back on the track in one jump usually. If the sleigh runner cut off, the sleigh would tip until the edge of the rack contacted the snow. Sometimes a driver would have to pull it quite a way before the team got the sleigh back on the road.

So their teams kept their head where they could see and walked at the same rate the team who made the road. That way they stepped in the same tracks, and they never had any trouble except they stopped several times to let the horses get their wind. They made excellent time because the horses were toughened from hard work and grain. By shortly after noon, they stopped on the South Fork of Otter Creek and watered the horses again and rested a few minutes, then went on to Randolph. They had made such good time; they continued south, finally stopping at the Cox Ranch in Woodruff. They stabled and fed the horses and harnessed up so that as they finished breakfast the next morning, they were ready to hook up and go, though not such an early start. It was okay, for there was no canyon to cross on this day.

A few miles North of Evanston, Almy was busy—lots of men working in the coal mines. A new bridge spanned Bear River. No snow on it, so they found a place and crossed on the ice. Bare ground or bridges made horses really work to drag a loaded sleigh.

At the railroad station they found their fur man. He had already bought a few hides and fur. He was several hours going over the Pope's loads. He was very impressed with quality and kept a notebook where he noted the number and price.

Finally after tallying everything, he said, "Four hundred fourteen dollars."

John said, "Write out two checks. Give Dad one hundred and fifty of that. I'll take the rest."

John's check was two hundred and sixty-four dollars. They drove the empty sleighs to the livery barn and took care of the horses, then walked back to the hotel and took a room. A café at the hotel seemed like a good place to eat. It was dark outside. Robert and John ate a good supper and signed the bill with the room number. They would pay it all when they checked out. On a napkin while drinking their coffee, John figured thirty dollars a month top wages. Forty-four dollars represented thirteen months of wages working on a ranch.

The next morning at breakfast, the fur man came into the café and said he was ordered by his company to give an extra fifty dollars. "When I wired the quality of your fur, they responded that Pope's were valued customers and to pay you more." The furrier grinned, eager to make out the check.

John said, "Make it to Robert." So his dad received about six month's wages. John felt good about his trapping venture! They walked back to the livery and hooked up and went to the loading docks at the back of Beckwith and Louder's store and gave a clerk the order. As busy employees loaded the sleighs, John went into the bank and cashed his check.

When the sleighs were loaded and secured, they gave the check the Garden City store had sent, filling in the amount. John told his dad to start for home. "I'll be along just after I settle our bill," he called. He paid in cash, a buck fifty for meals and room. John grinned, for all things considered, the expenses were low, and this emprise had only cost him lots and lots of hard work.

When John T. crossed Woodruff Creek, his dad was still ahead three-eighths of a mile or so. They got to Randolph late that night, and Randolph Stewart put them up. Next morning they left early and made good time, except for a few rest stops. They got home a couple of hours after dark. It was the next morning before the two loads of freight were delivered to the store. John bought a couple of boxes of 44-40's, and a razor, for he was beyond the peach fuzz stage now. He also bought a new scarf. He always wore one around his neck. After cleaning up, he borrowed the covered buggy and made a trip to Fish Haven, for he'd been thinking about a pretty little gal named Charlotte Ann Stock most of the way.

John asked and was directed to the Stock home. When Mr. Stock answered the door, John grabbed his hat off and asked if Charlotte was home.

Come in," the father said, mustache twitching, then Charlotte's father sat at the table with some papers, studying. Charlotte's mother was preparing a meal.

"Will you stay for supper?"

John's boots tapped nervously against the floor. "No disrespect, ma'am, but I don't even know if she'll have anything to do with me. I only met her that night at the dance."

The woman smiled. "I'll set a place for you, because she'll be glad you came. She's got that buck-toothed Randal kid in there, just trying to get rid of him, but he's determined. She talked about you for a week or two, and when you didn't come, she felt bad."

John felt his neck grow red, and he fidgeted with the hat in his hand.

"Come sit down. Tell me about yourself."

So Pope talked to Charlotte's folks long enough to get thinking a lot of them. Suddenly Charlotte broke into the kitchen and saw John sitting there all relaxed. She froze in place for a minute, then with a voice not quite normal, she said, "You came!"

Charlotte stepped toward him a few steps. He stood up and held his hands out. She ran into his arms and held him a minute, heart beating wildly. The action filled young John with hearty encouragement! John saw the kid from the dance watching from the door, mouth drooping dumbly.

John said, "If you can't see how this is, then you aint as smart as you ought to be."

The kid fumbled for his coat and hat, and went out into the winter's eve, slamming the door behind him.

"Thank you for coming back! What took you so long?"

"I went trapping for awhile. I finally hauled the fur to Evanston and just got back last night. So I'm here now . . ."

"What have you been trapping?" Mr. Stock asked.

"About anything with fur, I guess."

"Like what?" Charlotte persisted.

"I trapped coyotes 'til I got snowed out, then I trapped muskrats and mink."

"Did you really catch a coyote or so?"

"Oh, yeah, it kept me busy all day and half the night, running traps and skinning and stretching 'em for quite awhile."

Charlotte's father seemed intrigued. "I've tried to catch them, but I never caught one in my life. I drug a dead sheep up on the Red Hill and set about four traps around it. I hid the traps and stakes and next morning I could see a coyote sitting up there so I thought I had one. I went right up, but he was gone. The coyotes had a beaten trail around the sheep, but all about two feet out from my traps. Not one came any closer. They must be smart."

"They really suspect something when you bait your traps that way. They have a really good nose and they smell your traps."

"How many did you trap?"

"Sixty-five."

"Coyotes?"

"Yes."

"Good hell! Will you show me how?"

"Sure. The Shoshone Indians taught me to trap. I dipped my traps, stakes, and chains in wax. The smell doesn't come through the wax. Then I always wear moccasins or rubber boots and always wear gloves. If you touch a trap with a bare hand, they'll smell it, and you don't catch much. Once you get one, then save the urine from the animal and use it for a lure. Sprinkle a little around your trap. The coyote will smell it and come sniffing around, and you catch him."

"What else did you catch?"

"I had two wolves."

"Again I say, 'good hell!'"

"A lion, two bobcats, fifteen mink, and six hundred muskrats; we freighted two loads of fur to the railroad in Evanston, Wyoming."

Mr. Stock blinked as John rattled the numbers and John again felt most encouraged as the man said, "That's quite ambitious, Pope."

Mrs. Stock brought the dinner, and they asked John to pray. He was happy to be well-practiced. The meal consisted of fried trout and potatoes—and tasted delicious.

Mr. Stock said the fish was his specialty. He freighted a few loads of trout each year and got good money for them, too.

Charlotte smiled across the table. "I might like a fur muff, or a collar, or something."

"I've pretty much pulled all my traps for the winter, but I'll think on it."

So John knew he would be trapping some place and he was eager to get started!

This was a strange experience, and it was too cold to walk out with Charlotte, but she really seemed to like him. So before he left, he asked if it would be all right to call again.

"You'd better."

Her folks said, "Please do."

When John put on his coat and fastened the gun over it, picked up the hat, and stepped out, Charlotte came with him. She grabbed him around the neck and kissed him fair and square.

"I've never kissed a girl before," he said. "Does that mean we're engaged or something?"

She pulled his head down, and they kissed a long wet one. "Tell me what that meant to you?" She whispered before turning for the house.

John ran out to the buggy. No matter how cold the weather was, he'd be too hot to cool off before he got home! He let his team have their heads and before long, they were on a high trot that was the fastest he'd let them go since he bought them, for fear they might run, but he didn't care tonight. "Tonight we are celebrating, my fine, faithful friends!" The horses' heads bobbed in reply for they were happy for their master!

The next morning as he curried the team and his colt, Sarah LeDuc stepped into the barn and asked him about the night before.

"It was fun."

Sarah's black eyes sparked, and brows arched pleasantly. "*Fun?* I see . . ."

"If I trap some fur could you make a shawl or muff for Charlotte?"

"Yes son, it sounds *fun.*" John joined his mother in a chuckle, and he knew his eyes were shining, shamelessly belying his feelings for the lovely girl from Fish Haven, Idaho.

So, he took snares and traps to try to catch a girl. In a week, bucking drifted snow to his butt to set traps on a rocky cedar ridge north of town, he finally had two coyotes and three bobcats, one really big one. His mother gave an order for items from the store—harness oil, baking soda, kerosene, waxed silk tread, a sewing awl, and five yards of dark material.

John bought it, and as he was leaving the store keeper said he needed another load of supplies. "I will pay you fifteen dollars if you'll make the trip." So, John left the next morning on another adventure to Evanston, alone this time.

He was back in five days with the freight. He was only home a day when he was visited by some of his dad's friends from St. Charles. The Pope's were again hired to bring freight to the store in St. Charles. The list and check was left with them. The next morning before light, they were on another trip. John took his father this time, and it seemed that news was spreading: John T. Pope was freighting for pay.

Six days later, they delivered the freight and unloaded it in St. Charles. They spent the night there. On the way home, John stopped in Fish Haven to check on his only girl, and she was happy enough to receive him.

He continued to work with the colt until spring. Sarah made a short, waist length bobcat fur coat with a coyote fur collar and sleeve cuffs, as well as coyote fur trim around the bottom of the coat. It was quite a heavy coat, luxuriously lined with the dark material from the store. John made a trip northward to the Stock residence. The present was all wrapped in gray wrapping paper from the store, and Charlotte opened it with a look of awe on her face. She squealed with delight, and then planted a kiss square on his mouth. He knew that he had truly trapped a gal, and he enjoyed another merry trip back home.

Spring work was hard. Pope's sowed about ten acres of wheat, five of oats, and an acre of potatoes. They planted a couple more rows of raspberries as well as everything else.

The day came for Stock's to pick him up to go fishing. Mr. Stock came along with another man from Fish Haven, in a light wagon, with a spring seat in front. John T. jumped up, and they trotted out to the south.

"Where are we going?"

"To the Big Spring Creek, on the south end of the lake. It's by far the best fishery on Bear Lake."

"Fish Haven Creek, I thought, was really good."

"Yeah, it's good. A lot of fish spawn in the little creek. You can catch a mess with your hands or shoot them, but up here, I'll show you how to fill this wagon box in thirty minutes. Then I can take them north and sell them for spending money."

John T. saw the big net in the back, so he already figured out about what would happen. When they neared the gap, Pope spotted the big Indian tipis.

"This will be a bit tricky."

"What's the matter?"

"Well, there's a big bunch of Indians camped there already. They'll have their drying racks full of fish, and they might think we're being pushy."

Stock slowed his team to a walk. "They're friendly Indians, aren't they?"

"Yes, but their superstitious and notional."

"Notional?"

"You know—they get certain notions about things."

As they drew nearer, again John sensed danger. He could see dust in the air over the mountains above Laketown as they neared Rendezvous Beach. He could see Indians coming into the valley from the southwest. The Indian Trail through the cedar was full of Indians in single file, stretching as far as two miles. All was covered by moving Indians. John figured by the dust in the air that a large group was already in the valley.

A sense of alarm rang in his bloodstream. "I don't like this much! These Indians are Utes. If my hunch is right, the bunch coming in from the southeast is Shoshones."

"Another bunch?"

"Didn't you notice the dust?" John pointed them out and the other men saw them, but still drove forward. Charlotte's father just didn't get the danger.

"Shoshones and Utes don't get along. They steal each other's horses, and fight over ground."

By now the fishing party was nearing the creek. There was a large group of Indians scurrying around. Suddenly a Shoshone brave, riding buck-naked, came screaming around a clump of trees. He was mounted on a pinto horse on a dead run, lance held upright with a bloody man's head impaled on the top. The head was still bleeding down over the bloody rider, bathing him in gore, and his horse as well, staining them red. This Indian was screaming like a banshee, riding right past the wagon and on along the beach to the west. Pope jumped from the seat to the back of the wagon where he could shoot if necessary.

Stock nearly upset the wagon getting it turned so fast. He used his whip on the horses, and they went out of there on a run. They passed the screaming Indian coming back up the beach. Pope, standing in the back of the wagon, held onto the back of the seat and watched as the tipis came down. Before they got back to the gap, not one Ute tipi remained standing.

John Pope said, "That was the Shoshone's way of telling the Utes to clear the hell out! It's really not as safe around them as you think. I worked for the BQ ranch last year, and while I was freighting from Evanston, the ranch had a crew building a canal from Twin Creeks into the ranch. One group of teams was plowing and scraping and another bunch was building the diversion dam. Camped nearby on Twin Creek, a bunch of Shoshone were camped, and they watched the work with amusement and some of them made fun of the hard work which must have seemed like foolishness to them."

Stock and the other man nodded, wanting to hear more. "Go on," Charlotte's father urged.

"When the dam was completed, they turned the creek into the canal, and the Indians watched in amazement as the creek began to dry below and flow in the new ditch. They went crazy and starting shooting at the ranch workers who made a running fight out of it. They were chased to the ranch. The surveyor was killed. One horse was killed and several men and horses were wounded with arrows. The Shoshone cried that it was bad medicine to make water run up hill."

"I've had enough dealings with them to know enough to watch them. Their beliefs and everything is very different from ours."

The Stock Family was trying to make a place for their family as was everyone in these far off, isolated settlements of Bear Lake. Because so many left after the first winter, and because there was so little money, Brigham Young and Apostle Charles C. Rich tried to establish the United Order, and a modified version was tried in Bear Lake. Each ward or branch in the valley was encouraged to have a co-op. This would provide employment. The Stake itself started a dairy operated by the Kunz Family from Bern. They made the best cheese. Almost every family in the stake owned a cow in the dairy. Some had a bunch.

The Paris Ward built a slaughter house. No family could eat a beef before it spoiled because of no existing refrigeration or electricity. By distributing the meat to everyone, it was cleaned up, and nothing wasted.

Another ward built a tannery, because the settlers needed the leather badly. Cobbler shops, saddle and harness shops all needed these items in the frontier. A grist mill was built by Phineas W. Cook in Swan Creek, between Garden City and Fish Haven.

Every family raised enough wheat and corn for their bread and meal. Now they sacked the grain and hauled it to the mill, waited while it was ground, and then loaded their flour and cracked wheat. The hulls were sacked separately for the chickens and feed for stock. They didn't have to grind it in coffee mills anymore.

Garden City Ward had a shingle mill. Everyone was paid in scrip since there was almost no cash. So in the fall as all the kids, as well as the adults, in the Pope family needed new shoes, they took the scrip they had been receiving from dairy cows, and their work on the mill, etc., and they went north to Paris. They bought new shoes and boots from the cobbler shops. They could pay in scrip. One team went on north to the dairy. The whole Nounan Valley was a dairy operation. Pope's brought back huge longhorn cheeses, which would last the family the whole winter. The longer it was kept in the cellar, the better it got. All was paid with scrip.

One day out of every ten, individuals worked on the projects that were needed to improve the settlements. So, timber was stacked in the tithing yard. Bridges were built. Rock was quarried and hauled. One day a week belonged to the Lord. So, John T. Pope, free spirit, Kid Pope, pistoleer, Indian expert, teamster, freighter, packer, trapper, and drover, was seeing the value of the church organization first hand. He saw his dad watch out for a few who didn't have much. He would take flour once in a while, or a piece of meat to them. John T. knew that in the case of one or two of these families, the men were just too lazy to do anything.

"I think you should let those lazy men starve! Until they learn how to work, why should they beg their way into favor?"

Robert just said, "Son, the wife and kids are in need, so I'll do what I can."

John would laugh the rest of his life about a conversation he heard from one family. It went like this: "Eden, go borrow a team and get us some wood!"

"God damn it, Martha, you know I aint got no wood."

John T. wouldn't have loaned his team to anyone else anyway. So he went out himself and brought a load of wood to this family. So, the creator was shaping a life and preparing Kid Pope to be able to help another community, on the fringe of the wild frontier, to overthrow the outlaw stronghold existing there. He was learning about settling, bringing electricity, oil roads, peace, and so forth to communities. It's good we don't know our future, and John was often thankful that he hadn't been granted a peek into his.

Chapter Six

Building a Future

YOUNG POPE KNEW HE wanted a wife. He might have swelling of the neck or maybe this was love. Whatever, he knew he'd like a family. He'd have to try to earn enough to get a milk cow or two. He had a runaway team that hadn't run away since he'd owned them. He had a two-year old colt. His old saddle horse should go to his dad for the horse he had ridden away on to Texas. He could haul the logs and build a house and barn and get fixed up if maybe he could file on a spot of ground. So no sooner thought of, but John bowed his neck and went back up on the mountain and cut a load of building logs and hauled them into his dad's yard. By Saturday night he had enough logs to put up a cabin.

He rode his colt to church in Fish Haven on Sunday. He met Charlotte, and had dinner at the Stock's home. Everyone was talking about an accident up Fish Haven Canyon. A log fell on a young man, killing him instantly. They had buried him the day before. His pregnant wife was looking for help to move her belongings back to Salt Lake. So John said, "I'll take my team and help. I guess what I'm doing can wait a week."

Charlotte walked with him to the new widow's camp and introduced him. "I'm awful sorry, ma'am, and I'd be happy to help if I could."

"My husband and I had a lot on the north end of town, on the lower side of the road. We've partially built some corrals. We were still living in a tent, but we've hauled logs and planned to start work on our cabin. I will give it to you, lot, logs, and all, if you'll take me and my belongings home to Salt Lake. I am eager to get back to my parents."

"I'm happy to do it for nothing, "John said.

"But the lot and logs are no good to me now! The lot can't really be mine until I've lived there for two years and made improvements. That dream is gone now—I just want to go home."

Charlotte whispered, "Not un-chaperoned, you won't take her home."

John grinned at his girl. "Charlotte Ann would feel much better if I brought my dad or one of my brothers to drive your wagon. I'll be here in the morning. We'll load your trunks, bedding, and supplies, and if there's room in one wagon, we'll make a bed for you so you can sleep right inside. It will take us five days to get you home."

As John walked Charlotte home he inspected the widow's partially built corrals and lot, carefully eying the stack of logs. "Charlotte, do you think you could live here?" That was like a proposal, and the kiss that followed felt like a definite yes answer.

On the way home that night, John kept urging his colt to hurry. When he broke into a trot, John would jerk his head down, trying to teach him to walk fast. Shorty wanted to hurry home too, so after one of the jerk backs, he hit that pace. John had never ridden a pacer before. He knew he was going pretty fast and so smooth he leaned out to try to see what he was doing. He couldn't quite tell. He was afraid the colt would become winded with this new gate, but he didn't. John began falling in love with his colt.

As soon as he got home, he ran in to get some help from his family. It was decided that Dick could make the trip. They had to shorten the reach in John's wagon and load the covered wagon box. They packed their bed rolls and grub box. Dick took his rifle and some heavy coats.

Next morning they were off by four, reaching Fish Haven at five-thirty. Mary was packed and waiting. Two trunks went on the wagon, but the tent, two chairs, a table, bedding, a spinning wheel, rifle and shotgun. A plow, a broad axe, and sledge hammer were still waiting to be loaded.

On inspiration, John asked, "What will you take for all this stuff? I'll give you twenty dollars for the plow, axe, and hammer."

"Do you want the spinning wheel?"

"I guess I do."

"Give me fifteen more. And five for the tent?"

John pulled off his money belt and extracted fifty dollars. "That sure loaded us up fast didn't it? Any cooking utensils and firearms you want to sell? I'll give a fair price."

Mary pulled a heavy Dutch oven toward its new owner, and then pushed the shotgun in his direction. "Ten more for these?"

Dick grinned at the exchanging business deals. "There's wheeling and dealing in Fish Haven this morning, and if yer sellin' old John's a buyin'!"

As soon as Mary's team was harnessed and hooked up, they were ready to go. They stopped at Pope's for dinner, and that night they camped up Cottonwood on a meadow. They had a supper and were soon asleep. Next morning, they got away good time, camped that night above Huntsville and went on to Ogden the next morning, making camp about fifteen miles further on. They rolled up to Mary's folks' home early the next morning. There were many tears shed by Mary and her family.

On the return trip, John stopped in Ogden to buy a load of lumber that had just come in on the railroad. He tried to judge so as not to get too much weight to roll home. The two boxes of nails would really help, but were heavy.

"Well, well, well," Dick observed smoothly. Somebody I know must be pretty hot for house of his own."

John said, "Hell, a covered wagon box or tent is good for me, but I need to have a good woman to sleep with me. They mostly don't do tents, I guess."

Dick laughed 'til John thought he'd fall out and get run over.

John finally said, "I never slept with any woman, or even close to it, but I've been kissed a few times lately, and it gave me the damnedest urge to do things, and think things I shouldn't have been thinking . . ."

Before he could finish, Dick busted out again. John clamped his mouth shut, the hell with him, and no more words to anyone! But Dick couldn't stop. When he did reign in the laughter it was only to draw decent wind, and then he'd cut loose again.

That night on the way up the left fork of Monte Cristo, they had to stop every few minutes to let the team get their wind. They spotted a bunch of pine hens. So John handed the lines to Dick and got out.

Dick said, "I've wanted to see you shoot, but why not from here?"

"The last time I shot over my horses' heads I deafened them for about a week."

John walked ahead, watching the hens. Suddenly he drew and fired in a smooth motion, shooting a head off one. He stepped ahead several steps quickly, then repeated the fire, and the second hen's head disappeared. Two flew. The first got about five feet off the ground when it went down in a stream of feathers. The fourth was hit as it reached some aspen and the bird bounced from branch to branch as it fell. John gathered up the four and came back to the wagon. Tossing in the grouse, he said, "Supper."

"I'm glad they're not geese."

This time John laughed, remembering the stinking miseries of picking feathers and floating down. Dick grinned at his brother's reaction and said, "Everybody said you could shoot like that. How do you do it without aiming?"

John shrugged. "I've been carrying an iron since I was eight years old. I practiced a lot those first years. A friend of mine from Texas showed me how to grab the pistol from the holster and shoot in one motion. Then I practiced thirty minutes every day since. I concentrated on each shot. I knew where every bullet was going."

"I don't have an idea how those last two shots were so close together. If I hadn't known better, I would have thought someone else had fired almost the same time."

Dick peeled and cleaned the chickens as they traveled that afternoon. They camped early that night, just after crossing Blacksmith Fork Creek. The pine hens were delicious! They saved enough for breakfast. The brothers spent their last night on Big Spring Creek, and the next day they were home free.

John stopped by the new lot and unloaded his lumber. He walked around, looking at the logs that were hauled, and surveyed the natural spring under the hill. As he was trying to visualize just where to build, Charlotte came walking up.

"So you got Mary home alright?"

"Yes. Dick helped me. We didn't have much to haul."

"How come she left the tent?"

"I bought it."

"What for?"

"It's a good place to keep stuff while the house goes up."

"What stuff?"

"Go look."

Charlotte's skirts swished gracefully as she stepped over to the tent and looked in. "You bought all this?"

"Yes."

"Wow!"

"Do you approve or not?"

She nodded vigorously with a big smile. "I almost can't wait to pop biscuits in that Dutch oven!"

"Well Charlotte, I've often heard that the way to a man's heart is through his Dutch oven." Charlotte smiled again, and then poked around the tent, examining the bargains. John continued, "The corral is half built. We'll need to crib the spring and dig another place a ways down for the animals to drink. We can haul water from the spring."

"We have a spring?" She walked down and looked.

"That's why nobody's built here already. I grubbed sage brush 'til I looked like a sage brush when we settled in Randolph! We got nothing but grass here. It's nice! I wondered what it would be like to build by that cottonwood tree over there and leave it for shade."

"Oh?" She walked back up to see. "Yes, that might be nice," she called back, smiling smugly at the exciting plans tumbling around in John Pope's head.

That's when the three loads of logs, and four men to help build a house, came rolling in—his dad and brothers and three teams. John stepped up and told his dad what he had in mind.

Robert said, "We will need some rock to set the bottom logs on, as well and the joist. What are you going to use for the joist?"

"I thought small logs or poles. What do you think?"

"Wow! Now I know why you brought so many planks. A plank floor on those poles will work. You'll have the plushest house in the settlement."

"We'll need some for the door, and frames for the windows as well."

"I get windows," Charlotte whispered, smiling again. "I get windows *and* a floor!"

Charlotte knew where they could pick up some rock, so Charlotte, John, and Dick jumped in a wagon and went after rock, leaving Robert, Rob, and George to start on things. They stopped in front of the Stock's home a minute to tell her mother where they were going. A little ways south, they turned west, rolling up a gradual hill through the sage brush and serviceberries. They drove to a knoll where nothing was growing because of the flat slate rock. There was about an acre of the stuff.

They drove around it looking for the best place to start. John wished he had brought a shovel. The shale was layered. On the west side they found where others had hauled a few loads. John positioned the wagon so they could pick up a rock, turn and place it in the back of the wagon. In about forty-five minutes they had all they dared haul and started back.

When they got back, they were amazed to see Charlotte's dad, uncle, and three other neighbors who claimed to have come to the barn raising. They had an old black horse dragging logs up to men with broad axes on either end of the logs. They would unhook the chain, and kiss to the horse, and he would walk back around. Somebody would hook onto another log. They had the barn up five logs high already.

About that time a buggy pulled in and four women got out, Charlotte's mother included. They found the table and chairs in a few minutes and dinner was cooking on hooks over a fire, along with a big coffee pot.

Charlotte showed off the spring. The women raved over it, claiming it was a good spring, and Charlotte's feet swayed with excitement, making her skirts swish back and forth. Everybody was so busy John forgot his job for awhile, but finally he started unloading rock. By seven that night the corral was finished, the barn was done, and part of the roof and the floor of the house was nailed down, all level and squared. The crew left, but Charlotte lingered.

"You better have meant it when you asked if I would live here, John T. Pope."

"Well Charlotte Ann Stock, I don't know if I'm man enough for you."

"I'll bet you are! Anyway, I want you more than anything else in this world."

By the next night the house was built. It was the only house in the town with a shingled roof and good plank floor. Most had dirt roofs and floors. The men had managed to split enough poles to cover the roof of the barn. The poles were cut straight enough with the broad axe so they fit snugly, nailed together like a narrow plank. The pitch was really steep so it might drip a bit, but most would run off. From inside looking up you could see a few cracks and stuff, but it felt snug and warm.

A manger ran down one side with several petitions. Along the back of the barn pegs were fitted into the wall to hang harnesses, collars, and other tack. The gate in the corral was three bars to slide in or out and drop to open. The barn door would have to be built and hung when they could get lumber again.

The only lumber was built on the pit mill. A log would be drug up and rolled so one end was over the pit. With one man down in the pit and one up above, they sawed the log with a cross cut saw, lengthwise. The man on the bottom had a lot of sawdust to put up with as well as being down in the pit with no wind.

John's forty acre field that came with the lot was above the road and a ways north. Since these pieces had to be fenced, he was able, by making a three way trade with some friends who helped build his house to get his forty acres next to his lot north. Then instead of staying on the hill, he ran his fence clear to the lake. His neighbor on the south had already fenced his lot, so John simply ran his fence on to the lake and the front fence parallel to the two track dirt road.

It was a hell of a lot of work to haul a load of poles and then build a fence that day. The next day he would go back for another load. He built a buck stand three pole fence. It looked pretty, but later when he got sheep he had to tighten it all the way around.

John married Charlotte in Fish Haven. The bishop performed the ceremony, and it was for time, only. Neither of them wanted to wait any longer, and the Endowment House was clear in Salt Lake City. Everybody needed and wanted lumber, so John took Charlotte with him for another load of lumber.

Robert decided to go with them as well since everybody needed lumber. John's family sent three outfits, and so four loads of lumber came back. John killed a couple of ducks at Big Spring Creek. They made an early camp that night and cooked the meat and potatoes. Charlotte made baking powder biscuits. When John crawled into the back of the wagon with Charlotte that night, he saw Dick watching and remembered the laughing on the last trip. Now John laughed until Charlotte was ready to shoot him, not knowing the joke. John killed sage hens and pine hens on the trip so they had meat both ways.

Pope's kept their lumber, but John sold his load in Fish Haven for forty dollars.

"Oops!" Charlotte reached for the twenty dollar profit, delighted by the ambition of her new husband.

John made five trips in five weeks. He made twenty dollars for three trips, but the fourth and fifth he had to trade; a milk cow with one trip and forty head of sheep on the next run. He'd have to thin off the coyotes again this fall to maintain his profits.

He went to his dad's and borrowed a hay rack. He bought a scythe and pitch fork and started on the forty acres of hay. He used a rope net to stack it. The net was placed on the floor of the rack then loaded with the pitch fork about a ton to a load John would pull the rack up to the stack, and then throw the ropes attached to the net over the stack. He'd then unhook the team, pull them around to the other side of the stack, hook to the ropes and pull the hay out of the rack and drag it on the stack. At that point John pitched the hay around, stacking it while getting the net free. Everything could be straightened out on the rack floor for another load that afternoon.

The hay down on the lakeshore was mostly tullies and coarse hay, but it would winter cows and horses well enough. Hay on the slope to the lake was fine, good quality. John figured he'd have more than enough hay if he could just get it put up. He worked for about a month steady, with Sundays off. Four loads went in the tithing yard. Then he spent a couple of days more and decided he had enough, and left the rest for his dad.

John's dad and brothers started hauling right away so they took their rack and John's net. A couple of his brothers spent full time on the scythes. Three hay racks made a load a day.

John dug a hole and built a back house over it with a pole frame and green willows nailed close together on the frame. A door of the same was hung on leather hinges. It mostly stayed part way open, but he covered the roof with hay to hold it in place. He ran wire back and forth over the top. He built a crib of logs around the spring and dug the water hole for the stock below.

Fall was coming on. He got wax and treated his traps. He still had to haul some wood for winter. He took Old Shorty out for reconnaissance. He finally found the aspens he was looking for and started hauling wood. He broke it up as he hauled and after a few days, he took a sack of traps and snares with him and spent about three hours setting traps, and then getting a load of wood to take home, and the next day he was back for more wood. He set more traps and snares and brought three coyotes home on the wood. He was busy skinning and stretching fur. Next morning a repeat, but he brought five coyotes home.

In two weeks he quit hauling wood and concentrated on trapping. He went higher in the cedars and rocks, hoping to get a bobcat or so. He was rewarded right away with a big bobcat. When he got snowed out, he had a hundred and ten coyotes and twelve bobcats. He'd watched his mother work with fur, so he worked with it, increasing its value.

John went to the lakeshore along Fish Haven Creek back to his own place and caught thirty muskrats and four mink. He had to move a quite a ways further north to find where the muskrats were thick enough to do much with them. He picked up a few all along the lake shore though and finally found where they were thick—right in the bottom of St. Charles Creek. He picked up two big river otter in snares along the creek as well as four coyotes and a mountain lion. In a week there he picked up over one hundred rats, twelve beaver, twelve coyotes, a mountain lion, otters and about twelve more mink. He got home the last night with traps as well as fur. Now he had to freight it. He talked with his mother, and she wrote to the furrier again. He worked the fur over.

His dad-in-law wanted him to see if he could get a stove, either a pot bellied, or cook stove. He told John he'd watch out for Charlotte who was too sick to go while he freighted. His dad showed up the next morning. He said the furrier would be in Evanston the next three days so they had to load up and go. They packed up fur and grain and hay and left before Christmas. They put up that night in Randolph, left early the next morning for Evanston. They found the fur man, and he spent a couple of hours totaling up everything. He finally wired New York and talked to the boss. "I will pay four hundred twenty-five." John said to give a hundred to his dad, but Robert wouldn't take it. He took only twenty-five dollars for freight.

They took the horses to the livery barn and got a room in the hotel. They were almost too tired to sleep. The next morning they took the sleighs around to Beckwith and Louder. Robert gave them his list, but John asked about stoves. They looked at cook stoves. John spent fifty dollars on two big cook ranges with enough pipe and elbows and hardware to set them up. They had breakfast while they got loaded and secured. John walked to the bank and cashed his check, then went to the hotel and paid three dollars for meals and beds. They kept the money in the bank for the stoves. Beckwith Bank and Beckwith and Louder Store were nearly one and the same. Three hundred forty dollars went into his belt, seven dollars in his pocket for Charlotte.

John got information on costs of a stationary steam engine and a saw mill. It would cost about seven hundred. Maybe he could get a co-op going so they could have the lumber they needed. He figured they had almost enough logs in the tithing yard to build the church in Fish Haven, but they'd have to have a bunch of lumber. Hauling it over one hundred miles and a mountain didn't make sense, especially having to pay so much for it. The best stand of timber in the world was within a few miles from Fish Haven, free for the taking. John's creative mind was working out a solution to the problem. Three days later he walked into his home again.

"You are looking better, Charlotte! I hope you are not allergic to me." His bride smiled, shaking her head demurely. "Well, I bought a present for us—and one for your parents. Let's take theirs over to them, shall we?"

Charlotte agreed and snuggled inside her warm fur coat and John drove the sleigh right to the Stock's front door. Everyone came out to see. "I'm here with a cook stove, Mother Stock! Let's get a couple of men to help me lift it!" In a few minutes, with a man lifting on each side, and on the back, John could lift the other end enough to slide it a few inches at a time. It barely fit through the door.

After setting it where they thought it should be, they put the chimney on and ran it up a length. They then added an elbow and took it to the side of the room where it would have to go through the logs. A big wood bit was brought out, also wood chisels, and in a few minutes the logs were notched big enough to put the pipe through. They fastened another elbow and enough pipe to reach higher than the house and topped it with a weather cap. Within minutes a piece of wood was shaved up into a handful of shavings and dropped into the new range. Fine kindling went in next, and the fire started. It only took a few minutes to feel the warmth begin to come from the stove. A few bigger chunks went in and it never missed a beat. It was soon hot in there. The coffee pot went on and many smiles radiated with the heat.

Everyone went back to Pope's and helped get the stove set up there. The chimney went straight up and through the roof lumber so it was an easier operation.

John said, "Merry Christmas, Charlotte. I probably won't be able to match this again."

Charlotte shrugged. "So what? I couldn't care! I should only need one stove!"

John smiled as they snuggled in bed that night, for Charlotte seemed very content. She sighed once, whispering, "I have a beautiful fur coat . . . and windows, and a floor . . . and a stove."

Sunday in priesthood meeting, John took a few minutes explaining his thinking on the saw mill. All the men were excited, but fourteen men would have to put fifty dollars in to make it happen. It was more than they wanted to do. John explained, "It's even a little worse than this because we'll have to freight it from Evanston. But it puts the new church in our grasp as well as our homes and furniture, bridge plank, head gates, and whatever!"

Everyone was excited about getting stoves for their homes, but John knew if they were squirming about the saw mill, they couldn't afford stoves either, so his mind spun on other options. However, the storekeeper asked John to bring two new stoves and hardware for a complete set-up.

"They cost me twenty-five dollars apiece. I won't make the trip for less than twenty so you'll have to ask forty apiece to come out."

The storekeeper agreed and John took his money and set out again, freighting iron stoves. While they were loading up, John went into the bank and talked to the A. C. Beckwith Bank president, asking if he would loan him the money to buy the engine and mill. When John told of his collateral, and that he'd only need to borrow three hundred of the total sum, he was assured he could have all he needed.

"My next question then, is how much will I need to charge in order to pay for the mill and make a bit in the process?"

The banker's head bent and he scratched a pencil against paper. "Five dollars a thousand board feet would get you out of the obligation in a short time."

John nodded, figuring things in his head.

"If you decide to do it, I'll loan you a heavy duty sleigh to haul it on. You can put as many teams up front as you need."

That seemed to top off John's wish list like a fat, red cherry. So John ordered the engine and mill. The whole outfit would be ready to go in a week! They would send a man with the rig to get set up. It came with a belt and extra blade and files. So John, his brother Rob, and Dad Pope took one sleigh and two teams leading behind. When Pope's arrived in Evanston, A. C. Beckwith himself came out to watch. His big mule teams came around pulling the big rig. John was disappointed to see that the engine alone loaded the sleigh. So A.C. ordered another sleigh to be brought around the mill, and accessories were loaded and Pope's teams hooked on it. Four teams were hooked on to pull the engine, and three on the mill. One would have done on the mill, but it really looked impressive. A lot of people came to see them off that morning.

"I appreciate your help, Mr. Beckwith." John shook hands with the obliging banker and businessman.

"Not at all, Pope! I enjoy seeing a young man that's full of scrap! You are a forward thinker."

When the impressive teams and their loads finally reached Fish Haven, they took the rig up to the timberline above town. There was a lot of room for stacking logs, and with all hands on deck they set it up.

Four teams went on to timber and felled logs. Another hauled a load of dry aspen wood, while others hauled water from the creek. When everything was operating, the felled logs were being sawed, cut into lumber which was carried to the big sleigh and stacked so it couldn't warp. Each of the tall trees had to be cut in lengths, twelve, fourteen, or sixteen feet, which was as long as the log carriage. By the first night a lot of lumber was already sawed and stacked.

John watched and listened and asked a lot of questions. Then the fire was let out on the engine and the water drained from the boiler. When they got to town, each man who helped that day got some lumber. They were all happy with that.

John told his dad-in-law to to keep track and charge each man two-and-a-half cents a thousand feet for awhile, until it was paid for. "Then we can lower costs when we can."

John and his dad and brothers took the mules and rig back to Evanston and brought back another load of freight—buckets and barrels to haul water to the boiler. John went up every day for a week hauling logs down from the timber and piling it to dry. By then he had enough out to fill some big orders and to build a shed over his saw and engine. John T. Pope was in the lumber business!

Once again the family rallied to help with the framework of the shed. They started fire in the engine and filled the boiler, and while water was heating, one team went for a load of logs while the other pulled several into position and logged them to length. It took an hour to get the steam going, so another load of logs were hauled from the timber. By eleven o'clock they started sawing six by sixes for a frame, two by sixes for rafters, and by the time the sun was directly overhead, a large crew was putting up the shelter shed, and John sawed sheeting to cover the rafters. Boards on the back were nailed on, and others to keep everything braced. Now John felt his investment was protected from the elements.

Word was out and people started coming with their logs from St. Charles, Bloomington, or Laketown. The old mill began to be busy every day, and people would come with logs and go home with lumber and slabs. Keeping the sawdust out of their way was a trial. But by spring, John had recouped his four hundred dollar outlay.

John hired a man to lamb his sheep that spring because he was too busy. By the first of June, he had enough to pay the bank plus four hundred to put in the bank on interest, and another three hundred to carry again. Business was going well and John trained a man to run the mill.

The church got its lumber for free. Everyone else paid cash, and so it was enough to pay wages plus put thirty dollars a month or so in John's pocket. He traded wood to the Relief Society for them shearing his sheep. John had observed them gleaning little bits of wool off brush and fence poles, or wherever the sheep had scratched some off.

The Relief Society sisters, of course, made their husbands do the shearing, and while the shearing was being done, John got some to help him dock the lambs. He had about sixty lambs. He kept the two bucks in after shearing them. Then he had the mill cut a load of lumber on his wage and he took it to Randolph and stacked it for sale at the old store, then went on to Evanston and checked at the store to see if the new McCormick Deering Mowers were in yet. Beckwith had taken the first two car loads himself.

"We'll have another load in tomorrow," the storekeeper said.

"Save me two of them."

As he went through his business, he decided to trade his light Nebeker wagon for a heavy duty new Studebaker Freight Hauler with wider bunks. Beckwith threw in a box with a spring seat, larger built, which would be good for hauling lumber and also this load of freight. "Yes sir, young Pope, you are a forward thinker you are, and we like doing business with you!"

Up the street at the Blythe and Pixley Store, he bought a pedal grind stone to sharpen things on.

Next day when the train pulled in, John was waiting with grindstone in front. They rolled on one machine, one tongue to the back, and the next back, astraddle the tongue of the first. They came with oil cans in holders and two knives a piece, also a box with extra sections and rivets. This would revolutionize the haying from now on. "Now the scythe can stay in the shed where it belongs." John triumphed, pleased with his purchases. John bought a large coil of rope to secure the load with, and a bucket of grease and a gallon of oil. Then he pulled away, without as much as a squeak from the new wagon. He camped on Otter Creek that night and slept late. He was tired. He'd been wound as tight as a spring. He really needed to relax and unwind and enjoy a little.

The next morning, as John was near the top, he saw something going up a draw a ways from the road. He thought it was a big brindle bull for a few minutes. The beast caught his smell and raised his head to look. John stopped as well because he was looking at a big grizzly. For an instant, they both held their breath, and then the big bear whirled and ran down the hill toward Randolph. John told his team that thing looked as big as a bull, too.

John unloaded one mower in his dad's yard and took the other home. He spent a few days with his wife, and she was thrilled to have him around, as she was nearly ready to have a baby.

John was eager to try his new investment and hooked up to the mower and let the cutter bar down. "Talk about cutting hay!" John laughed at the new delight! He put the cutter bar back up and drove to Laketown. He went to Ira Nebeker's ranch and asked for a job cutting hay.

Ira looked it over. "Does it work?"

"Does it work?" John asked. "Let me show you." So he pulled into a big meadow across from their house and started to mow. He cut about an acre that night because Ira nodded his approval and hollered, "Keep a going; you've got a job with me!" The next morning, he was mowing by eight, quit for dinner at noon, and changed hay knives. Ira went north to try to hire Robert or someone to bring the other mower, also to bring the grease, oil, and the grind stone. John could cut eight to ten acres a day. With Robert and John together, they averaged about twenty acres a day.

About a month later, when they quit custom cutting to go harvest their own hay, Ira had eight hundred ton of hay stacked in about twenty different yards. Ira said he had ordered a bunch of mowers for himself and others in his area. John took a ton of oats for part payment. Ira gave John and Robert each a hundred dollars for man, team, and machine for the month. Young John Pope began to influence his community in a way . . . and he became a father, for Charlotte had a baby boy. The baby's grandpa, Bishop Robert M. Pope blessed the boy in sacrament meeting, giving him the name of John William Pope.

The mill was still busy, and now John and his dad went to their own communities and began mowing, drawing crowds to see the machines at work. Also several neighbors offered to stack if he would mow for them as well. Another month of haying and every bit of hay was cut, also they cut many acres of oats, barley, and wheat which was stacked until they could get it thrashed.

In the early autumn John took two days preparing traps, and getting a cover on a wagon rack. He spent another day stringing traps, and snares. Coyotes weren't as thick, but bobcats were more plentiful on ridge tops and rocky cliffs. Of course his catch for three weeks was down from the previous year, but he had snared three wolves which accounted for less coyotes. He had two dozen cats and one lion, so more expensive fur was up. John brought a few chickens home each day; his favorite food in the entire world.

He moved his traps south and set a string from Round Valley to Long Ridge. Cook's offered him a place to stay and a barn to treat fur in. They said they would pay twenty dollars apiece bounty for coyotes and cats, for they were in dire need of predator control. The bounty was in addition to what he could sell it for. The Cook's had two thousand sheep and predators were plaguing. The extra week in this virgin area netted about sixty more coyotes plus another five bobcats. P. W. Cook hauled a load of fur to the Pope's in Garden City for John.

In the middle of the next week it snowed. John pulled the foot traps and part of his snares, and then spent all day setting for rats and mink in the bottoms. They were really thick. Every other day he ran the snares. Two weeks later he had another wolf, twenty-five more coyotes, and eight more cats. He stayed with it 'til the muskrats were thinned out. Then he pulled all traps and snares, and loaded everything up. Cooks hauled part of his fur for him. They said they counted about a hundred predators. John said, "Keep some of that for helping me transport fur, and for giving me a place to stay." He was told that they would be glad to have him do this as often as possible, and that the wolf alone was worth thirty dollars to them.

After Christmas, John and Robert made another trip to Evanston, where they settled on five hundred and ninety dollars for the fur. He gave his dad ninety and put five hundred in the bank. They hauled freight back to their frontier communities. John worked in the mill until spring. The wood he cut to burn was slabs, cut to stove length in the mill and loaded on his sleigh. What a neat easy way to get his wood! He laughed to himself when he thought of the hours of agony he went through, trying to decide to go in debt that far. It had tripled what it cost and he had only charged half of what Beckwith advised, and besides it was free to the church.

Fish Haven was getting ready to start building the chapel. They needed rock and cement. The sand and gravel along the lake shore was clean and good to mix it, and free for the hauling. They would need a drop-bottom wagon box, so it would run out by itself. He talked it over with the blacksmith. He built six hinges. John went to the mill and had planks sawed the right length, also two-by-sixes to make it high enough and wide enough. John cut some two-by-fours, and then stopped at the store, buying all the bolts they had in stock, and a sturdy chain, thirty feet long. Then back to the blacksmith shop where he found out they needed bed pieces to be high enough of the standard to work. The blacksmith kept the plank while John went back to the mill for twelve-by-four square bed pieces.

After all day, John and the blacksmith had a gravel box on the wagon with a self dump. The two inside bottom plank were on hinges. When they were down, it left a twenty-four inch wide hole in the floor, full length. A chain ran from a pipe on one side, around and under the box, and up to a ratchet on a pipe on the other side so the bottom planks could be pulled up and closed. "See," the blacksmith muttered. "It holds the gravel until the chain is released and the gravel falls out." It was a nifty set-up, and only a small amount of sand would be left along the sides of the box, but it could be quickly raked out in a matter of minutes.

The men studied their work. The blacksmith had a flash of inspiration, and two planks were fastened in so the sides sloped right to the dump door. As the possibilities were realized, the men got excited. One man had worked construction in Ohio. He said, "We used a hoot to load gravel with a scraper, no shovels."

"What's a hoot?" The men asked.

Turns out, the hoot was a ramp of planks built on a solid frame with a pulley and a cable that ran back to the scraper. A man held the scraper handles. The team on whip would drag the load of gravel to the top where it was dumped in the wagon. Other teams and scrapers were dragging gravel to the bottom of the hoot. The top hung over for the wagon to drive right under it. John said, "Get anything you need from the mill and build a hoot. Maybe someday we'll get a church built."

Cement would all have to be freighted from Evanston; a huge undertaking for free, yet the blessings of the Lord could surely be counted as wages. Another problem was that they really couldn't haul it before they needed it because cement needed a place to keep it dry. "If I saw the wood is anyone willing to build a shed to keep cement in?" Once again volunteers came forward and the lumber was cut. Next day John took two teams and big freight wagon, but instead of taking his father with him on this trip, John invited his mother, Sarah LeDuc.

She seemed pleased with the invitation. "What will you do with *me* along?"

"I want to show you the railroad, Mother, and the big China Town at Evanston. We shall visit all along the way."

"Yes, I'll come with you, and I am proud that you are hauling for the Lord." They camped on Otter Creek and enjoyed sage hens for supper and breakfast.

Sarah asked to stop in Randolph to say hello to close friends. She was introduced to a six-year old boy she had delivered. Everyone made a big fuss over Sarah, for she had doctored many, and was well respected. That night after dark, they put the horses away at the livery then walked to the hotel where John had two rooms. He escorted his mother into the café. They sat up and drank a few cups of coffee after the apple pie. "I'm living the high life now," she said, all eyes, for Sarah had never eaten out in her life. Next morning after breakfast John walked with her to Beckwith and Louder, and she strolled up and down the aisles, and looked for at least an hour. Then they walked on up to Blythe and Pixley and looked awhile again. John said, "If there's anything you want or could use, I will buy it for you."

Sarah protested, for she couldn't have him buying anything for her. He walked her across the tracks and they went to several businesses in China Town. Sarah was really glad to leave there, for it was all so strange and foreign to anything she'd ever known. A long train was coming in from the east so they watched it pass. John said, "They travel fast. If we got on and left here today, we could be in Omaha, Nebraska, by tomorrow night."

"Oh no! When we came in 1860, it took us all summer to go that far. We were very tired every night."

At noon they walked into another café for dinner. Sarah remarked, "I shall have to hire a servant after this trip," and John laughed at his mother's humor. After dinner, John had his team brought out, and the wagon was parked at the dock of Beckwith and Louder's store. They put on forty hundred pound sacks of cement and rolled out of town, stopping over at Woodruff Creek. The next morning they went on up Otter Creek and over to Laketown, and stayed one night there.

Sarah rode on to Fish Haven where she would stay with John and Charlotte for a night or two to get acquainted with her grandson, handsome little J.W.

John took everyone on a picnic the next day up Fish Haven Canyon. They spread a blanket and kicked back for a while. They ate Dutch oven bread, and fried potatoes, pine hen, and coffee. It was fun.

On the way home they stopped and John showed off the mill. "Why son, however have you done all this?"

"I tried to get men to put in and start another co-op. but everybody was broke, so I bought it myself."

"How much did you have to give for it?"

"Seven hundred dollars."

"Where did you come up with that much?"

"I borrowed it at the bank in Evanston."

Charlotte cut into the conversation, "John Theodore Pope! You never told me we were in debt. That's awful. Did you mortgage the farm to get it?"

"Yes, I did, but it's paid for now."

"How could you ever come up with so much?" Sarah asked incredulously.

"I've been scrounging day and night for a year. I got five hundred for the fur sold last winter. The mill is paying dividends along. Church lumber is free. I only charged one-half of what the bank suggested, so it's been busy and everybody looks more prosperous. It was a very good thing to do because now we are hauling cement for a church! When the cement is here, then they can start pouring the footings. I can saw the lumber as fast as it is needed. We'll have a church for everyone to take pride in."

Charlotte was looking at John with new appreciation. "I'm glad I didn't know all the details, for I'd have worried myself into a dither."

"Mother was so amazed at the big city and everything. If everybody wanted to go back for another load, we could go before you get too far along. We'd have to get your dad to do our chores and watch for us. Maybe we could get Dick and Robert to go, too."

Charlotte finally said yes, and once again they made the trip with John's brother Rob driving the other rig. They spent another day in Evanston, this time Charlotte was oohing over everything. John bought a wheelbarrow and hand crank cement mixer which was loaded on the top of the cement—forty hundred on the big wagon, and twenty on the other.

They picnicked and camped out, eating sage chicken and enjoying a good visit. So Pope's had five ton of cement and all the lumber donated for the new church. They also made the trip back to Evanston to pick up a hay rake John had ordered. With mower and rake, they were really able to put up hay.

John went to Laketown and worked for Ira again. He had a bunch of mowers of his own, this year. Now John's rake was the new rage. Ira went to Evanston and ordered himself some. When the hay was stacked in Laketown, they went to South Eden and stacked that as well. So John went home to his own work with his rake, all paid for. Boy, with that rake, John pulled big piles of hay into the yard where a hired hand pitched it up and stacked it while he went for another big load. After a week or so, that was done. John and his hired man raked and mowed most of the hay in Fish Haven, always using the owner's team on one or the other machine.

During trapping season he took extra traps and snares, and Sarah went to cook for him and help with pelts. She stayed on the ranch cold days and worked on the fur.

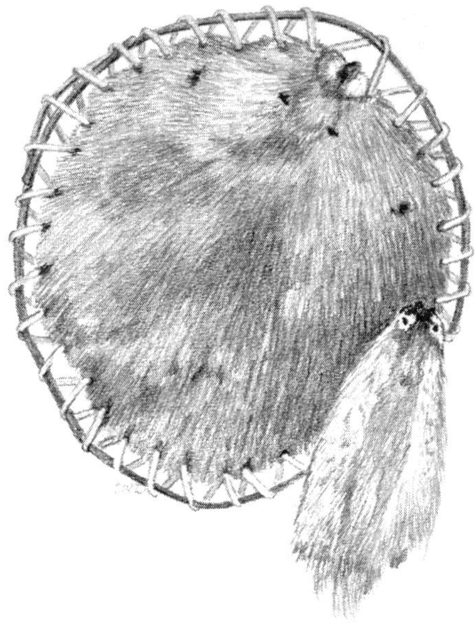

After nearly a month, they pulled traps and went to the bottoms for muskrats and mink. He ran the snares every three days for a couple of weeks. He took three wolves on Twin Peaks, a lynx, and nineteen bobcats. Now the snow brought him to the muskrats, and when they started slowing down, he pulled out. Cook's had hauled a couple of loads home for him but Sarah knew exactly what he had—one hundred forty coyotes, two hundred and twenty rats, several beaver, twenty-two mink, twenty cats, and three wolves. He netted six hundred dollars after the long haul with two rigs.

Thirty-two dollars from Cook's went to Sarah, along with another five for her midwife skills, for John and Charlotte welcomed another addition to their family, a daughter this time, Charlotte May. "Our little Lottie May is as beautiful as a picture," John said, holding a finger out to a small, dimpled fist.

The mill was still busy and John worked the rest of the winter in the mill. That spring after a long family council at John's parents' home, it was decided to try to sell out their places in Bear Lake and try the Uintah Basin. "It is just beginning to settle," Robert explained. "We need to go where there's room enough for all you boys to have a place."

Charlotte was both eager and hesitant to leave. "But John, what about the church? Our place? And everything we've built?"

"That's the pioneering way, Charlotte! That's what our parents have done, again and again, is it not?"

John went to Paris to the stake president and explained his situation. "I wondered if the stake would be interested in buying my mill. Everyone in the stake is getting lumber there."

The president listened, and in the end, John took six hundred for the mill. He sold the rake and mower to Nat Hodges for a hundred dollars. His sheep now numbered a hundred and ten head, ewes with wool, the milk cow, house, spring, water rights, and all improvements brought six hundred from a new convert.

Chapter Seven

Goodbye, Bear Lake

"WELL HERE WE ARE Charlotte, starting for the Uintah Basin with almost everything we started with in the beginning—a wagon, a team, a tent, and Old Shorty."

"No," Charlotte pressed, "we now have two children."

John's parents and some of his brothers made up the small wagon train, consisting of four teams, and four covered wagons. They drove about twenty head of horses, one buggy with a small team, and thirty cows. Teddy Longhurst had married John's sister Adaline, and they decided to emigrate with the rest of the family. Rob had married Polly Calder, and they stayed with the place in Garden City.

Teddy volunteered to drive John's team so John could drive horses or cattle and scout the trail. John's old runaways were getting plenty of age on them, so John had quit worrying about them running away. He was on the look for good young colts to break while he had the old horses to hook them up with.

The Stock family hated to see John and Charlotte leave, and there had been many farewells from everyone. John told all the neighbors that lumber and logs and cement, the dump bottom wagon box, and hoot were all donated for them. "I'm going to pray for you that you will be able to finish that house to the Lord. And I'll be back in a year or so and check it out, okay?" Several men with tears in their eyes promised to do it.

The Pope's in Garden City had the goodbyes said and the wagon train rolled onto Laketown. They camped up to the head of Laketown Canyon on the spring. They hobbled teams, built a long rope corral for the horse heard. The cattle were tired. Dick and Rock shot a mess of chickens. They cleaned them on the creek, then after supper, they left the big pan of cooked chicken under the lid for breakfast. They set up the tent. Charlotte, John, and the kids slept in it. In the middle of the night, John awoke with Charlotte shaking him. "There's something out there John, I heard the pan crash."

He rolled to the door and pulled the flap open, seeing a big bear cleaning up the chicken. As the bear turned his head, Pope's gun roared, and the bear's nose went into the dirt immediately "Everything's all right now. We just had an unwelcome guest eating our breakfast. I need someone to light a lantern."

As soon as a lantern was lit and carried out, someone poked the bear with a rifle barrel. It was dead of lead in the brain. They had kept a horse saddled and staked out to help get things rounded up next morning. They brought him around and drug the bear to a big aspen by the creek. Four men with sharp knives went to work on the bear. Everyone else went back to sleep. Sarah LeDuc came down and showed where to split the hide so it could be made into a rug. Everyone took a leg and started to skin. Forty-five minutes later the bear was hanging in the aspen, minus his hide and innards. This bear was a butter fat, black bear. His last year's coat had been shed. The new coat was about an inch long, black, shiny and beautiful.

Sarah made them peg the hide out tight and scrape off all excess fat. Everyone went back to sleep for an hour or so. They slept in a bit that first morning. A fire was built up good, and a big back strap was cut up into chops.

Several pieces of the fat meat on the shoulder went into the Dutch oven. The fat began to melt out. When plenty of rendered fat was in the pot, the chops were added, and a spoonful of salt and a bit of pepper. The meat smelled like mutton as it cooked.

Sarah made a couple of men help her with the hide. The lips were split and thinned. The cartilage came out of the ears. All the grease and flesh was scraped off. The lot of the horses and cattle grazed up the creek on good meadow grass.

Robert said, "I know why it smells like mutton. It is. Nat Hodges had his sheep up here at Twin Peaks for awhile this spring. A bear kept getting them 'til they had to move them."

Everybody tanked up on bear meat and most really liked it. It tasted of mutton, but with a wild flavor, too. They decided to stay a day, render as much of the bear grease as they could, and let Sarah work on the blanket. Lye was made with wood ashes in a little water. The hide, which had been drying fast without any flesh, was treated with weak lye every hour or so which made it dry even faster. When it was looking quite white, that night she had Marcellus split the skull with an axe. Sarah used the brains to spread like a paste all over the hide.

The next morning while hooking up and getting ready to roll, they built a rack of dry aspen and stretched the blanket to it and tied it to the side of a wagon. They had about eight gallons of bear grease. This cooled very white. It looked and smelled like mutton grease. It would make good soap if nothing else.

They stopped in Randolph a short time, camped that night on Saleratus Creek. Cattle and horses seemed tired so they rested them awhile. That night they camped on a small creek just north of Almy Creek which seemed to come down north of the Evanston Butte. They decided to let the wagons roll through Evanston, but drive the horses and cattle through the east of the ridge at Almy, and cross the tracks two or three miles east of Evanston, so they wouldn't panic them in all the busy hubbub of Evanston.

Charlotte said to John, "I'm certain you should have stopped to say goodbye to the folks at Beckwith and Louder. They will probably think you died."

That night they camped on the Old Mormon Trail on water, about twelve miles east of town, and the next day they took the livestock around Ft. Bridger. John stopped and talked to some guys to see what they knew of the way south into the Uintah Basin. One officer from the post told him they could ride over the mountains on horseback on a military road they had blazed, but they couldn't make it with wagons. An old cowboy told him to go southeast and go past Lone Tree, through some badlands, and down a creek past a few ranches until they reached the Green River, then down the river a few miles there was a good crossing. The river was wide and shallow and swift, but he could cross the river with wagons if was not too high.

He said, "If you come to a big rocky canyon, you've gone past the crossing. The road goes down the river a way, then turns east up to the ranch. Keep to the south as much as you can. There is a two-track wagon road. In some places it's kinda steep. Go about fifteen miles or a few more. It will take you back to the bottom, then you go about forty miles east into Colorado. There is a deep canyon, but you'll be able to turn south again, and then follow the road to the White River all the way back west into the Basin. It's a roundabout way, but to go over the mountains is impossible."

John memorized his directions and the Pope's rolled on. Looking south to the big mountain, with the forests of trees running clear down into the bottoms, was pretty impressive. While they were surveying the view, five men came out of the draw and rode toward them with rifles across their saddle horses. They wore beaver hats pulled low.

"Dick," John whispered loudly, "Get your rifle, and tell Rock and Marcellus, as well. These guys want trouble, I'm afraid." The men had stopped the cattle and were looking through them.

John loped toward them. "Howdy," he called.

Nobody answered, but John heard the man with the black beard say, "Yep, just like I told ya. They're all mine. Let's look at the horses. Hell, they got my cows! They probably took my horses, too."

John said, "I sure hope you never had too much dinner."

"Haw, Haw. What difference does that make to you, kid?"

"The last men I killed were full. My shells opened 'em up. The smell of vomit, heave, and shit made me so sick I had a hard time going through their pockets."

"There's no way in hell you can get five of us."

"Well, I figure I can get at least two. My brothers back there are good shots. They are just waiting to see what you are gonna do. Which one of you big, brave, rustling, no goods wants to go first? Make a move."

Black beard threw his rifle up. Pope's pistol materialized and went off. The bullet smashed into the action of black beard's Winchester causing two shells to explode in the magazine. The shell ricocheted up, cutting through the top of the hand and thumb. The exploding magazine sent powder and particles of brass raining down, cutting his chaps up some, and drawing blood from his thigh in four or five places. It stung his horse bad, causing him to jump high, leaving black beard eighteen inches above the saddle. When the horse hit, he ducked back hard, throwing this tub of meanness on his head. The horse then bucked back the way they had come, stirrups popping, reigns flying. John had immediately looked to the other four. All were frozen with a look of horror on their faces. "Drop the rifles."

They let loose quickly. Pope motioned with his chin. "Starting on this side, one at a time, pull and drop your pistols." That was soon done. "Now get down, turn your horses loose, and see what's wrong with the ugly, bearded clown."

The first man to reach the unconscious outlaw bent down.

John said, "Ease out his pistol and hand it over."

John kicked the pistols away from them. Marcellus walked over and picked up the rifles and put them in the wagon, as well as the pistols.

"Now you retreat thirty feet and sit down in the grass!" They did as told. Black beard was sound asleep, so Sarah came forward with a case of the doctor stuff she always carried on midwife trips. She poured a dash of whiskey on his wounded hand.

He groaned a bit but didn't wake. She was going to sew the thumb back in place, but the bullet had gone lengthwise through, carrying about three-fourths of an inch of bone away, so she rinsed a knife blade in alcohol, leaving a strip of skin, and what flesh was still attached to it. She cut the part off, then pulled the skin over the stub and sewed it on, leaving him a short stub. Sarah took a bit of gauze and bandaged it up. She made a sling and told the remaining bad guys to keep it elevated, to keep him quiet and let him rest.

She said, "He has a concussion, and I don't know about his neck. If you brought him a doctor it would be good."

Robert had been watching and listening. Before the wagon train rolled away he called, "Rustlers are hanged where I come from. Count your blessings! You've caused us a half a day's travel and a scare to the women and kids. We'll keep your irons for a trade off; but, try anything again and we'll string ya! I don't think I could talk him out of it again."

"Who the hell is he?"

Young Marcellus boasted, "He's my brother! He's the most dangerous gunman anywhere."

"He got a name?"

No response.

During the 1890's the State of Wyoming was almost completely controlled by outlaws. A. C. Beckwith gathered as many big ranchers as possible together. They formed the Wyoming Stock Growers Association. Acting for the association, A. C. Beckwith gathered an army, equipped them, loaded them on a train and sent them to K.C., where they unloaded and embarked on a trip into the Hole in the Wall. Beckwith's army was shot up and soundly defeated by outlaws.

Later on A. C. Beckwith again, acting for the Association, hired ruthless Tom Horn as a range detective to ride the grub line in Wyoming, and on into the Brown's Hole. When Horn determined the ranchers he was staying with had rustled B.Q. beef, he shot them in the backs, or from ambush. He was paid five hundred dollars for each outlaw killed. A. C. Beckwith paid Tom Horn from his bank in Evanston. A.C. Beckwith was a victim without a doubt, being robbed and plundered with every rustled beef, but Horn's habit of back shooting was cold, yellow cowardice, and not in keeping with American justice.

Into this mix rolled a Mormon family at a critical time when they could make a big difference, tipping the scales to good, bringing peace and law to the wildest, most lawless place on earth. The Lord had prepared John Pope to do a work from his earliest year in the Basin.

That night they camped on water, a little east and south of Mt. View. They rolled southeast from there, continuing on past the badlands to water before stopping that night.

When they finally killed some sage chickens, Marcellus, Rock, and Dick all appropriated pistols from the wagon and began building holsters for them. Dick fancied the shoulder holster. Most of this bunch of outlaws shot a colt 45 with four-and-one-half inch barrels. John's brothers were quite awkward with them at first, but he coached each one for a while. They didn't have extra shells so they unloaded the weapons, and began practicing and dry firing—pointing and shooting, clicking on the empty. (By the time they rolled into Ashley Valley ten days later, they were quite improved, being at least as good, and a shade faster, than most. The rifles were two Springfield Falling Block 45-70's, army issue, with saddle ring and leather loop; one Marlin Lever action repeater 45-60 caliber, and one Winchester leaver 38-55.)

That night they camped on the other side of the river. The next morning they stayed in camp three or four hours while the kids fished, using meat from an antelope shot the day before for bait. They had so much fun they stayed in this beautiful spot long enough to cook fish and eat an early dinner before rolling the wagons. Everyone had stories about the big one that got away. Sarah Leduc had worked on the bear skin every stop. Now it was completely tanned and it made a beautiful, soft blanket, very heavy.

John T. had ridden Old Shorty out before daylight. Now he guided them on their way about twenty miles to the next camp. From here they traveled east about twelve miles coming down into Brown's Hole and the Green River, where they spent another night. John rode a block or so up river to the John Jarvie Ranch. John Jarvie had a small store where John purchased shells for the new shooters as well as some staples, such as coffee and so forth.

After visiting an hour or so, John came away with directions east and south into Colorado, through some narrow canyons with sheer cliffs, Indian ruins, and petroglyphs, lizards, horny toads, blow snakes, and an occasional a rattler. The White River flowing west was very pretty by comparison! Now all they had to do was follow it west a couple of days, then a short day north into Ashley Valley. This route, they learned later, was called the Cherokee Trail by people in the Basin. There was a natural pass without having to build a dug way and cut trees to get over the mountain.

Ashley Valley only had a few permanent settlers. People had been coming and going for four years, but only a few stayed because of the outlaw element, and Indians. Sarah LeDuc said she couldn't believe things were green instead of gray—creosote instead of sagebrush. "I actually miss our Bear Lake sagebrush and the lake."

The ground was sand, alkali, or rock. John's young wife sighed wistfully. "The mountains seem far away, too." Charlotte was used to living in the shadows of high timber-covered mountains, west of Fish Haven, where the hills ran clear to the lake in places. "Welcome to forgotten Utah . . . or wherever in the world we are."

As camp was set up on water a few miles from town, John and Robert rode into town to see what things were like. They needed to know where to camp, what ground was available to homestead, and get information about range timber, and so forth. What about church? Chickens hadn't been so plentiful lately. Popes had lived on them for years. They needed to watch for meat.

What they learned was a bit discouraging in a way. "This community was not colonized by Mormons. A few families had come in 1875 to build cabins and try to start ranching. They were spread out here and there on water. Everyone was building for himself and trying to start his ranch.

In 1880, and 1881, an Indian war in Colorado put everyone on alert. The big Uintah Reservation was almost next door. They were a notional bunch. These early settlers were forever watching their stock. If anything strayed a little, the Indians ate it or stole it.

When news of the Colorado Indian War broke, people panicked. Most of them numbered the logs on their houses, took them apart, loaded them up and moved into Ashley where they put the houses up in a square and constructed a fort—Fort Ashley. By concentrating numbers at the fort, they felt a little comfort and protection.

This whole region had been a hideout for train robbers, bank robbers, and rustlers. Almost anyone wanted by the law came into this area. The law and posses got into this wild, God forsaken country, and because they knew Wyoming, Colorado, and Utah were close by, they were outnumbered by outlaws. Too often, they were glad to turn around and go home. If they got in very far, they had nightmares about it for years.

In1882, 1883, and 1884, a few more people had drifted into Ashley. Outlaws were organized into gangs. They needed supplies so they helped a few folks financially start a couple of small stores and a couple of bars. People built in a willy-nilly way. There was no pattern, nor wide streets plotted out in this place as most Utah towns were.

"There's no order to anything," Robert mused.

"Yeah, the only order seems out-of-order," John observed wryly.

Mail started coming in from Ft. Duchesne. This new community was called Ashley Center. After a while someone in the mail department hadn't liked the word *center*, and so they started calling it Vernal. The community had to build a jail, but the constable was treated badly. Prisoners were turned loose, and the jail burned down. This was repeated three times over a five year period. There were good folks who wanted law and order, but they were intimidated by outlaw gangs. Most all gangs were in the Wild Bunch. This group was the elite, and was only here once in a while.

Butch Cassidy and Sundance had a couple of hideouts in the Hole, also known as Brown's Park. They had one cave well supplied, known only to themselves. Butch's gang members fluctuated, depending on what they were going to do or if they were partying after a successful robbery.

They had horses left at various ranches for relays in case they had a long way to go fast.

Butch spent several years in Lander, Wyoming, owner and operator of a large cattle ranch. However, he was buying stolen cattle, altering the brands and laundering money for rustlers. He sold thousands of calves in a couple of years. He was liked by neighbors and was respected until the Wyoming Stock Growers Association investigated.

Butch Cassidy rode back to the outlaw lair one jump ahead of a posse. As the posse followed for one hundred and fifty miles, the small ranches they rode past were the very people who had rustled and sold cattle to Butch in the first place. The posse was in enemy territory. They were lucky to quit and backtrack in time to save themselves from becoming buzzard bait.

Butch had been foreman of a big ranch in Alma, New Mexico, and was loved by the owner. He was always welcome after he went back on the Outlaw Trail. On several occasions they made large robberies on mining payrolls in Utah or Colorado. Because of horses along to relay, they rode around the clock and were seen by influential people in Alma, New Mexico, where they made it a point to cash a check or write a letter and post it or something so when they came to trial, they were acquitted because it was impossible to be in two places at once. Nobody could travel that far in that time in those days.

Most people in Ashley Valley knew Butch. He stopped in for a few days every once in a while. He helped finance something, or in general was generous with other people's money.

John said, "It's weird that there's not a land office in town to file homesteads, water, or mining claims." People knew the preemption laws and figured if they were in possession and had been there a while, that they would be given deeds to their places. Most had filed in the town office building, built of logs. It doubled as a court house.

After a family discussion, it was decided to file here, and also in Salt Lake, if they found something. One fellow told Robert it was free range, and if there wasn't a house or a fence, just move on. Water had been brought to the fort in a canal so they would have water in case of an attack. The system of ditches in Vernal was for culinary use, not irrigation. This was the culinary water for Vernal until well into the 1920's. It ran through corrals, and stock was watered all along, so it must be boiled. (Popes were later able to encourage and organize an irrigation company to build diversion dams and canals. As water for irrigation came, the whole scene changed. Crops grew and people with ambition began prospering. Honest people created an economy of happy people that attracted other people of religion to settle.)

They camped for several days where they were while they rode around talking to people and looking at prospects. Robert decided to homestead on the west end of town, kind of the end of the canal, so the water flowing through Vernal was diverted out onto sloping ground and irrigated about twenty acres, softening the ground so it could be plowed. They filed on the homestead in Vernal and got the description. They filed on the water from the culinary canal and were immediately told this wasn't done in Vernal. Robert insisted, and it was filed. The office lady said it wouldn't make any difference, though.

Chapter Eight

A Lawless Frontier

POPE'S BROUGHT A WORLD of experience. Robert was a former bishop of two settlements. So in 1883, the LDS Church helped set up Vernal as a town. The town wasn't officially incorporated until 1897. Under their suggestions and help, an irrigation company was organized with shares for users. Shares were assessed and the money was used to clean and enlarge ditches, and build diversion dams. Shareholders could work out their assessment costs, giving employment. Water was legally filed on. Records started being kept. Stockholders voted officers to do jobs, bringing order to the chaos that prevailed before their arrival.

John Pope purchased about twenty acres from a resident, who had a house in Vernal and had previously been filed on, and it would be deeded if, and when, the government caught up. He purchased water shares as well, as it was improved and developed. He gave up forty dollars for this unimproved piece of ground on the edge of town.

Pope's took teams and wagons up Dry Fork and brought four loads of building logs. Robert and sons continued to haul logs while John took his freight wagon to Price for lumber. He got a look at "The Strip" and Nine Mile Canyon which was actually closer to *Sixty* Mile Canyon. There was a passable two track road around sheer cliffs, petroglyphs, outlaw hideouts, but a trail for sure.

Pope got back with four head of horses on a wagon and a big load of lumber—plank and sheeting. He had purchased a team in Price from a newcomer who had bought a store so he wouldn't need the team anymore.

Also, John built an ingenious device to rest his horses on the steep pitch out of nine-mile. It was simply a cedar post chained to the axel in two places so it drug along behind the wheels. He'd kiss to the horses, and they would really get for a ways before they ran out of wind. John would holler, "Whoa!"

The horses would stop and the big load could pull them back a foot or so, and then the load would hit John's post and quit pulling on the horses so that they could stand and get their wind. In this way, he was able to bring much bigger loads through to Vernal. It took John eight days to make the round trip.

Robert and brothers had almost hauled enough logs for the houses they would need right now, and so they sent two more wagons back to Price with John. They brought three more loads of lumber.

John was getting tired of freighting, but he went back and got the stoves he had ordered—three nice kitchen ranges with pipes and accessories. They had lots of chrome, looking really sharp with warming ovens and reservoirs. When they got back to Vernal, Robert had one cabin up with a plank floor and door step. There was lumber and shakes for a shingle roof.

A stove went inside. Wow, the envy of the other women of the community! Charlotte smiled at John. "Beckwith and Louder's loss is certainly some Price storekeeper's gain! We will be happy to cook on stoves again!" There weren't many women living in Vernal. The first white woman came into the valley in 1878.

Charlotte was eager for them to start on her home the next day. She missed her home in Bear Lake, and roughing it was difficult with a little family and another one on the way.

To the Pope's it was just as important to have a barn and corral as a house. Horses were their living, their transportation, their means of getting work done.

John walked uptown to a store after work that night to hopefully buy some nails. As he was nearing the store, a gunshot rang out. Just as he was almost to the store, another shot sounded, then several men came spilling out of the bar, two doors down. As John watched, a man raised a pistol and fired in the air, then laughed loudly. About this time, John saw the law, Sheriff Sterling D. Colton, hurrying up to see what the fuss was. Sterling was sheriff of Uintah County, Utah Territory. John could see the roughnecks planned on either killing the Sheriff or humiliating him if possible. They spread apart a bit so he was boxed in as he came up.

Sheriff Colton asked, "What's all the shooting and noise about?"

One man whose back was to Pope said, "Hell, it's not against the law to shoot is it?"

The voice of this bully sounded familiar to John, and he stepped closer. From the sheriff's face, Pope knew he had figured out his danger and was trying to withdraw. John knew they planned to take his guns and humiliate him some way.

The bully said, "Try for your gun. I'd like to be the man that killed the sheriff of Uintah County!"

"Why don't you try *me*?" John's voice came from behind the outlaw.

The man whirled with a look of sheer terror on his face.

John said, "Sheriff, back up a few steps. You accidently let a couple of guys get behind you there." The sheriff was happy to step away from the fire, so to speak. "All right black beard. Let's see your magic on me! I'll just finish what I started one other day. What about your tough friends?"

Black beard's eyes shifted sideways, wondering how much thunder his friends were willing to raise.

Pope continued, "I take you one or all. Have at it."

Black beard suddenly was having trouble standing up. He grabbed the tie post. His breath became loud and almost like a broken, winded horse. He threw up a couple of times.

Pope said, "Take him and get out of here! If you try anything more around here, I'll take a hand in it, and enjoy doing it."

After they rode away, Sterling was shaking, but not as bad as black beard. The shivering sheriff thanked John.

"Hell, they would have killed me for sure. I didn't want this job! They wrote me in and elected me. I wish I could quit right now. I want you to be my deputy."

John nearly laughed. "I really haven't got time. I'm building a house and trying to get enough stuff to get my family through the winter. If you get in trouble though, I'll try to help out. But I aint got time."

"Those men were really afraid of you. Why?"

"Chicken shits, I guess."

"Not them. I thought ol' Gus was gonna die. They knew you from somewhere else."

Pope smiled and went in the store. The sheriff tagged along. He said, "They don't pay much, but if you'll be my deputy, I'll see you get thirty dollars a month and practice ammo."

"A few weeks more I'll have a house built. Then if I'm not freighting or looking for a place to homestead to start a ranch, I'll help you. If you have trouble like tonight, send word. I'll come immediately." For some reason John thought of coyotes in sheep and said, "I don't like predators."

John spent two weeks working with his dad and brothers, staying in his own bed with his wife and kids. It was wonderful!

After getting squared around with the work in Vernal, John saddled Old Shorty, took a pack horse and rode up to the store. The sheriff hailed him. So after tying his horses to the tie post, he walked over to talk to him. The sheriff wanted John to come to work. They were talking about the outlaws and trouble Sheriff Sterling was having.

Suddenly a shot sounded in the store. A man came running out, jumped on a horse, and went tearing out of town on a dead run. Pope ran across the road to the store. John Harter, the store keeper was down and bleeding.

Harter gasped, "Jack Davis just shot me without warning and ran away."

Sheriff Sterling asked a young man to get a doctor quick. He turned to John and said, "You come with me."

John went to the tie post, left the pack horse, jumped on Old Shorty and went pacing out of town. John stayed on the traveled roadway. Jack Davis had gone across rocks and cactus and creosote brush.

John saw the sheriff come running out of town on a horse borrowed from a tie post. He was on a high run on Davis's tracks. When the horse hit a badger hole and went head over heels, Pope kept watch until he saw the sheriff get up. When the horse got on his feet, he was bad lame. John could see others coming from town, so he figured the sheriff would get a horse someplace.

John studied the direction of Davis. He could see his dust. He had taken a rough, circuitous route, thinking he would be out of sight and maybe get to ambush the sheriff. On the other hand, Pope on the smooth road was catching up pretty fast. The trail Davis was on was coming toward Pope's road. He would be on the brow of a hill, maybe three hundred feet higher than the road. When Davis came in sight, he was only three hundred yards away. His horse was winded, and lathered, fighting the rough trail.

When he saw John, he started to shoot at him. He wasn't coming too close, shooting from the back of a hurrying horse, and having to turn and throw the shots back. John kissed to his big horse, eager and still fresh. Shorty came on a high run, closing the distance fast. As the outlaw was nearing some cover, John stopped quickly, and stepped away from his horse so he wouldn't hurt his ears. He didn't want to hurt the outlaw's horse either. He figured about four feet hold over so if he missed, it wouldn't kill the horse. He fired. He saw Davis lurch sideways, make a grab for the horn but missed catching it. The horse went on without him. Pope heard a "Thwack" of the bullet hitting flesh. Pope's shot was true, but he saw Davis go behind a rock on his hands and knees.

Pope crouched down low and ran forward about another seventy yards or so, stopping where he could see all sides of the rock Davis had taken refuge behind. Then, he took cover, got comfortable, and kept his pistol cocked, holding it out over the rock. He stayed in this position for about fifteen minutes. Soon John's brother George came riding around the point of the hill on Davis's trail. John yelled and stopped him before he rode into the ambush waiting up there.

About that time a hat appeared on a gun barrel. John was looking over his colt at it. It continued to go higher until the gun barrel was in view.

John yelled, "Stick your head in that hat, and I'll take it off!"

Davis yelled, "I'm bleeding to death. I'm through."

"Throw out your guns. Be sure I can see them."

They came.

Then John said, "Now you come on the other side."

Davis did as he was told. He was pretty bloody, but it was a flesh wound.

When the Sheriff arrived, George and John had Davis on his horse. John had his guns and a lariat rope around his neck.

"There he is, Sheriff. You can take him back or hang him. It's all up to you."

Sheriff said, "A jury could do the hanging."

George spoke up saying, "John Harter should be on that jury if he lives."

When they got to town with the prisoner, the doctor who was treating John Harter came to check and patch up Jack Davis.

Harter would live. Davis would later be tried and sentenced by a District Court in Provo to five years in the Salt Lake penitentiary.

Sheriff Sterling asked John to please come help him.

John's answer was that he wanted to look for a ranch prospect first, but that he had been thinking about the job. He said when he had filed and improved it some, he'd come help once in a while. "I actually got a kick out catching Jack Davis for ya."

Sheriff asked, "Did you shoot him with the rifle or pistol?"

"The pistol."

"How far away was Davis when you knocked him off his horse?"

"I judged about two hundred yards."

"How many shots did you shoot?"

"I lucked out and hit him the first shot."

Someone listening said from the side, "I doubt if Butch Cassidy himself could do that on the first shot."

"I just got lucky, I guess."

They went in the store for supplies for the pack trip. He was still starting on his trip that morning and needed several items. John Harter's partner filled his order. He packed the horse with supplies he'd need for a week and rode out.

John camped on water that night about ten miles from Ashley. Next day he rode into Brown's Hole and crossed the river. He followed the river to Red Creek. He remembered crossing Red Creek when they were on the way from Bear Lake. They had crossed it upstream a ways and he had kept it in mind to check out.

Red Creek came from the mountain to the north. This south facing slope in this deep canyon would make wonderful winter range. Another plus for Pope was that sage brush grew here instead of so much creosote. There was also an abundance of his favorite food, sage hens.

John T. camped on a little meadow on a bench a ways from the river, got a sagebrush fire going, boiled his coffee, and fried chicken. Oh, it felt good to be alone and at peace. He paused to thank his maker on his knees for everything and asked for help in choosing his spot to homestead. He also asked for help in guiding him to do what his maker would have him do. He asked the Lord to bless his wife and family, to bless his dad who was once again the ecclesiastical leader of the frontier community in helping and influencing people to do better. There was so much to do and so little time to do it.

He slept well and awoke later than usual. He saddled up after breakfast, left his camp and hobbled his pack horse. He then rode up the mountain to see if it would work how he figured. It turned out to be bigger up there than he thought. He went through a narrows of sorts. Rocky ledges were on both sides of him, creating a narrows about one third of a mile across. The narrows emptied into a cluster of meadow ground. This was a little valley about a mile wide, between the edges, with a series of seeps and small springs that watered the grass which was ripe and brown now. It was good hay, but that wasn't what he was thinking.

By filing a homestead in the narrows, he could run a fence between the ledges in the narrows, build a dam in the creek, and water a small crop. He could build a house, and corral, and make enough improvements to prove up on the homestead of three hundred sixty acres. He would file on all the water in Red Creek and all the grass. He could prove beneficial use through stock water, as well as irrigation on a few acres by the house. He could also spread water out up above to make even more grass.

John sat on his horse up on the upper reaches of the creek. Looking south he thought he could see at least a hundred miles. The mountains had deep canyons. The colors were fantastic! Rocky ledges hedged this high mountain valley. There would be a minimum of fencing along the bottom. He'd have a private range that would run at least fifty head, year around, maybe even a hundred, but that would be seen later. The best part, they wouldn't be mixing with other herds. He could probably have private pasture where rustlers wouldn't be so apt to steal them. At least they would have to drive the cattle out the bottom to do the job which would be over his private land.

John got back to camp that night, excited at the prospects. The next morning he looked where the fence would run, then built a pile of rocks on the line. Into the rocks he put his handkerchief with the JT connected, written in charcoal. It was put in the middle of the pile under a flat rock. This was the way claims were marked in those days.

John rode to Carter, Wyoming, and got a liveryman to keep his horses for about a week. He took the train to Cheyenne where water was filed. He registered his brand in Wyoming, as well as grass, and went to the land office where he filed the homestead.

He took the train to Salt Lake where all this was filed there, as well as in Utah Territory. (Statehood wasn't granted until 1876.) On the chance he might be locating in Colorado, he made the trip horseback from Brown's Hole, to Denver, where everything was filed again, for the third time. His stake on Red Creek was nestled in that iffy, tri-territory area, and John had to be sure. Then he rode home. He had been gone one month, and when he rode into the yard Charlotte nearly pulled him off Old Shorty, so eager was she to see her husband.

After several kisses she cried, "Rob and Polly are the smart ones! Polly's in beautiful Bear Lake and she knows where her husband is at night! What on earth are we *doing* here?"

"We are making a future for our family, Charlotte."

She nodded, but stubbornly jutted out a bottom lip and said, "Making a future was easier in the past." John laughed and scooped her in his arms once again.

He stayed a few days and helped Sheriff Sterling move five men who were trouble hunters. Pope suggested Vernal would be way too little for him and them both. The next morning, they were gone. Pope's reputation had grown huge in a short time among outlaws and settlers alike.

John visited with his father and brothers. They were really busy, but he was able to hire a couple of kids that were seventeen years old to go back out to fence his homestead and make improvements. He took his covered wagon and four planks, a bunch of nail blanks and four large rolls of wire. He bought wire pinchers, another axe, and a bunch of supplies. The young men threw their bed rolls in. John tied Shorty behind, and they took the Cherokee Trail back the way the Pope's came into Vernal.

Seven days later, they lifted the wagon box off the wagon onto four rocks to camp in until a house could be built there. They took the running gears, minus the box, and drove about fifteen miles east to a nice stand of poles on the river there. They cut and trimmed the poles until dark. They drank coffee and ate pine hens for supper and breakfast. They loaded a huge load of poles and went back to their camp on Red Creek. By night they had a cabin built to the square; it was small, only ten by ten.

The next day saw the cabin complete, with a tiny window on each side, covered by a plank shutter, a plank door on leather hinges in front, and a large flat rock for the step. Split poles were nailed close together for the roof.

After lifting the wood rack back on the running gears, a couple of loads of dirt was hauled and shoveled on top to make a dirt roof. Cracks were battened with strips of willows and limbs, nailed in. These were whittled and fitted fairly tight. They used the last of the poles on the fence, and then went for more poles and posts. They were gone from Vernal for two and a half months.

A corral was built, fences were up, and about ten acres was under irrigation above the house. A dam and short ditch was built onto it. Also, more diversion dams and ditches were in use up high. John thought this would maybe, over time, water an extra twenty acres or so. He rode down to Jarvie's Store one day and found a small camp stove and was able to buy it, with pipe enough to install, as well as a coal oil lantern. With this, his ranch house became both warm and comfortable.

Upon returning to Vernal John paid his young friends sixty dollars each for their help. They said they would love to work for him anytime.

Pope met the shock of his life. In his absence, the Territorial County Election of 1890 was held. John T. Pope had been elected sheriff of Uintah County! Nobody would run for the job. John's name was written in, and he was unanimously elected.

"How the hell has this happened?" John asked Charlotte.

"I figured you must be out campaigning," she answered drolly.

His mouth twitched with a smile. "No . . . I was out building a future for our—"

"I know, I know! You were out building a future for our family, but don't you see? We can't build a future here!"

"Why not?"

"Because the present keeps getting in the way!"

"Oh Charlotte . . . you do beat all."

John knew deep down that Charlotte's sarcasm was a hundred percent true. If the lawless territory didn't shape up today, there really wouldn't be a tomorrow, and he just couldn't bear the thoughts of all of this being in vain.

CHAPTER NINE

Thick as Thieves

IF IT HADN'T BEEN for his brothers, things could have gotten way out of hand. Jim McKee and his gang had moved in for the winter. They were going to take Vernal and have their fun with it. John's brothers had kept things in hand 'til he could get back. So now he'd simply run them the hell out or kill them.

"No, no," Dick said. He thought now John was back they could handle them without anyone being killed.

"What's your idea?"

"The McKee outfit spends lots of time in the bars. To find out which bar Jim McKee is in, John, you could just walk in the front door, walk up to Jim and put him under arrest. If he resisted, I would lay him out. See, I would slip in the back door and up to him while he watched you."

John said, "It is not my way to get too close or to put my back to any of the rest of the gang."

"What if Marcellus, Rock, and George cover with shotguns from the doors and window?"

John looked at these brothers and asked, "Will you shoot to kill if something goes wrong?"

No hesitation. "Yes sir!"

"Okay. They'll want me to come get close. Somebody will try to bag me to keep me from drawing my weapon while Jim pulls his to shoot me, so Dick, don't hold back. Hit him as hard as you can."

"I'll probably kill him if I do that."

John said, "If you don't, we might all be killed, along with a bunch of others, in the cross fire in that smoky little bar. After the first shots, nobody in there will be able to see anything but black powder smoke."

"I never would of thought of that. You talk like you've been in something like this before."

John never answered. "Have you got that many shotguns?"

Dick said, "There's enough at the jail."

"Okay. Get 'em and load them with buckshot. Take extra shells. Reload as soon as you shoot because if gang members come out the doors, or from the other saloon, you better be able to shoot, otherwise I lose my brothers that I love."

Twenty minutes later, everything was ready.

"Mother will kill you if anything happens to me," Marcellus teased.

"If anything happens to you, Marcellus, then that means I'm already dead." John's words rang with a serious clamor in the ears of his brothers.

George indicated the closest bar was where Jim was. So everyone scattered to get into position. John waited a few minutes, strolled up to the bar, and stepped in. He saw the situation was just about what he told Dick it would be.

"Jim McKee!" John barked, sounding authoritative. Everything became quiet. Jim stood a bit straighter, staring at John as he approached to about arms length.

"You're under arrest."

"Like hell!" Jim went for his pistol. Someone grabbed John from behind. Everything was playing out as John predicted, but because he was looking for this very scenario, he was able to get a hand on Jim and push him back a little. In doing this, he pivoted clear around.

Whack! Dick must have hit Jim. Now out of the grasp of the man behind him, John drew is pistol like a flash, sticking it under the man's nose who had grabbed him. John's thumb held the hammer back. A lot of shotguns cocked, and two brothers stepped through the door. McKee's gang, seeing Jim laid out cold, and the odds all in Pope's corner, put their hands up. John told two of his brothers to go to the other bar and round up the rest of the gang before they heard of the incident and cut out of town.

John had the bartender gather the guns and put them on the bar till morning. The gang was marched to jail and locked up. Jim McKee was hauled to a doctor's office and left in the Dr.'s custody till morning, as well.

Next morning court was held for eighteen men. All had to pay fines and some were given jail sentences. John had all their guns on a bench outside the courthouse door. After paying their fines, each came to get his gun. After pointing out which was his, Pope would open the load gate, and drop shells in a keep box. He also shucked shells from their belts, giving the empty guns back to them.

He said, "The Vernal area will be extremely hard on your health and welfare, if you boys catch my drift."

It was a couple of weeks before Jim was good enough to ride away. The Jim McKee Gang never bothered Vernal again. However, individual outlaws had a bad grudge against John T. Pope, for he was getting to be a dumb nuisance.

Word came to John that he was needed home, so he walked down to find Charlotte in labor. His mother had him run some errands for her. He figured to keep him busy, but he sent up a lot of silent prayers on behalf of Charlotte and the new baby. The prayers were answered and tiny Charles Theodore Pope joined the family.

John knelt by his wife as she laid the new babe against her breast. "You're not the only one making improvements, John T. Pope!"

"I should say I'm not! Well done, Charlotte." John kissed his wife and new son. "You're building a future for us, too, I see."

Everything worked well. Quiet came after the McKee Gang broke up. Robert Pope didn't have enough hay for his cow herd to last the winter, so John offered his Red Creek pasture to him at least until spring. So a cattle drive ensued. Robert sent fifty cows. They took salt and a covered wagon for a chuck wagon and went back down the Cherokee Trail. It took about ten days to trail them in there. Robert was impressed by the nice, comfortable place! Cows were gaunt and hungry when they arrived, but in a few days they were full, and completely satisfied. John stayed on at Red Creek 'til someone could come replace him.

An interesting visit from Ann Bassett occurred the second day. Pope was dragging a couple of cedar posts down with a lariat on Old Shorty to help build a shelter for his horse. He spotted her horse tied in front of his cabin. He dragged the posts up to the corral, dismounted, took his rope off, and re-coiled it then tied it back in place on the saddle. He unsaddled and led his horse into the corral, pulled the bridle off, slid a couple of bars in place, and turned to go into the cabin. Ann Bassett was leaning against the side of his cabin smiling at him.

He startled a bit. She laughed at his reaction. "Surely you saw my horse out here."

"Oh, I saw your horse all right. And I knew I had company, but when I turned to go you were close enough to touch, and I was looking at a beautiful face in these dirty cowboy clothes. It's like seeing a ghost or something. The last thing I ever expected to see was a girl—there's one hundred miles of empty land out there. Where did you drop from?"

Ann laughed again, but longer, and there was a bit of mean raucousness in it. She had a pretty sounding voice and a good laugh until this last, almost mocking challenge, something John could hear—and maybe his subconscious was at work.

John had done his homework on the neighbors—and this is what he knew about Ann Bassett: she was petite, only five foot, two inches tall, and maybe a hundred and fifteen pounds, fully clothed. Ann and her sister, Josie Bassett, had hair-pulling fights over Butch Cassidy. Ann later became sweet on the Sundance Kid, but Butch would do if Sundance wasn't around. She was called Queen Ann Bassett by ranchers. She was arrested and tried for rustling in Colorado, but as the trial approached, she made bail and while in town, she bought the best and prettiest dresses. She had her hair marcelled and cheeks and lips powdered and pink. She was on good behavior and considered very beautiful and gracious by everyone. As a result, the jury wouldn't convict her of rustling! She was pardoned and released.

Ann's eyes flirted shamelessly, wanting in on his thoughts. "How did you know I was a girl?"

"When I saw those big grey eyes peering under long pretty lashes, smooth skin, and full lips, I knew instantly. You were a pretty young gal disguised as a dirty 'ol cowboy. Even your clothes let you down. No man I ever saw filled his clothes the same way you do."

"Hell, I can outride, out shoot, and out rope any man I know, and maybe two."

John said, "Yes and out swear, out talk, and out lie most of them, I'll bet." She was getting a retort ready so John said, "But can you cook?"

"Not worth a damn."

"I'll peel these chickens I got this morning, and you can prove it."

"Sage chickens? What's wrong with beef? How can ranchers make a living if everybody eats chicken all the time? Everybody likes beef best, but not jerky."

"If I killed a beef, I only get a few days to use it up, then to save the rest I have to build racks and make jerky. Man would wear all his teeth to stubs chewing jerky all the time."

Ann laughed merrily this time. "I can make coffee. Where do you keep it?"

"There's a can on the shelf by the stove. I made a fresh pot this morning, just add more grounds and water."

"You like it strong and bitter I see."

"Yes ma'am."

She stepped out and said, "Anything wrong with using the Dutch oven out here?"

"Not a thing. Throw an armful of sagebrush in the pit, put some of the cedar limbs over it, and light it up."

She had a good fire going when he got his chicken ready. She was making baking powder biscuits. She said, "Set it in the Dutch oven, and I'll cook for us."

"You don't cook, remember?"

"I said I don't cook worth a damn, but I get me by my way, okay?"

"I appreciate it. Yes ma'am."

John sat on the step watching her get dinner, wondering what to do with her. She acted like she was going to move right in. He might have to cut and run at any time! She was way beyond any experience John had ever had with another woman. He knew she was enjoying his uncomfortable position. What to do? Charlotte Ann Stock would have torn Ann Bassett to pieces in a second's time had she seen her stirring supper in her husband's Dutch oven. That would have solved the problem.

Ann made good biscuits. She fished the meat out of the oven and made gravy. John really enjoyed a good dinner with Ann, but still his mind spun. "I found out you can cook after all. I guess you better tell me who you are. Of course I don't want a jealous husband or posse to come after me for taking advantage of a pretty gal."

"I'm Ann Bassett. Who are you?"

"I'm John Pope. I am a new neighbor, I guess. I've got some complaints from the Two Bar Ranch about Ann Bassett rustling cattle. Tell me it's not true."

"I've never rustled any of their dumb cows, but I've shot some and drove some in the river. They don't think anybody has any right to run cows in the Diamond Hills but them. They keep getting more and more cattle, trying to crowd us out."

"How long have you been up here, in Brown's Hole, I mean?"

"I was raised here. I was the first white baby born in Brown's Park."

"Well, Ann, I think you've established some rights of your own if you've been there that long. I don't know if you filed on your place or any water holes or not. If not, do it now. If you are the first to file on the water right in your area, then that legally establishes your claim to the range. I'm Sheriff John T. Pope, and I'll consider you a good friend, and I'll ignore the complaints from the Two Bar for awhile—until you get your land and water filed. If it happens that the Two Bar hasn't filed the water on your range, then it's yours, and I'd have to arrest them instead of you in case of trouble."

"I didn't know I was talking to the *law*." She heavily buttered the word at the end of the sentence, coating it in ways that made John squirm.

"I'm glad you did. I really need to know what's going on around out here."

"I'll do the dishes before I go."

"No, leave them for me, but get something and take some of the chicken with you. I'll have to heat a bit of water. You just take the chicken and head on out. It must be ten or twelve miles home. It'll get dark on you unless you hurry. Where will you cross the river?"

"The Jarvie Crossing. I have the best horse in the whole world. He'll take me home."

The next day another visitor stopped by for a visit, a man named Butch Cassidy. He stepped off his tall thoroughbred and walked up, looking inside the open door. "Howdy."

John said, "Come in and have a hot cup with me."

Butch stepped in and glanced around.

John said, "Yes, it's hot in here with the door closed. I've had the beans cooking since early this morning. They've soaked all night, so maybe we can share a bean in a few minutes."

"Ann told me we had new neighbors in Brown's Hole."

"Yes, she stopped for a visit yesterday. Pretty gal."

"She was my gal for awhile there. Both she and her sister Josie had a few fights over me. Now they're both looking elsewhere, I guess. She's taken up with Sundance now, course if he's not around, I'll do—and Matt Rash, she steps with him a bit. She likes men, if you know what I mean, and she's much too hospitable to make a feller go without."

"When she found out I was sheriff, she sure lost all interest in me."

Butch laughed out, "Pretty good, at that."

"I advised her to file on all the water on her old range, also on the ranch unless it was already filed. If the Two Bar filed a prior claim on the water, I'm afraid she would legally lose it to the Two Bar. Will you follow through and see that it's filed?"

Butch said, "Hell yes. You would think I'd have known to do that much."

"We generally try to fight our own battles, and so we war on our own and fail to comply with laws." John handed Butch a spoon since he was on the side of the fire. "Try the beans. See if we gotta cook something else for dinner."

Butch stood up and pulled a glove from a back pocket, folding it over the pot handle. He lifted the lid and ladled a spoon full. Sitting back down, he blew on the beans a while. He finally got some in his mouth and he declared they were cooked well enough for him. Both men got a bowl and spoon, and a fork for the pork. The men were quiet while eating beans and fresh side. As they began to get full, chatter started again. After the meal, dishes were done and Butch was on his way out.

Pope said, "I went over things in my office in Vernal, Cassidy, and I don't have anything on you. As far as I'm concerned, you have complete amnesty. Please don't do anything to circulate a warrant to my office for your arrest. I *will* do my job."

Butch answered, "John T. Pope, you serve a warrant on me, and I'll kill you." He turned the horse and rode away.

John watched him ride away on the tall, superb horse. He thought he would probably have to give Butch the chance. John knew he would be fast, but thought in his heart he could beat him. Butch, as far as he knew, had never killed a man. He was generous and he had many friends, but he just didn't seem to want to change. It was only a matter of time.

A magpie landed out a ways looking for scraps. Pope threw his draw and fired, killing the bird. He thought, "I'm purty good shooting magpies and chickens, but they aint shooting back. If I have to face Butch or Sundance or both, I'll have to throw down on them like shooting a magpie."

That night Rock rode up on one of the three years olds they were breaking.

"Any trouble with the colt?"

"No. He'll be broke after today. I trotted him for hours. I left Vernal before light this morning. He didn't like the ferry, but I got him loaded before he got his wind. Maybe next time he'll just get on."

They had supper by light of the lantern, and visited awhile.

"I've got some interesting neighbors up here in Red Creek, Rock."

"Yeah?"

"Just—watch yourself. Don't let some little gal all dressed in cowboy clothes ride in here and hoodwink you." Rock gave his word.

Next morning John pulled out before light. He was ferried over and riding away from the river by first light. He arrived home, where he was welcomed by his wife and young family, and John tried to get acquainted with his newest. He was talking and playing with kids 'til late and the laughter sounded good to him.

After a good night's sleep, John went out and milked cows, did the chores, and came inside to a good woman, cooking breakfast. A man really appreciates the differences after batching for a while. After visiting with Charlotte he walked to the jail to look through his mail and catch up on circulars and posters. One poster gave a five hundred dollar dead or alive reward for Carl Bitner, a murderer from Colorado. "I could use that reward," John thought. Then he wondered if lawmen could collect rewards or just bounty hunters. He'd have to ask about it if anyone knew.

He walked to his dad's home and went in to visit a bit. They asked about the cattle. John said they were rested, and full, and really looking good.

"You know I like my place out there. It's the nicest winter set up I've seen. It is lots warmer in that canyon than down here. I haven't seen snow stay for more than day. Good water, grass, protection, and for a bachelor, my cabin is perfect."

Robert laughed and laughed. "I'm glad you said that. My conscience has been bothering me for dragging my family from Bear Lake. It's taken us awhile to get established. And my younger kids are being raised with the roughest kinds of people in the world and some of the best."

John walked home and did chores. He rode out a ways for the milk cows, brought them home and milked, and walked in to supper. Before he had time to eat, there was a loud knock at the door.

"Oh good," Charlotte muttered. "It's the present calling."

Charlotte's words were like a prophecy, for a neighbor had his horse tied to the hitching rail in front of the store. When he came out with his packages, his horse was gone. It had been stolen.

John took a lantern and lighted it. He walked out to see the tracks. The horse had been missing awhile already, and other horses had been here since, so it took about five minutes before John got a good clear print of one hind foot. The mad and excited owner said it was his. "I shod her myself!"

"A mare?"

"Yes."

"How big?"

"About a thousand pounds."

"She's tall?"

"No, she's kind of a gentle, little, heavy-set mare. Kids can ride her."

"Branded?"

"Yes, with the Lazy A on the right front shoulder."

"Color?"

"Dark bay."

Pope had been walking north while talking. Finally on the edge of town, he found where the horse had left the other tracks. So Pope knew where to start the next morning.

Pope directed, "File a complaint with the judge, and I'll get on the tracks in the morning when I can see."

Several people had told him that it was impossible to track in this infernal country. "It is either all rock, or sand, or alkali, and prickly pear." John thought he'd find out in the morning.

Daylight next morning found him riding Old Shorty north on the trail through miles of creosote and sagebrush into Ashley Creek. The tracks didn't emerge across as it should have, so Pope rode down the bank a ways, carefully watching. He found where the rider had come out across the creek. The rider had then gone into a dry creek bed of cobble rock. However, Pope could see places marked by the shoes, and he followed as fast as old Shorty wanted to go through the rock.

He emerged finally, then went through a tangle of buffalo brush, crossed a canal and into Steinaker Draw. He continued through a few miles of cedars, across a field, and into Frank Boan's Corral. John tied his horse and walked to the house, muttering, "What the hell?" He knocked and Frank answered the door, put his hat on, and stepped out without really opening up very much. Pope wondered if the outlaw was in the house.

Frank said, "You must have got caught out last night to be showing up this early clear out here."

Pope said, "Truth is, Frank, a horse was stolen in town last night. I've tracked it right into your corral. Tell me what you know about it."

"Please Pope, don't ask me that. All I've got for me and my family is right here and on the range. If I throw in with the law, I wouldn't last long. What would happen to my family if I got eliminated? You can see how things are, can't you Pope? Please don't ask me any questions."

"Yes, I know that, but quietly tell me where he is. I'll sneak back and get him. We've got to put an end to this childish bunch of steal thieves. I'll keep your name out of it. Okay?"

"Your word's good enough for me. Don't look that direction. He's up the draw in back of the house. He's got plenty of guns. Please be careful."

So John untied his horse, mounted up, and waved calling, "Sorry you couldn't help me, Boan!"

Old Shorty hit fast pace, thinking of home, but after getting out of sight, John started a circuitous route to another draw that looked like it would come out somewhere close to the draw the outlaw was hiding in. He took it in a hidden spot near the top. John tethered his horse and, hanging bridle on the horn, went on afoot. He could see Frank's ranch below, no dust, so he must still be up here. So crouching low, he crossed the saddle from his draw to the one the outlaw was hiding in. John advanced a step, quietly listening. Another step. His eyes were busy as well as his ears. He tried hard to concentrate on this job, but his mind was flying a thousand miles an minute. Finally, he took the step that brought the stolen mare in sight. She was tied to some sparse brush, just standing, hip shod on three legs. She was saddled, bridled, and waiting patiently—perfect bait for a sniper bullet for anyone approaching her. John took another quiet step, then another. He figured his man to be watching from the rocks directly in front of him. Three more slow quiet steps, and standing straight up, he could see the horse thief. As John watched, he saw the man's head nod a bit, he was dozing off. So Pope made himself concentrate on no noise, but he was able to close the distance fairly fast. He took the rifle in his left hand and began to lift it out of the thief's hands. The outlaw's eyes sprang open and he was looking into the barrel of Pope's colt.

"Just let go and keep them in the air. Lay over on your stomach!" Pope pulled the outlaw's pistol out and stuck it in his belt. He put his own pistol in the holster. He took a pair of handcuffs from his coat pocket and locked one on the outlaw's wrist. Pulling that arm behind the prisoner, he handcuffed both hands behind his back. Then, with the prisoner's rifle in one hand, he pulled him off the ground and sent him after the horse. The horse thief went down the hill very slowly.

Pope said, "Step it up a bit."

"Why? I'm in no hurry."

"Well," Pope said, "I killed the last horse thief I went after. My job all pays the same whether I kill you or bring you to trial. If I kill you, you won't steal anymore of anything from anybody. And I save the expense of trial, and or, burial for the county. So step it up a little."

He stopped along and got the slip knot undone by turning his back and looking over his shoulder.

"Okay. Lead her right back up past here and go on up in front of me."

When they got to Old Shorty, Pope stopped him. He bridled his horse, and before going, he unlocked the left cuff and locked it on the saddle horn, thus locking the thief's right hand. Then he took the outlaw back to Vernal to jail. People were watching their newly elected sheriff bring his prisoner through town. Something new was happening around here. Real law had arrived in the Basin.

Pope's mind had been worrying over how intimidated residents were by outlaws. He realized he was all alone here for a while. A good thought was the fact that he could track in the Basin. Bless those Shoshone friends who spent weeks trying to teach him and test his tracking skills! So the outlaw was brought before the judge and evidence submitted: the horse disappeared and Pope had tracked it to where it was recovered with the thief hidden, watching it. It was a simple case.

The Judge said he'd have to release the prisoner because all the evidence was all circumstantial. Pope needed witnesses! Now John had made a promise to Frank Boan and so he kept it. When Pope gave the prisoner his guns, he said, "I'm new to this job, but I found out that the best way to take care of you two-bit bad men is just to kill you. So here are your guns. If you don't want to have to try to face me with them, get the hell away, just as far and fast as you can go."

John didn't know if all this had done any good or not, except he had recovered the stolen horse, and the owner was really thankful. Maybe some of the people would begin to trust in the law and begin resisting this evil blight which had fastened itself to this forgotten and rugged part of the world. Honest people were so intimidated by outlaws; they didn't dare even report activities to the law. Many times Butch Cassidy and other outlaws had been generous with others and they felt they owed them, and tended to sympathize with them. So John T. Pope had a job just to win the trust of honest people, and win the fight for order and freedom to be able to resist evil, and keep the property a person earned by the sweat and sacrifice of time and tears! Someday people would live here in happiness, be able to turn cows on the range, and round them up in the fall without having to keep all the outlaws fat! That was John's vision for the Uintah Basin.

John had to battle outlaws and scared judges, judges that were afraid to curtail the rights of punks, and afraid for their own jobs. As he thought about it, he began to see the scope of his job in a much expanded and bigger way. He was more quiet and thoughtful that night at supper. After dishes were done and kids off to bed, Charlotte came over and sat down on his knee. She put an arm around his neck. "Why are you so sad?" He laughed and tried to make it seem like nothing, but finally tried to explain the glimpses, or vision, he had of the importance of his job. He now knew he had more to do than he thought. Charlotte listened quietly.

Next morning he thanked deity for such a wonderful family and wife who had lifted him into a happy place again. Before he was through with his morning coffee, a homesteader was knocking on his door. So he listened a minute and went for his horse. Charlotte quickly put a sandwich together for him. "It was nice meeting you," she whispered with a smile while putting the sandwich in his pack.

John rode out, with the homesteader riding one of Pope's horses. John told him he could use him until his own horses were recovered. Someone had taken this homesteader's horses from his corral the night before. He had a saddle horse, a black gelding, about eleven hundred pounds with a triangle brand on the left shoulder, and a white snip on his nose. His team was bays, tall horses, and one had a sore neck from the collar. They were about twelve hundred pounds apiece. They both had their manes roached off with collar marks and the triangle brand.

These were the homesteader's only horses. He didn't know what he'd do without them. So Pope dismounted and went over things. He got good clear looks at all three of the horses' tracks, also a good look at boot tracks. The perpetrator wore high, under-slung rider heels, about size nine. They had metal plates on the heel and toe. This bad man had tied his horse to the corral, walked in, caught the horses, tied them to teach other's tails, led them out, mounted his own horse, which apparently was a small horse with size zero shoes, and led them away.

John let Old Shorty pace about fifteen miles from the corral. He came to the spot where they spent the night. John got down and checked. The fire was cold, so the thief was still a quite a way ahead, but he had switched horses. He followed tracks clear over Diamond Mountain. His adversary was avoiding any ranches or camps. It was getting dark that night when he came in sight of a cabin on the other side of the river. The horses John could see in the corral matched as near as he could tell, to the ones he'd been following. The rowboat usually left here by the Bassett's, to cross the river with, was pulled up on the sandbar on the other side. So Pope decided to cross and get up close, and make his arrest the next morning. He took his boots, sox, and pants off and tied them up, and then crossed the river.

It was too damn cold for this! John's teeth were chattering. He finally got dressed again and ate his sandwich. He untied his coat from behind the saddle, then unsaddled and used the blankets and ground sheets to wrap in. He didn't dare light a fire so he lay and shivered awhile. When he finally started to get warm, he almost dropped to sleep. John shook himself. No sleep tonight! If he went to sleep he might lose his man. So he got up and walked about a mile down to the cabin, very quietly and slowly he moved into the corral.

John struck a match, sure enough, triangle brands. These were the horses he'd followed over the mountain and into the hole. So he moved quietly out front, finally fixed a comfortable seat behind the woodpile in front of the house. His quarry didn't stir 'til after it was full light. Finally, he came out the door to do a bathroom chore and John threw a pair of handcuffs to him, startling him half out of his wits.

"Snap them on!"

Buckskin Ed Carouthers looked with dull eyes toward Pope.

"Put em on Ed."

Ed continued to crouch, hands close to pistols.

"Grab em Ed and I'll have the excuse I need to rid the country of your bad smell."

Finally Ed bent over and picked up the cuffs.

"Now lock em on ya, Ed."

He did.

"Undo the pistol belts."

He finally complied.

"Okay, Ed, come around here and get an armful of wood. Carry it in and we'll have a cup of coffee before we start back to Ashley Valley."

Buckskin said, "I aint got no coffee."

Pope said, "Start the fire. There's always coffee in the cupboard. This is a line cabin of Bassett's."

So while John watched, Ed made coffee. He thought his nick name fit him well. He always wore the buckskin trousers. They were so soiled and greasy they looked stiff and black in places where his knees bent. They were wrinkled in back and the knees stuck out in front, making him appear like he was always ready to jump.

After about four cups, John was ready. He picked up the pistols and watched Ed saddle his horse. He caught the others and tied them tail to tail. While he made the horses ready, John mounted Ed's horse and made him walk about a mile to where John had left Old Shorty, still staked on good grass. John saddled his own good horse, rolled his coat in the ground sheet and tied it behind, on top of the saddle bags where Ed's pistols were now stashed. They rode back, picked up the horses, and rode to the boat. John bobbed Old Shorty's tail and tied Buckskin Ed's horse to it, then handed the reins to Ed.

"All right Ed, I'll get in and take the oars. You push us off and jump in and lead the horses. Can you do that?"

No response from Ed.

So Pope got in and took the oars, watching Ed, until he pushed them into the currant and jumped in.

Pope pulled hard on one oar, a couple of times, and then stuck out for the other shore. He heard the last horse jump in, and a couple of more hard pulls and he'd be close. Suddenly, the handcuffs and hands of Buckskin Ed dropped over Pope's head. He had a pocket knife in one hand and tried to slit John's throat.

The dirty outlaw yanked back violently, sticking the blade in John's throat. John had grabbed his wrist when he saw the knife coming. John reared back with a force, throwing his weight into Ed, and his gun went off, shooting straight up into Ed's body. Pope didn't remember drawing it, but after most of a lifetime of practice, it was an automatic reaction. His next shot was up into Ed's face. John then wrenched the cuffs off over his head. John rolled Ed off into the river.

John got back on the seat to pull ashore. Before he reached the bank he was coughing blood. Ed's short bladed knife had cut into his wind pipe, and blood was trickling into his lungs. What to do now? First things first.

John pulled the boat up onto shore. Old Shorty brought the other horses over. John untied the bandana he always wore around his neck, and felt his neck while coughing. He was bleeding, but it wasn't squirting, so he knew an artery hadn't been cut. He decided to try lying upside down, letting the blood run the other way. He lay down on the river bank with his head way lower than his feet and legs. He lay on his stomach and in a few minutes, was able to quit coughing. As he lay there, he took his bandana and washed it in the river until the blood was gone. He looked at it. Ed's knife had cut through the fabric, leaving a ragged hole in his bandana. However, he couldn't help thinking it had protected him somewhat. About five minutes later, no blood was running any more, it had been running off his chin when he first lay down, then it dripped awhile, but he wasn't bleeding now.

John hated the taste of blood. His throat quit hurting so much. He sat up slowly so he wouldn't start the blood running again. He pulled off his shirt and washed it in the river until he couldn't detect any blood, then spread it out to dry over a bush. He washed his face, especially his chin and chest. John was mad at himself. He should have known! But he had handcuffs on Ed and had given him the horses to lead, and he just had given Buckskin Ed the benefit of the doubt. That was a wrong move, but John bet this wouldn't happen again.

John got his clean handkerchief out and tried to feel his neck, and then he put the handkerchief against the wounded throat and tied his bandana around it, holding it in place. He finally dragged the boat out a ways and then mounted up and started home. He'd lost his hat in the scuffle. He had a headache. He'd lost a half a day and he could taste blood, all in all, not a good day for the sheriff.

Late that afternoon, he shot a pine hen. Things were looking up when he came to a spring; he called stop, staked his horses out, and got wood enough to last the night, and started a fire. He always kept a salt shaker in the saddle bag, so Pope skewered half the chicken on a willow and started it cooking. When it was done and salted good, he ate every bite, cleaned off all the bones. It hurt a bit to swallow, but he was hungry. After he had eaten, he went to sleep. It was necessary, for he'd been up all the night before, staking out a louse.

He slept all night and it was after sun up when he came to. He built the fire again, and cooked the other half of the pine hen. After a good breakfast he saddled up and rode on over the mountain. The snow was above the horse's knees all the way, so he had to stop often to let the horses' blow. It was good to get back down into the Basin where most of the snow was gone. He rode through the cedars, as always, and noticed a dust a mile or so ahead.

A man on a horse with a lead horse was quartering toward him. Pope looked close, wondering about anybody out here going this direction. He pulled his horses off the trail a ways, into the cedars and waited to see who was traveling out here. The man came on through the saddle that separated them. As he climbed the hill up into the scattered cedar near Pope, Pope left the other horses and rode to meet him. When the man saw him, he startled and looked quickly around like some guilty person, thinking he might be surrounded.

"Howdy."

The man sat uneasily, his eyes shifting around.

"Traveling far?"

Still no answer. Pope's ire started up. He was sore and tired and cold! Now he stepped off his horse on the right side, keeping his right hand free to draw if necessary. He walked a step or two closer. This guy was way too nervous.

The rider said, "That's close enough right there."

"So you *can* talk."

"Get back on your horse and go on about your business, and I'll do the same."

John said, "It's my business to check on your business."

"You aint gonna live long then."

"Maybe not, but tell me your name, where you are going, and why."

"Who the hell do you think you are?"

"I'm John T. Pope, sheriff."

The guy jerked his pistol. He got it out when John's bullet hit him in the throat. He slid off his horse, dead as a can of corned beef.

His horse was a big black mount. It shied back a bit then stood still. Pope walked forward, wondering why. He looked at this guy. His hat had fallen clear when he fell. He had a streak of white hair in one lock on the left side, and John remembered the wanted poster offering five hundred, dead or alive, Carl Bitner. That white lock of hair was part of the poster's description.

"I could sure use that reward." John unfastened the gun belt, pulled it off, took the gun from his hand, and returned it to the holster. He found the wanted poster in his shirt pocket. He went through the front pockets, finding thirty dollars in change. Things looked kinda full around his middle. Pope felt around. He was carrying a money belt, so in a minute he had that off. It was actually packed. The first pocket held five hundred bucks. So Pope dropped all this stuff in his saddlebags. He picked up the hat and tried it on. It was a little big, but it sure beat nothing in the brisk air. It looked like an almost new hat.

Sheriff Pope dropped a rope on the outlaw, dragging him down off the hill to a short rocky outcrop. He got off, took his rope off, and rolled the guy off the rock. He then found a flat rock and covered most of him. John saw couple of smaller rocks and this fellow wouldn't be found. Pope pulled his new hat off and said, "Heavenly Father, I have been sheriff for a short time, and already I've shot a few men. I could have used a reward for this guy, but it is not worth trying to claim it. Please do what you can for them and please forgive me. I don't think Uintah County can afford court and burials and everything, so maybe in a way, this is the only way justice can be done. Help me get home safely; I pray the name of Jesus Christ, amen."

John put his hat on and walked back up, took Bitner's horses and tied them behind the other bunch, then started home. It was after dark by a couple of hours when he rode up to the homesteader's cabin. He knocked and got this fellow out with a lantern to claim his horses. He was so glad to have them back!

"Sheriff, I didn't think I'd ever see them again!" He choked up trying to thank John. John told him to buy a shotgun, load it with buckshot, and kill any horse stealers that came around again.

John never told a soul about any of this trip or activity. When Charlotte asked about his neck, John told her he got poked with some grease wood while riding along the river. He doubted she bought the story, but he also knew she didn't want the truth, not on this one.

A month or so later, Charlie Crouse came to Vernal asking for Buckskin Ed. Nobody seemed to know anything, so he looked John up and wondered what became of Ed Carouthers? John said, "You better not have anything to do with him. He'll get you in trouble for sure."

Charlie said, "He was going to bring me a team of horses about a month ago. Nobody seems to know where he went."

"Where did he get a team?" Pope asked.

"He told me he had a good gentle team, so I offered a hundred dollars for them. I can't believe he'd turn that offer down."

"He probably lost them in a card game. Anyway, the last time I saw him, he was heading out for California."

John didn't say he took the river route.

A few days later another character of Brown's Hole of that time showed up with the truth about the whole matter. Speck Williams rode into Vernal and started telling everyone that he found Buckskin Ed's body caught in some driftwood down Lodore Canyon. "Yes suh, Buckskin Ed was wearing handcuffs. Yes suh, he sho' was."

Most people in Vernal and the surrounding area called Speck Williams the Speckled Nigger, which was not politically incorrect at the time. Almost everyone tried to befriend him. He had been a slave in the south during his boyhood. He had ridden on a raid or two with the Jessie James Gang. He had been kicked around from here to there, still with a fearful dread of being taken back into slavery. Speck lived alone mostly. He jigged or speared suckers out of the Green River to live on. The suckers congregated under driftwood which explains why he found Buckskin Ed.

Chapter Ten

A Friend at First is a Friend at Last

THAT SPRING ANOTHER ADVENTURE began which took Sheriff Pope the most of a month to solve. Elisha Driscall, a rancher living on the Henry's Fork on the north side of the Uintah Mountains, near the Utah State line, but in Wyoming, walked into Sheriff Pope's office in Vernal, introduced himself and asked for help. John had been watching him closely as he talked. He knew the man from somewhere.

"How can I help you?"

"I have a horse ranch over there with good stock. Outlaws decided they needed horses worse than me. They drove about fifty head out of a pasture into Utah."

When Driscall discovered they were missing, he immediately set out to get them back. He followed them zigzagging back and forth on the big mountain, finally coming down the south side into the Basin. He succeeded in following them to a point about seven miles northeast of Vernal.

He said, "Tracking is tougher over here, and I will need help in getting them back."

"Yes sir, Mr. Driscall, you came to the right place for help. Can I first ask you a question? Mr. Driscall, were you with Captain Conner at the Battle of Bear River?"

The man's brows furrowed together, being quite astonished by the question. "Yes, I was there."

"Were you on guard over the morgue wagons containing dead soldiers?"

"Yes, I was there."

"Do you remember a little boy in Smithfield, Utah, who asked to see the bodies?"

"Yes, I remember the lad—he was just a young scrap."

"You pulled the cover back and let him see in and then fished out a service revolver?"

Driscall's forehead wrinkled. "Surely you can't be that kid, can you?"

"Yes sir, at your service. Now I'll try to pay you back for your kindness to me. Your white hair and beard kinda threw me, but that face has been stamped in my memory."

"Well, let me shake your hand! When they directed me to your office, I didn't expect to find a friend from so many years ago. My friends just call me Lige."

"I guess it has been twenty-two years ago. Okay," Pope said, "let's go over to see the judge. You swear to a complaint charging John Doe and Richard Doe with stealing horses and get a warrant to arrest, and we'll be on our way."

John saddled Old Shorty, and put a packsaddle on one of the extra horses he had confiscated just lately, and then went to the store and bought supplies; two pounds of coffee, a slab of bacon, two dozen eggs, a can of shortening, salt, pepper, canned peaches, milk, and beans. Pope bought an extra water bag, and threw in an extra box of shells. They rode out to where Elisha had tracked the horses to, then followed their tracks south until dark.

They camped on the Green River, south of Vernal. They rolled in a blanket, using their saddles as pillows. They had an early breakfast and got back on the trail. They went southwest to nearly the Ouray Indian Agency; there it turned west to Lake Fork where they had camped. They followed on west up the Duchesne River a few miles where it turned south again. They camped there, having made a long hard day of it. Good water and grass made their mounts content. The thieves were staying away from ranches and Indian camps. Next morning they started early, following the trail into the mountains. Again, Pope and Driscall found where the thieves had spent the night and John got off and studied the area pretty good. There were three men with the stolen horses. The trail turned back to the south.

John said, "I see what you meant by zigzagging now. They are killing time. I haven't figured why, yet. There is no pattern at all to where they are heading."

"They seem to scatter around like a herd of damn chipmunks."

John laughed with his friend, picturing such a sight in his mind.

They followed on south to the top of the mountain. The horses separated in seemingly all directions. Now what? They camped that night and rode in a large circle. No Trail. So one more night they camped and Pope said, "We can't track the herd, so I'm going to track one horse 'til we find him anyway."

They were out of supplies. Elisha looked used up, but he'd go 'til it killed him. So Pope took them back to where the tracks had been together. He picked one he could recognize from all the rest and started to track it around the mountain. While tracking this horse through the trees, and a myriad of other tracks, he slowly pushed along. They met an Indian on a horse and tried to talk to him, but, "Me heap no savvy."

Driscall spoke fluent Ute language, but he got the same results. John was sitting Old Shorty between the Indian and Elisha. Elisha knew the Indian could understand him. Old Driscall was almost worn out. He was hungry and grouchy.

"You red son-of-a-bitch!" He jerked his pistol, pointing it at the Indian. John bumped his arm up as it went off, making Driscall miss. As the shot rang out, the Indian's horse jumped and the Indian went out of there, whipping and spurring.

John said, "For hell's sake Lige, don't shoot again. If we kill an Indian, it'll cause so much trouble for us we'll never find your horses."

"Maybe so, but the idea of a dammed Indian acting like that when a man's starving to death . . . at least he could have told us where to find a ranch or something."

"You heard the man, he didn't savvy." Pope laughed at his ill humored companion until Lige's mood lightened by a degree.

In about an hour, the track led into some timber, and John killed four pine hens.

Lige said, "Please don't ever let me make you made at me. I didn't think it was possible to shoot that fast and straight."

While they cleaned chickens and started a fire, Pope replied, "That's what you get for giving a pistol to a young boy."

They again set out on the tracks and followed to a place they could see to the south and east. Pope knew where he was. He was recognizing landmarks, so once again they dropped the tracks and went to a ranch and asked if they could have food and stay the night. The old rancher said, "I don't keep strangers."

Driscall said, "We want supper and breakfast and we're going to get it."

John fed and watered the horses, and when he got back, he found supper cooking. They ate supper, went back to their horses and rolled in blankets. After breakfast the next morning, they asked what the bill was.

"Five Dollars," the man said.

Lige handed him the five dollars and said, "I would rather have given you ten dollars and been treated like a white man than how you have treated us."

As they rode away, John turned to Elisha with a big grin on his face and said, "Partner, we've been out here going up and down, round and around so long—just look at us. Our horses are starting to show wear of this trip, we look like a couple of outlaws on the run. I can't blame that guy for treating us like he did."

The men went back to their tracking.

"Nobody else in the world could stay on a track like you do Pope, and I'll bet nobody else in the world will hang on until no hope exists. There aint no give or quit in you, is there John?"

"You are just buttering me up so I'll stay with it."

They laughed. Things didn't get so tough that a sense of humor didn't show.

A couple of more days of pine hens and tough hard tracking brought them suddenly back onto the trail of the horse herd again. They were in the mountains west of the road from Vernal to Price. What a puzzle that had been, but now the horses seemed to all be back together and leaving an easy to follow trail.

Elisha spotted a ranch in a canyon so they rode down and bought what supplies the rancher could spare. They rode back, intersecting the trail. Then got on it at a pace and trotted. They put in some long miles crossing the road from Vernal to Price, then east a few miles, then south to Nine Mile Creek. There the horse herd and outlaws had stayed for several days. When John and Elisha pulled out the next morning on the tracks, they were fresh for the first time, now they went north.

John knew he was close now. It was time to be vigilant, lest they be ambushed, or be seen by the outlaws who might bolt, and he would lose them. The track doubled back again, going parallel, almost on the same track made going south a couple or three weeks before. So Pope rode west of the trail which was in the open. He and Lish hurried east in cover until they cut the trail.

Pope thought they might be looking for a place to cross the Green River to join the Outlaw Trail which ran from Canada to Mexico, but they didn't, continuing on this wander about merry-go-round it seemed like they had been on. So Pope and Lige camped on the banks of the Green River. The next morning they followed a fresh trail within four miles west of Ouray Indian Agency. The wind had blown the day before. Yet there was no dust in these tracks. They continued north up River, they stayed clear of Jensen and any ranches, then crossed the Indian ford on the Green River.

Driscall's hair and whiskers were white. They had been sleeping on the ground and riding hard 'til it's a wonder he hadn't collapsed. One meal a day seemed to agree, though. So after another camp, they followed on that night. They camped about five miles southwest of the now famous dinosaur beds. The horses had crossed at this ford. Again, Pope and Lige resumed the chase. They were within five miles of the outlaws because they found their last night's camp.

They went east by Cucklebar Springs, then south. When Pope got out of the canyon south of the Cucklebar, he spotted the stolen herd going into a draw a few miles ahead. They let the horses water up at Powder Springs and went on. So John knew they knew the country. He'd probably be making dry camp tonight, so all canteens and the bag was filled with water. Then, they rode hard to cut them off, crawling up on Dead Man Ridge to wait for them.

The group of men and horses finally came along and made camp on Dead Man Ridge about a half mile or so from John's planned ambush. So Pope and Lige went back to their horses for the night. In a few hours, they moved their horses as close as possible, and then staked them out. Taking rifles, they quietly worked within fifty yards from the sleeping outlaws.

After light came, the outlaws got up and started a fire.

Pope hollered, "Hands up!"

Instead, every man went for a shooting iron. After a short volley of shots, the outlaws lay dead. Only one of them got off a shot before being smashed down with 44 slugs. Pope said, "You can serve them warrants now Lige, if ya want."

"I guess I'll use 'em for bum wipe. I've been tempted to about fifteen times since we started this chase."

Pope stripped pistols off them and went through pockets. He came up with almost two hundred dollars. Also, he knew the men as Cassidy gunmen. He told Elisha he'd bet these fellows had been supplied by other men out of the gang from time to time. He said, "When we lost the trail and had to follow one track for awhile, I suspected these three had help from several other men, making it easier to scatter a few horses for each man."

After a hearty breakfast, Pope had Lige help carry rocks and they covered the outlaws' bodies in shallow graves on Dead Man Ridge.

Pope took off his hat and Elisha seeing, pulled his off as well. Pope said a short honest prayer of thanks for helping bring the men to justice.

Elisha wiped his brow and both eyes. "You are a scrap, John Pope! I don't figure how a man can shoot like you do and pray like you do! You are a walking contradiction of a man, but God love you! God *bless* you, for you are as true as any friend I've ever ridden with."

After they were saddled up ready to go, Pope said, "I guess that's what I do to all horse thieves." He handed Lige the money from their pockets. "That'll pay for your times and trouble they caused you."

Lige said, "You put it in your pocket. I owe all to you."

"You paid me when you befriended a little boy years ago. Anyway, I seem to confiscate a lot from the fellas I shoot. I'll help you get your horses home."

The next night they camped on the Green River. They crossed the next morning and drove north up Brash Creek, north of Vernal, 'til they came to the trail the horses had been driven in on. When they hit this trail, every horse turned on it toward home.

Lige said, "They'll go back home now. It will be easy to follow them on home so why don't you go home?"

Sheriff Pope shook hands with the man. "Don't mind if I do," but he insisted that Elisha take the two outlaw packhorses, and he gave Lige his pick of of their guns. Driscall took one pistol and some the ammo, and finally took their saddle horses as well.

So a month after leaving, he rode home to a worried, frustrated wife and a loving family.

Of course, he never told a soul of this, but much later graves were found on Dead Man Ridge, and Pope, on being asked by some of his brothers who were beginning to see a pattern, fessed up to shooting the thieves after a month's chase. "It was all in self defense."

How many times John Pope saved the county the expense of a trial is anyone's guess.

Chapter Eleven

Wanted!

JOHN WAS ABLE TO stay home a few days, catch up on correspondence and paper work and try to catch up on family news, as well as become better acquainted with his newest daughter, little Hazel Sarah. Tiny Francis Lavina was so fascinated by this new sister; she could scarcely leave her alone.

Robert said no one had been to Red Creek for a spell, but he had plenty of pasture in Ashley Valley for his cows now if they could spare a few men to bring them back.

John said he would be glad to go. He wanted to see how the place had taken the fifty cows and calves through winter and spring. He asked if his dad wanted to sell the calves.

"Leave them there and just bring the cows home? Yes, I could use the money, and I was wondering where I'd ever sell them."

They talked it over. It would take about five days to wean the calves.

John said, "I'll get the blacksmith to make a brand for me. I'll try to hire a bit of help and if a brother or two could come, we could brand the calves and when they quit bawling and settle down, bring the cattle home. I might have to fix the fence a bit to keep the calves from mixing up with their mothers until they are weaned."

"I'd feel better if we drove around, rather than swim and then come over that mean, rocky, mountain."

"Figure on three weeks, then, to get back."

Rock said a lot of cows had already calved. They had kicked the yearlings off already.

In those days, the bulls stayed with the cows year around, especially in wild regions where cattle grazed year around. At that time only a few fields were fenced. Everything else was wide open.

Some people had brought in a few short horn cows for milk cows. They also made good range cattle and a few of the short horn cross bulls were starting to show up. Most of the cattle were Texas long horns or at least they were the dominant foundation.

John gave his dad a thousand dollars for the calves and Robert agreed to send help when the steers were two or three years old to get them to market.

John walked to the blacksmith shop where he had an interesting conversation. The blacksmith said, "I'll do it for five dollars because iron is hard to come by. But you shouldn't be out walking around in plain sight like this."

"Why not?"

"I got word from a little bird that you are worth twenty-five hundred dollars, dead. The Wild Bunch will guarantee payment. All they need is the news that you are dead."

Pope asked, "Did you think you'd try to collect on that reward?"

No, but gosh damn, I mean, you're worth at least seven years of wages at thirty dollars a month."

Pope whistled. "Not bad, eh, for an uneducated farm boy? I wonder how many good honest folks will succumb to the lure of all the filthy lucre and be killed trying to collect on me?"

As John walked out with the brand JT, he was watchful and thinking from now on he'd go different ways, not get in habits that someone would be able to lay for him.

He knocked on the door of one of the young men who helped him build his Red Creek place and offered him a job.

"I'd like to go, Sheriff, but I don't have a horse." Jesse Freestone was a good kid, willing, eager, and strong, and his friend was of equal caliber.

"I'll provide the horses for both you and your friend, Ray Dickory, if you want to go."

"I figure me and Dickory are itchin' to get to it, Sheriff Pope. And thanks for the invite!"

Pope walked in the store and asked about net wire. He bought six rolls plus a box of staples. Surely they could staple the wire on the poles and make a pig-tight fence to wean the calves.

So after preparations for the trip were made, John let two brothers and his two hired men take the church wagon and supplies, along with good, trusted, mounts from the remuda. He spent one more day with Charlotte, and then rode out about four in the morning and down to the ferry.

John could tell by the way people looked at him and their actions they knew of the reward. If they wanted to collect, they had to earn it because he seemed to always be facing them. His reputation ruled out, nobody would dare draw. "If they catch me it will have to be from ambush."

John arrived three days ahead of his help. He rode north through the cattle. They were fat and happy. The green feed was up six inches already. It was really a little better than he figured because the hay that grew on the meadows from the year before was only about half used. Where the cattle had taken it, they took it all, but there were big patches that hadn't been touched. Where the cattle had cleaned the hay off, new green growth was coming good, so that's where the cattle were spending most of their time, keeping it down.

John wished he had a mowing machine for a couple of days. If the old hay was cut and stacked, then three times more grass could grow. He could see cows had cleaned a good percentage of the grass that grew on the hills and brush surrounding the meadows. It was more tender than old dry hay, he guessed.

John took careful stock of all and drug a couple of piles of sagebrush down to the corral for firewood, branding, and cooking. He unsaddled and swept the cabin out, and carried a bucket of water. John cleaned a chicken, but left it soaking and simply opened a can of peaches for supper along with a couple of hot cups of coffee. He went to bed with the sun.

Since the sun tucked him in, he arose with it the next morning. John saddled up and rode around, scouting for tracks, drug up a dead cottonwood limb, then cut a couple of cedars and drug them down for wood. He walked out on a hill a ways and saw a man approaching from the river. He was well mounted on a tall buckskin gelding. The man was well dressed and rode like a cowboy. He carried a rope, but a rifle stock stuck up through the lariat. Pope watched him ride closer. When he was about a block away, he stopped his horse and looked all around himself. John saw him pull his pistol and check it, then put it back.

John decided to edge into the draw behind him and scoot down close to the house. He was barely back when this fellow came riding up.

"Hello," the man hollered.

"Hello your own self." Matt Warner whirled to face him. John laughed. "Didn't mean to scare you, but I didn't want to be pinned anywhere with only one hole. What can I do for you?"

"I'm Matt Warner. I heard you were out to your ranch, so I came over to welcome my neighbor."

"Get down, take your horse around and give him some oats. I'll start a fire and we'll put a pot on and have a cup of coffee."

When he came back, John had a fire in the pit and the Dutch oven ready to cook the chicken. Now he cooked the other chicken as well. John added potatoes, sliced thin, and diced an onion in with the chicken, letting them cook together.

"Why don't you grab a couple of benches from the house? Put them here in the shade." Pope also had Matt help him move a table up close to put the food on, and they sat and talked while the chicken and coffee cooked. Matt was about John's age and likeable.

John said, "I heard you married a girl from Montpelier, Idaho."

"I sure did. How did you know about that?"

"I'm from Bear Lake, myself. I listen to talk. They say you and your buddy robbed the bank in Telluride, Colorado, rode out with a posse on your heels. You made it into Star Valley in a big snow storm which discouraged the posse. You stayed up there and really had a time, huh?"

"Yes, it's true. Me and Tom McCarty done some shenanigans together, I tell you that."

"The Mormons settled Afton that summer for the first time. P. W. Cook, one of our neighbors from Garden City, took a young polygamist wife from Garden City up there and built a grist mill in Afton. You and your buddy decided to liven up the party. Bought a cabin and went to Montpelier and brought a load of whiskey to open a bar. Tell me about Whiskey Flats."

"I was just a stupid kid. It's all true. One of the barrels of whiskey sprang a leak while jouncing along over rocks. So we tried to keep it from all wasting by drinking all we could. We got so damn drunk!" Matt paused to chuckle. "The only reason we didn't freeze to death in the snow up there is because the alcohol wouldn't freeze, I guess. Anyway, we started the bar. We had one hundred dollar bills pinned up in back of the bar, even a couple of thousand dollar bills."

"You got tired of looking at each other and rode to Montpelier for girls?"

"Yes, it's true and the gal I married was way better than me. I married Rose Rummel, and she was only fourteen years old at the time. If the law would let me, I'd reform for her. Hell, I really love her. She's stayed with me through a lot."

"I'm the law here. As far as I'm concerned you never done anything wrong. Of course, if warrants come in for things you might do from *now* on, I'll come serve them. So change your ways! You are free to start all over again. You are free to prove to your beloved Rose just how much you are done being a pain-in-the-butt thorn."

Warner's head bent as he chewed on Pope's words. "That's really white of you Pope."

"I've heard some good things that you did. That first year in Afton, snow was deeper and came quicker than anyone anticipated. The storekeeper there had stocked things really well, but he saw a way to make big bucks so he doubled the prices on everything. The Mormons were in trouble. I guess you must have known their plight because you called a meeting at the store for all men and bishops. You told the bishops to take inventory of all the goods in the store. The store keeper tried to interfere. You pulled your colt and told the people to get what they needed to have. The bishops dispersed things and you paid for it!"

Matt Warner smiled at the recollection, "Yes, but not at the price the store keeper wanted."

"And in coining your own phrase, 'that *was white of you*, Matt.'"

"I guess I made a few friends."

"You did, and one of them was me when I heard what happened. How is your wife doing anyway?"

"Not good. We can't find a doctor who will do anything but amputate her leg."

"Cancer on it, huh?"

"That's what they call it, I guess."

"Grab some plates, utensils and cups. This grub is done to a turn." John picked up coffee and poured the cups full. They filled their plates and began to sip and eat as it cooled enough.

"I've got sugar if you want it."

"No thanks. I drink for the coffee, not the knickknacks."

John got a good laugh out of that. "I've never heard sugar be referred to as a knickknack before!"

After the dishes were done, Matt rolled a cigarette. They sat in the shade talking. John said, "I heard the Wild Bunch put out a big reward for my head. So, I'm worth more dead than alive to anyone who can collect. In the process a lot of men will die trying."

Matt Warner's head jerked up and the men studied each other for a long moment. John continued, "I know you could use that money with your wife's health problems and all. So I'm going to shoot some targets with you. I figure Butch, and maybe Sundance, might be a bit faster than you. I think in a shootout, you could have a good chance of killing either one because you are steady and you'd probably take some lead and still take them." Matt's mouth pulled into a taught line, but he didn't interrupt.

"I think I'm faster and better than *any* of you, so if you get me, it'll be in the back. There are some empty cans in the hole over there, why don't you fish out a half dozen of them? Just carry them out as far as you want wherever it's comfortable for you. Leave them about a foot apart."

Matt did as bidden. He came back with a look of exalting, like he'd show this sheriff something.

"Okay Warner, stand by me, face the cans and count to three, and shoot the three cans on your side and I'll take the three on my side."

So Matt said, "Let me get the strap off that holds my pistol down."

"Go ahead. I always do mine during my draw."

Matt's eyes rolled at the confident sheriff's comment, but he let it bounce, ready to show what he had. "Ready."

"One, two, three."

Bang! Pope's first can flew out of the way. *Bang! Bang!* Pope's second can flew at the same time Matt's first can was hit. *Bang!* Pope's third can flew sideways, then *bang!* Matt's last shot missed. Matt looked at the first two cans. They were both holed, but the cans stayed put. His third shot missed, trying to hurry.

John T. Pope's shots had delivered with fiery precision and hell's own fury. Matt Warner blinked his eyes at the three dead cans. Matt said, "I wouldn't have believed any man could get in action that fast, especially with a strap in place! How did you make them fly like that?"

"I always shoot them on the band that fastens the bottom onto the can. It makes it fun to shoot and see them fly away."

Matt walked around and checked them. They were all hit in the middle bottom which nearly flattened them.

"Matt, I only did this to save you or your partners from learning the hard way."

"How in the hell did a little Bear Lake Mormon come to be such a gunman?"

"I carried a 44 pistol since I was eight years old. I had an ex Texas Ranger work with me. I've practiced for fifteen minutes a day for twelve years or so. I've worked for law enforcement before. I killed men before

I was twenty years old. I realize your fellows have been bosses around here. You've had a sanctuary from the law. You hate to see the law come and change it. I know that, but get a ranch or a real job, and quit trying to live off other men's hard work and money! You've got to change, or move, or *die* . . . because the law is now beginning to come here. Can you understand that?"

"I've got to think about that a bit. I can see it will, eventually."

"Well, Matt, I haven't talked so hard or long forever, but I like you. If I can help you, I will. Take care of your wife. I'll say a prayer for you!"

Matt shook hands with John, saddled up, and left.

It was two days before the branding crew got in. They had supper and visited a bit. The next day they worked on the fence. Night found the fence in good shape, so the day after the men rounded up the cattle, held them on the fence while the cows were let out through the gate, and everything else was held along the fence. The new calves were let out with their mothers. They started roping calves and dragging them to the fire where they were branded. It was a job that took 'til nearly dark. Forty-eight calves were branded, thirty heifers, and sixteen steers. John kept two of the biggest best males as bulls. It's funny, but a man usually wanted more steers than heifers because they were worth a tad more and that was his cash crop, but John was glad for more heifers this year because they would be the foundation for his cattle herd. Boy, it was noisy trying to sleep with the cowboy music going to close and loud, calves crying for their moms, cows bawling for their calves.

John did ask his maker to help the fence hold. When daylight came, cows were walking a worn trail back and forth along the fence. Calves had a worn trail on the other side. If the fence held about three more days, the animals would quiet down some. John gave a brand new ten dollar bill to his brother and told him to go buy fish line and hooks at the Jarvie Store. He and the rest dug for worms along the irrigation ditch. They found a bunch, then went down to the river and rode up the banks until they found some birch bushes. They all cut a pole, tied some line and a hook. They had a blast, finally catching enough for breakfast and supper. It was a successful night of fishing, and the sport of it felt good. While they were fishing, John killed a mess of chickens for the next day. The men were able to stay away from the tiresome noise of lowing cattle this way, and the break was refreshing. John noted the younger men, Jesse and Ray, really seemed pleased to have had a break, and they wrestled and played in the grass like kids. Notching bark from green willows, John showed them how to make willow whistles and they both had to have one.

That night, John stood watching the silhouettes of his calves beneath a bright moon. He felt pride and accomplishment in fulfilling his dream. He was a rancher!

Three days later the cows were rounded up and started home. John helped them get away; rode along about five miles, then rode back to Red Creek. He let the calves trail down to the fence to bawl once in a while for another day, but with their mothers long gone, it got quiet again. He went over and fixed the fence around his little field and watered it. Then he saddled up and rode back to the bustle of the big city, being ever vigilant for snipers.

After a few days at home, once again trouble came, from Indians this time. The settlers distrusted the red men. The Indians outnumbered whites by many times. The Indians grew up knowing Indian laws which made no sense to the settlers at all. Indians were taught to steal from other tribes and whatever they found that man had left out there, unprotected, was used as their own. Stealing and eating white man's livestock was *not* wrong in an Indian's eyes. There was honor in it! Settlers had cried and complained for a couple of years about stealing by the Indians. Now, they had law in Vernal, and wanted to test it out to see if the white man's laws could help protect settlers' property.

The constable handed Sheriff Pope a warrant for the arrest of an Indian from White Rocks. Wapsock had stolen a horse from one of the ranches. Pope knew the United States government was supposed to supply food for the Indians as part of the treaty made with these Utes. Pope inquired and found out issue day, because he knew all he could get out of the Indians was, "Heap no savvy." He would never find Wapsock. On issue day, Pope arrived on the reservation early, along with a deputy from Vernal. John talked to the Indian Agent and asked Colonel Waugh to point out Wapsock. He did. Then he showed him the warrant.

The agent said, "It is impossible to arrest him."

"What about getting troops from the post to hand the Indians?"

"It is possible they would butcher us all before the troops could arrive. You'd start a war."

"Okay," Pope looked to his deputy. "Are you ready for a little run?"

He looked a bit confused, but said, "I'll do whatever you say."

"Lead that extra horse over close to me."

Pope pulled a pair of handcuffs and started playing with them as he sauntered up to Wapsock. Suddenly, he slapped Wapsock's left wrist with the cuffs which locked on his wrist. Pope yanked him, staggering up to the horse, where the other cuff slipped the saddle horn, thus locking him to the horse.

Pope said, "Start out," and as the horse started forward, Pope threw the legs of Wapsock up, and the captured Indian straddled the saddle, and then John grabbed his good old horse and made a flying mount as they left there on a run. Pope saw a look of amazement on Indian faces as they went away from them. It took a moment for the Indians to realize what had happened, then a few minutes to get mounts ready to start a pursuit.

Deputy Christensen was riding in the lead, leading the horse carrying Wapsock. Pope rode to the side, whipping the two horses ahead and to the side, trying for more speed. About a half mile south of the agency, the road crossed the Uintah River. Brush grew along the river. There Pope guided his little group back up stream, in the brush past the Agency, and then took a trail leading to Dry Fork to the northeast. When they rode to open country, they could see clouds of dust on the road to Vernal, east of White Rocks Agency.

They were congratulating themselves for fooling them when Pope saw dust coming on their own trail so they had to spur and whip the extra horse carrying the Indian. John said, "Try for Cedar Mountain. Then I'll make a fight of it. I won't turn the Indian loose until they kill me."

So when they got to the cedars, Pope jumped off, and went down to start a war, if necessary. He told his deputy, "If you hear me shoot, kill this son-of-a-bitch, and we'll try to get away if possible."

"No savvy *that,*" Wapsock cried, not especially fond of the sheriff's orders to his deputy.

John ran down the hill a ways, and stopped behind a cedar. A lone Indian came racing up the trail. When he was within thirty feet, Pope stepped out with his rifle leveled half. This Indian jerked his horse to a stop.

The rider yelled, "Mike Ticaboo!" (Indian words for "Hello Friend").

"Mike Ticaboo, be dammed," The sheriff called. "Where are you going?"

"I'm going to Vernal to talk for Wapsock."

"Do you need that rifle to talk with? Just drop it to the ground, and the belt of shells."

The English-obliging Indian did as he was told.

"All right, Big Joe, ride up the trail a piece."

John picked up his rifle and shells, and then they took both Indians to Vernal with them.

Big Joe was the only Indian to notice their trail. When they reached town, it was nearly full of Indians.

John rode up to Big Joe, unloaded his rifle, gave it back and turned him loose. A half dozen Indians came up to John and offered six horses for Wapsock.

The fearless Sheriff said, "I will remember this talk, and the trial will be fair, but white man's laws *have* to apply. Wapsock will have to stand trial for stealing."

There was discontent, and much of, "Heap, no savvy," muttered through the group.

Wapsock was tried and convicted, but before the judge passed sentence, John interceded for the Indians.

John said the courts of white people should have justice for all, including red men. All he wanted was right and justice. The judge was determined to inter Wapsock for a term in prison, but Pope pressed, "According to white laws, that would be expected. But by Indian law, they should be able to rectify the wrong done. Chiefs who were waiting outside had offered six horses for the one taken. Besides, they promised to make a good Indian out of him. They would keep him from getting back in trouble. That is more than fair and just! The just, fair, way for the Indian is better for us as well! Judge, have you noticed the amount of armed Indians in town? If we lock up Wapsock and something starts out there—are there enough white men to defend this town? Even if we do, how many will die for nothing?"

The Judge wasn't afraid of the Indians, but he told Pope to take care of it.

So Pope walked out and told the chiefs to bring back the horse Wapsock stole, or one equally as good. "Keep Wapsock out of trouble!" Then he took off the handcuffs and let the happy Indian go. The chiefs said it was fair and they were very impressed with white man's laws.

"We like Pope," they said.

Friends were made by the handling of the affair. Many cattle and horses were saved for settlers because Pope's actions made a valuable, lasting, trusted friendship between the reds and white men's law.

Chapter Twelve

No Peace for a Peace Officer

SELDOM HAD A DAY gone by without trouble but John's deputy took good care of things in Vernal while John was tracking down bad men out of town. But a man named Sprague had drifted into Vernal and started gambling at Charley Crouse's bar. Charley had a ranch in Brown's Hole, but the Wild Bunch had established him in the bar where he was bartender. Hired men kept his ranch for him. Sprague gambled and drank, and after a while too much whiskey got him in trouble. Sprague managed to get off a shot in the fight between himself and a man he was playing poker with, wounding his opponent quite badly. Pope's deputy immediately got on the scene and arrested Sprague for being drunk and disorderly and attempted murder.

Taken before the Judge, a hearing was set for the next morning. Charley Crouse went to Sprague's hearing. He was bonded for one thousand dollars, and set free until morning. Charley found John T. and asked for his help in finding and bringing back the dirty s.o.b.—for Sprague had skipped. So Sheriff Pope saddled up once again. They found where he left town and Pope followed his track with his big horse pacing. Charley was standing in the stirrups, hanging on to the horn with both hands, roughly trotting through hot hours of sagebrush, greasewood, and shadescale. They rode through flats and desert, finally coming to Fort Duchesne.

As John and tuckered Charley rode up, a celebration of some kind was going on. There were a lot of men and Indians congregated around the parade ground. Pope thought maybe there was some horse racing or something. As John rode in, he spotted Sprague in the first cluster of men he came to. Pope rode up to the group and told Sprague he was under arrest. Sprague grabbed his pistol and had it half out when he realized he was looking in the barrel of Pope's pistol. Sprague froze for a minute and Pope said, "Pull it on out and drop it."

He did.

Pope swung his left leg up over the saddle horn and swells, kicked his right foot out of the stirrup and slid to the ground, facing the group. He handed the handcuffs to Sprague, and had him lock them on each wrist. Sheriff Pope pushed Sprague back a step and picked up his pistol, shoving it in his belt. About that time, the officer of the day came walking up.

"What's going on here?"

"I'm taking my prisoner, a rascal who jumped his bond and ran away. We've tracked him all day. We've found him here. We're taking him back to face charges of assault with intent to kill."

The officer of the day, assuming a very important air, said, "Like hell you are. You're taking those cuffs off that man and turning him loose."

"No I'm not. I came to take him back to answer a charge of attempted murder."

"What the hell business have you got, coming onto a government post, making an arrest of anyone?"

Sheriff Pope pulled the warrant of arrest from his pocket and showed it to the officer, saying, "This shows I'm no imposter. I'm an elected official with a job I'm going to do."

John turned, grabbed the saddle horn, and vaulted astride. He said, "I'm leaving the prisoner with Charley and you while I go see the commanding officer. Old shorty started off.

The officer of the day yelled, "Stop!" Instead, Pope hit a high run. The officer ordered his guards to aim.

Pope slid off on the side of the horse, standing in one stirrup and crouching completely out of sight like a trick rider. He approached the headquarters building on a run, stopped in a cloud of dust, and stepped into the outer office in two running steps and met the orderly.

"Is the commander in?"

"Yes, but you don't want to see him. He's in an awful mood."

Pope stepped across to the door and rang the bell.

Colonel Randlett opened the door, saying, "Now what the hell do you want?"

John looked at his man a moment and said, "I came on business and I expected to meet a gentleman." Pope turned and walked back to his horse. Before he got that far, the orderly was calling after him.

"The colonel wishes to see you, sir!"

So Pope walked back.

Colonel said, "So you expected to meet a gentleman did you?"

"Yes sir, I did."

"Okay. Who are you, and what kind of business are you on?" The officer was speaking in a much changed manner.

"I'm Sheriff John T. Pope of Uintah County." He showed his badge and the warrant for Sprague.

The Colonel read the warrant and asked if he knew where he was. John answered, "Yes I've got him handcuffed in that bunch of men over there."

"Well, if you know where he is, why don't you take him and go?"

"Because the officer of the day stopped me."

The commanding officer had heard enough. He put on his hat. They walked back to the parade ground with Pope leading his horse. By the time they got there, Pope had told everything.

Now Colonel Randlett let loose on the officer of the day. He called him every profane name Sheriff Pope had ever heard and a few that were new to him. He'd try to remember so he could tell this story some time. Next, Randlett ordered ten men to go as guards to assist the sheriff on the way back to Vernal. They hooked up to an army ambulance with several seats and loaded the prisoner.

Pope and Crouse tied their horses behind. On the way back, Crouse said, "This is saving my life Pope."

"How's that?"

"We'll, if I'd a had to stand in the stirrups and trot all the way home to keep up to that giant horse of yours, I just would have died."

Sprague kept complaining and groaning as they rode along. He said he was sick, and had a headache.

"You might just be hung over." John took Sprague's handcuffs off to try to relieve him, but as they were rolling along, the prisoner suddenly rolled out, and picked up a rock to heave at John. John quickly shot him in the thigh, taking the fight out of him. "Congratulations, idiot, now you have something to complain about!"

It took all the fight out of Sprague. He was subdued on trial day where he was found guilty of attempted murder and sentenced to most of his life in jail.

Taxes in Uintah County were new. A few paid. Many ranchers didn't think they were getting anything from the County so why pay taxes to them? Not only couldn't the county get taxes, they couldn't find out how many cows and stock citizens owned or where they ran them. So Sheriff Pope was asked to collect taxes for the county.

So in his typical cowboy way, he deputized a big crew, and they went out on roundup time with all the cattlemen associations. Once out there, they got a count on, as near as possible, each brand. Then they gathered enough cattle to pay the taxes if paid in cash.

The range lay in Wyoming and Utah in winter. This high mountain was covered in deep snow. Feed was lush in the summer and cattle did well. Winter range was in Uintah County, where snow seldom got so deep that cattle couldn't graze on it. Throughout the winter, it was an ideal set up if a few problems could be worked out. Now the Sheriff's Department had enough of the rancher's cattle separated to pay tax debts, but ranchers wouldn't give in. They were determined to resist.

Pope was determined everyone pay their fair share. Now Pope tried to reason with them, to no avail. Pope had stationed Dick Pope and a large group of deputies around the herd with the orders to shoot to kill if a fight started. One rancher, whose herd had been cut, rode up and started cutting a steer out of the tax herd. Sheriff rode over by him and cracked him over the head with is pistol, then cut the steer back in. Ranchers riding to the rescue, with rifles in the ready, were warned by an old guy that there would be a blood bath if they went after the cattle, showing them how Pope had positioned guns if trouble came. The ranchers then wanted to dicker. They offered to give notes, payable when the cattle were sold in the fall as security for the confiscated cattle. But Sheriff Pope already had the cattle, and knowing how hard it might be to collect the notes, refused the notes. Then George Finch rode forward and offered to back the notes. John knew George had always paid his taxes. He believed him to be honest and worth a bunch of dough, so notes were made out on notebook paper or whatever people had, and when notes were made out and signed, then George countersigned all notes and Pope collected them and turned the cattle free.

That fall all the taxes were paid. That pretty much ended the trouble of collecting taxes. It was comforting to know everyone was paying their fair share. Not a big item, but interesting to think a young Bear Lake or Bear River cowboy would live through such an eventual experience with Indians, outlaws, ranchers, all with a price on his head, ranging from two to four thousand dollars. This young man seemed fearless! He didn't seem to care what others said or thought. He was as fast with his pistol as a striking rattlesnake. He was literally bringing law to a lawless land. Almost every other day another experience helped eradicate the old government of robbers and replaced it with freedom. The old system kept people fearful to resist the robbers or else, but now even though this young sheriff had a reward on his head; people were starting to come forth to help because they knew he was helping them.

Pope was shot at from ambush five or six times, and each time outlaws died in their attempts. He traveled at night if possible. He went different ways each time and always went home a different way as well. He was careful and fearless.

One day in the early spring, Pope was riding the main road to Jensen, a little settlement on the west bank of the Green River, about fourteen miles east of Vernal. About half way from Ashley Creek, was a little oasis of green berry bushes in the desert, Pope had a thick leather vest on as he approached the creek. A shot rang out. It cut his vest clear across the chest; it cut through his shirt as well, and burned him like fire across his chest and breast bone. His horse took off. John bent down like he was wounded and trying to hang on. When he went into the trees, he stopped, tied his horse, pulled the Winchester and went up the creek hunting these fellows.

After about an hour of *Indianing* through the trees he heard a couple of guys talking. One coward said, "He's dead. I tell you. My shot went right through both lungs."

The other guy said, "Let's go get him then."

"Why? I don't need to see him."

"How are we going to collect the reward if we don't take something back?"

"Listen, they say he never misses. I don't want to make a target of myself by approaching too quickly."

"Hell, it has been a couple of hours, I bet. Let's go take his gun belt and hat. Then we can claim the rest before somebody else comes down the road."

"Okay."

They finally came out of the brush a few steps, and Pope paid them for the pain in his chest. These were a few of the hired killers who fill unmarked graves. Nobody but John T. Pope ever knew their fate. The men who would have paid the reward didn't know how much Pope knew or what he guessed.

Sheriff Pope got tired of delivering prisoners. It ate up a lot of time in trips and trials. He felt drudgery in delivering prisoners and especially having to stay for days to testify in different trials, which most times took place in Provo. Every dirty job fell on the sheriff! Once he was dispatched to take two prisoners to the penitentiary at the last minute. Another man was added, an insane man. Jon Hayworthy was always funny in the head, but hadn't been dangerous. He had grown very large and strong. One day neighbors heard his father screaming for help. Two men raced to the Hayworthy home where they could hear banging and scuffling going on. They reached the scene just as John slammed his father down on his back and raised a large butcher knife.

"I'll kill you, I'll kill you!"

Hayworthy's dad was screaming in terror. When the neighbor men tackled Jon, they got way more of a fight than they thought, because of his size and crazy condition. It was all the three men could do to finally take the knife away and tie Jon up. Afterwards, a doctor declared him criminally insane.

They asked Pope to deliver him to the mental hospital in Provo. So Pope had the prisoners all handcuffed, seated on a middle seat in the spring wagon. Jon Hayworthy was handcuffed on the front seat by the driver. John T. sat in back where he could keep an eye on all. They would catch the train in Price and disembark in Provo. Things went well until a stop at Fort Duchesne, where they stopped for a break to eat, and feed and water the horses.

When they left out of there, the driver had swilled several too many drinks. He was so drunk as to be almost useless. As they were driving through the desert, they met a fruit peddler and Sheriff Pope bought some apples from him. As they resumed the journey, Pope handed out an apple apiece for everyone. The driver pulled a pocket knife out and peeled his apple and ate it, then handed the knife to Jon. He peeled his apple but kept the knife. The sheriff was watching and wondered what the best way would be to get the knife back. He knew if Hayworthy showed fight, that the drunken little driver wouldn't be any help, or the handcuffed prisoners. While the sheriff was thinking about it, the driver held out his hand and asked for his knife back. Jon Hayworthy said, "Sure, I'll give it to you right now."

Hayworthy rose to a standing position, towering over the driver like a giant. He raised the knife in both hands.

Whack!

Sheriff Pope's pistol hit Hayworthy on top of the head, dropping him instantly on the dash board, where Pope, leaning between outlaws, grabbed him and laid him kind of sideways so he didn't fall on the double trees. That might have caused a runaway. Jon's head was bleeding, but Pope told the driver to go on.

"The longer he sleeps the better," Pope said. The other prisoners watched with wide eyes, and the incident was like a tonic, sobering the driver instantly.

When they reached Price several days later, Jon Hayworthy was awake, but very contrary, not cooperating with things at all.

When Pope delivered the inmates to the mental hospital, they refused to give Pope a receipt for the inmate because they thought the scalp wound might prove fatal.

Sheriff Pope said, "You've got him, not me, so my job is done whether or not I get the receipt. That little bump on his head saved another man's life. So if he dies from it, it's probably a good thing." About a week later, the receipt came in the mail to Sheriff Pope saying the inmate had been delivered.

Chapter Thirteen

Trouble at Red Creek

After one of the jobs in Provo that had seemed to be extra long, John had been wondering about his cattle in Red Creek so when he got back to Vernal, he decided he'd better ride out to Brown's Hole, after only a short stay with his family.

"I want to go this time, Dad." Charles was earnest, smile wide, eyes shining. "I want to go see our ranch. I can help you rope calves or anything!" John would like to have taken his son with him, but it wasn't safe—not with the price tag riding like a target on his head.

"You're the man here when I'm gone, Charles. I need you to help J.W. with everything. Take good care of your mother, brothers, and little sisters. You've got lots of chores around here, and I'm counting on you. You're my deputy of the home front, Charles."

John thought of his son's request again and again as he rode. Old Shorty's hooves clipped against brush and rock, keeping steady time like a metronome. John rode up in sight of his place and saw smoke coming out of his chimney. He was instantly grateful his son wasn't with him! John was always wary of being ambushed, but he'd never had anyone move in before. As he approached carefully, he could smell sheep. Also, the gate bars were open. A couple of dogs started barking and came out real unfriendly like. John noticed his wood pile had been mostly used up and then he saw a few sheep in the alfalfa field. All of a sudden Pope's temper started giving him a hell of a lot of trouble. A black rage began smoldering.

A Mexican herder came out of the house with a rifle in his hands. "Go way. Why you come here?"

Pope was too mad to answer such a stupid idiot, so he rode on by, and up to see what was going on in the range. All the lower end of his ranch was covered with sheep. He rounded up sheep and began driving them out. His cattle were gone! Pope was thinking the Wild Bunch had maybe got this herd here some way.

Here came the herder and his dogs on a camp horse, waving the rifle. Pope knew he'd have to keep his eye on the idiot. He was getting several hundred sheep together, and had them started the right way. John was picking more up as they came down. Once again, the herder came up, yelling to stop.

"Could you understand English if I bothered to talk to you?"

"Si, mucho comprendo Ingles, si!"

John sincerely doubted it. "Your sheep have eaten most of the salt I bought for my cows."

"Si."

"You burned most of my firewood."

"Si."

"Yes! You drove my cows away from my property."

"No I drive only from government land. Sheep have as much right to government land as cattle." The broken English gushed from ignorant lips.

"This is *my* private filed homestead! *My* land! *My* water!" John thumped on his chest, trying to illustrate the finer points of ownership. "*Mine!* It's filed and proven. So you are a stinking, black-hearted steal thief who doesn't know enough to pound sand!"

The Mexican said, "You can't take sheep."

For one who *mucho comprendo Ingles*, he seemed dumb as a post, and slow to boot! "Why not? You took my cows!"

"My boss no lie!"

"Yeah, where the hell *is* your boss? He's the one that needs killing, right along with the men who put him up to this."

As they were getting closer to the gate with a fair size herd of sheep, the herder was getting more agitated, especially since his dogs were working for Pope.

The Mexican came up missing, so as John had time, he looked around and saw the man had dismounted, and was starting to raise the rifle.

Pope jerked his horse back, whirling Old Shorty to face the Mexican. The gun went off, hitting Pope's saddle horn, and fragments of lead stung Pope a bit, but Pope's gun exploded next, taking the herder between the eyes.

Damn it! What to do with him now?

Pope's rage still went on. Killing this idiot hadn't solved anything, but John didn't want him found here, so he put a lariat on the Mexican's boots and drug him out of the gate. John tied his horse to go look in the house. There was a mess.

He spent a few minutes straightening things out, eliminating evidence of the Mexican's sloppy existence. John saw his shovel leaned up against the barn; he glanced around and decided the herder's refuse hole would make a suitable burial plot. John enlarged it a little, cleaned it out, and drug the herder over. He didn't think the dimwit would have anything, but he went through his pockets and, surprise, he had three twenty dollar gold coins, new mint. He'd been paid to do this! The coins would be from a mine payroll robbery in Colorado. John had seen posters on it and was asked to be on the watch for the gold to show anyway. John's mind spun and his jaws clenched tighter and tighter.

The brains behind the government of outlaw's had been trying to buy his death. Now they determined to use *his* own resources to pay the assassins for *his* head! Again, a wave of rage washed over him. He stomped the dirt down on the herder harder than necessary, but he was mad enough to stomp! Then he stepped over and dug another hole for cans and trash. He shoveled the excess dirt on the grave, and then smoothed things down a bit. He realized the herder's horse was here. He didn't want anything left on his place, to make anyone looking for the herder, to think that anything had happened. If anything, let them think the Mexican had taken his money and rode home with it.

He walked up and caught the horse and led him down to the house; put the Mexican's pannier on over the saddle, then loaded blankets and anything that had belonged to the herder, including the rifle. Then he led the horse through the gate and fastened the bars.

John mounted up and started after his cattle. There were no tracks, but John had expected that. He rode in a circle about a mile and still no tracks. He now had a couple of dogs to feed; therefore he knew they had used the sheep to cover the tracks. They had come in from the northeast over a high steep mountain. He didn't know if they drove the cattle out and then brought the sheep over their track to obliterate tracks, or if they drove the cattle out after the sheep arrived then drove back and forth over the trail with the sheep to cover it.

Whatever, the day was spent. The sun was setting and John found a bench and made a dry camp. He figured they might be as much as thirty days ahead. He was so aggravated he didn't bother to eat before sleeping that night. He made peace with his maker after confessing his rage and killing the Mexican herder. He even prayed for himself that night. He asked for forgiveness and for help to get the cattle found and returned. He prayed for his family who didn't see much of him anymore. He asked for understanding to help him to control the rage that almost caused anxiety. He finally closed in the name of Jesus Christ, but his mind was working like lightening going back over what had happened.

How could he have avoided killing the herder? Did these sheep men really believe they had as much right to things as men who had legally filed on ground, grass, and water; many having deeds recorded in county, and who were paying taxes on the land and the stock? If they did, then America wasn't the land of opportunity that he and his folks had thought.

Pope thought of stories of his mother's father. He had been a great French soldier, and after his return home, the king of France had given a large tract of land to show his appreciation for LeDuc's service. So his grandfather was a landed man. He was an aristocrat, definitely the high class in France. He was expected to lease farms to serfs, or members of the lower class, then he was given a percent of their income for rent, then he had to give about seventy percent of that to the king because the land was still his. He remembered Uncle Charles LeDuc had told him that when his dad came to America to trap, he didn't bring much because it wasn't his. It was the king's! Uncle Charles said a couple of his sisters still thought that someone had stolen his riches; that some sinister bad thing had caused him to lose his fortune, but Charles said he gave it up for his own choice to come to America where a man could own and control property himself. The American government actually encouraged people to own land so it could be put on tax rolls and the land would be improved and become more fruitful.

The government passed homestead laws. They gave one section of ground of every township to the state to help fund education. Most of the ranchers of any size in the Basin were leasing at least a section of ground from the state. Some had more than one; also many had bought homesteads from others who had proved up. Many ranchers had their kids, members of their family, file on choice pieces of range so ownership of private land was checker boarded in with government land.

Pope had a knot in his stomach from the idiocy of everything. He couldn't sleep. His mind was working this over. He knew George Washington, this nation's father, had a large plantation. He was aristocracy, so why did he sign the Declaration of Independence? Why did George Washington put himself in harm's way of England, the most powerful nation on earth? Because England *claimed* America! Washington's farm belonged to the king of England, damn it! He became General of the Army of the Colonies. George Washington was a patriot! He believed a man should be entitled to own land.

The Continental Congress was so afraid they would become like the social countries of the world that they limited their power, not raising any taxes at all. So Washington fought eight long years for no pay. When soldiers came to join, he'd say, "We can't pay you. We've got no uniforms or guns. Bring your own. But if you stay with me, how would you like to own your place yourself? I'll see you get your deeds to your places." So people fought for the freedom to own and control property.

If the Mexicans actually thought they had rights to graze anywhere they wanted to, then it seemed like they believed in a despotic government which is when the king or government owns everything. Citizens just work for them. A lot of people seemed to want to be told what do to and how to do it. Others wanted to steal from honest workers.

Someday, John guessed, when he quit sheriffing, he'd become a lawyer and work on cases of government verses private individuals. An awful lot of his time as a new sheriff had been spent settling domestic arguments over water. It tickled John when people became educated as to the real water laws vs. stealing. Once the system was established and running, they were able to regulate and run the irrigation company themselves without help from the sheriff all the time, even though a bunch of people on different systems seemed to get a bit more than their share.

Pope suddenly laughed out loud as his thoughts were taking him through a whirlwind of things, but one of the sayings so often heard lately was, *'Highority was better than a priority.'* In other words, to live at the big end or beginning of the canal was better than being at the end of the ditch, even though the man on the end owned most of the water. People on the top seemed to get enough. Prior appropriation laws were laws regulating water in eighteen western states.

East of the Rocky Mountains, irrigation wasn't worried about because rain irrigated crops. In California the 49ers, prospecting, filed mining claims. The first to file owned that spot with known size, usually he needed water to wash the impurities from the gold so he filed on water. The first to file on the water owned the water as long as he put it to beneficial use. It was his.

The State of California adopted this law and sent officers to enforce the laws; otherwise the man with the fastest gun owned what he wanted. So water was regulated by state. If a man quit using his water benefit, then a juror appropriator would own the water. So the western states all adopted these water laws, with various degrees of difference, depending on the states. The Federal Government of the United States gave its stamp of approval.

John thought "I legally filed on Red Creek. Nobody owns the water but me! I'm owner as well as law officer. I did what I did protecting property and life!" What about his homestead? Legally filed and recorded. "What else can I do?"

Back east as large sections of land were opened for homesteading, a land office was opened. People filed the land and officers were checking to see if they were working and using the land. If they were, then they were given a deed to the property which was filed with the county. There were always people who lived and worked land that they never filed. They were called squatters, but as the section became settled up, the last thing officers from the land office did was take deeds to land being squatted on, and gave it to the squatters since over years they had acquired rights to their places. These were called the old redemption laws. Then the land office closed and moved to the next section.

It was late and Pope knew he was wrestling with his conscience. This Mexican should still be alive, yet he'd shot and hit John's saddle horn and tore it loose. The hell with it! John went to sleep.

When he woke, it was getting light. He got up, saddled and packed and rode off, the dogs following faithfully. Pope thought they must not have thought much of the herder. They were working for him even before the old Mexican was killed. Pope thought, "I'll find something for them to eat in a bit. Sure enough, about full daylight, they came to a prairie dog town and Pope killed one. Watching close, he got a second shot and both dogs got a prairie dog to eat.

About ten o'clock, he came to a small spring where he called a halt. He hadn't eaten in over two days. He soon had a fire going and coffee heating. He got into the pannier and brought out a small Dutch oven, put some water in it, and got it in the coals, then cut up the sage chicken he killed the night before, salted and peppered it, and dropped it in the oven. A camp robber swooped in and landed about twenty feet away and Pope drew and killed it, practicing, but now the dogs went out to fight over it. Pope decided he couldn't wait for the chicken and opened a can of beans with his knife and ate them off the knife blade.

He could see lots of chips and fire rock. This spring had been used much by Indian hunting parties, for hundreds of years probably. While waiting for the chicken, he walked a pretty good circle, and found a fire from the camp of sheep or cows, or both. Tracks were tromped out, but he was sure they had stayed on water at least two or three days. He walked back, got his cup and poured some coffee, pulled the lid off the chicken and got a big piece of breast. It was still a little chewy, but he enjoyed it anyway. About the fourth cup of coffee, the chicken was tender and done to a turn. Pope filled up tight.

John then scraped out the last of the chicken to the dogs and rinsed the coffee pot and scoured the oven, packed them away, filled the canteen and water bag, bridled up, and rode on. The tracks, they seemed to be working east through cedars into the big canyon. He came to a small stream in the canyon and found another camp. He rode on until coming to a branch of the canyon. One canyon came in from the east and the sheep had come down it. Before following on, he rode up the straight fork and presto, cattle tracks.

His cattle had been driven on west up this main canyon. It wasn't as steep as most of the canyons in the Basin, but grass grew on the sides. A guy could slip out anywhere, but huge areas were covered with cedars and sagebrush. A long eared jack rabbit came streaming passed with two dogs in close pursuit. *Bang.* Mr. Rabbit went end over end, and the dogs began scattering fur, tearing him up as Pope leisurely reloaded and returned the pistol to his side. They camped on a meadow that night with good water and grass. It looked like the rustlers had camped here two or three days before. He knew about five men had brought them to this point.

The next morning when Pope left, he found where three rustlers had ridden west toward the big ridge. Now only two men were with the cattle. He was still way behind, but he was gaining about five days at least. They were letting the cattle drift and feed slowly along because the tracks were spread even up the side hills a ways, and about three miles further along, he found another camp—another day closer.

Pope wondered if he was going to catch up in time to save any cattle or what he'd do to these thieves when he caught up. His rage—even thought out and under control, was burning him like a fire. He knew these fellows with the cows weren't the brains. They were only puppets being maneuvered by the puppet master, pulling the strings. Still, everyone eliminated brought him closer to a shot at Mr. Big. That's the shot he wanted so badly.

Pope continued to track. He lived on chickens. He ran out of coffee about seven days later, but he was getting close. His dogs ate squirrels, rabbits, left over chicken and whatever Pope killed for them. He had no use for them, but they had adopted him and were company.

On the fifteenth day, Pope found where a group of riders came in from the west. There were about five horses Pope figured. Two were pack horses and they had spent some time here, then they split the cattle in half. One group went on northeast with three men, and two men and pack horse took the others east. Pope stayed with these two who had apparently received a pack horse of supplies. This was definitely a planned attack on Pope by more than a random rustler gang. These men were organized, working together as a big group. One thing on his side, they thought their tracks had been covered. No one could have followed them here. But Pope tracked like the Shoshone Indians who had trained him. And he was close enough to start looking for an ambush.

He followed on 'til dark and camped on a big hog back with a dry camp. Next morning he moved out at first light and traveled over this big hill for several miles. As they descended, a valley came into view with some nice meadows, a cabin, a barn, and corrals. Smoke came from the chimney and John could see his cattle grazing in the meadow. A pasture held five horses close to the corral. This was a pretty picture, but the cattle belonged a hundred miles or more on Red Creek, not on this place. How to do this now? No mistakes. Then the burning rage started jabbing him. He rode down behind the barn and tied up and walked around the corral to the house. He could smell meat cooking. He heard a loud laugh from inside and some talking that he couldn't distinguish through the door.

John opened the door and stepped in and kicked the door shut behind him. Two bearded, rough looking men were looking at him in amazement. One stood at the stove with a fork in his hand, the other sat at the table on a bench. The man by the stove said, "You ever heard of knocking?"

Pope answered, "Only heads." Then he said, "Very carefully produce a bill of sale for the cattle out there."

"You go to hell."

"Yes, I'm afraid that is going to happen for killing rustlers. I hope you're heeled and ready to make a fight for your lives."

Both men grabbed for iron. Pope killed the cook. He turned to the other man who had been hampered from making a smooth draw because of the table. He was barely visible through the smoke as Pope's second shot took him out. He reached back and opened the door to get rid of the smoke and realized he was still mad, but at least he was rid of some of his antagonists. Pope stepped up and waved the door back and forth, drawing some of the smoke out, then he stepped in and grabbed a man by his heels and drug him out. He went back and did the same with the other. He then checked the meat on the stove. Pope put a bit more pepper and salt on it and left it to finish cooking.

He went and found a shovel and came back with shovels full of dust to cover the blood on the floor. After about four trips, it looked and began to smell better inside. The meat was done, so Pope got a fork and took the pan to the table where he began to eat the meat. It was mutton, not Pope's favorite, but it was sure good to have meat again. After about cleaning up the whole pan, he went back to the stove and looked in the oven. They had a loaf of bread cooking in there. It was black on top, and it hadn't risen very well, but Pope was glad to have it for a sandwich for later on.

He took the pan out for the dogs, but found them licking blood and brains from his victims. Pope couldn't watch that, and he gagged some from the gore.

He remembered a hole that was dug back toward the corral. He thought on seeing it that they were probably digging a place for a latrine, so he stripped the pistol from one, then grabbing his heels, he hauled him out there to the hole. John went through his pockets and found about three hundred and fifty dollars. He went back and got the other guy. He had thirty-six. Both had nice colt 45's. They both went in the hole they dug themselves. Pope covered them with the shovel.

John went through things in the cabin. He came up with four new pair of socks. Boy, Pope was glad for that. He traded the camp horse for a good looking bay horse to carry the pack with. He found a nearly new saddle in the barn. It wasn't a form fitter, but fit him well. Since the horn was bent and torn loose on his own saddle, he decided to try it. He hoped it wouldn't hurt the horse's back. Some did.

He put his bags and outfit on. He took pistols and ammo. He found a box of 44-40s which he appropriated as well. He stocked the pack with supplies from the house and then he rode back to where the outlaws had split up and went after the other bunch. He ran out of daylight before getting back, but didn't need light since he knew where they split. He camped on the trail of his cattle.

He followed all day. He went past one camp and close to forty miles from where he left his cattle the day before, made camp on the trail. The next morning about ten miles from camp, he spotted his cattle being herded east by three men and four horses. He rode east off the tracks, and made an attempt to get ahead of this bunch to ambush them, but the country was so open he couldn't get by without being seen. So he worked as close as possible and watched his chance.

They soon quit for the night. Pope ate the last of the hard bread. He left his horses staked on grass. He tied the dogs as well and walked closer in the twilight, carrying his rifle as well as the pistol. Pope knew these men would fight so he came prepared to give them one. He worked his way to within twenty yards of the sleeping camp. He didn't have much cover, so he scooped out a bit of dirt with his knife. He made a depression several inches deep. As he loosed the dirt, he scraped it toward the outlaws, making a mound to shoot over, and a depression to lay in for the security it might afford. He had plenty of time to kill before morning, so it was deep enough for real protection by then.

After the men were all up, standing or squatting around the fire, a couple with cups in hand, Pope yelled, "Hands up. Don't move."

They froze only a split second and everyone went for their guns. Pope fired three shots. The first before anyone had a gun out, the second about the time of the first shot from the rustlers sounded, and the third about the time the second shot hit the dirt John had scooped up. Now it was quiet. Pope looked at the poor mislead bunch of would-be bad men. It was amazing how fast they repented.

John T. walked down and went through pockets. He had another three hundred and fifty dollars. He knew all these gunslingers of Cassidy's. He lifted a pistol off one of the dead outlaws and fired a shot, then put it back in his hand. He walked around and made sure all their guns had fired. It made it look like they may have had a disagreement and fought it out. The coffee in the pot and bacon in the pan was ready and Pope ate it all. He took their pack horse and pack, loading all their food and coffee. All the rest of the horses were turned loose. He walked, leading the pack horse back to the place he'd left his horses, and dogs, and pack. He loaded up, saddled up, and went after his cattle. There was only eleven head here. He must have lost some someplace, and as he rode past the outlaw camp, it gave him an eerie feeling. His cows seemed willing to go. They wanted to go home.

They drove south for a change that felt good. On the second day of the trail home, they picked up fifteen head that were left in the meadow. John had found sixteen of thirty that were driven away a month or so ago. Now all he had to do was follow them home. The dogs were willing to work which made for easy driving. Pope let them graze along easy. He killed a chicken a day for meat, and a jack rabbit or prairie dog for the dogs. Sometimes they caught something on their own.

They gradually wore this bloody trip down to home. Pope was instantly mad every time he thought of the injustice of an ignorant sheep herder! John T. wondered if Cassidy was the brains behind this caper, or if some other brain thought it up. Whatever! Cassidy's gang wasn't as big as it used to be. John T. rode around and let the bars down to his ranch at Red Creek. The cattle filed in. Pope unloaded the things out of his pack that he'd need on the ranch. He put the bars up and rode for home. He was ferried over before dark, and then rode all night to arrive in the morning about daylight.

Chapter Fourteen

Shenanigans

John went home. He took all he sweaty worn clothes off and took a bath, the first in a month of Sundays it seemed. After he smelled better, Charlotte treated him to a real homecoming.

Pope stayed home for two days, lying around with Charlotte and the kids. He said if he stayed out of sight, nobody would know where he was so they couldn't shoot him or hand him a job. The deputy seemed to have things under control, but all good things come to an end.

The judge knocked on his door with a warrant for the three McKee Brothers. They had run a whole herd of sheep over a cliff in McKee draw, killing them all.

Whoa. "Who has signed the complaint?"

"Ford Childress."

"Who's he?"

"He owns the sheep."

"Oh." Pope's eyes narrowed a little. "Who witnessed this terrible deed?"

"I don't know. Why?"

"Because," Pope said, "The McKee draw is named after the McKee brothers' dad. I've known them ever since I've been here, that the McKee's own the draw. So why would anyone take horses or cattle or sheep or anything else on the McKee's property? Maybe they are just trying to precipitate a war or at least cause trouble enough to private property owners to get their name on the land themselves. Unless Childress has got a witness, it won't do me any good to go out there. McKee's are my neighbors. They've been good neighbors to me, and personally I'll testify for McKee's and against the sheep herder who owns no land and is stealing other's feed wherever he goes."

The judge hesitated, "What about the warrant?"

"It was conjured up on the man's desperation on losing his sheep. But even if they killed the sheep, it was done defending their property. But anyone might have killed them. I don't know any rancher in Brown's Hole who wants sheep around. So save me the wear and tear of that ride. Tell Ford Childress that John T. Pope said to put that warrant where it stays dark all the time. Tell him John T. Pope is worth twenty-five hundred dollars to him dead, if he can collect, and I hope he'll come to get the reward! It would give me great pleasure to be able to have an excuse to kill that black-hearted steal thief. So tell him to bring his gun!"

The judge's eyes were wide and he was backing up. He said, "Maybe one of your deputies . . ."

"Why don't you do it, Judge? If you were more interested in justice and less on pomp and routine, this county would be better off!" John's jaws worked fiercely, and the cords in his neck were bulging at his sudden upset.

John closed the door and he was mad all over again. He stepped to a window and watched the judge walk away. His kids were playing with the dogs. They would throw a stick and one dog would run and get it and bring it back. That dumb dog would play with the kids as long as they would pay attention. The other was a bit standoffish. Charlotte spoke from behind him making him startle a bit.

"You were awful rough on him, John."

"Yes, I guess I was."

"I really think you need to go apologize."

"Even if I have to ride away again?"

"Probably."

"I'm weary of riding away, Charlotte." John reached a hand up to the coat rack for his hat and walked out. He had new clothes.

"Goodbye Daddy," Hazel called.

"Be a good girl, little sunshine!"

"I will. I got me a dog now." The little girl was well content. John heard her say, "Throw it again, Charles, only farther this time!"

John had nearly two blocks to walk. He got out in the middle of the road and walked the distance with an attitude. He walked up to the house and knocked on the door. The judge opened, and seeing Pope, stepped back alertly.

Pope pulled his hat off and said, "I came to apologize for your treatment in my house. I shouldn't have said anything to you."

The judge said, "You are forgiven."

"Thank you, Frank. I've been under a bit of strain. I chased rustlers for nearly two months, and I guess, as you could tell, am prejudiced in this deal. I'm tired of trying to walk where my neighbors won't shoot for the money on my head. So I just sauntered up here hoping somebody would take shot. If they hit, my troubles are over. If they miss, then their troubles are over. Do you still think it is the right thing to serve these papers?"

"I don't know after listening to you."

"Okay," Pope said, "I'll take it and serve it if you think, but I think the Wild Bunch is stirring trouble with these sheep to divert attention from themselves for some reason. The McKee's aren't the only place fed off and wrecked by this bunch of sheep. For one thing, while a rancher is trying to get rid of the sheep, rustlers are driving his cattle off, drifting them out of the country, covering their tracks with sheep tracks. Listen Judge, will you be hearing this case yourself or will they send this to Provo where city lawyers and judges can rule on things foreign to their understanding?"

The Judge stood tall, almost unblinking. He said, "It would probably go to Provo."

"Would you give me papers on Ford Childress first? Let me bring him here for some questions about himself, whether he has any property or not? Whether it is leased or deeded? Who brought him here? And what they are paying him for his charade? Who his witnesses would be?"

"Why not? Nobody ever questioned a complaint before."

"I've got a horse with good common sense. He doesn't do things backwards. The sheep man Ford is the cause of this, not the ranchers. Where was Ford when this alleged crime took place? Why didn't he stop it? If he tried, why is he here alive? Hell, if the McKee's did that, they wouldn't have left a live witness! You know that don't you? Give me the paper on Ford Childress. I'll bring him to you and we'll get some questions answered. If he's legitimate, it'll be a surprise, but if he's like I say, lacking witnesses or property, his papers won't do any good."

The judge filled out the complaint from Pope, and Pope signed it. "Okay, now do you know where he's staying?"

"No."

Pope put the warrant in his shirt pocket and said, "I'll find him." He walked down the road to the store, stepped in and asked if anyone had seen Ford Childress. No one knew a thing. John bought a large piece of black licorice and left, chewing on it.

He went to the bar and noticed the back door open. The bartender leaned on the bar, "Well Sheriff, we don't see much of you around here."

"No. Have you seen Ford Childress?"

The bartender's forehead furrowed like he was trying to think. "I guess I don't know him."

"Who just left the back door as I came up front? Don't try any of that no savvy stuff because I know you know."

He finally said, "Ford."

"What did he run for?"

"Hell, I guess he didn't want to talk to you."

"He knew it was me coming?"

"Yes."

"How?"

"He asked me to tell him if you came out of the judge's house and started coming this way."

"Sounds like a real innocent feller. Thanks." John closed the door as he went out.

Ford's tracks were here in the dirt. He might as well have signed his signature for the sheriff to follow. He had run-over heels, holes in half soles in about size ten boots, with pretty deep tracks. Pope followed behind the buildings about fifty yards and came to the place his horse had been tied. Now Pope looked the horse tracks over. The shoes were worn almost smooth, very little heel or toe left on number one shoes, and they were narrow. Pope took another bite of licorice. He followed the horse around into the road and saw he had been kicked onto a lope.

Pope walked down the board walk to the store. He stepped back in and bought about a pound of jerky and a half pound of coffee, as well as a double handful of dried parched corn. Carrying the three sacks, he walked to the jail, chewing his licorice. Rock met him in the door. Pope looked at Pope and John said, "Hell Rock, you look tougher than any of the Wild Bunch. When did you start growing whiskers? You didn't let that little cowgirl hoodwink you, I hope."

"No! Nothing like that!" Rock said, "I'd like to look and be just like you."

"Thanks, but be a better man than me. Are you still working on the draw?"

Rock grabbed the four and a half inch barrel colt 45, and it came out fast.

"That was good. You're as good as or better than they are, so keep practicing and make up your mind in a scrap to win. I've already done that. Rock, I've got to go back. I'm on the tracks of a shyster. Would you go out and catch the bay horse for me? He's in the jail corral."

Rock grinned. "Shyster, huh?"

John nodded solemnly.

"What's wrong with Old Shorty?" Rock asked.

"He's been on the road for nearly two months, I'll give him a rest I guess." While Pope worked on a saddle, taking up the stirrups for his short legs, and tying bags, blanket, poncho, and ground sheet, he picked a couple of blankets and tried to remember which bridle had belonged to the bay. He remembered he didn't have his matches packed from his roll, so he got a box off the back of the stove, and filled his canteen. They started saddling, and the bay stepped away and rolled his eyes, and snorted.

John said, "Hell I wish I didn't have to put this outfit on here if he decides to buck. He didn't tighten the cinch 'til he led him around a ways, but he had a hump in his back and rolling the white in his eyes.

Rock said, "Nobody's rode him for a long time. Guess he can't stand prosperity."

John yanked the cinch up then again, he was still humped up.

"Let me top him off for ya," Rock offered.

"Okay. I've got a long ways to go. I think I don't need this."

Rock put the bridle reins around his neck. The bay rolled his eye and stepped away. Rock stayed close and walked him sideways into the side of the jail. He had one hand on the reins and the other on the horn when the horse touched the jail. The bay jumped about a foot ahead. Rock's foot went in the stirrup, and he was on, just getting his other stirrup when Ol' Bay realized he was already up. He jumped four or five stiff little jumps and stopped, but Rock's spurs hit him, bringing a lunge ahead. His head was broke to the bridle too good to get wound up, so the horse started walking away. The saddle still stood up on the horse's back, and he was rolling his eye and taking steps like he was walking on eggs.

John watched while Rock gave him a bit of exercise about a hundred yards up the road. He kicked him on a lope which only went a couple of yards and Ol' Bay busted. He went high and swapped ends, and bucked hard back up the road to the jail. He started trying to stop. Every time he slowed down, those spurs would sing as they raked him and pretty soon they went out of there on a run about a half mile then came back part way on a lope, then a walk. Ol' Bay was sweating it up, and trying to breathe air he hadn't seen before, when Rock crawled off, "There ya are big brother. He's all fixed."

"Thanks, all I needed today was to get bucked off and my old neck broke. That was fun to watch that ride. You must have been practicing more than your draw."

John mounted and rode to Ford's tracks. Now to see what he had in his mind. Ford Childress couldn't possibly be anything but a trouble maker. John and Charlotte had a bunch of sheep once. They didn't pasture anybody but their own pasture. Charlotte had spent one-half her time chasing them to get them back in the pasture and fix the fence. They never had wire there at the time, either.

Pope thought Cooks had run two herds of sheep. They never bothered anyone because they owned a lot of ground and water also. Nat Hodges had had over a thousand head. They didn't try to sheep off neighbors. Maybe the Wild Bunch put Childress up to ruining him, and that's all. "He sure is running from something or leading me into an ambush for the reward."

That was always in the back of his mind. John rode the tracks until dark. He hadn't been trying to hide his tracks so Pope made an easy job of following. Ford was definitely going to Brown's Park. It got dark while they were on the mountain so he made a dry camp. He staked Ol' Bay good—didn't need him to get away. If he'd been riding Old Shorty, he might have caught up by now. He chewed on some jerky, then some licorice. He'd forgotten it. He listened to the night sounds on the mountain until sleep finally came.

Next morning at first light he was riding. The tracks went down Sears Canyon. Pope looked at it a bit apprehensively. So he asked for help from the source of his help in the past. He began to ride over to one side of the canyon or the other, not staying on the tracks. He stayed alert. It was impossible to ride under cover all the way. He went slow and used what he could.

Bam! Ol' Bay went on his belly so fast, John rolled off and behind the horse. That shot had come from in front. *Bam!* Another bullet zinged into the bay. *Bam!* Another shot splintered the stock of John's rifle. He hadn't had a chance to pull it. Everything went down so fast. *Bam!* Pope was laying flat behind the dead horse which still faced ahead. *Bam!* The shots were coming so fast he couldn't get a peek to see what was happening. *Bam!* Pope's pistol was in his hand. *Bam!* Automatic reaction to draw it. *Bam!* That shot went into Ol' Bay. *Bam!* Pope was trying to look between the horse's legs which were sticking out. *Bam!* Pope was trying to see something and he heard a shell being pushed into the rifle. Was he empty?

Pope looked up. Ford Childress was walking toward him, loading the rifle so John rolled over in the clear and killed him. Pope looked at the horse. His rifle was busted. His horse was dead. The saddle was busted to all to hell, broken tree, leather cut and wrinkled. But he was alive! John took his roll off the saddle and bags. He loosed the cinch and pulled the saddle blankets loose. Everything was ready to pick up if he could find Ford's horse. As he walked passed this guy, he stopped long enough to go through pockets. He had ten shiny twenty dollar gold pieces. So, he got paid for causing trouble, plus about six dollars in change. Pope walked on by, watching for the horse tracks as much as he could. About a block down the canyon and around a bend he found the mount, an old grey horse, a bit potbellied like his former master. Pope looked in his mouth, smooth and long toothed just like he looked. He was about right for his kids, maybe. Wouldn't the kids squeal over another present?

John took the blankets from Ol' Bay, put them in place, and then he picked up the saddle. He was impressed. It was like his form fitter, but the seat was longer. Like his saddle, the horn came out a ways forward, leaning forward. It was much bigger around the top, not like the Mexican horn, but at least two and one-half inches across the cap. It was covered and wrapped with rawhide. It hadn't been cared for, but it was exactly what he was looking for, so he threw it on and cinched up, then spent about fifteen minutes taking the strings out of the stirrups, measured with a stick and put one stitch on each side while he mounted and made sure what would fit. The skirts were extra long and square.

He finished lacing up and rode back up to the stuff he left up there. He picked up this fellow's rifle, a 45-70 lever action marlin. He put it in the bucket, after finding Ford's shells and reloading it. He wasn't going to bury Ford, but he couldn't feed the ravens and crows, magpies and vultures. He rolled him off the trail and carried rocks until he was covered. He took his rifle and latigos, and strings with Conchos, and lariat—even the stirrups would do. He rode about a mile on down to the Crouse place to see if they might invite him to dinner. His conscience didn't bother him, no not a bit. This wasn't like it had been when he killed the herder.

John rode into the Crouse Ranch. A bunch of chickens had the run of things around there. John noticed good corrals and wing fences, a large barn and a two room cabin, a bunk cabin with room for about six bunks, and a nice buggy was parked near the house. An outhouse was built downwind of the houses and a large garden grew with a lot of weeds in a fenced field north of the house. A small chicken coop with a door propped open wide enough for the chickens to come and go. A Mexican man and woman were working in the garden with hoes. Smoke curled from the chimney. Pope got down, tied at the tie post and hollered, "Anybody home?"

Charley came to the door. "Well, hello Sheriff. Come in. Dinner will be ready in a few minutes. Where did you get that fine young colt?"

Pope laughed, "I guess I inherited him. Feller tried to collect a reward up there. He missed me, but he hit my horse. So I had to borrow him or walk."

"Oh, he beats walking, that's for sure. I thought you had a lot of hardware on there."

"Yes, I tried to take what I could use. How are things in the ranching business in this neck of the woods?"

"Okay. There's a pack of wolves around. I've heard 'em a few times, and they killed a few calves on the Two Bar. If we don't rid ourselves of them, we'll catch grief next winter."

"If I had time, I'd come catch 'em for ya."

"You trap?"

"I can catch coyotes and wolves. I trapped several winters and made good money."

"Ranchers would make it worth your time if you could catch 'em."

Pope was watching a buxom woman working at the stove and wondered if this was Charley's wife. She soon started carrying food to the table which was already set, and Pope sat up and enjoyed a really good dinner; fresh peas and carrots and new potatoes in gravy with roast beef. It was really delicious. He went out with Charley after dinner and looked at the horses. He didn't want to buy a horse, but Charley wanted to sell. A brown horse caught John's eye. He looked at his teeth and figured him to be about six years old. He had hard back hooves and was shod. Charley asked fifty dollars. Pope offered thirty.

"Maybe forty-five?" Crouse dickered.

"Thirty-five."

"Or maybe forty?"

"Okay, forty it is." Pope transferred the saddle to the brown horse. Charley loaned a saddle to carry stuff on. He told John to leave the saddle at his bar. So he rode out about four o'clock. He rode all night which works against ambushers and worked for John. He rode into Vernal after daylight, going home and to bed where he slept the clock around.

After waking and a hearty breakfast, he told Charlotte he still didn't know exactly what happened, but his conscience was clear, and he was in better spirits again. Pope spent a few days home. The dogs loved his kids and vice versa. He led the old grey horse out and let the kids ride. The old horse took care not to step on them and tolerated their abuse. He seemed to be glad to be here. By the next afternoon, the sheriff saw his neighbors as well as his own kids on him, all riding bareback, and the old Gray was careful with them. "Looks like I lucked out getting a dandy kid horse."

"And dandy kids," Charlotte said softly, stepping to the window to watch with him.

"Oh hell yes! The best kids in the world!"

The kids would lead old Gray to a fence, and then climb up, and aboard the patient horse. He would go about any place with them. They guided him easily, which beat a lot of corral balky ponies Pope had experienced. A lot of horses ridden by kids, and even some women, learn to take advantage. They get bad habits sometimes, but old Gray would raise the kids.

Chapter Fifteen

Back to Business at Hand

JOHN GOT THE WARRANT for Butch and Sundance for robbing the Montpelier Bank. He spent quite a lot of time riding and talking to people in Brown's Park, and at the Strip, trying to locate them so he could serve the warrants. Many times after a successful caper, a group of them would have a party to celebrate. Many times they rode east to Baggs to party. Stories were told for years of the money won, lost, and of fun that was had during these times. So when Pope got word they were going to the Strip to party, he knew his chance had come. He had promised Butch that he'd give warning first, so they could meet fair and settle things. So John had ridden Old Shorty on his last ride, and John would miss him the rest of his life.

Pope didn't really know, but it was said, and he couldn't find any evidence to prove that LeRoy Parker, Alias Butch Cassidy, ever killed anyone. He seemed to be a likeable, well set up young man that you might meet at a Sunday in church. Once again John couldn't tell if Butch was the true leader of the organized outlaws or Wild Bunch, but it was believed he was by everyone around here. If he was, what's the difference of him killing someone or putting a price on someone's head? John had received news that he was worth four thousand dollars, dead now. Butch was running and staying behind the scene while gunmen from his Wild Bunch killed people, every so often, in various capers all over the West.

If Butch was the brains and boss of these thieves, then he was responsible for bringing the sheep and stealing his cows. He was responsible for at least seven deaths that John could think of in that escapade alone. What's worse, it caused John a bit of suffering mentally for awhile. But John reasoned, "Where does the buck stop?"

He wanted to have law and order. He wanted justice. He wanted people to be able to raise their cattle, and horses, and families, without being robbed blind, and their kids led the wrong way. "In the simple mind of a self and home educated rancher, the leaders of this Wild Bunch should be the targets." So John started hunting Butch and Sundance, not only for killing Old Shorty, but for what they tried to do, and were trying to do to John.

"Without the head the snake becomes harmless," the sheriff said, and so he strongly felt.

Matt Warner was in jail with William Wall. Many of Butch's close associates had been put under while trying to do his bidding. Now to find them was a problem because they seemed to have so many friends, and the Wild Bunch came and went from any direction. They had not any particular home.

John Pope walked to his office where all the information on outlaws was stored. Maybe he was overlooking something. He started through everything he had. Sheriff Sterling D. Cotton had put as much material together as possible on Butch. Richard Pope kept everything from Pinkerton, and circulars, so he had a nice dossier.

"Dick, let's go over what we know of Cassidy. Let's dig into the file."

Dick pulled up a chair, and began reading. "The largest gang of outlaws ever seen was organized in Utah, Wyoming, and Colorado. The organizer and undisputed leader is Butch Cassidy. They operate on a large scale, being bold and spectacular, and their innumerable hideouts are practically impregnable."

John listened to the rich timbre of his brother's voice as he continued, "George LeRoy Parker's grandpa died on Rocky Hill, nearly to the summit of South Pass, Wyoming, in 1856. He was a member of the Willie Handcart Company. He had been president of the Mormon mission in Preston England."

"So he was of good stock. Too bad Butch decided to shy away from his teachings."

Dick nodded. "His grandma was Ann Hartley and she and their small children survived the handcart trek. Maximilian was his oldest boy. The family buried Robert in the snow and pushed on. With aid from Utah, they made it in and settled in American Fork. In 1865 Maximilian married Ann Campbell and settled in Circle Valley where they raised a family of seven children. George LeRoy was born 1867. His father bought the old Jim Marshall ranch, twelve miles south of Circleville."

"Go on."

"Mike Cassidy worked on the ranch and George LeRoy's dad kept him on. Mike had been building himself a herd by branding mavericks. He ran them in the place now known as Bryce Canyon. From Mike Cassidy, young George received an education in rusting and horse stealing. George LeRoy's boyhood hero was Mike Cassidy. George learned to rope, and ride, doing cinch ring or wire branding. And he learned to shoot. Before he was sixteen George LeRoy Parker was the best shot in Circle Valley."

John poured a glass of water, listening to his brother, straining the information for anything helpful.

"He stands five feet and nine inches, weighs a hundred and fifty-five pounds, or thereabouts."

John knew that much, for he'd certainly met the outlaw on more than one occasion. "I wish I would have had papers on him sooner."

"Mike Cassidy's herd got so big it was being noticed so he moved it to the Henry Mountains, near the Colorado River. George was hired to herd cattle in what is now the Robbers Roost area. Mike got in trouble with the law and left ahead of a posse for Mexico. George took his name, George Cassidy. A few days later he was arrested for stealing horses. He escaped and went to Colorado. One of his friends had an old needle gun with a bad kick. He called it Butch. George was conned into trying it. It kicked him down and into a water hole so everyone nicknamed him Butch. He started small, Butch Cassidy."

"He should have learned to honor his own name, damn it!"

Again Dick nodded, and kept reading until the dossier was closed.

Of course, the reason John was going over this was to find a clue where he might locate him. He knew Butch might be in Montana, or New Mexico, or anywhere pulling another robbery. John would go anywhere within a hundred and fifty miles or so, even though his authority was in Uintah County only. After reading and realizing the scope of Butch's experiences, he decided once he got his trail, he'd stay with it.

It was time to check his cattle anyway. So John saddled up once again, and taking a pack horse, he visited the store where he purchased a brass Navy telescope. John put it in his saddle bag so he could draw it anytime. He packed a hundred snares. He rode north through Steinaker and began to climb northeast.

He stopped up on the side of the mountains and let his horses rest a bit. Taking the telescope, he sat where he could rest the telescope and watched his back trail. *Nothing*. He could see Vernal and even his own place with the glass. He camped a bit farther along and was at peace out here on the mountain. Next morning he packed up and rode east, then southeast to the back of Diamond Mountain. He watched for tracks of game as well as livestock. He rode around a bit to Matt's place. It was undisturbed. He rode on over toward the Hole. This was such a beautiful summer range. He saw occasional cattle. The range was stalked, but there was good grass, and it was still green and growing up here. John knew Butch had a cabin above the Bassett Ranch which was well supplied in case they needed to hide out.

John cut back and forth as much as possible while descending. He didn't find the cabin or cave, but he knew it was close. He made camp on a small spring above Bassett's Ranch. The next morning he rode out 'til he found a place. He could see the ranch. John tied the horses, and taking the telescope, went to a place where he could see everyone going or coming around the ranch. He sat and watched for a couple of hours. He saw Ann ride out on her horse toward the southwest.

After a while he got tired of spying on nothing, so he mounted and rode to the river, crossed at the Jarvie Crossing and rode to his own ranch on Red Creek. He unpacked, unsaddled, and grained the horses. It was kind of dark already, so he lit the coal oil lamp and got supper by opening a can of tomatoes and eating them cold with a bit of salt and pepper.

Next morning he started a fire and sliced bacon in a pan. John fried a nice bunch of bacon, fished it onto his plate, and then broke three eggs in the grease. When it was mostly cooked, he pushed the pan back off the heat, and poured his cup full of coffee. He fished his eggs onto his plate with the bacon, and had a nice breakfast while keeping an eye out for anyone. After saving the grease in any empty can, he cleaned the dishes and cleaned up the house. He rode up to see how his cattle were doing. There was lots of grass and the feed was almost too good. He could pasture more cattle, but he was raising more. He had over twenty calves.

John decided to brand. No help, but the calves were small. He rounded them all up and drove them down into the field by the house. The corral wasn't big enough. Then he got the brand and carried several arms full of wood and got the fire going. John put the brand in. It would take awhile before the fire got hot enough to heat the branding iron. He sharpened his pocket knife, went into the house and got a pigging string. He continued to put fuel on the fire. John worked with his rope, tightened the cinch and got the lariat unlimbered. He was definitely out of practice, but he wasn't a novice, so in a couple of minutes, he brought a calf as close as he dared. The calf's mother followed closely.

John tied a rein on the rope. The first several calves he brought down, so he would face a calf and not a stampede. The heifers only needed a brand. The bulls, he cut, making them steers. So it was a routine that lasted 'til almost dark. Drag a calf down, get off, throw him, tie him with the pigging string, take the rope off, bring the red hot brand, and burn it deep enough to show forever.

Each time a calf was branded another piece of wood or two was put on the fire. If a calf was a bull, it took a little more time. With another man helping, it would have only taken an hour, but alone it was a job.

John knew it was work, he branded at least twice a year, and it discouraged the honest rustlers because they rode around the range. When they found slick salves, even if they were on mother's, if they were old enough to live without their mothers, they were branded, then penned up long enough to wean them. After a week, the cow would leave and the rustlers had another calf to sell that fall. With branded calves, chances were good that they would be left alone, except serious rustlers altered brands or branded with an iron that would cover the brand. These serious rustlers were more apt to be daring. So smoothly they altered brands on cattle then they would drive in from a long ways away so locals wouldn't be apt of notice.

After John finished the job, he drove the cattle back up to the range and closed the field gate. It was late and John was tired, so he tended his horse, pulled his boots off, unbuckled his gun, loosened his pants and rolled in a blanket on the bunk and slept hard all night.

When he awoke, the sun was already up. He lay on the bunk half awake, not wanting to move. Coyotes were howling around him. He could see his breath, so it was a pretty cold morning. That was a bit of a worry about branding. If it stayed hot, the flies might get to new branded calves, but it was cold enough he thought. Finally, he rolled off the bunk, stood, and tucked his shirt in his Levis. He pulled the boots on and then the pistol was buckled on.

John stepped out and went quickly around the house to make it a bit harder for someone trying to collect a bounty. John didn't know about trapping yet, the fur wasn't quite prime. Butch and his confederates must have gone a ways out of the country. John was hungry enough to eat a horse so he started his fire and sliced bacon. He also sliced a potato in thin slices and salted and peppered it a bit, and fried it in the bacon grease. When it was done and browned, he dropped three eggs in. So he had his big tin plate full of good food. By the time he'd eaten that and washed it down with four cups of coffee he was in a good mood. He cleaned up and packed and saddled up. He left the snares in case he could get back in about a month. He'd catch these predators before they ate his calves.

John rode out about ten o'clock, going west to where the Pope's came in when they came from Bear Lake. He turned north and rode a few miles and then climbed up the ridge to the east, northeast. John knew this land was claimed by the Middlesex Cattle Co., an English outfit. They hated the Bassett's because they pushed cattle into Brown's Park trying to establish rights there, and Ann drove them into Colorado—what she didn't shoot, or drive into the river to be washed down Lodore Canyon and drowned. Ann didn't just drift them a way, but followed them one hundred miles or so. John thought as a landowner, his sympathies were with Ann.

John saw a huge flock of chickens that afternoon. The whole ridge was covered with chickens for a half a mile as they started walking to get out of his way. It looked like the hill was moving. It made John dizzy, like water moving or something. John picked out a young one and shot its head off. He took time to throw insides out, and then put it in the pack to be enjoyed later.

He stopped on a high place and looked the country over. What a sight! The river could be seen in several places coming down from the north. The high Uinta Mountains were covered with timber and a bit of snow to the west, Diamond Mountain to his southwest. If he followed this ridge far enough north, he'd be at the Green River. John had thought often of the outlaws who had come in from the west to help the ones who stole his cows. They had ridden down off of this very ridge, fifteen or twenty miles ahead, and way further east. He wished now he had back tracked them to see if they had a base of operations up here somewhere.

John loved to ride the country and do as he was doing now. "Forget hauling prisoners, arresting drunks, and arbitrating fights over water, or having a horse shot out from under you." This was recreation to Pope. So he camped on the first water he came to, settled in camp and enjoyed the sage hen for supper. Next day he rode further north, and then swung west. He'd passed a lot of cattle for several days.

He suddenly came to fresh horse tracks. Someone had come in from the east and rode down this draw that very morning, so Pope turned to follow. About a mile, he came on the top of another hollow. Below him, about one hundred and fifty yards away, three men were going to brand a critter; they had ropes on, head and heels. Another fellow was off his horse, encircled with a bit of smoke coming from a fire. He didn't have it started long enough to be hot yet. Pope rode down on them. When he was about seventy-five yards away, someone saw him and spread the word. The roper on Pope's side turned to look. The man by the fire stood up and came toward him a few steps. Pope rode to within twenty yards.

The fire man said, "That's close enough. You can't come in here now."

"Ill clear out alright but, please tell me why you would be branding that big cow? She's surely not a maverick." Pope threw his left leg over the horn, kicked the right foot free and dropped to the ground in front of them.

The fire man said, "You must want to die. I'm gonna shoot your ears off if you don't git!"

John advanced a few more careful steps. Fire man went for his gun. Pope beat him so far that he should have quit, but he kept it coming, so John killed him. By then both ropers had pulled pistols. John shot the close roper. The other shot, but his horse was fussing, and he shot the crown off John's hat. Before he got the second shot off, he was done. The cow went helling out of there, dragging the lariat on her horns. She had kicked the other rope off the hind legs. Pope now had a sickening feeling. What had happened here?

He saw the Two Bar brand on the cow as she ran away. These men were altering a few brands. The Two Bar was a really big outfit. By altering a few, if a man was a good artist, when roundup time came, these fellows' ranches would be running a few more, and the Two Bar a few less.

John said, "I'm sorry men. I hope you were all single and ready to meet our maker. If you would have stopped when I had you beat, we might have had a friendly discussion and departed friends."

John hated to go up and look at them. He hadn't recognized any of them. Of course, he was probably one hundred miles from home. John walked up and went through pockets. The three men had over a grand on them. Honest ranchers just didn't have that kind of money! There was a wash about fifty yards ahead, and those men were buried there. John took horses, guns, saddles, and ropes. He left the brand in the fire. The horses were tied to the tail of his pack horse, and then another tied to his. John had a nice string of horses.

He headed down and crossed the river at the crossing they had used when they came in from Bear Lake. He spent the night, rode over the mountain the next day to Vernal, arriving after dark. Next morning he told his Charlotte that he thought they should go visit her folks.

"I need a vacation. If we go, would it be alright to take my folks as well?"

Charlotte started to cry, and could scarcely control herself. Two days later, before somebody needed the sheriff again, Robert and Sarah, and John, Charlotte, and little family drove out of Vernal in a covered wagon.

Chapter Sixteen

Timeout

SARAH LEDUC AND CHARLOTTE got to see Myton and the Strip. It was a lawless, savage place and wild as they had thought it to be.

"If I was Lot's wife, I'd never glance backwards at such an ill reputed place!" Sarah declared.

Robert chuckled and rubbed his whiskers. "No, Babylon would not appeal to you, Mother, and Sodom and Gomorrah be damned!"

"It *was* nasty," Charlotte agreed. She was still pale from the sight of the painted ladies, all shamelessly advertising their wares, calling boldly to drunkards and fools. "My word, don't they have dishes to wash and butter to churn? Who has the time to act like that?"

They drove west to Price. John took the new road over the mountain to Price, rather than Nine Mile Canyon. "Isn't this the wrong way to Bear Lake?" Sarah asked.

"Depends," John teased. It took four days on this trip to Price. John found hotel rooms for everyone. He bought round trip train tickets to Montpelier, Idaho.

The young Pope children cheered for the adventure of a train ride! The railroad agreed to haul the team and wagon as well, which was a common practice for railroads in those days. The Pope's ate plenty of cheese, jerky, bread and jam. It was a novelty to have a place for a bathroom break inside the train. The kids loved it, often dreaming up reasons why they had to go again. The women thought they could get used to it really easy, as well.

Both Sarah and Charlotte were afraid of such speed. When the train reached Spanish Fork, Robert and Sarah were all eyes! They were trying to see something the same as it was when they came west. Back then, Mormons were at war with the United States, and the Saints, in compliance with Brigham Young's Scorched Earth Policy, left Salt Lake and came south where they stayed a short time.

John T. had been born in American fork, so all eyes were watching out the windows as they traveled north through Springville, Provo, Orem, and American Fork. "There are so many orchards and hay stack crops!" Robert's neck craned to see. The cities were scattered with so much good irrigated crop land, fenced fields, and milk cows. It looked like the Garden of Eden.

As they went along, Sarah LeDuc pointed things out to John's kids and told stories about the pioneer trials, here in the *olden days*. J.W. and Lottie May were old enough to appreciate the stories of their grandparents, and to see for themselves how things had changed. Charles and Frank pretended their hands were pistols, and they shot things out the windows, randomly taking imaginary aim.

There was a fifteen minute stop in Salt Lake, fifteen minutes in Ogden, five minutes in Brigham City, five minutes in Tremonton, and a few water stops and side track stops for passing trains. It was a way dark night again so seats were laid back a bit, and kids went to sleep mostly thinking the train was even more fun than the hotel. The adults dozed along as much as possible. They had to wake up to change trains in McCammon, Idaho.

The stock car and flat car with Pope's team and wagon were cut off the train they had been on, then they were added a new train in about thirty minutes, and the family was chugging along up the grade past Lava, on up the Portneuf River, past Bancroft, Chesterfield, and through Soda Springs. They had a water stop at Soda, then down grade along the Bear River into Montpelier.

J.W. and Lottie May were extremely excited to be so close to "home," for they had cousins, and grandparents, and relatives, all living "back home." Charles Theodore, Franklin Arthur, Francis Lavina, Hazel Sarah, and baby Hattie Marie didn't know the difference.

"Golly, I thought we wuz just home," Francis whispered to Frank.

It took about thirty minutes to get the team and wagon unloaded off the train and another fifteen for John to harness and hook up. John drove to the depot, and everyone came out and got in. It was chilly this early.

"Montpelier has grown at least three or four times in size since the railroad came to town!" Robert cried. They left Montpelier on a trot west. "Oh what an improvement! A good new bridge across the Bear River." They stopped the other side of Ovid. There was good grass here, and water. They unbridled the team and led them to water, grained them and left them eating while they built a fire and fried bacon, eggs, and potatoes. The kids needed to be fed. They were beginning to think they would never get there. They put the team in a livery barn in Paris that night. They took two rooms in the hotel and ate supper and breakfast at the café in Paris. They drove out of Paris in good time. They went though Bloomington. South Bloomington Creek was bridged. Worm Creek had a good bridge. St. Charles Creek was bridged, along with both forks.

Little Hazel asked, "Dad, why is everything so green around here?" The family got a good chuckle out of her sweet innocence.

What memories came flooding back! Popes had been among the first to build a house here! As they came to people on the road, Robert inquired about old friends. Some were still here, in fact most of the families were here. John T. had trapped the mouth of St. Charles Creek and took loads of fur out of here years back. "I've brought in my share of beaver and muskrat from that creek, kids." The Pope's were anxious to get to Fish Haven to Charlotte's folks again, so they drove on through St. Charles to Fish Haven.

John and Charlotte stopped a few minutes in front of their old home and farm. Charlotte wiped a tear or two.

"Yep, I remember playing on the steps right there," Lottie said.

Then they stopped in front of the new chapel. 1885 was on the front of the building. They had left in 1884 for the Basin. Now John's eyes were full of tears! He could remember the terrific rush to get it built. All the cement he freighted and the mixer! The huge pile of logs, hauled to the lot, the dump box to haul gravel, the saw mill, and the steam engine. John's life was a puzzle to himself. He hoped the difference he made wherever he went was positive, because he sure as hell made one.

When they pulled up in front of the Stock's home, Charlotte ran up the steps and into the house. John heard squealing and a bit of a commotion. He dismounted and had the kids all out when the door flew back open and Charlotte's mother came out to see her grandkids, some of them for the first time in this life. The smaller kids were hanging back behind John, hanging on his legs.

John said, "This is your grandma. Come give her a hug."

As the kids stepped forward, John noticed how much they'd grown—how tall J.W. was, and what a beautiful young woman Lottie May was becoming. The last couple of years had done amazing things to the oldest two. John vowed to somehow spend more time with all of them.

He was glad he had brought them back. John needed a break from his quest to catch Butch, Harry Longabaugh, aka the Sundance Kid, and Elza Lay. There were thousands of outlaws down there, but those were the brains of the organization. Once they were gone, the battle would be mostly won. Still a mop-up action and fight, the war would never be as hard after that battle was won.

The family was standing outside, getting acquainted again for about fifteen minutes. When Charlotte's dad came home, he had about twelve trout, from three to fifteen pounds, probably averaging ten pounds apiece. Fish were cleaned, and supper was ready to be cooked. Mr. Stock still did commercial fishing on the lake and did well.

Pope's brought out the Dutch oven and fry pan as well as the big camp coffee pot to help with cooking. A fire was put together outside. The coffee pot and Dutch oven went in right away, about a pound of lard went into the Dutch oven where it melted and got hot. They said it was ready. They brought a dish pan full of trout they had filleted. The bones out, it was cut in pieces about the size of Charlotte's hand. It was rolled in salt, pepper, and corn meal, and about half was put in the oven at once. Potatoes and scones came from the stove inside the house. The porch was the right height for a seat. So after Robert said a prayer on the food, everyone started filling plates. The team was in a little pasture west of the house so the wagon tongue made a seat for several, as well as chairs that had been carried out. It was a great feast and reunion.

John noticed Charlotte's father watching him, eyes scrutinizing. "Have you killed any bad men, lately?"

"That's the only kind I do kill." The answer was blunt, but John would trade subtle answers to subtle questions. He knew Charlotte's parents were wishful that he was a common, ordinary fellow. But John thought, "If they only knew."

Robert and Sarah took a bed in the wagon that night. The kids stayed in the tent. John and Charlotte took the extra bed in the house. John didn't think Charlotte would ever come to bed, she and her mother stayed up and chattered like canaries 'til way late.

The next morning after breakfast, John harnessed up and hooked up again and trotted out to Garden City. Charlotte and the kids stayed behind to be with her mom and dad for awhile. John hoped he wouldn't lose it again like he had while looking at the chapel. When they got to Garden City, it was really good to see his brother Rob, and his wife Polly. Oh my, he had a well behaved and a good family! Celia, Edith, Burt, and Royal Robert, called Rile or Riley, they were a great bunch. "If you folks aren't too tired of camping out, then we'd like to join you," Rob said. "It's been a while since we've been anywhere."

Rob and Polly's family squealed with excitement, eager for an adventure, too, and wanting time alone with their grandparents and famous Uncle John, the brave sheriff. They ran around, finding neighbors to do their chores, Riley hooked a team to a wagon, saddled horses, and loaded shotguns while Celia and Edith packed pots and pans and food.

The family camped out that night on the lake, north of Laketown, and visited and told stories around the campfire 'til quite late.

John noticed his nephew Riley kept sidling closer to him as they joked around the fire. "Did you really turn that judge's nose?"

The question caught John a bit by surprise, but of course Sarah had been corresponding to Rob's family. "I did!"

"Tell us," Riley begged, so John told the story, surprised by the rapt attention his nephews and nieces paid to him.

The next morning they drove through Laketown, stopped at the Irwin store and got everything they could possibly use. The drive up the new Laketown Canyon road was steep and twisty, and so narrow in some places it would put a wheel in the creek then they went up left hand fork and over the top, going on down to water. By the time they got there, they had plenty of sage hens to last for supper and breakfast. So camp was made, fire started, horses watered and grained and staked on grass. So for three days, they lay around and visited, and ate the food Pope's had lived on for a long time—sage hens.

"Uncle John, tell us about your ranch on Red Creek," Riley coaxed. "Tell us about your horses and stock." John wished it might have been possible for Charlotte and his own kids to be with them *and* in Fish

Haven at the same time. J.W. would have gotten a kick out of Riley. For Riley's rapt attention and interest, John told stories.

Pope's loved to camp out, and picnic and shoot, cook in Dutch ovens, and tell stories. The youngsters were riding all over the hills and racing. Rob's family was horsemen. They traded horses with Indians, and other ranchers, so they seemed to collect some with bad habits. They were always trying to break horses of hanging back, corral balkiness, or running away, rearing or bucking, kicking, not standing while a rider mounted, not leading well. So they devised all kinds of tricks to break horses of these bad habits.

Things they tried out sometimes worked and some not, but as they were camping, stories of these trials and errors were told, resulting in a lot of laughter and fun. Mules had been the most stubborn.

Riley shared a story. "The harder I tried to break a bucking mule, the harder it bucked! Pope's are like mules. We won't give up, so I *could* stay on, but each new thing I tried found the mule learning to buck harder. He seemed to be learning the fastest." Riley paused, letting his family laugh. John grinned, for his nephew would be a charactered storyteller, and he had the wit and timing for it!

"We try all kinds of tricks while working with horses," Riley went on. "Sometimes we tie one foot up. Sometimes horses repent, but when they hang to their bad habits, they are soon bucking in someone else's remuda, and then we trade for a different headache to figure out."

It was so refreshing for John to listen to stories and laugh, to be with family and remember. Many stories were related by Robert and Sarah of the Vernal area—of outlaws, Matt Warner and Bill Wall's incarceration, and John delivering them to prison, of shootouts and arrests of outlaws by John T. All these things were new to the Bear Lake Pope's, and young Rile was riveted by them all. John T. only told about things already talked about by his folks. He was quiet about ninety-nine percent of the experiences he had had. However, he told of mining, and Indians, and potential of the Ashley Valley area. He told more of his Red Creek Ranch and how he thought it was an ideal set up for a small operator who wanted to be private and not mixed with neighbors. He grazed summer and winter. He didn't have to put up much hay. This was as foreign to a Bear Laker as a different country could have been.

Bear Lake, with long winters and snow, the folks had to put up at least two tons of hay for each cow, with extra for horses, sheep, and even pigs and chickens needed a bit of hay. A Bear Laker spent the summer stacking hay and the winter pitching it out to the livestock.

Rob teased his brother. "A man's muscles would get puny with no hay to pitch! How many cows are you running?"

"Seventy-five head," John said. It was a small operation, but it was larger than most Bear Lake places.

Bear Lake had some good ranches and some big ranches, but all were expensive to operate because of labor to do so much work. Time passed so pleasantly, and time to break camp and go back to work rolled around too fast. At daybreak, down came the big tent, everything was stored in the wagons, except kids on horseback, teams and harnesses. So Pope's rolled back up Six Mile Canyon, down Left Hand, and then Laketown Canyon. They got back to Garden City late afternoon. Everyone helped with chores, had supper, and stayed up late telling stories.

It was decided that the Popes should get together at least every two years, and to keep in touch through the mail. They all loved the outdoors, having spent all of their lives pioneering. A tradition was started.

The Pope family acquired three of the big old longhorn cheeses to take back to Vernal with them. They picked up John T.'s family in Fish Haven, and journeyed north to camp on Bloomington Creek. Hazel kept waving most of the way, somehow believing her grandpa and grandma were still watching.

Late the next afternoon, they boarded a train to take them back to Price. It was a vacation from danger and continuous, monotonous watch care which seemed to have worn the sheriff to a fine tune. John wondered if the strain of having a reward to twenty-five hundred to four thousand dollars on his head made him more trigger happy. Could he have not been so bloody under other circumstances? John T. Pope was glad he kept quiet about most of the killing he had done. His reputation was already way too big. As they arrived in Price, while waiting for the wagon outfit to be unloaded, John walked uptown to talk to several friends to see about outlaw activity anywhere.

Organized outlaws were a menace. John knew now that to control this bunch, the leader of this army of outlaws would have to be arrested, or killed, or run off. It was easier thought about than done, but he'd have to find him somehow. Once Butch was out of the way, the price on his head would be gone because who was to pay? Nobody had heard or seen neither hide nor hair of him for awhile. So he went back, asked if they would like to spend the night in a hotel since it was getting late already.

John went to the hotel, got rooms for everyone. They ate in a café. That was a really big splurge for the family.

"We're rich now," Francis whispered to Hazel. Lottie May overheard and flashed a radiant smile at her father.

John T. got tired of waiting during trials in Provo, in delivering prisoners, and feeding them. He was proud to have those he loved the most in the whole world to share with him here, though. He watched his kids marvel at everything so new to them. He ordered pie ala mode for the bunch. They had a good night, had a good breakfast before rolling out. He took them home through Nine Mile Canyon. The kids were all trying to be the first to see the Indian art on the rocks. Nearly everyone was the first to spot a picture or two before long because the canyon was so long and picturesque.

"I just don't know how long our ride would be if this was called Ten Mile Canyon," J.W. quipped, bringing laughter to the bunch.

Three days passed before they were home and back to the old jobs. The horses were showing the trip by the time they got to Vernal, having traveled thirty miles a day. John got only one night at home before the judge showed up with another warrant.

Chapter Seventeen

Hot on the Trail

John saddled up and rode toward Brown's Hole. He was always alert to ambush and made his own way away from traveled roads or trails. He camped on the mountain that night, waking to a light drizzle and fog. He crossed the river on the ferry and rode on to Red Creek. Boy, the cattle were fat. Calves had really grown. He had about seven or eight small slicks. It would be a lot easier if they were branded before they were stolen. If it wasn't raining in the morning, he'd take time to brand the slicks before they got too big to handle. So after breakfast, he went out and saddled up. It looked like it would be all right. He hauled wood for about an hour first, still no rain, so he opened the field, went up and around his cattle. They were a little slow to get in, but he finally got them. He caught the first calf after dinner because by the time the fire was hot, quite a lot of time elapsed. It was three o'clock by the time his cattle were driven back to grass. John rode down to Jarvie's Store. He could tell by tracks, other people had been there earlier that day. He hollered and stepped up, knocked on the door and stepped in just as John Jarvie was reaching to open the door.

"Howdy."

"Well Sheriff Pope, what can I do for ya?"

"Have you got a hot cup and maybe something to eat?"

"Will beef stew do?" Jarvie waited for a head nod. "Wonderful! Sit up to the table there."

Jarvie carried silverware and plates to the table, then went back for cups and a coffee pot. So Pope found himself being waited on. After eating a couple of pieces of sliced bread and butter, a couple of bowls of beef stew, and about four cups of coffee, Jarvie said, "You can eat all a man can cook, can't you Sheriff?"

"I was too lazy to cook breakfast this morning. Too hungry. By the tracks, I'm not the first customers you've had today."

"No—Butch Cassidy, Harry Longabaugh, and another older man stopped by awhile this morning."

"Yeah? Say, where were they headed?"

"I kinda figured maybe Bassett's. They were in no hurry."

"Thanks for the meal, what do I owe you?"

"Twenty-Five cents. You probably ate fifty cents worth, but twenty-five cents will do 'er."

Pope flipped a quarter in Jarvie's direction, thanking him again. He stepped on the horse, turned and followed the tracks out of the yard. John got down and studied the tracks, then got in a hurry following them. After about five miles, they crossed the river, so John crossed as well. It was getting dusk, but he followed along as far as he could see. He got off his horse, knelt down, and holding the reins in one hand, and his hat in the other, he offered a heartfelt prayer, thanking his Father for the vacation, for his health and life, for Red Creek, the work done, for his family. He explained that he was trying to catch Butch to bring peace to this part of the country. He thought he'd killed way too many all ready. He would try to capture him. He asked for help also to protect him in this job. He asked for guidance. At the conclusion of the prayer, he put the hat back on and stood thinking for a while.

He was pretty sure they had gone to Basset's, but they might have been heading up to one of his hideouts. Well, if he went on to Basset's and got the drop in the morning that would be lucky. If he went there and Butch wasn't there, he could track him on tomorrow. He didn't think anyone suspected him to be out here, therefore, they wouldn't be ready for him. So John mounted up and rode on toward the ranch. About three-quarters of a mile from the ranch, John dismounted, unsaddled, took the bridle, and replaced it with a leather halter, using his lariat as a tether rope. He led his horse to the river to drink, then came back and staked him in a cottonwood grove where he could graze on grass. He got two pair of handcuffs from the saddlebags. He had thoroughly cased this ranch with a telescope, as well as buying a horse here once, so he knew the lay of the ranch. John decided to approach from above, down over the little knoll immediately above, to the west of the ranch.

It was really dark, so John found a stick to use to check where to put his feet as well as a shepherd's staff. He made his approach in a circuitous route, leading up hill; it would take him around the pasture and garden, north of the buildings.

He moved slow and quiet as possible. Ranch dogs were barking at some pest. Coyotes were noisy as well. The dogs worried John because if they heard or smelled him, he wouldn't be able to get close enough to surprise them in the morning. Not a window with any light showing. It was so black, that after getting on the knoll, he wasn't sure he was where he thought. So he began working down closer. About ten minutes later, he heard a door slam, straight in front of him. He stood and listened for a few moments. Somebody was going to the back house, maybe?

His thought had been to hide in the barn, and when Butch and Sundance came for their horses he could handcuff them and try to get away without being shot by Ann. She would be dangerous. Now something was warning him. *Don't go in the barn.* Wonder if somebody might be bunked in there? It was more complicated than slipping up on a camp. He'd done that successfully a few times. John T. knew in his heart that Butch and Sundance would show fight rather than submit to handcuffs. So why not just shoot with a rifle from ambush as they rode away in the morning? John thought he couldn't live with himself after doing something like that. His soul was pained enough over men he had killed before, all either in self defense or because they chose to fight rather than submit. "So, let's keep it that way."

He was tired standing there so he started moving forward again. He felt with the staff, then step up a step, then again. He reached the staff out, no rock or brush so he stepped forward carefully with the left foot as it came down, it went right into a badger hole. He was able to get it up and take a long step to avoid the hole, but being out of balance he had to take three quick steps. His spurs jangled a bit and chaps scuffled through sage brush. That instant, a blinding flash and a gun went off, not more than thirty feet in front of him. He felt the wind of the bullet pass his face.

Three more shots rang out so fast after the first that it was almost a continuous roll of shots. The last three were from his colt, one at the flash, one right and one left. Now Pope was kneeling, watching—staring at total darkness, listening. He began to feel the rage coming again. He would have put a lookout on the knoll himself. He should have come from below!

"Bart! Bart, what's wrong?"

It sounded like Butch hollering. Then Pope heard them talking amongst themselves. Sundance said, "I was just leaning against the fence out here. I think one shot was Bart's. Three more fired from someone else, or several somebody's. He was fanning it, or maybe it was too fast for one."

"Posse, do you think?"

"I don't know, but maybe, I guess. Saddle up."

Ann said, "Damn it to hell, I'm coming with you!"

John could hear them in the barn, but couldn't tell what was said. In about a minute, he heard them riding out south. They would be circling back west. He had tracking to do tomorrow. In the meantime, he had to stay alive. Had he hit Bart? Was Bart waiting for him to make some more noise so he could shoot again? Or was he through? Whatever, he was quiet.

John checked his colt again. He had reloaded after shooting which was his habit, but in the excitement, he forgot. He began hitching forward a bit, very quietly. He wanted to be out of here before they started shooting with rifles from the ranch. After about thirty minutes of careful hard work, John reached a hand out to get a good hold of something to hitch up a bit more and felt a spur sticking up. Bart was belly down in scrubby brush. John came to his feet, colt in hand, stepped forward and reached down, checking his heart beat at his throat. None! He grabbed an arm and dragged him out of the brush. He put his colt back and went through pockets. There was sixty dollars, but John went on and found he carried a money belt. It was well packed, so he dropped it over his head and one arm. He pulled his belt and scabbard from the colt out, and then spent about ten minutes on hands and knees until he found the colt. He placed it in its scabbard; put this gun belt round his neck as he had done with the money belt.

He left Bart for the ranch to bury and started back to his horse. He couldn't find his staff in the dark, so he went on, not being so concerned about being quiet now. The dogs were having a field day with barking, but that's as far as their bravery went. John carefully walked back to his horse. He started a fire and got some coffee started. He pulled a can of peaches out of a saddlebag, opened them with his knife, and ate them with the knife as well, except the juice, that he drank from the can. He led the horse to water again and saddled up after some coffee.

He rode back across the same trail as before. He wanted to get past the ranch before daylight. He barely made it. He rode on, watching for tracks as he could see close now that daylight had come. Pope came to track again. Only one and it was Ann Bassets' mount, so Bart had been the older man who came in with Butch and Sundance. John T.'s mind was working on the way things were working. He came to Brown Hole, hoping to get a lead on Butch Cassidy as well as check on his ranch and cattle. He was able to finish branding.

Jarvie had been really closed mouthed about things except Butch's crew heading to Bassett's. John T.'s mind was warning him something wasn't right, but what? What was happening he didn't know about? He had followed the tracks west about a mile, then back north and down a natural pass into the canyon where he had been ambushed by a sheep man.

John pulled the telescope and tied his horse. For about an hour he had studied the lay of the land. As he lay in the shade with the telescope, his mind went back over things. Meeting with Butch's bunch was almost miraculous. Jarvie probably would be guarded in anything said to a sheriff. To have a guard out in the dark, and another outside listening at the same time was most unusual in the least. Why were these men so jumpy?

What John didn't know was Tom Horn had been to work here.

If John had been here at the right time, and trusted by these folks, he would have tracked Tom Horn down and brought him to trial himself, or killed him, but as it happened, both John T. and Butch had arrived to the aftermath of several of Horn's bloody executions. Butch heard the story from Jarvie, as well as Ann and her family. Ann was in shock and mourning. Matt Rash rode up to his summer cabin on Cold Spring Mountain where he was found dead with a bullet through the back. This murder stunned the entire area. Ann was the most grief stricken to lose her recent fiancé. Matt had been taking her to parties and dances in Craig Colorado, as well as the Hole.

Followed closely by Matt's murder was that of Isom Dart's murder at his cabin. This murder was heart breaking for Ann as well because he had looked out for her since she was a baby. Isom Dart's real name was Ned Huddleston. Isom was a black man and a former slave. He joined the Tip Gault Gang in 1875, soon after arriving in the Hole. Later Isom got acquainted with the Basset's and soon moved to the Basset Ranch, cutting firewood, carrying water, cooking, and tending to the five small children whom he loved dearly. Isom was an expert horse trainer, and trained the getaway horses for the Wild Bunch. Both of these senseless, bloody killings were like family members of Ann's, and both men were shot in the back from ambush. Ann didn't know, nor anyone else, who had committed these cowardly attacks. Pope was mentioned as maybe, but Butch said it didn't fit Pope's profile. All his victims were shot from the front with a gun in their hands.

So Tom Horn had been hired by A. C. Beckwith for the Wyoming Livestock Growers, to assassinate rustlers, and was paid five hundred a piece for this bloody work by Beckwith himself, from his bank in Evanston, Wyoming. All this was unbeknownst to anyone in this area, John T. Pope being in the dark the furthest.

John T. wanted Butch. Butch was the uncontested leader of the outlaws. So John wanted to follow right across the canyon. He could see the tracks all the way. On the other hand, something was making them extra careful. They wanted John at least as bad as he wanted them. They were masters of ambush.

John had a scar across his chest, especially his breastbone. He had a scar on his throat. He had another scar in the calf of his leg, had one saddle ruined, and two horses shot out from under him. With that kind of record, he guessed as bad as he wanted them, he would go up the canyon in the dark, and then he would cut their tracks on the other side. He suspected they would stop on the rim in a hideout they had someplace up there. John had spent one day once before fooling around without finding it. But as long as John stayed around when they decided to move, John would find them. He had complete confidence in his ability to find them and bring justice.

So he laid in the shade and studied every hiding place for signs of their presence. He hadn't had any sleep and the warm weather finally made him drowsy enough that he dropped off and slept soundly for a couple of hours. He awoke with a start. He looked at the sun. It was behind a cloud, but showed through enough it must be noon or so. He looked all around himself, backed away from the edge of the canyon so he could look back down his back trail. It was a rocky, steep area. No way over south of the canyon, north of the canyon was rocky and open from the rim for at least a mile. It was easy to see why they built a hideout up there. They could host a standoff of all the Ute Indians on the whole reservation from the rim.

After watching for a time, John decided to unsaddle and stake his horse on grass for awhile, so he led his horse to the only clump of trees, unsaddled, and staked on some grass, turned to walk back to watch when he almost touched a big old porcupine. He wondered what the sound of a gunshot would do to those he was pursuing. Or was he the one being hunted now?

John pulled his pistol and shot this old porky's head. He took time to borrow long saddle strings and fastened to the porky's legs, drug him out, and hung him up and field dressed him in about five minutes. He'd never skinned a porcupine, so he dug the wire pinchers out of his saddle bags and took hold of the skin with them, then pulling it out, he was able, with his sharp pocket knife, to separate him from his hide, head, feet, and tail.

While the porcupine hung, cooling in the wind, John took his glass back down and watched awhile. Not seeing anything, he came back to the pile of dead trees, gathered a big armful of dry sticks, and piled them against the cliff wall below his observation spot. Now he built a fire of dry twigs and pieces. He built it up good, and then carried some rocks, leaning them up against the wall, making reflector walls on both sides. He cut a couple of green sticks as big as a husky Indian lance, skewered the porcupine on both, carried them over, and put them across the reflector walls he built, letting the porky dangle almost in the fire. He continued to gather dry wood and keep the fire going. When the fat was frying out and dripping in the coals, the fire would flare and dance. His porky was salted and turned on the sticks several times. Before dark, the meat was browned and was very juicy and good. It was a bit greasy, but when a man is hungry, a porcupine is an animal you can kill with a club, if necessary, and it can save your life.

Of course, John T. had coffee, and he lay around watching while he ate all he could hold. Then, he looked through his stuff, finding one extra pair of clean socks. He spent about twenty minutes cutting all the meat off the bones and packing two sox sacks full of well cooked, salted meat, and packed one in each saddle bag. He didn't have room, so he took out the money belt. He had worn one a quite a bit years ago. He tried it, and by making another hole, it would take up to fit. Before he put it on, he went through it. Wow! There was thirty three hundred dollars, all in one hundred dollar bills. Probably Bart's share of a job he had helped Butch with.

Where had they been? They had been gone quite a while. Mine payroll? A bank? Not a train, John knew, Butch had sworn off train robberies. Assuming they each got an equal cut and there were only three of them, ten thousand dollars was a pretty big heist, however, Bart may have money here from several robberies, and Butch probably had more than the three men helping in the caper. It would be interesting to know how much money Butch had stolen in the last ten years.

Pope couldn't begin to guess. If a man like Butch would have put his mind and energy to building, or following good pursuits instead of tearing down, and stealing, and intimidating, he could have accomplished about anything he had tried in life.

As John put the saddle string back in place, and the blankets, then threw the heavy saddle up, he said, "I'm sorry Dobbin, I'll water you later. There's a spring I know of on the other side about eight miles from here. We can water there."

It was starting to get dark. Pope watched closely with the glass, one last sweep before starting on. Oops! What was that? Pope swung back a bit and sure enough, in the last of the light, he could see a man struggling up the steep trail across the canyon carrying a rifle. A little too much hurry now would have cost him his life!

John pulled off his hat, bowed his head, and thanked his maker for his life. Then he swung up and started down the trail into the canyon while he could see the trail close up. As he descended, full dark came, especially in the depths of the canyon. John let his horse take his head. He kept it down, almost sliding in places to the bottom, and then turned up the canyon toward home.

Pope let the horse pick the way at his own speed. Several hours later, Dobbin stopped and put his head down, so John stuck a match and sure enough, the spring.

John dismounted once again. He slipped off the bridle which was simply put on over the halter. He loosened the cinches and unsaddled while his horse filled on water. He soon had the horse tethered on grass. He pulled off his boots, loosened his belts, wrapped in the ground sheet, covered with a saddle blanket and used the saddle as a pillow. In a few minutes he was sound asleep.

He awoke with a chill. It was really cold up here on top of the mountain. Morning was beginning to light the sky. John decided it was too cold without a fire, so he unrolled, shook out his boots and pulled them on. He adjusted his money belt, then pulled pants up, tucked his shirt in and buttoned up. He pulled the slicker off the back of his saddle. He could use anything to keep body heat. But as he carried wood from a dead pole a few yards away, he worked up some heat. He started a fire, filled his coffee pot with water, dropped a handful of coffee in, and put the pot in the fire. Several more trips and he gathered enough wood. He fished a sack of salty porcupine and skewered a piece with a stick, propped it above the flame. It was already cooked, but it would taste better hot on a cold morning.

When John had a good breakfast with his coffee, the sun was burning through the fog. He packed back up again, and rode a little north of east, back toward the rim where John suspected Butch's hideout to be.

When within about a mile of the rim, in a thick stand of timber, Douglas fir here—a great stand of saw logs, John smiled as he thought of his old saw mill and steam engine for stationary power. Man what an investment that had been! He stood as if in a trance for a minute with this smile as he remembered loads of lumber, sawed day after day. Those were the golden days of his life.

He staked his horse and pulled the rifle from the saddle. His 44-40 had the stock blown off, so he adopted the 45-90. It was full, nine shells in all. He had also swapped his pistol, which was getting a little loose after all these years, for a colt 45. He had traded 44-40 shells in his belt for colt 45 shells making it tight again. This 45 fit his holster perfectly, but it had been worked on by an expert gunsmith. It was new, yet so smooth and quiet. If anything, John was even faster with it. The 45-90 was much heavier and good for long range shooting.

A lot of people thought it was too much gun, but Pope liked it the more he used it. With 500 grain shells, it would have worked well on elephants. But John loaded with 350 grain, hard lead. Flat nosed bullets shot quite flat for the caliber, and at the time of black powder, he had shot quite a bit at a thousand yards. Pope knew as he used and practiced, he would be able to hit quite accurately at a lot of ranges. Marcellus had a Sharps 45-110. It was very good for long range shooting. John knew in his heart he wouldn't shoot any of this bunch in an ambush, only in a fair gunfight, if it came. Butch and Sundance both carried 45-90's.

John was nearing the rim. Careful now. There were several up-thrusts of rock along the rim and John theorized that they would have someone watching from up there. They would be able to see along on his side in places too, so cautious and careful, slow moving from here on. Trust Butch to pick a spot where he could duck and run away from with perfect cover, as well as see and defend easily.

Pope came up through the trees as close as he could get, still using trees as cover, then using the telescope, he glassed the up-thrusts of rock for awhile. He watched the rim and could detect no smoke, nothing. Finally, getting on hands and knees, he crawled to the rim. From here, he could see forever, the river and the Bassett's ranch, cliffs, and mountains. John was the most blessed and luckiest person in the entire world to be able to lay up here and enjoy the beautiful scenery. Clouds cast shadows on the mountains across the river and kept the colors and scenes changing. John thought if he could paint this, it wouldn't seem real. No picture could paint or capture the size and grandeur! He knew some of the mountains. Those he was looking at were at least one hundred miles away. A long ways away a whistle sounded which seemed to be louder and louder. John looked back in time to see a pine hen fly up from a bush as a huge Golden Eagle plowed in where it had been. The chicken flew up into a pine tree with ruffled feathers, watching down as the eagle stood up and walked out of the bush and flew lazily along the rim to the south.

John marveled at how far he must have dived to hear the wind whistling so long and loud, just to miss the quarry by inches. He was thinking of this as he watched the eagle swoop up to land on the farthest up-thrust of cliff along the rim, but before it landed it suddenly veered off, flapping hard to get some height and distance from something up there which scared it. He watched the eagle fly back west until it was out of sight behind the trees on this huge old mountain.

John was talking to himself. "I'll bet a nickel that was a lookout for Butch, or Butch himself. If it was Butch, he wouldn't be happy to be betrayed by that big old golden eagle which could be seen by anyone watching for miles. It could have been a lion, or a lynx cat that scared it, but not likely. Now . . . what to do?"

John just didn't want to try to brace them in their hideout because the chance of getting in there unseen was really almost zero. If Butch thought his hideout was compromised now however, he would probably leave. Then John could follow until his chance came. He was nearly sure Butch knew he was out here watching. So after another thirty minutes of watching, he crawled back to timber, and then walked back to his horse which took a little while to find in the heavy timber. He got his tracks finally and soon picked up his horse.

John rode back to the spring where he watered his horse, filled his canteens, tried to cover his tracks some, then rode out a mile or so, and found a good grassy spot and camped. If Butch did break camp and come this way, he didn't want him catching John asleep by the spring, so the move made sense.

He started a fire and made a final meal of salty porcupine, which he was fast growing tired of. Next morning, he broke camp and rode at daylight back up toward the rim, then rode south toward the canyon, staying just out of sight of the rim in case they were still up watching. When John came to the trail out of the canyon, bingo! Tracks. John got down and studied them. He couldn't tell if they were made last night or this morning. He walked along the trail going west into the timber looking thoughtfully ahead. He mounted again and rode north of the trail for awhile, then came carefully back and crossed it, rode south a short distance. When he was quite close to the spring, he tied his horse and approached carefully on the chance they might be camped here, but they had watered there and gone on. Tracks were probably made this morning. So John went carefully ahead, but soon left the trail, riding north of it a ways. He rode fast for a couple of hours hoping maybe to get ahead. When he started back he was surprised to cut their tracks so soon. They were north of the trail as well, and all still ahead.

He wouldn't have been surprised if someone had been waiting on the trail to ambush him, but they were still together, but were they swinging north to bypass Vernal, maybe, or what?

By late afternoon, they were getting off the mountain. It was cedars now and dust betrayed a person's travel unless they were careful and slow. Pope saw a bit of dust a few times, several miles ahead. He began watching his back trail more now as well. Things were different in the desert. Finally, before dark, John made another swing north and picked up their tracks. They were still going west southwest toward Myton? The Strip? Nine Mile? Pope suspected a change after dark. They would spend the night with some friends while he made a dry camp.

He had no doubt he would catch them someplace though. So he began to look for grass for his horse tonight. He picked a secluded spot to camp, made a fire and made coffee, getting low. He chewed a handful of parched corn and a piece of jerky with the coffee. Next morning he dug his next to last can of peaches out. It was good to the last drop. He threw the can at a badger hole, drew his pistol in practice, but didn't fire.

John rode west then began to swing north when he cut a track headed straight for Vernal—one horse. John got down and followed afoot for nearly a hundred yards before he got a good track to study. It was Butch or Sundance, probably Butch. Harry and Ann were pretty close lovers. They would be together someplace. Maybe this was his chance to get Butch Cassidy. He began following.

As he topped a slight knoll, he stopped to look around when he spotted a little dust puff on his trail that could have been a bit of wind or something. Then he saw it again. Now while he followed one, the other was following him. So John dismounted and tied his horse. He walked back to a huge old cedar. He stepped up close to it, watching his back trail. Oops, he forgot to bring his handcuffs. They would probably fight anyway. So he stood his ground. About fifteen minutes, he could see a horse coming through the cedar. His rider carried a rifle in hand and was concentrating on the tracks. As he came around the last cedar into the clearing, Pope swore and stepped out.

"Tonagets, dam you!" yelled Pope.

The Indian looked surprised, then tried to bring his rifle into position to shoot only to see the blinding spot of Pope's fast draw and knew he couldn't win. Instead, he opened his mount and let out a blood curdling war cry, while kicking his mount in the flanks. John could have killed him, and thought he probably should have, but this Ute went away from there, laying over the withers of his horse, going over and under with the rifle and screeching and yelling.

Tonagets! Pope ran for his horse. He couldn't let this pup go now. He'd have a mess with the whole tribe! *Damn it!* He'd have to come back for Butch later. As he followed Tonagets along on a lope, he thought back of the trouble he'd had with him before.

Several years earlier Tonagets got some firewater with a hunting party, up Dry Fork. He got too drunk. He killed a settler's horse. Pope eventually got the paper to serve on him. They had come back off the mountain and camped not far from Vernal when John T. and a deputy rode up. John looked around until he spotted Tonagets. Pope knew him even before as a savage, wild man. So he told the deputy, "Things might get a little wild, so be ready to shoot. If they see you are ready and believe you'll shoot, they will stay in line. Okay?"

So Pope watched his chance and as Tonagets walked to the outside of the group, Pope grabbed him, carried him a step, then slammed him down hard on his back, landing in his belly with a knee. It took his wind so bad Tonagets passed out long enough for Pope to secure the handcuffs. He looked up to see another buck pull a gun. Pope drew his pistol fast and hollered loudly to back off, which they did. His deputy had a sickly look on his face. He later told John he just completely misjudged and didn't do as he was told.

Pope said, "All's well that ends well. I'll bring Rock or Marcellus or Dick next time."

Pope began to talk to the chiefs and told them Tonagets would get a long stay in the jail unless the horse he killed was replaced by as good of one, or a better one. He said they were fair and good men. All he wanted was for fair treatment for everyone. So two ponies, one of them Tonagets' own mount were brought up. Pope took the handcuffs off of Tonagets. He grunted a bit, then as he rubbed his wrists, he looked at Pope and said, "Me kill'um you some day."

As Pope thought of this, he said out loud, "You sullen, sulky, wild son-of-a-bitch." Tonagets now galloped all the way into the agency at White Rock.

Pope slowed to a walk and came into the agency a little behind Tonagets. The sulky Ute had a gallon crock of whisky in his hands and was yelling, "There's the paleface dog that sell me fire water!"

Sheriff Pope looked at Agent Waugh in an amused, quiet voice, "You don't believe that do you?"

"I really don't know," Waugh replied.

"Well, I'll kill the red snake for you."

He made a lightening draw and pointed the pistol. Tonagets dropped the crock, threw both hands up and yelled, "No, No, you no sell'um me firewater."

Pope's pistol went off, smashing the crock into pieces. Tonagets jumped about three feet in the air. Indians were ducking for cover in every direction. Tonagets continued to yell, "You no sell'um me firewater!"

Waugh tried to retreat to his quarters, hooked his heels on the stoop and sat down. His eyes were open all the way.

Pope said, "Over the last six years, I've been out here to bring peace and justice for the Indians, doing *your* job for you at least fifty times or more! You're no good. If I have to come again, I'll be after you, not the Indians. If they were rid of you, they might get a good agent. If not, he couldn't be worse."

Pope pulled his horse around and rode away. He saw one of the chiefs watching with a smile on his face. Pope's anger was soon gone; thinking of the smile on the old chief's face was like a tonic because very seldom did you see them smile. These Utes were usually stoic, and about all anyone heard from them was a grunt. So a mad was replaced with good humor. Pope found himself laughing out loud as he thought of Tonagets, both hands high, yelling as loud as he could, "You no sell'um me firewater!"

Pope then laughed outright as he thought of Indian Agent Waugh. Pope had no idea if he was Chinese or what, but when his life was endangered, his eyes were just as round as anyone's. "Why does our government always manage to hire these idiots?" Pope wondered. "I bet he's not even a citizen of the United States, and he's set up out here with the power of a dictator over the oldest citizens of the United States. It's an outrage, really."

Again Pope laughed and he thought he had just resigned from a responsibility which had cost him a lot of time. He had been able to help bring justice to everyone and safety for white men by his treatment and understanding of the Indians.

Pope asked, "Why am I going so slow?"

He stopped laughing at himself this time because his thoughts had diverted his attention to the things happening around him. He picked up his horse's foot. He'd lost a shoe and his hoof had chipped deep in a couple of places while chasing the Indian. John looked toward Vernal and guessed it to be at least ten miles, and at least that far to where he left Butch's tracks. There were a couple of hours of daylight left so he stepped back on and let his mount shuffle along the dusty road toward Vernal. He wasn't limping much, but he was being extra careful where he put the foot down. Pope let him take his head and time.

John watched a dust coming from the south. When he got closer, it turned into a big load of wood pulled by a pair of big gray percherons. The man pulled into the road a few hundred yards behind John but had soon caught up. John got over so he could pass.

"Hello Sheriff. You don't seem in such a hurry today."

"No. My horse threw a shoe, and I didn't want to lame him. I've been on the road for nearly three weeks, so he's wearing down."

"Where's your big pacer you used to ride?"

"He died."

"Oh, well everybody has to do it I guess."

"I wish I had him back."

"Hell, I'll sell you one that looks a lot like him only bigger."

"What is he?" Pope asked.

"He's part Percheron, out of a work mare of my neighbor's, but she only weighed about eleven hundred and fifty pounds, maybe twelve hundred. She was a good old mare. This colt didn't match anything he had, and he was scared of him, so he brought him over to me to break him and try to sell. He's about four years old. He probably weighs fourteen hundred, but he's tall. He looks like a saddle horse, but he's got good bones."

"How much?"

"He wanted fifty."

"Good broke horses don't bring more than that."

"Okay, but I've worked him a little. I can ride him with the harness on."

Pope reached in his pocket and drew out two twenty dollar gold pieces. He scrounged until he got a full fifty, and then said, "If I pay you, will you bring him to the jail in town, in the morning by eight o'clock? I'll be there."

It got full dark before John unsaddled and fed his horse at home. He knocked on his front door and waited until the door opened a bit suddenly. Kids started to yell, and John was nearly swarmed under. Squeals and laughter! Girls all naturally know how to squeal. So he sat on a chair inside the kitchen and listened to each one and gave attention and hugs for each kid, then stood up to embrace Charlotte Ann. In a few minutes, she started getting supper for him. Since everyone else had already eaten, John ate a good home cooked meal, the first for many days. He topped it off with a piece of German chocolate cake; a specialty of Charlotte's when she had plenty of cream and eggs.

Next morning it was really hard to get the mattress off his back, but he did chores, milked the cows. Over a bucket of milk, he thought "No wonder I like chocolate cake."

He left right after breakfast and led ol' Dobbin to the blacksmith shop, then walked to the jail to find his bronc-busting brother doing deputy chores. He was hoping he would be. He told Rock about buying the horse. "If you'll top him for me, and he acts alright, I'll take him. If not, I'll pay you to break him for me, and I'll take a different one."

The horse was delivered and Rock put his saddle on him. The only bridle that would let out to fit was Old Shorty's, so it was put over the halter. He mounted by stepping up on John's knee then going on up into the saddle.

The colt seemed gentle enough, but he wasn't shod. He didn't know straight up, so Pope saddled Rock's horse at his suggestion, and rode him. Rock begged to go along, for the day at least, so they rode out together, Rock riding Shorty the Second.

"He's a Shorty, all right. He's got the longest legs on a horse I've ever seen. He's got foot round bone, no hair on the front of his foot, quit a lot on his fetlocks. I'll bet he'll need a bigger shoe than a number three, and they will probably do for a year or so. Some of these horses grow 'til they are seven or eight years old, so you never know. Clydesdales and Shirer have a lot of hair all around their feet, but they have flat bone in their legs, pretty big and adequate, but flat. Percherons and Belgians have round bone, but the Percherons make the best saddle horses. It's always Percherons that girls do tricks on in circus shows, and they seem to have a little more action and finesse than Belgians who make bulling pulling horses. They'll crowd and bull, but pull, oh my hell, those Belgians can pull."

John was thinking Rock talked a lot, but the conversation was pleasant, and he enjoyed hearing how much knowledge his brother had about horses.

When they came to the track, they turned on it and started following it across Steinaker Draw to an older ranch a few miles east of Vernal.

"Who are we after today?"

John T. said quietly, "Butch Cassidy." He then put a finger across his lips and up to his nose to signal quiet.

Rock looked stunned. They rode up to the corral on the track. John tied his horse to the gate and walked up to the house and knocked. It was quiet so he knocked again.

The door opened about six inches and an older woman said, "What do you want?"

"I've been to this ranch a few times when I was greeted and treated well. I was inclined to believe you were very hospitable until today. What's wrong?"

"You've come at a bad time. I can't talk today."

"Well, it's a ways from town. I don't come out this way very often. Besides I'm on the tracks of Butch Cassidy. I've followed him a long ways, right to your corral. Is he the reason you can't talk?"

After a long hesitation, she said, "Yes."

He said, "Have him step out here. I have a paper to serve on him for robbery of the Montpelier bank. Can he hear me, ma'am?" John asked.

"No."

"Do you know it is against the law to harbor or help a criminal, ma'am?"

"No."

"Will you open the door so I can look for myself?"

"Oh please don't," she wailed.

"Why not?"

"Because I'm so ashamed! I've treated you so bad. Butch left when he saw you ride in. I was supposed to delay you a minute. I guess I did that."

"You did. His horse is still in the corral. How did he go?"

"He's kept a few horses here for years. He traded horses and was saddled ready to go out by the orchard. He expected you last night."

Pope was walking back to his horse. He said, "I've got more to do than just chase him all over hell."

So he mounted and they rode around the orchard. Sure enough, he found where Butch's horse had been tied. So Pope once again got down and checked the tracks carefully, memorizing differences. He could recognize it wherever he went. They tracked him to Vernal, but he left the road and went around the north side of town, then turned and rode right up the road through Vernal.

John knew most trackers would give up trying to follow a track through a town where numerous horses were traveling every direction. He wasn't most trackers. Besides, Butch's horse was the last horse up the road. So John and Rock rode slowly forward. Rock looked like a former knight, riding a jousting horse which had to be big to carry all the armor.

To an outlaw, they must have looked like hell on horseback.

Pope watched the track, Rock watched everything else. He followed right to a hitch post in front of a bar. So John dismounted. He guessed Butch had given up running and was going to have it out right here. He braced himself, stepped up, and pushed the swinging doors open and stepped in. It took a minute to get his eyes adjusted to the semi darkness. A card game was going at a table in the back. Two men set at a table with a bottle between them. They stared at Pope. A young woman, quite pretty with a little too much paint, and a hard look about her, stood at the bar. The bartender was polishing glasses behind the bar. But no Butch Cassidy.

Pope looked at the girl and said, "Did someone go out that back door in the last five or ten minutes?"

"Are you Sheriff Pope?"

"Yes."

"Why concern yourself about the back door? I'd like to spend a bunch of time with you."

John stepped almost across to the door and turned to the bartender, "Did Butch just leave by this door?"

"Yes, but let him go. One of you will be killed."

"Yes, unless he gives up and comes to jail peaceably."

He pushed the back door open and came out slow, watching for a shot at anytime. Nothing. John stepped out and knelt down, studying his track. He slowly followed it to the back of the store about fifty yards from where he came from the bar. He had mounted another horse that had been left for him, probably by the friend at the ranch. They tracked him from this morning. That's why Butch had circled and come in from the west to give the old rancher time to leave his horse for him. They planned this all the time, but Pope wasn't supposed to get his track again, but he had it.

So John walked through the store and hollered at Rock who was still watching the other horse. He untied John's horse without dismounting and led it up to the store. John said, "He's out of here on a different horse so we'll have to follow. "Do you like licorice?"

"Yes."

"I'll be right back."

John stepped in and bought two pounds of coffee, at least a pound of jerky, a couple of chunks of chocolate, four cans of peaches, a can of salt, and a handful of licorice. He had the store keeper put it in two cotton sacks. He also got two boxes of .45 long colt shells. He saw a big winter overcoat hanging on a nail by the door. He looked at it and asked how much.

"Six dollars fifty."

Pope bought it because it was getting cold nights. Better than a good blanket.

When Rock saw all the stuff, he said, "Maybe we better get another pack horse."

John said, "Let's see if we can carry it like this. If we can, it'll be easier or quicker starting anyway."

So they divided up the lot and filled their saddle bags. Rock took the two sacks and tied them on top of the saddlebags,

"Can you roll this big coat and tie it across the cantle of your saddle? Make bucking swells for ya."

So Pope and Pope rode out of Vernal on Butch Cassidy's tracks. That night they camped on the White River, heading east. Butch had really been standing in the stirrups. John and Rock staked horses on grass and lay awake for awhile drinking coffee and visiting.

The Next morning while packing up, Rock suggested he take his horse back since Shorty Two hadn't acted up. So John put all his stuff on his new giant horse. Rock mounted his and watched to see what John would do. He put reins around his neck, and holding them with a handful of mane in his left hand, he reached way high to grab the horn, sprang in the air, got his foot in the stirrup and swung on, making it look easy. When his foot went in the stirrup, Shorty Two started to walk, so he finished mounting on the go.

Rock said, "How do you jump so high?"

"I think I use my arms to pull me some. I don't know. I practiced a long time on tall horses. I've always been short. I've learned to make do."

Butch's tracks turned south a bit over the hill from the river to a cabin on a spring by an aspen grove. Rock said, "That's a pretty sight."

John was watching and didn't answer. John reached down and drew out the telescope. Through the scope, Pope could see tracks leading east up the draw from the house. So trying to stay out of range of the cabin, they rode east and south to cut the track, which were now three tracks. John rode along as fast as he could urge Shorty Two to walk. Rock's horse had a good walk but when John was urging a little, old Shorty Two had such long legs, he could walk a bit faster without looking like he was trying at all. He naturally held his head too high, but after observing all day, John decided it was natural for him. He never stumbled. His hooves were black and hard. He had never been shod, so John hoped he'd be all right 'til he could shoe him.

Rock said, "I wonder who Butch is traveling with?"

"Sundance and Queen Ann Bassett."

Rock whistled. "Oh just small chumps."

John smiled, "Yeah," and then he chuckled, for these *chumps* were a downright notorious trio.

"I heard Queen Ann Bassett uses an alias occasionally."

"Oh?"

"Etta Place."

"Etta Place? That's right damn interesting."

"Well there have been a few circulars show up wherein Butch and Sundance have been spotted with a petite, lovely woman. You claim to have seen her ride out with them. Now who do you figure that woman is?

"Given her history with the men, and her ability to clean up, I'd say Ann Bassett is enjoying her charade."

"Maybe she likes being a girl," Rock said.

They were deep in Colorado. John had no authority here except as a citizen. It got dark on them and they got a good place with water, grass, and wood. They built a fire, unpacked, watered the horses, made coffee and ate jerky and a piece of chocolate, apiece.

"What about Butch now?"

"Let him go, I guess. I hope he just keeps riding. He's not welcome in my area any longer, and I'll never quit chasing him if he comes back. I believe he's figured that out."

Rock was disappointed, since they'd been so close. "It's too bad."

"Just let them keep riding. That's as good as anything."

Next day they rode into Rifle, Colorado. John saw a blacksmith shop. They rode on to the edge of town. Tracks from Butch's bunch turned into a livery barn where they traded for fresh horses and rode off again. The hostler told John they got in the night before and then rode on after dark. So John T. rode back to the blacksmith shop and hired the smithy to shoe Shorty Two. While he shod the horse, they walked to an eating house pointed out by the smithy. They had T-bone beef steak, and apple pie.

Rock asked, "How can we ride? I'm gonna bust. I'll swear I swelled up after I was done eating."

John got a laugh out of Rock trying to stick his belly out to show how full he was. His belt buckle stuck out further because he had very little stomach.

They strolled back to their horses. John paid the smithy, asking, "How was he to shoe?"

"He was gentle enough, but he wanted to lay on me too much."

"What size shoes did he take?"

Size twos on the front. I made the back shoes. They are a bit smaller."

"They sure look good on there! Thanks."

So they rode for home going back toward Brown's Hole. It was a nice ride. They camped that night, not too far out of the Hole. The next morning they rode to Red Creek and checked the cattle. They were doing well.

They rode back to Jarvie's before heading home.

John Jarvie finally told John of the murders of Matt Rash and Isom Dart. Both were shot in the back. No wonder Butch and his comrades were so jumpy. John told what he had done. "I wish you would have told me before. Maybe I could have tracked the skunk Tom Horn down myself."

Pope's crossed the river and rode over the mountain in the dark. They arrived in Vernal just before daylight, so they unpacked and fed the horses.

John said, "Come over to the café with me. We'll drink a hot cup or two and see what else looks good."

Rock asked John while they were eating breakfast, "How many times have you crossed that mountain in the dark?"

"I don't remember, but I used to always travel at night or go a different way each time so none could collect the bounty on me. I don't know how far Butch will go before he stops, but if people find out he's gone, then nobody can pay the bounty. I won't have to sneak around anymore. He may come back, but things are changing and I'll get him next time."

Several days later a letter came to Sheriff Pope, addressed to Vernal, Utah.

It said, *"Lay off Pope. I don't want to kill you. Butch"*

It was posted in Alma, New Mexico.

Sheriff Pope smiled. "Run Butch, just you run."

Chapter Eighteen

Lost Holiday

Law had truly arrived in this corner of the world. John arrived at home to stay for a few days after the marathon chasing of Butch. John knew outlaws would continue to come here for refuge from the law, but word would eventually spread around that you came at your own peril; you kept a low profile, and stayed clean in Ashley Valley.

John T. Pope was satisfied that Butch would find new stomping grounds. He felt a happy, euphoric feeling about the outcome because he hadn't had to kill but one man. He would always wonder about Butch and crew, and always perused the circulars, scouting for information on Butch, Sundance, and the lovely Etta Place. "School teacher my eye!" John said to Dick one day. "Queen of the rustlers is more like it."

"Queen of the outlaws now, and I wager she likes being a girl."

Winter was coming. The Uintas looked white. It was cold in the Basin. It was one of those kinds of winters. It was a time most men stayed out of the weather as much as possible. But the county had paper to serve on outlaws.

The first was for John Hill and Billy Roberts. These were known bad men so were watched closely. They just couldn't stay straight. Pope got the warrants for them with crazy instructions. The county treasure was empty—too many lawsuits and prisoners to house and try had sapped the county's money set aside for this legal department. Pope was told if they were slipping out, to just let them go to save the expense of trials and everything. If they were here, he was to arrest them and bring them to jail.

With this crazy instruction, Pope would have just ignored it for awhile, but the next warrant was for J. Gilford. Gilford had run up lots of bills and was leaving the country. A lot of irate, unpaid people were being left behind. Pope was glad Shorty Two had had a few days rest and grain, because the only way John could catch J. Gilford was to catch the stage which Gilford had taken to Price—the only road not closed.

Pope wore long johns, cap, mittens, the sheep skin coat, a bandana around his ears, and the wide beaver hat pulled low. His tall horse started down the road, reaching out with a long stride. John was warm. His pistol was outside his coat as always.

He traveled to the Strip. He had missed the stage change of horses here, but stepped into the bar to see if he could get something to eat. As his eyes adjusted to the light he saw that Joe Hill and bad Billy Roberts were standing at the bar. They turned, facing Sheriff Pope. John stepped up and asked if the bartender would make a sandwich that he could take with him. He then bought a round of drinks for all inside. Joe and Billy seemed plenty willing to drink.

"Good hell, it is raining outlaws," John thought. Pope didn't have time to fool with Joe and Billy now if he could catch the stage. Taking the sandwich, after paying for the drinks and food, he mounted and went out as fast as he could. He was hoping to overtake the stage at Wells, the last stop for a man and fresh horses before the final leg to Price.

Sheriff Pope came up on the stop. He could see the stage had fresh horses being hooked up to it. Pope stepped off his horse and went into the hall where men were standing around having already finished their meal. John spotted Gilford, walked up and handed him the warrant, and then waited for him to read it.

Gilford turned to John T. "You got me. I didn't think anybody would come after me in a cold storm."

Pope replied, "I didn't want to."

"Let's go, then."

"My horse gets grain, water, and an hour's rest. Also, I'll have to round up an outfit for you, so sit down and don't go anywhere. Have you got warm clothes enough?"

"I've got a heavy overcoat."

"You'll need mittens and a cap. How are your feet?"

"I have wool socks and new boots. They are part of the bill I owe."

"I'll be back with what you need."

John turned and went to the man running the stage stop to get a horse, saddle, mittens and cap for his prisoner. He felt annoyed that he had to be responsible for such things, for babysitting dishonest people, but he had to transport Gilford somehow, and he couldn't have his prisoner's flesh freezing. John borrowed these items for a bit of rent money, five dollars. He would send them back on the next stage.

He then went out and led Shorty Two to the stable, unbridled him and gave him a drink, then about two gallon of oats, and loosened the cinch. The stable hand started saddling a horse for the prisoner. Pope visited the outhouse for daily chores, and then he went into the hall for a couple of cups of coffee and a donut. The boss came in with mittens and cap with ear flaps which could be tied above the head or let down and tied if the wind was bad.

By ten o'clock the next morning they reached the Duchesne Bridge on the Duchesne River. Here they watered and grained the horses. John Gilford was almost sitting on the stove trying to get rid of the cold while Pope was getting horses tended and ready to go again.

John also was watching a couple of riders coming down the road. He looked with his telescope for a minute and recognized Joe Hill and Billy Roberts. So Pope walked over to the bridge and waited for these self-confessed gunmen and outlaws to come around the bend onto the bridge. He stepped out, holding his colt in his hand and he said loudly, "Put your hands up and quick."

The surprise and shock of Sheriff Pope's sudden appearance with a drawn pistol unnerved these desperadoes and their hands automatically reached up.

"Now Hill, throw your gun over here."

He did.

"Roberts, now you throw yours over."

Very reluctantly, he complied.

Sheriff then threw a pair of handcuffs to each man, saying, "Lock these on your wrists. No monkey business."

After they did this, Pope had them hold up their hands and demonstrate that they were tight enough.

"Now Hill, reach down and slide your rifle carefully out and hand it to me stock first." Pope took the rifle cautiously, stepped back looking at it. "Roberts, now you throw yours over." Pope took the rifle, looking at it with an appreciative glance. He put his pistol back in the holster and picked up these prisoners' pistols off the bridge. He turned and walked back to his horse. He put the pistols in his saddle bags. He worked on Roberts' horse's tail a minute, bobbing it up short, and tied his reins to the tail of Roberts' horse. He then bobbed up the tail of Gilford's horse and tied Roberts' mount to it. Next, he unloaded the rifles, putting all the shells in his saddle bags and gave the rifles back to carry in their scabbards.

Pope looked around, "Ready to go?" He couldn't think of anything he'd forgotten. John hollered at Gilford, "Let's go. We're all waiting."

Roberts said, "You're a tough bugger today aint ya Pope?"

"I guess so."

"Yesterday at the Strip when we were ready, you weren't so tough then, huh?"

No answer.

"So why didn't you take us yesterday?"

Pope said, "Lead out Gilford, and knock on it as much as you can. Maybe we'll get back in daylight."

They started with Pope on the back to watch everything.

"Big tough Pope! I don't think you wanted to try us when we had an even break. Did you Pope?"

No answer for a minute. But before Roberts started again, John T. said louder than his usual way, "Billy, I'll say this one time, so dig the wax out. It might save your life. Yesterday at the bar you had some fighting whiskey in your veins. So I'd have killed you both. That was what the county wanted me to do to save the expense of a trial and jail. But I didn't want your killing on my conscience. I've already saved the county many thousands this way. Yesterday I had to catch the stage at Wells to get Gilford. I was in a hurry. I knew where you were so I figured to get you today. Now, if you keep that noise going, I'm gonna stop, give you your gun, and save the county their money. You hear? Billy, you hear that?"

"Yes."

"Okay then, you shut up!"

It was quiet except for squeaky saddles and groans from prisoners not as tough in the cold as they would like people to think they naturally were.

The procession rode into Vernal about sundown. As they passed Mona's Donut Shop, the attorney was just coming out. He watched the prisoners ride by and said, "You got all three rascals! I'm surprised you got them already, Sheriff."

"I'll bet you are. I've ridden more than one hundred and fifty miles since I left here yesterday morning! I've had no sleep. It's cold. Those fellows have tried my patience. If you want to help, step back in there and ask Mona to fix supper for this bunch, and I'll be back to get it and pay her. I'll talk later." He rode on, noting the man turned back inside Mona's.

John was really glad to see Dick at the jail. He took the prisoners to their cells and helped tend horses. They already had several prisoners in the jail. John told Dick he thought Mona would have supper for them, but coffee would be appreciated because they were all cold. John walked to Mona's while Dick took care of things at the jail. When John entered the café, Mona had a big slab of prime rib dished up with mashed potatoes and gravy and coffee. John cleaned up every bite, along with a roll and butter, then the third cup with apple pie.

Mona put six dinners in the basket, and covered them with the dish towel. When John paid, he had a couple of dollars change coming. He said, "You keep it with my thanks for helping out."

Mona was stunned because if you ever got a tip those days, it was a nickel. Mostly nobody tipped.

After chuck at the jail, John laid down on the cot for a little rest, but because he could tell how tired he was, he said, "You better come take care in the morning, Dick, because I've been about forty hours without sleep and I've rode over a hundred fifty miles. I'll never wake unless someone comes and stirs around here a bit."

It was eleven o'clock before John woke up the next day.

Dick said, "I stirred and rattled dishes, hauled ashes, chopped wood. I thought you were going to sleep all day."

"Well nature and all the coffee I drank got me up." John went outside for about ten minutes. When he came back, he got close to the stove. "Someday I'll invent an outhouse with heat."

Before John walked home that day, he poured Shorty Two about two gallon of oats, curried him, and talked to him, then went home.

Charlotte and the kids were glad he was home. He told the kids about his long ride in the cold, about catching the stage at Wells and taking John Gilford prisoner, and then catching Joe Hill and Billy Roberts. J.W. and Charles especially liked hearing the stories, and asked for lots of details, like, "What kind of pistols did they carry?" and things like that. J.W. always wanted to know about their horses, and if they could keep up to whatever his dad was riding. The kids just knew their dad was the best sheriff in the world.

Joe Hill and Billy Roberts were later tried, convicted, and sentenced from one to twenty years in the state pen for grand larceny. They served a couple of years and were paroled. The next Sheriff Pope heard of them, they had killed Sheriff Tyler and his deputy, Jenkins, in the southern part of Utah, and were running ahead of the posse. "Oh boy," Pope thought, "I could have saved the county the expense of the trial, and it would have saved at least two lives. If I see them, I'll remember to take care of it now."

Pope slept well and until ten the next day. He wrestled with his boys and teased the girls. He stayed in and made a nuisance of himself 'til Charlotte was glad when he walked up to grain his horse and check on things at the jail.

Ah-oh. The attorney and whiny neighbor, Hal Carroll were hurrying up to the jail with a warrant in hand. John grained Shorty Two while waiting for them. They came huffing up and handed Pope the warrant for Zeb Edwards. Sheriff asked, "You know where he lives?"

"No."

Pope pointed at the Uinta Mountains to the north. He lives on the other side of the Uintas, up Burnt Fork."

"Hal Carroll has a bill that has to be collected now!" responded the attorney.

The bill was for thirty dollars and John Pope nearly choked. Carroll had received a letter from Edwards saying, *"Find enclosed $30 which I owe you."* Carroll said there was no money in the letter and made a complaint to that effect, claiming Edwards was guilty of using the mail to defraud. The warrant was issued against Edwards to that effect and was given to Sheriff Pope to serve.

The Sheriff said, "Edwards probably discovered he had failed to put the money in and if you'll wait a minute, it will come. Also, it's a dangerous journey over the mountain this time of year, unless you go on snowshoes. Snow will be from six to twenty feet deep up there. It is ten thousand feet at the highest point. How can you justify that trip for thirty dollars? What if I pay the thirty dollars myself, and then collect from Edwards when I see him next summer?"

Carroll was adamant in his demands. He not only wanted his money but to apprehend the crook as he called him. "Remember, Sheriff, you're a sworn officer of the law and the public's servant. So, it's *your* duty to serve the warrant even if it is dangerous or painful. Now I *demand* you execute your duty!"

"Hell, you're a little weasel! You aint a patch to the man you accuse of being a crook! You don't want justice or you would take the money! You expect everyone is as crooked as you are. Now I give you a promised fact, if I hurt my horse or Zeb Edwards while bringing him back, I'll take it out of your hide. I'd suggest you find a new locality to settle in."

"Is that a threat?" Carroll turned to his petty-flogging lawyer. "I want you to remember Pope threatened me."

The attorney said, "Maybe you should take the money, Hal."

"No, absolutely not."

John T. said, "You can call it a threat if you want. It's a true promised fact, and I suggest you start hunting a better local because you just showed me your size—snakes are a step up from you, Hal, and I step on every little snake I see."

Turning to the attorney John said, "I'll keep an itemized bill for the expense of bringing Zeb back, which I am sure the county will be glad to pay. Also, when its proven Zeb is innocent, the county will be expected to buy a railroad ticket from Price to Carter for Zeb and his mount, otherwise he will be hopelessly locked on the wrong side of the mountain 'til spring."

"Wait a minute. The county is broke. I can't speak for them."

"Oh, but you can, and will, because you approve every legal expense paid by Uintah County. I know you want justice for all, so before I leave for Zeb Edwards, you will write a statement to that effect. Also, if me and Zeb get stuck up there and die or are caught in an avalanche or something, our families are to be taken care of by the county for a reasonable time, or be subject to wrongful death suits. You seem to agree with Carroll so fast, you write it on the pad and sign it! Someday maybe we'll get someone with a little common sense and enough guts to stand for truth and forget this *idiocy*!" John T. was wound up and did get his pad written on a bit before the men sneaked out of the jail and left.

John sat down and looked at what was written. *"Sheriff John T. Pope is entitled to be reimbursed for expenses incurred in bringing Zeb Edwards to trial. Also, the county will be responsible for the care of their families if they should be killed crossing the Uinta Mountains. Signed, County Attorney."*

After reading the pad, John smiled. He felt better having this note written and signed by the attorney. He'd been mad as hell, and would spend a thousand dollars to collect thirty, which he would have paid himself. This was complete lunacy. Now he started thinking of the trip. Should he leave now and try to cross the top in the dark? The valley and south side 'til you got high was mostly bare. Pope decided that by leaving by three in the morning, it would put him in the deeper snow by daylight, so to be ready, he filled two cotton sacks each one-half full of oats for the horse. He pulled the rifle and scabbard off the saddle. He walked down to Mona's to get a last big meal before he left. She packed a couple of sandwiches for him while he ate a rack of lamb ribs and drank a bunch of her coffee.

When he walked out carrying his lunch and supper for prisoners, he met Dick.

"I read the pad in the jail. What's up?" So Dick walked back with him to the jail while John explained. Then John asked if Dick would keep the pad. John told Dick he had no idea how much snow was up there. He said a cloud had hung up there ever since it got cold.

"That old mountain seems to make its own weather, so if it's too deep, I'll come back down to Price and ride the train which will really please the County Commissioners—three tickets, from Price to Carter and back, then back to Carter."

Dick laughed. "How did you get the attorney to sign this pad?"

"I was mad."

Dick got a bigger laugh. He laughed 'til tears were streaming down his face. He'd seen John mad before. Nobody stood in his way when he was angry. Dick continued laughing. He thought everybody who ever faced Pope when he was mad wondered if he would pull the gun and shoot them.

Two in the morning found Pope dressing by the light of a coal oil lantern in the jail. He pulled on a new pair of wool socks, pulling the tops up over the long johns, and then his garter around his calves held the socks. A wool shirt was tucked in a pair of overalls. Folding the pant legs back on his calves, the sixteen inch mule eared boots went on over top, leaving pants tucked neatly in the boots. He tied a bandana around his neck and another over his ears. His big beaver hat and the sheepskin coat were put on last.

Dick had led Shorty Two down to water while John was getting gussied up. When he got back, John had poured about two gallons of oats for him. While the horse ate, they saddled up and loaded the other sack on the back of the saddle.

Dick said, "Hell, John, that's too much grain. You might founder him."

"If it was barley, yes, but oats just gives him more energy, and that's what he needs anyway. He's a big horse. He needs a lot."

"Yes, he's getting bigger all the time with you graining him so much."

"I bought and paid for the oats, so I'll feed my horse as damn much as I please!"

"Okay. I was just joking." Dick peered sideways at his brother. His own good nature was less prone to temper, but he appreciated John's sand. "I hope nobody gives you any lip today."

John laughed. "Why?"

"Your humor aint the best and you're just as apt to shoot as not."

"That's because I'm being sent on a wild goose chase of complete nonsense. Damned idiots."

Dick watched John bridle and mount up. He looked little on Shorty Two, but Dick knew nobody teased John T. Pope about his horse. As John rode away, Dick hurried back inside to the fire. As he stood near the stove, warming up a bit, he said a prayer for John. Dick knew John would take care of himself, but he was the only man in Vernal who would have tried this, and the only man who might pull it off.

The next morning at first light John was high in the Uinta Mountains. Snow was up to Shorty Two's belly. They were getting close to the pass on the divide. John got off and pulled a sack down and backed Shorty Two back a few steps and poured grain in a track. He pulled the bit out of Shorty Two's mouth so he could eat. While he ate grain, John slipped a bare hand in a coat pocket for one the Mona's sandwiches. So far old Shorty Two hadn't sweated a hair or even puffed. He didn't lunge in drifts, just walked through them like they weren't there.

Pope was standing in snow eating Mona's sandwich, wondering. Snow was about to his waist on the level. The huge Pines were heavy with snow. Once in a while some would fall. John remembered horses, soft from not enough use; they would give out half way up the bare side. Now he thought maybe he'd make it over. So after a twenty minute break, he was back on top and riding northeast through the pines and snow. It was snowing a bit and wind was moaning in the trees. Snow was nearly gone where the wind could get at it on the divide, ten thousand feet up.

As he started off the top, he waded into deep snow. Shorty Two held his head high anyway, but his head and John was about all that stuck up out of the drift. Shorty Two continued to wallow through until he went about fifty yards or so, and then he was in thick pine, and the snow was about like the other side. So he continued his relentless march through trees and snow. Snow was deep, but it was a gradual down grade now for ten miles or so. John got to the Edwards' place about three o'clock in the afternoon. Zeb was glad to see Pope, so John unsaddled in the barn. He fed Shorty Two and watered him.

John handed Zeb the warrant. He read it and got red in the face. "I remember writing out the check right in the post office in Mt. View! In fact, I usually write on the stub, so I might have proof I made out the check."

Zeb looked in a drawer and found his checkbook. He opened it and found the check written out, but not torn out of the checkbook. He had written on the stub. It was signed and dated and everything, but not torn off.

"Hell," Zeb said, "I was visiting with the post mistress. I'm getting old I guess. Now what do we do?"

"Do you have a big, strong, work horse that's been working and full of grain?"

"Yes."

"Can you ride him?"

"Yes."

"Then we can probably make it back over the mountain if it doesn't storm. Can you leave or do you have stock to tend?"

"My stock, except for my team, is being fed down in town by a neighbor I bought hay from."

"Do you have enough warm clothes for the trip, if even we get stuck for a while?"

"Yes."

John paid Zeb ten dollars for feed, food, and lodging. They had supper, went to bed for a few hours, got the horses ready, as well as fed and watered. Zeb left one half of his team with access to the haystack. You could see very little, but John started Shorty Two back on the trail he made going in. He gave him his head and let him pick his way. The further they went, the harder the snow fell. After a couple of hours, the wind was moaning really loud, snow was falling out of the trees, and being blown around. Another hour and the storm was an all out blizzard. Pope had faith in Zeb's ability to survive in the mountains. He had lived up here for twenty years.

So when Zeb yelled at him, it kind of spooked Pope to hear Zeb say, "I'm lost. I hope you know where you're going, 'cuz I can't tell nothin.' I can build a shelter if you want to stop."

"This storm might last a week. We better move if we can, so we don't get stuck up here."

"The only way I can go is in your tracks, so go ahead."

So Shorty Two moved along like a V Blade, with Zeb's horse following one or two steps behind. When they came out on the top of the divide, the wind had cleaned the top of its snow for fifty yards or so. Pope knew it was downhill from here. He knew Shorty Two was on the road home, so he just sat back and let things happen.

It never got really light in the big storm all day. Finally at dusk, it quit snowing. There was a little gusty wind, but horses were tired. Pope knew the Davis Ranch lay right ahead, so they rode there. The Davis Family was surprised to see folks out in the weather, but glad for the company. The Davis boys tended the horses, watered, fed, and grained them, then blanketed them for the night. John insisted they take ten bucks for everything, supper, breakfast, and a good visit. Pope knew in his heart these were hard working pioneer families. They were the best kind of people in the world.

Zeb told the Davis Family that John guided him over that mountain in a blinding blizzard. He explained that he couldn't have done anything except make a shelter and wait it out.

My horse just walked back on our trail going in." John really knew he couldn't tell where he was until they crossed the divide. Also, he didn't mention the prayers he'd said. They left the Davis Ranch the next morning and arrived in Vernal about four hours later.

They stayed in the jail that night, after having a good meal at Mona's. After breakfast next morning, a hearing was held. The case was thrown out of court for lack of just cause, and Edwards was released.

Pope and Edwards rode out early the next morning for Price, where they arrived the second day. John bought Zeb a ticket to Carter for him and his horse. It cost Uintah County at least sixty dollars to recover the thirty dollars for Hal Carroll.

Before Pope left Price, he went to the newspaper office and said he wanted an article printed in the paper. A correspondent came with a pad and listened to John tell what had happened. After he wrote it, Pope read it and made corrections. Names were named and blame put where it should be, especially concerning Hal Carroll. Pope said anyone doing business with Carroll should pay in cash and be sure to get and keep a receipt. The paper would be out the next day. Pope paid for fifteen copies. The newspaper office promised to ship the papers on the stage to Mona's. Pope felt good. He knew Carroll would be finished in Vernal after people read the article.

John was riding east into Nine Mile Canyon when he noticed a horse ahead, and it looked like somebody was down.

"Oh boy, I hope he's alive." Pope thought, "No telling what might happen out here." Pope and Zeb had been blessed to get through without more trouble, and Pope hated to see anyone in a bad way.

As John Pope rode up, he noted the brand on a superb, tall, thoroughbred gelding. It was not a local brand Pope knelt down and felt the young man's pulse in the throat. Good, he had one.

"Can you hear?" John asked.

The young man rolled to his side revealing a drawn and cocked pistol, pointed at John. The young man grinned, showing crocodile teeth, but no mirth. "I can hear, see, smell, and feel. That's more than you'll be doing in a few minutes."

"I'll bet I know where you're from and who sent you," John said conversationally.

"Where?"

"You are from New Mexico, and Butch Cassidy sent you."

"Why would you think that?"

"Because I just ran Butch out of here, and he landed down there. Your brand isn't local. I read the sign right, huh?"

"Yeah, you read it pretty good."

"I'd like to know what he's going to pay you for my scalp."

"Oh, I just wanted the reputation I'll get by being the man who killed John Pope."

"One more question then. What's your name?"

"Call me Kid Reader."

"Is that what you want on your headstone?"

"It don't even matter to me what goes o—"

Pope drew and fired. Kid's gun went off, burning John's ribs, and shooting through his coat and shirt in two places. Pope looked all around. Nobody was in sight. He felt in the Kid's pockets. There was three hundred sixty-five dollars, a big Bowie knife in a scabbard on the top of one boot, a derringer, and a 41 colt in his vest pocket. Pope pulled the pistol belt off and put his pistol in its place, and put all this stuff in his saddle bag. He dragged this kid to the cliff, laid him under an overhang, and rolled several big rocks in on top. Then, catching this big bay gelding, he led out east toward home.

It was hot in this canyon. Then he remembered he'd had a bit of a workout, but it wasn't as cold as he'd been through for a while. He made it to the stage stop at Myton after dark. John stabled and fed his horses, took a room, and had supper. The next morning he woke early and went out and watered his horses, then grained and saddled them. He went in and had about three cups of coffee with fresh side and fried potatoes.

"Good cold weather grub," Pope observed.

The cook agreed. John paid the bill and rode out before light. He got to Vernal in the light just before sundown, rode to the jail, unsaddled and fed the horses, carried the rifle, saddle bags, and everything belonging to Kid Reader inside where he went through it all.

The rifle was a new cartridge size to John, a 25-35. As Pope looked it over, he thought it was too small a caliber for most things. It would be a good varmint gun, maybe, but John was intrigued by it. He'd go shoot this one day soon. It might have a better trajectory than most big caliber rifles of the time. There were two boxes of shells for it in the bags. There was also one box of .45 long colts and one box of .41 caliber pistol shells. Pope pulled the derringer out, checking how it worked. There were two one-and-a-half inch barrels over and under a latch which let him break it open to load. As Pope pointed it and handled it, he knew it might save a life at close range, but impossible to hit much with it at more than twenty feet. Everything was new.

Of course Kid Reader was new too. He couldn't have been more than twenty years old. The big Bowie knife had a twelve inch blade, a brass guard, and bone handle. It was sharp as a razor and handmade. John set it in the silverware drawer. There was not a letter or address or anything more than what the kid had told him. The Texans had called him Kid Pope, so John guessed every young gunslinger was called Kid. Everyone knew of Billy the Kid, and of course, the Sundance Kid.

At the jail, he barely got things put away when Dick stepped in with a big pot of stew. "I've brought supper for the prisoners. I'm glad to see you back and the fire built up again. If we don't keep the fire going, we might freeze a prisoner or two."

"They complain all the time," John said, "I guess if we ever build another jail we'll build it with their comfort in mind."

"Oh, by the way John, if you're going home, you'll want to stop at the store for a Christmas present for Charlotte. You missed Christmas and New Years with all of your traveling around this year. Also, you'll owe your dad for remembering your family with candy and a big ham."

Damn it! Missed Christmas? "I owe you for reminding me. Thanks Dick."

John left the jail and walked quickly to the store. He had no idea what to get, so he explained his dilemma to the store keeper who saw an opportunity to make a big sale.

"I got a new Singer sewing machine, treadle made, with all the attachments for fifty dollars."

"Think Charlotte would like that?"

"Women are crazy for them. Nobody can afford them, though."

"Will you deliver it tonight, within the hour, if I buy?"

"Yes sir!"

"It's no good without thread and cloth. Put a spool of every color thread you have in a box."

"Okay, six spools."

"Now, have you got denim cloth?"

"There is probably six yards left on this roll."

"Okay, I'll take that. You have white?"

"Yes."

"Give me that and a roll of blue and one of red."

"That's another five dollars."

"Also, bring a sack of chocolate candy, a buck's worth, and another sack of hard-tack, peppermint sticks, and licorice."

It turned out the storekeeper asked John's help to load a two wheeled cart with the stuff and pulled it by hand to his front door where he knocked like a stranger. Charles opened the door. John and the storekeeper had the sewing machine in hand, one on either end. They carried it in.

John looked at a bewildered family and asked, "Where do you want this contraption?"

"What is it?"

The storekeeper said, "This is the best sewing machine money can buy—a Singer treadle model."

"Just set it here 'til you demonstrate how it works. Then we'll know where to put it."

John sent the kids out for the rest of the stuff. They came in with it and found the candy with squeals only kids can give. An after-Christmas Christmas party began in John T. Pope's house. That night at eleven o'clock, Charlotte still sat at the sewing machine, squinting by the soft lantern light. John never knew when she came to bed. He had fallen asleep.

John was up and chores done before Charlotte woke the next morning. "Good morning sleepyhead. I don't know how you strain this milk."

"I'll get that." Charlotte came quickly. As she came past the stove, she said, "Oh, a nice fire already." She threw her arms around John's neck and gave him a long big kiss. The kids turned away.

Lottie May said, "Yuck!" But John embraced his wife, and they both enjoyed a minute of time in each other's arms.

"I didn't know I missed Christmas 'til I got back last night. So I came home by way of the store. I hope someday I can make it up to you to all you've had to do alone. I'm proud of you and love you very much."

After breakfast, Charlotte showed off a shirt she'd made for John T. "All it lacks are buttons. I used an old worn out shirt as a pattern."

"Can't tell it from a store bought. Wow! Thank you. I'll get you some buttons and other stuff."

John hurried up to the store and he bought all the buttons the store had. The storekeeper said he'd get an order in the mail and should have more thread, buttons, pins, and material in about three weeks.

"Order in ribbon and trim, and all those sewing notions women can't live without. My Charlotte shouldn't be without a one."

Chapter Nineteen

Winter

THE ICY SEASON SAW John out on horseback almost all winter. One thing after another kept him out in the blustery, chilled weather. Marshall Wayman of the White Rocks Indian Agency came to Vernal with a prisoner to be locked up. This prisoner was wanted for stealing horses in Idaho.

Marshall Wayman recognized him from circulars sent by the Sherriff's Union and arrested him, but had no place to lock him up while awaiting authorities from Idaho to come get the prisoner and horses. So Dick locked him up, along with some other prisoners.

Several days later, on February twenty-second, a cold, blizzardy, Sunday morning, Sheriff Pope arrived at the jail with breakfast for his prisoners. The doors to all the cells were unlocked. The prisoner from Idaho was gone, but other prisoners were still in their cells.

"What happened?" John asked while re-securing the jail.

One prisoner, Wallace Eisler, spoke up, "Somebody came in the night with a key, and unlocked all of our cells and told us to take off. He said nobody could track us in this storm. He seemed to know the new prisoner, and old Idaho, he left with the man that unlocked us."

All of these men were incarcerated for serious crimes. John could have had a real catastrophe on his hands! While the men ate, John carefully took a description of the stranger. "Why didn't you men go them?"

"Idaho didn't know you like we do! Nobody ever got away from Sheriff John T. Pope in any weather. We only had one way to go—and after stealing another horse, all the roads would be closed anyhow. We'd either freeze to death or you'd be apt to kill us when you caught up."

"Yeah," wily Patch Perkins agreed. "We had the advantage on Idaho. He thinks he's tough, but we know what we were up against. I'd hate to be in his shoes right now."

Sheriff Pope bundled up for the weather, took his big horse, and left Dick to sort out the jails lock and key mess. "Better get new ones, Dick."

John picked up Marshall Wayman and they went after the escaped prisoner and his accomplice. "The only way they could go is across the Green River into Colorado."

At the river John talked to rancher. "Oh I saw a couple of guys, alright. They had a fire on the other bank for awhile. I figured they were trying to dry out a bit after swimming their horses across the ol' Green."

John said, "I'll give you ten dollars if you will row us across so we can stay dry. I know you keep a boat."

"Yes, it's in the shed, there. I'll take the ten, but you drag it down and launch it, then drag it out about twenty feet and tip it upside down after you cross. When you come back, it'll be ready for you to use, and then put it in the shed when you're done. I'll stay in and watch out my window. It's warmer that way."

John paid the rancher. Then he rode to the shed, and leaning way down from the saddle, without dismounting, he grabbed a rope which fastened to the bow, and was coiled on top. John made sure it was straight, then he backed Old Shorty Two back a few steps, took a turn on his horn, then turned his horse around and walked to the river with the boat sliding smoothly along in the snow behind them. The oars rode in their locks.

The men were soon across the river, dry and ready to go. They inspected the area where the escapee and his accomplice had dried their clothing. Their trail led out plain in the snow. The temperature was about zero. John kissed to his horse and picked up to a fast trot. By standing in the stirrups and leaning on the front, he could handle this gait okay. It was rough, but a lot smoother than a slower trot. Old Shorty Two stuck his head out and sprang along, trotting like an elk with a long stride. Marshall Wayman's horse loped quite fast to keep pace. They traveled this way about ten miles before Marshall's horse began to labor. They cut back to a walk and both men were warm as toast, despite the temperature outside. Riding fast was a workout, and their blood was circulating plenty fine.

The trail they followed was getting quite fresh. Where the wind was blowing and moving snow continually, the tracks were blown full, but most places it was easy tracking.

By the time it was full dark they were about twenty-five miles from the crossing on the Green. Marshall Wayman said, "I believe we better make camp and get a fresh start tomorrow.

"No, let's go on to the K Ranch. I've stayed there many times and they will be there because they think they out-distanced us, and out-toughed us. They are wrong on both counts! We'll take them there if they don't stop before they get there. If they do, we'll take them any minute."

"How far to the ranch?"

"About four miles."

Marshall Wayman groaned. "Hell, I think they damn near did out-tough me! My toes are frozen, my fingers are frozen, and my butt hurts! I'm tired and I never had a chase like this before!"

"Welcome to my club," Sheriff John T. Pope said merrily. "I've been out all winter so far! I kind of think if riding and bucking cold weather gets a man in shape then I'm about there. It makes my face dark as any Indian's. The rest of me is white. Pull my hat off and my forehead is white. I look like a Pinto!" Both men laughed at that. John said, "I will let you take my mittens for awhile and I'll wear your gloves. It'll get your hands warm," so they traded as they rode along.

John said, "Get a pair of boots made a size too big then wear a pair of wool socks. If you keep your feet dry they will stay warm." About twenty minutes later John asked, "Are your fingers warm yet?"

"Yes, and I'm gonna buy me a pair of these mittens!"

"Trade me back, we're here. This little narrow house here is the bunkhouse. They will be in there now. I'm going to the foreman and get a lantern then I'll go in the front door. When I'm inside, you open the back door and step in. We'll have them in a spot."

John rode on to the main house while Marshall Wayman tied his horse and ran up and down the path a few trips, trying to get blood circulating through his feet again. He ran out of wind, but continued to walk until a lantern approached.

Marshall Wayman hurried to the back door when he knew Sheriff Pope was inside. He opened the back door and stepped in, right on someone's face that was sleeping on the floor by the stove. The fellow let out an oath of filthy words as loud as he could, while grabbing his head with both hands. Marshall Wayman fell against a bunk, trying to keep his balance.

Sheriff Pope held the lantern high with his left hand, and checked the faces. He recognized the Idaho man, just as he awoke from the big noise. Idaho grabbed for his gun under his pillow and Sheriff Pope's hand flashed in a fast draw and he hollered, "Whoa!"

Idaho froze, having his pistol in hand, but not yet pulled out. He was looking in the muzzle of Pope's colt and knew that to continue to pull the gun was instant death, so he let go. His jail-breaking accomplice was still swearing about the "sharp shod jaybird" that danced on his face. His face was bleeding a little.

John T. handcuffed these men and Marshall Wayman added a cuff on their ankles, with the other end on the chain between the hand cuff s of the other outlaw. In this way they were shackled and rigged.

John retrieved their guns, then said, "Try to get some sleep; it will be a long day tomorrow." The lawmen left the bunkhouse, then tended their horses, and fixed a bed in the hay of the big barn.

John replayed the events in his mind, finally collapsing to the hay in roaring laughter.

Wayman arched a brow. "What's so funny?"

"What's so funny?" John gasped. "You stepping all over that damned infernal puke, that's what was funny!" The image cut into John's visual and he bellowed again, laughing until he wiped tears from his cheeks.

"Hell, it was worse than stepping on a cat," Wayman said. "My feet were numb with the cold, and his stupid face really threw me off kilter. I damn near fell on him!"

John mimicked the stepped-on bad man, using some of the colorful adjectives, ending with, *"that bumbling, sharp-shod jaybird!"*

The lawmen laughed themselves to sleep, with John thinking he couldn't wait to tell his boys and brothers about this trip.

Next morning John awoke early and went to his horse, watered, and grained him. He was all saddled up and ready to go when the breakfast bell started to ring. He went into the bunkhouse and unlocked the cuffs so the prisoners could dress, then snapped the cuffs on their wrists to allow them to walk in and eat breakfast. John offered to pay for everything and was refused.

"You are welcome here as always, Sheriff Pope."

"Thank you!" Sheriff nodded his appreciation to the rancher and his wife. "God bless the K Ranch."

After the meal John told the prisoners to saddle up.

"We're in Colorado. We don't have to go with the Utah authorities!"

Sheriff Pope said, "Since we formed the Sheriff's Union we work together between states and counties. Now you've got a choice, you can come and saddle up, and ride back like men, or I'll just turn your horses out. We'll drive them back and I'll put my rope on you and drag you back. Of course you can try to keep your feet and keep up but if you fall you'll slide through the snow pretty well. It's your choice, but you're going back even if you were in Hell, it's still my jurisdiction, I guess. Now move!"

The men jumped involuntarily. Marshall Wayman got his horse ready and turned to see John T. sitting on his horse, waiting with a disgusted look on his face. When the entourage was finally ready to go, John rode up to both men, and un-cuffed one wrist, then locked the cuffs on their saddle horns. "That's a nice looking boot print you've got right there," he said to the stepped on, bruised up, prisoner." Pope's eyes locked with Marshall Wayman's, and a smile twitched beneath his heavy mustache.

John borrowed a buggy whip from the K Ranch buggy, promising to bring it back later. He said to the outlaws, "Go for Vernal! We're right behind you. Any monkey business and I'll use this little whip on you."

They were locked back in their cells that night about eleven thirty, tired, cold, worse for the wear, but some wiser as to the grit and conviction of the sheriff of Uintah County.

John found that Dick had changed all the locks and keys. John stayed in the jail all night, and the prisoners were eventually taken back to Idaho and convicted of stealing horses.

John visited with a half a dozen different men from outlying ranches, and all worried about the weather—too much cold and snow too early. John said he figured if it got rough, they could put a trail herd together and drive southwest, maybe to Buckskin Wash or the San Rafael Swell. They might be able to take a trainload of feed to save them, as well.

Nobody checked on John's cattle, but him. Maybe this was a winter with enough snow to cover his feed. He decided he'd make another trip to Red Creek. He was thinking of this as he walked home with goodies and a sack of canned goods. Few people ever had canned goods at home. Pioneer families had root cellars and raised everything they ate. Canned goods were usually taken to cow camps, sheep camps, or mines. It was a special treat to have this for a change for Charlotte and the kids.

After dinner he told Charlotte of the worries and the talk he'd heard. She knew he'd have to check on their stock in Red Creek. John walked to the jail that afternoon, grained his horses and looked in on his prisoners. He then walked out back with Kid Reader's model 92 Winchester 25-35. It had a long octagon barrel and magazine, nice sights, and a smooth action.

He shot at a beer bottle at one hundred yards and busted it. He shot a rock at three hundred yards. The rock was about the size of a five gallon bucket. He hit the rock, but he had held at the top edge. He was impressed. It was a fast, flat shooting little rifle that had very little recoil. He decided to take it instead of his usual 45-90. He stopped on the way home to see if the store had any 25-35 shells. He ordered a case. He got home to find Charlotte making clothes for the kids. She loved her machine! She was learning fast, and was busy teaching Lottie May. Charlotte kept her instructions handy to study as she did various things with it.

Next morning John didn't get away until first light, with Shorty Two leading the tall bay with a well loaded packsaddle. John thought he'd try the mountain. If the snow was too deep, he'd go back, and go around through Colorado and in the back door. About one o'clock they were getting into timber. The snow was two feet deep. As Pope sat, giving the horses a blow, he could see tracks ahead. Something had crossed from the timber on the left toward the cedars on his right. They were going downhill. The tracks were a ways ahead, and he couldn't tell what had made the tracks.

When he reached the tracks, they were fresh. There were two sets of tracks about ten yards apart. The snow was deep enough to crumble in, not letting him see a clear print. As he rode along, he noted the long stride. It looked like a tail dragged snow a bit. These were way too big for coyotes, and deer didn't drag their tails.

After following for a couple of hundred yards, Pope knew he was following a pack of wolves. Two wolves were on each track, stepping in the same track as the leader. He remembered talk from last summer. Now deep snow was bringing them down for livestock. Pope knew with all the Utes hunting continually, and ranchers shooting game, the meat left for these big predators was rancher's livestock. He decided to follow and see where the tracks took him. If he could kill some of them, he would profit on the hide, and it might be his own cattle he'd save.

He pulled the rifle out and jacked a shell in the barrel and carried it in his hand. After about a mile, he was well down in the cedars in a series of draws or small canyons that ran off the mountain. Pope would cross a divide, then set and look with his telescope before riding to the top of the next hill. He would find where they crossed, then hurry on. This time he reached in a bag and opened a box of shells, putting a handful in his pocket before going over. Snow was only about eight inches deep on the level down here. It was bare in spots on slopes toward the south so he rode slowly ahead there, not seeing where they had crossed or went up the other side. When he was about a hundred yards from the bottom, he was watching and listening to some magpies in the cedars. He got thinking those birds were waiting for a turn to eat something down there. He crawled off his horse, he left both horses, and went on down afoot.

After about fifty yards downward, he got a small view in an alley through the cedars where he could see movement, but couldn't tell what; so he quietly moved straight toward them. The closer he got, the wider the alley. As he stood on a little ledge, he got a look at a dead cow being ripped at by four big gray wolves. John thought he might get closer, but from here he'd have a whole side hill to shoot at them if they ran that way. He sat down, got a good steady place to shoot over his knees, and waited for one to look up. In just a few seconds, a wolf raised his head. John took up the slack. *Pow!* That wolf went down. The one next to him ran up the hill a few jumps, looking back. It appeared almost as though the wolf was saying, "Here I am."

John shot again. Again a wolf went down. By this time, a big grey was up far enough to be in sight above the cedars, running straight uphill. The third shot broke a leg on this wolf, and he whirled to snap at whatever bit him. The other wolf went by running all out, so Pope held course and clipped that one in the back of the head. The wounded wolf started straight down the canyon. The last wolf was about two hundred yards away and John had to lead him a little. He missed twice. The third time he rolled the wounded one again. The wolf got up and ran a ways, but before John could shoot again, he pulled up to kick a couple of times in death.

John fed shells into the rifle until it was loaded again. Then he started back up for the horses. He marveled at how far it was up through the snow and mud and how fast he had come down. Had there been a bounty posted on wolves? John remembered talk but probably was out someplace when it was decided. The pelts should be worth quite a bit anyway.

If he tried to skin them here, they would be frozen before he got to number three. He decided to take them home to see if there was a bounty or not, and leave them inside 'til time to skin them. As he arrived at the first wolf, he looked in dismay. He forgot how big they were. This big male must weigh at least one hundred thirty pounds, and the three females would probably average a hundred pounds each.

Oh boy, this was no job for a man as small as he was. Pope smiled. In this dead weight sloppy condition, it would be hard. The bay didn't like this much either. Quickly Pope changed his saddle to the bay and the pack saddle to Shorty Two. He cut about three feet off his lariat. He then cut through the big wolf's gambles, slid the rope through and tied it loose so he had a loop to put over a fork of the tree of the pack saddle. He led old Shorty Two around on the downhill side and explained what he was going to try to do. He didn't think Shorty Two could understand, but knew he would try to cooperate.

He tied the lariat around the loop he'd made, put the end up around the saddle tree on the far side, then taking up slack with one hand, he lifted with the other. After a couple of tries, he had the wolf nearly off the ground. Finally, he bent over and got his arm around the neck of this giant carnivore, then lifted up. After a struggle, he managed to tie his rope around the wolf with Shorty Two holding him by the rope while Pope got the loop in the opposite fork of the saddle tree. He took the rope off and let him hang down. It was amazing to see how far down he came, even from the other side of the saddle.

He led Old Shorty Two up to the next wolf, cut another piece off his rope and repeated the loading process again. This wolf was probably thirty pounds lighter. Pope wasn't fresh anymore, so it was a strain. It looked much better to have a stabilizing load on the other side of the saddle.

He rode the bay up a hundred yards or so, to the next wolf. When the four were suspended from the four corners of the pack saddle, Pope knew he had between four hundred fifty and five hundred pounds loaded. A lot of horses would lie down. He tied his ground sheet around the load to stabilize it and keep it protected a bit. Then, he got on the bay and headed home.

Several people recognized him as he passed the ranch where he had once rescued horses from Buckskin Ed Carouthers, and hollered a hello. It was way dark when he got to town, but people spoke to him from several places as he passed. He stopped at Mona's. The newspapers were there. He took half a dozen and had Mona put some out for people to read in the café. He asked if she would post his article in a window and send the rest of the papers around town for everyone to read.

He then mounted up and made it to his mother's house before she went to sleep. The horses were tended and the wolves left on the porch for the night. They were already half frozen.

The next morning John T. and Sarah LeDuc had a nice visit over breakfast and coffee. John learned a lot of family news. He just missed a lot by living outdoors most of the time. Sarah said a fur dealer lived in Price. She had seen an advertisement. "John, if we can't sell these pelts for a good price I will tan them anyway, and they will still be valuable for any number of things."

John went to the county office to see if a bounty had been posted by the pest control board. Sure enough, there was a bounty of fifty dollars a piece on the wolves. They had to be seen by ten people to swear that they were taken in the county. John and Dick hooked up a team to a light spring wagon, went down to Sarah's and loaded all four wolves, then went to the City County Offices to have everyone come as witnesses that wanted to.

A couple of county commissioners came to see, and at a least forty people finally looked at the wolves. It caused quite a stir for people to see these feared killing machines up close and personal.

J.W., Charles, and Frank were delighted to be involved with the wolf proceedings, and bragged to each other about their dad as a mighty hunter.

John stepped into Mona's and ordered take out dinners for six, plus three more meals to go to jail for the prisoners there. While John got dinner, Dick took the wagon back and got Sarah to come with them to the jail where they had dinner together and skinned the four wolves. They stretched them to Sarah's parameters. John's boys were eager to learn and felt grown up being included. Every drop of grease or flesh was scraped from the pelts in the jail. With the fire cooking, they dried fast. John took a walk to the store for the ingredients Sarah needed to make a tanning solution which was mixed and applied.

Late that evening John bought supper for the three, Dick, Sarah, and himself. He'd sent the boys home earlier to do chores. John walked Sarah home while Dick took supper to the prisoners. John spent the night at his own home. He left again the next day for Brown's Park. This time he had a team, covered wagon, salt for stock, and grain. He tied a saddle horse behind. The long way was the best way, especially when the snow was deep and ice flows came down the river to capsize a ferry or at least freeze a man if he tried to swim.

As John neared Brown's Park, he began to relax. The canyon out of Colorado was almost bare and there seemed to be a warm draft coming from somewhere. The phantom of Brown's Hole was like an oasis. This was like a warm spot in the middle of the North Pole! Indians had wintered here for hundreds of years. Fur traders and trappers had also wintered here for many years. This place was much like the Wind Rivers in Wyoming. The Teton Mountains had snow most of the year. The Wind Rivers, the Sage, and Jackson Hole had hard winters. North of Jackson Hole over the pass in the Wind Rivers to Togwotee Pass would have twenty feet of snow, yet down river, twenty-five miles to where Dubois stands, there would be no snow and a warm wind seemed to prevail there. Shoshone Indians wintered there as long as anyone knew.

This place here was a kindred spot. It could be cold and stormy, but the warm wind came to melt the snow. John wondered where it could come from. With the snow drift on all sides and frigid air, John couldn't figure it out logically, but he said the Lord built it like this for a reason. As long as He willed it, it would be that way.

Chapter Twenty

Taking the Bull by the Horns

THE FIFTH NIGHT JOHN camped in his house on Red Creek. Most of the snow was melted. The cattle were doing well. It was such a relief to find things alright! Since the serious trouble that had once occurred on Red Creek, John found it a precious gift when all was well and he could relax. John drank coffee and enjoyed his home at Red Creek. He tilted back and watched out the open door as he recalled the fight to settle and built here. He remembered Ann Bassett, Matt Warner, and Butch Cassidy's visits. He had liked them all. He wondered what was next. Have I accomplished the job I had to do with these folks? What was in store in his future? He found himself smiling as he thought of Matt Warner. He had told Pope after his jail time, he would come back and take care of him. But he had been out for a few years working as a security guard at the mine and in law enforcement in Price, Utah. Would he still come back?

Pope knew Matt would never forget the lesson he taught him out front, here, shooting targets. Matt knew the only chance he had was to take Pope was from ambush. That was just not his way. John could eliminate him as a danger. Queen Ann Bassett may well come back sometime after she grew tired of Butch and Sundance, but John never considered her a threat. She could ride as good as most men. She could shoot, swear, or talk sweet as the occasion demanded. She could dress and act as tough as any man, or when dressed in her female togs, she was a petite five foot, two inch seductress. That she could take care of herself, he had no worries. For the present time, she seemed to be enjoying her charades as a school-teaching lady, Etta Place.

So what of Butch and Sundance? That was a real head scratcher! They might go into Mexico, but Pope felt they liked the good life too much. Mexico was poverty ridden and already overrun by desperados. After thinking it over from every angle, John thought they would go straight, change their names, buy a business, or ranch in Texas or Canada, and hopefully live good productive lives.

No more Kid Reader? For what reason? Kid Reader! The thought made John wince thinking how close this kid had come to getting him. Somehow he knew John was coming and had set the trap. John rode right into it. He knew the kid was going to shoot. He couldn't hope to draw and fire fast enough to beat an aimed, cocked pistol. He could kill this kid though. However, the "take him with me" mindset was not a very good option. Trying to make the kid's mind work at something else, he asked the questions. John, in getting up from checking his pulse let the big coat bulk out as much as he could and went for it. Pope couldn't tell in his memory if Kid's gun went off first or last, but the kid couldn't answer any more questions.

Pope's sheep hide coat had two bullet holes; his vest had two holes, his shirt two holes, his ribs a burn scar. If Pope hadn't of been bulked up by coats, he would be dead. The Kid put the shell through where he thought it would do the job.

John laughed. All the thinking didn't make any difference when the Lord took a hand. It was time for John T. Pope to thank the Creator for his life and family and ask for guidance in his future.

Next morning John rode through the cattle, checking each one carefully. The feed would last fine if not snowed on too deep. The cows had worked on the hay crop, cutting to the bottom in places when the snow covered things. Now they were working everywhere. With this worry put away, John harnessed the team, hooked up, and drove to Jarvie's for dinner.

John spent several hours visiting. He bought two boxes of 25-35 shells. The Two Bar had a 25-35. Jarvie was a good store man. If a man asked for something he didn't have, next time they came by, he'd have it. He had a ranch, a ferry over the river, his store or trading post, also some mining property. He had milk cows, chickens, pigs, and sheep. Thus there was fresh eggs, a huge root cellar, a large garden; and he raised a few acres of corn for the still. What anyone wanted, John Jarvie had it. He was really popular on dance nights as he played on the concertina or organ. Small ranches in this area got together nearly weekly to dance, visit, and drink some of Jarvie's corn.

Pope couldn't know as he enjoyed a visit that a few years later he would be doing other things than being the law, and that Jarvie would be robbed and murdered by a couple of bad actors from Rock Springs, Wyoming. His body would be dumped in a boat and pushed into the river where it would be found, caught on the east end of Lodore Canyon. John wouldn't have known that his friend Jarvie would be buried in the Lodore Cemetery. Perhaps, had he seen into the future, he would see that the two murderers would get away with the crime because John T. Pope wouldn't serve as the tough as brass sheriff of Uintah County forever.

As John drove out for Vernal, he had a feeling of change coming. He hoped the weather would soon change. It had been a long, cold, bad winter in the Uintah Basin; but it would still be a few weeks till spring. After an uneventful trip from Brown's Hole, John stayed home with his family a few days. He had promised himself he would do more of the things he wanted to do with his life from now on. He talked to Dick about finding a law book he could study, maybe several.

Dick asked what was in the wind, and John said, "I've got to take a test. If I pass the bar, I'll hang out a shingle. Also I'd like to run for county attorney. We need some horse sense around here for a change."

"Oh, hell," Dick said, "I don't think it will work."

"Why not?"

"I never heard of an uneducated fast gun passing anything, let alone a bar exam."

"Will you see what you can find?" John asked.

"Yes," Dick said, "but you're too good a sheriff to get out of this job. You're needed here."

John said, "As long as I'm needed, I'll stay; but you're doing this job as good as me now. Twenty years from now if I stay on at three hundred a year, where will I be? I'm tired, Dick. Is there something better for me or my family? When Butch pulled out, the price on my head seemed to go with him."

"So that's it," Dick teased. "Just as soon as that four thousand dollar price tag disappeared off your head you're not feeling worth a damn!" Dick slapped his leg, enjoying his humor.

The next day Dick had a book on law which the brothers began to read and study daily.

Spring finally started to come. One morning Sheriff Pope was sent for. He went as fast as he could walk to the home of Richard Veltman, who had been robbed. Veltman was one of the early settlers of Ashley Valley. He had his life's savings in what he thought was a safe place in his home. There was very little money those days and few people used banks. Richard Veltman had a little more than two thousand dollars in his secret hiding place. Someone had broke in and stolen it.

John Pope studied the place for awhile. He found how they broke in. They had walked around the house a few times, hunting a way in. Most of the ground was muddy, too squishy to hold a decent track, but John went all the way until he found a good track in the snow on the north side. After he looked at it awhile, he had a good idea what the man he would be hunting would look like. This man wore low shoes about size eight, not wide. The heel had been built up, or rebuilt, leaving a squiggly line which would be easy to tell. Pope knew the perpetrator was either a youngster or not too bright.

Anyone with any experience outdoors would never leave a track so obvious. Pope found an old crate and put it upside down over the track to protect it from melting a day or two while he looked for the thief. Everyone wore boots those days, most with spurs being almost a permanent fixture. Anyone with shoes was an immediate suspect.

John spent an hour circling the area in ever larger circles, hoping to find a track or an indication a horse had been tied near. Finally he walked to Mona's for a cup of coffee. He stood at the counter and talked to several men over his coffee and donuts. This had become a very popular and busy place about this time of day, but no shoes though.

He walked to the jail and looked at posters. Nobody like this was wanted for anything since the Sheriff's Union had been organized. He got letters and posters from sheriffs from three states, posting names and pictures of people to be on the lookout for. So he looked, but nothing. He walked around town a bit, loitering at the store and looking at people and their feet. He went home early and talked to his family for a while.

Charles became excited and asked his father to deputize him immediately. "Me and Frank will scour the town for the shoe-wearing steal thief, Dad!"

"Just don't be too obvious about it, or noisy. We don't want to scare them off."

John hadn't let anyone he started hunting get away yet. Usually given time and patience, he either got his man or their hide. Butch Cassidy had ridden away with Pope on his heels until he got so far from Utah, that John turned back. But he hadn't escaped yet because he was wanted everywhere.

After breakfast, John walked back to the jail and told Dick what to watch for, and caught him up on everything. He then began his rounds again. Nobody had ridden the stage out of town that wore shoes. John was sure the suspect was still in town. He tried to think of everything. Whoever had robbed the Veltman home was probably a resident of Vernal, or maybe a member of the family, because they knew no one was home at the time of the robbery. Also, they seemed to know what they were looking for with an idea of where to look. They had looked through a lot of stuff however, before finding it. Pope kept going through things in his mind while looking at feet.

John walked into Mona's and ordered a breaded pork chop with all the trimmings. After a good meal and several cups of coffee, the crowd began dwindling. Pope, still watching feet, moseyed out with a toothpick and leaned against an awning post while watching folks going and coming along the street. Finally he walked into the bar and spotted a man with shoes. Bingo! John knew the guy. He was a tough-luck local character, a neighbor of the Veltman's, and about thirty years old. He had worked for Veltman a bit over the years. He could have a bit of knowledge of the

Veltman's money and know where the man disappeared when he went to get money to pay his wages.

John watched him sitting alone playing solitaire for a minute before putting a hand on his shoulder. "Come with me. I've got something show you."

They walked together to the Veltman house, and John took him to the snow on the north side of the house and asked him to put a foot down in the snow very carefully, next to the crate which sat upside down there. Then, he had him lift his foot carefully and step back.

Then John said, "Look here." He bent down and lifted the box revealing a twin track to the one they had just made. John asked, "Do they look identical to you?"

"Well, yes. I guess it does."

"How many people do you think have the squiggle mark in the heel?"

"Probably nobody but me, I guess."

John was smiling at this fellow who wasn't much younger than himself, but who was sweating and having trouble meeting John's eyes. John knew he had his man—he also knew young Charles and Frank would be sad that this detective work was over.

John said in a quiet friendly way, "You're caught red handed, stealing the life savings of a pioneer family. How many years in jail would you sentence a man to for stealing an honest family's life savings?"

The fellow groaned and mumbled, "I don't know."

"If you were desperate and hungry and told these folks, do you think they would let you starve?"

"No. They would have worked me though."

"And they should," smiled Pope. "However, you didn't just take enough to eat and to get by with, you took it all. Why?"

"I don't know."

"I don't know how long you'll have to spend in jail, but unless we can do something to make the courts more lenient, I'll bet it will be many years."

He groaned again, and asked, "How can we do anything?"

John T. smiled at this fellow again and said, "We could pay all the money back. That would surely help."

"I can't pay it all back."

"Why not?"

"Well, I spent some already."

"How much?"

"Probably four-and-half or five dollars."

"Well, if that's all, I'll chip in that much, and you can owe me."

At this point the fellow shoulders dropped and he sobbed a time or two. He couldn't get control of his voice for several minutes.

So John said, "It's okay," patting his back. "While you get your composure, let's go pick up the money."

They walked together to this fellow's little cabin. It was very dirty and everything was in disarray. He walked to a cupboard and got a coffee can and brought it to John, handing it to him.

John took it and asked, "Didn't you take a two gallon crock with money in it from Veltman's?"

"Yes, but Dan took it."

"What you've given me in the coffee can is only one half of the money you stole then?"

"Even less because Dan counted it and gave me a thousand, so there's only nine hundred ninety-five there now, I guess."

Now John's mind kicked a gear or two, wondering how best to get the evidence to get justice done in a mess like this. Pope's heart was touched by this guy. Finally he said, "I believe it is best for you to come up to the jail with me while I try to figure out how to get evidence that Dan was involved so we can recover all the money. We want that, don't we?"

"Yes sir. Everybody's afraid of you, Sheriff. Now I'm not afraid of you anymore. I believe you are trying to help me. You're a friend."

"Thank you. You're my friend too. If we can get you out of this, maybe we can go fishing together or something once in a while."

"I promise Sheriff, I won't ever steal again."

"I believe you."

John made his prisoner comfortable, locked the money up, and then walked back to Mona's and ordered dinner for him and the prisoners. He couldn't remember seeing Dan for a long time, but now he was watching for him. John T. knew he'd have to be watchful and maybe even break the law a bit to get the evidence on Dan.

After supper, he carried a good hot meal back to his prisoner and sat and visited while he ate. He found out Dan lived alone and went to the bar to play cards and drink. He had no job and was always trying to figure how to make a score. John walked home. His family had chores done and was ready for bed. John and Charlotte got to bed, but John went over the events of the day, and how he still needed to recover half the money. Charlotte fell asleep listening, and when John discovered he was talking to himself, he shut up and soon slept as well.

Next morning, John got up to the jail after Dick had the prisoners fed, but they went over things together. John and Dick were going to look Dan's place over. If the money was found without a warrant, the judge might throw it out. If they got a warrant and didn't find the money, Dan would be warned and become even more evasive.

John said, "I'm going over and start watching. When he leaves, I'll go in and look around. Kinda keep an ear to the ground and maybe we'll get lucky."

About two o'clock in the afternoon, Dan came out, looked around, then locked the door, put the key on the window sill to one side, and walked up town. When he was out of sight, John moved up, took the key, opened the door, and stepped into the mess. Dan was a better housekeeper than his partner, though. John looked quickly around. He went to the unmade bed and looked around and under it, then systematically went through things in the bottom of the coat and overshoe closet. He found the money in the crock. Pope looked down the road. Nobody, so he carried the crock out, locked the door, hid the crock in some weeds outside, and hurried to get a search warrant.

John sent for Dick by having one of the attorney's workers go and bring Dick back. They took the warrant and went to Dan's. He was still gone, so they took the crock with them. Dick took it to the jail and John T. went in the bar after Dan, who was really drunk. John told Dan to come with him to the jail to see a friend of his. Dan didn't want to leave his bottle.

Pope said, "Bring it along. Your friend would like to share it with you."

"I aint got no friends."

"What about Virgil?"

A shadow crossed Dan's countenance at the mention of Virgil's name. "What's he in jail for?"

"He told me you'd know all about that."

"Well, I don't know nothin' about it."

"Don't you fellows play a hand of cards and maybe take a nip once in a while?"

"Yes, but he aint my friend. I don't know nothin' about any money."

Dick had come back from the jail stood listening. He began grinning, finding it difficult not laughing out.

John said, "It's sure funny where he ever got an idea like that, huh?"

"I don't know nothin', anyway."

"Well, let's go up and talk it over so you fellows can decide between yourselves. I hate to see such a beautiful friendship broken over a little disagreement."

Dan got sulky, "I aint goin' up there. I like it here."

John took hand cuffs out of his pocket and had one on a wrist before Dan realized he had no choice. With Dick's help, the other cuff went on the other wrist. John walked the bottle to the bar and said he didn't think he'd need that up to the jail after all. A derringer pistol was removed from

Dan's pocket, and they walked to the jail where Dan was charged with robbery. Both men were found guilty and sentenced, but the sentence was commuted because Veltman's money was all restored. Also, Pope had gone to work for them, getting the sentence commuted to community service, becoming gainfully employed, and leaving strong drink alone. As a result, both men's lives were changed for the better.

Charles and Frank were well involved with the Veltman case, claiming some kind of ownership in it, it being so local and all. Charlotte regaled stories of their detective work to John after the children were fast asleep. "Today Frank and Charles arrested the little Hatch girls and their kittens."

"On what grounds?"

"Drunk and disorderly." Charlotte giggled softly. "The Freestone twins were recently locked in the barn and Charles went to get the prisoners some supper while Frank kept watch. Meals were provided by Hazel's Donut Shop—Hazel's delicious homemade mud pies were the daily special."

"Oh those kids," John smiled.

"And the Miller's hired man is under surveillance."

"Why is that?"

"Frank claims he has a shifty eye."

John and Charlotte shared another quiet laugh.

"Well, God bless those kids, Charlotte! By hell, we'll have no shifty-eyed hands in our town!"

After the Veltman case, John T. got his hands on a criminal law book and studied it for a while. He worked on property law, easements, and water law. He was worried about a test he planned on taking as a result. He became well versed and well rounded in his knowledge of the law. Each day he rode out a ways because he learned early as a sheriff that he found out what was going on by being out on the ground among the people.

One evening riding back into Vernal, he saw two cowboys riding in from another quarter. As he neared, he realized they were strangers to him. He watched as they rode up to the store. Pope decided he needed a bit of licorice. He dismounted and tied up next to their horses at the hitch rail. Not local brands. He noted the brands to remember when he went through the posters from the Sheriff's Union. Inside he looked the men over. He watched while they made their purchases. They bought enough to last about three days if they were in a camp. It wouldn't last long enough, so they were traveling.

John T. was very suspicious and went up to the jail immediately after watching them ride out of town. He got out his latest stuff from the Sheriff's Union, and, in about twenty minutes, he came to a letter from Sheriff Ward of Evanston, Wyoming. The letter requested law enforcement to be on the lookout for stolen horses. The letter contained a perfect description of the men John had seen buying supplies at the store. The two men had stolen horses—about fifteen head. Their brands and a description of each horse were given. One of the horses he saw in front of the store matched one of the stolen horses listed in the letter. The brand was a match.

Pope made his outfit ready for an early go in the morning. He got so he hated the killing, but he enjoyed the excitement. He was still a young and strong man, so the riding and work was even fun. As the sun came up, John T. was already quite a ways down the trail. Prairie dogs barked at him as he rode down the track. Birds sang and played from the creosote brush. Several horned toads barely got out from under foot as his big horse was reaching out with a ground eating walk. All the reptiles were out trying for a little sun after a chilly night.

John couldn't help remembering so many trails from the last seven years. So many times he had been ambushed, so many graves. He tried not to be as vigilant as chances of being bushwhacked for money was not the threat it had once been, but habit is hard to break. John still practiced his fast draw. He was no better, but at least he kept his edge. Nobody else was any better, either, as long as he kept practicing.

Oops! Pope rode up to a place where they had left a bunch of horses to graze while they went for supplies. They had crossed everything on the old ferry near Jensen. Their tracks went south about five miles. He spotted the horses grazing along the river. He needed to get close. True to his character as a cowboy, not wanting to get off the horse until necessary, he rode around and came in quite close on low ground where he was out of sight.

He smelled cottonwood smoke. Finally, not daring to ride on, he tied his horse and walked, being sure to take the rifle and one extra box of shells. He hiked around the river bank on the sand until he was afraid he might spook their horses. He then crawled up the bank and looked over.

What a view! Horses were grazing in tall grass. Along the river a cottonwood grove nestled in the draw. In the edge of the grove was a classic dirt roofed log cabin about fifty yards in front of John. The sod on top of the roof was a deep green, growing through the dry grass from last summer. The door was ajar letting out heat from the stove. The smoke coming from the black metal chimney was grey white, and it was building a white cloud, leaving a layered look along the top of the cottonwood grove.

John had been in places like this before. Usually he wound up killing all. He wanted them for Sheriff Ward, alive if possible. John got the rifle in position. How he wished he'd brought the 45-90! He could put shells through the cabin about anywhere. The big 500 grain slugs were like artillery shells. The 25-35 would have to do. Finally he heard both men laughing in the cabin. He thought he'd heard voices, but wanted to be sure. He had them both inside.

Sheriff Pope yelled, "Come out without your guns."

"Like hell we will," sounded a yell from inside.

The other man yelled, "When hell freezes over."

"Come out, you're caught!"

"When you've got the guts to come get us, then we'll see."

"When I come get you like that, you both die. I'm trying to keep you alive. Come out!"

Suddenly, the cabin door was jerked shut. Pope had looked at it when standing open. One inch boards on a two by six frame. He put a shell through the door, next the only window, then decided on the chinking between the third log and fourth log from the floor. He carefully shot the chinking about two feet from the left side of the house, then about two feet further right. Next, almost to the door frame, then the other side of the door frame. Then he placed another shot about two feet over. He started taking chinking on the next log up, shooting in between the holes he'd made in the other row. His second shot on this row brought a banging and crashing inside. After the next shot, he heard them yelling.

He quit shooting while pushing shells into the magazine of his rifle. He yelled, "What did you say?"

"Stop shooting. We'll come out. Don't shoot no more!"

John said, "Push the door open."

It came open.

"Throw out your guns. Be sure I can see them."

Out came rifles, then pistols.

"Now keep your hands where I can see them. You come out."

Both men filed out of the cabin, the fight drained from them. There was a constant flow of blood from one man's hand.

Pope walked up on them quickly, tossing each a pair of handcuffs and had each man lock them on one wrist. Pope had the man not bleeding find an extra shirt or something for a bandage. He produced a clean shirt from a saddlebag. Pope soon had it torn in strips about three inches wide. He tied them together and put a knot on the pulse at the wrist, then wrapped around the wrist pulling it tight. When it was quite tight, the blood flow went from a flow to a slow drip from the stub of a thumb. It was shot off by Pope's shells flying through the interior of the cabin, scattering glass and sand from the chinking, and even ricocheting around inside off of furniture, and stoves, and whatever. The barrage John had laid down on the cabin had been unbearable. It was a miracle they came out with only one thumb shot off. Both had small cuts and slivers from flying debris inside.

After John stopped the flow, the thumb was bandaged by going over the stub, through the palm, around the back, over the stub and so on, until it was tight and secure. John said, "We will have to loosen the one around the wrist in about thirty minutes. By then the bleeding will have stopped. If not, we'll apply it again for thirty minutes more."

While John bandaged and cared for the wounded outlaw the other one saddled their horses. John walked them to a nearby tree and had them each put an arm around the trunk, taking a hand cuff hanging from a wrist of one man, clicked it on the other fellow's wrist. Leaving them standing fastened to the tree, he went inside the cabin and looked around.

What a mess! John picked up the guns, then jumped on a horse and rode back for his own horse. He was soon back. He put the extra pistols in his saddlebags, the rifles he unloaded, dropping the shells in his saddlebags as well. He put the rifles in the boots on their horses, and he walked back and unlocked the handcuff on each side of the tree, leaving one on each of their wrists. He had them mount up and snapped the other side of their cuffs to the saddle horn.

John T. Pope was a kind person, but also a hard man. He could get it done and these men knew it. John sent them to start the horses. They were going to take them to Vernal tonight, and Sheriff Ward could pick them up there and see they got to the people who really owned them.

As they followed the horses back to the old ferry, John kept them ahead a little but visited with them. One of them said, "I heard Sheriff Pope rode a giant horse. Why do you ride a work horse Sheriff?"

"He's half thoroughbred, but his feet are big enough not to go in every prairie dog hole or badger hole. He's got enough bottom to go over the mountains and back without any trouble. He out walks most horses. If I have to rope something, he can handle it if the manufacturer made strong enough, hard twists in the rope. He seems to understand English and tries to please me. Now I ask you, why not?"

"I thought he'd be rough to ride, that's all."

John let that ride until they got ferried over and were on the way to Vernal, when John said, "I had another big horse once that was as smooth as silk. The Wild Bunch killed him. I got this colt, hoping for another as good. He's not gaited like the first, that's for sure. When cutting out cows, this big horse will watch a cow. He can stop, whirl, and jump ahead. But he's rough enough. He separates the men from the boys. Few can ride him."

"Sheriff, how did you get on to us?"

"You removed all doubt when you decided to resist arrest."

That silenced the procession to the jail, where Dick helped get things done for awhile. A letter went out on the stage the next morning to Sheriff Ward of Evanston, telling him his prisoners and horses were locked up in Vernal, waiting for him to come get them and drive them home.

John thought about the ordeal he must have put these fellows through, shooting the cabin like that. He decided on his next trip to Red Creek, he would build an escape out the bottom or back of his cabin so this would never happen to him. His cabin was built with small logs, so rifle shells would go right through.

After a day home, he took his kids and some of their friends fishing. They took a buggy and team, a big fry pan, some flour, salt, pepper, and grease. John found himself busy baiting hooks, untangling line, cleaning, and frying trout. He wondered how a few kids could make so much noise and eat so many fish.

After he got them fed, everyone wanted fish to take to their families, so it was at least two and a half hours later before they could head home; each family would have a mess of fish. The kids were so wound up! John T. realized he had created a monster.

"When can we go fishing again?"

"Please take us fishing, Sheriff Pope."

"I caught the biggest one."

"I caught the most."

Francis listened to the others brag and had to get in the conversation. "I got the most snags!"

Frank rolled his eyes. "Snags are nothing to brag about, Francis!"

"Oh," the little golden haired girl persisted, "And me and Hazel caught two butterflies and a fuzzy caterpillar, huh Daddy? And we didn't even need a worm and a hook."

"Please Dad, can't we come again?"

John whittled the kids a willow whistle apiece before loading them up for home.

It's neat that after the Wild Bunch ordeal, Sheriff Pope could begin to mellow and relax a bit. He started to fish once in a while, pleasing his own kids and their friends as well.

One day a fight broke out in town between Harvey Gale, a known bully that was over six feet tall and weighed two hundred pounds, and August Darren, a younger man who stood about five feet, eight inches, and weighed only one hundred forty-five pounds or so. Harvey had been poking and pushing August, trying to start something. The store owner sent a young man for Sheriff Pope before the fight started.

Pope arrived in time to see August Darren suddenly fire a left fist, catching big Harvey flush on the nose, knocking him down. Blood was running, and it took the bully a minute to get up, and tears were filling his eyes, but he started throwing punches. August, who had stood quietly waiting for the bully to get up, went into action again, dodging, sparring, and keeping out of the bully's grasp. Bully landed a few, but in a minute he was down again, having taken the trouncing of his life. One of the bully's buddies went to the attorney, and a warrant was handed to John T. to serve.

John said, "I watched the whole thing. August Darren did the right thing. He did exactly what I thought I'd have to do one day."

The judge said, "Do it."

Pope served the warrant on August Darren. A hearing was convened. The judge heard the case. He turned to Darren and said in a severe tone, "I find Darren guilty of willfully and maliciously striking and knocking down one Harvey Gale several times, and I sentence him to serve ten days in custody of Sheriff Pope on a fishing trip."

A big grin broke out on the faces of August and John T. They looked at each other, enjoying the anticipation of such a recreational sentence.

One morning Billy Davis came running into Sheriff Pope's office. He tried to talk to Sheriff Pope, but was too excited and out of wind from running so far. It took time for him to settle down and get his breath.

"How old are you son?"

"I'm twelve years old sir."

Sheriff Pope said, "I was pretty much a grown man when I was your age, too. What's your name?"

"Billy Davis."

"Now, explain it all to me again.

"Ma's missing. Pa's killed her and hid her grave someplace."

"Are you sure?"

"I'm pretty sure."

"Did you see your dad kill your mother?"

"No, sir, but they been fighting a lot. Day before yesterday they had a bad argument. Ma was alright when I went to bed, but yesterday she was gone all day. Pa washed all their bedding and hung it out. He's never done that in my life. I asked him where ma went, and he said, 'She just left. Good riddance to bad rubbish.'"

"What makes you think she didn't go?"

"All her stuff is still there. She only had one good dress. It's still there. We don't know anybody much in Vernal. Where would she go? What would she do?"

"Okay, Billy, I believe you. What do you want me to do?"

"Find Ma's grave, I guess."

"If I find your dad killed your mother, then I'll have to arrest him for murder. Do you want that?"

"Yes sir. I do."

"What's your dad's name?"

"Ean Davis."

"Where is your place?"

"It's on the edge of town, on the northwest, a pretty run down outfit. I don't know how we'll make it without ma. She done all the work."

Sheriff Pope said, "I'm on your side all the way, but here's how things work with the law. I can't go look around your property without a search warrant. If I do, then evidence I find isn't allowed in court. If I go for a search warrant, the D.A. probably won't issue a warrant unless I have some evidence already. Do you feel safe at home?"

"Yes."

"I mean, would your dad do anything to you?"

"I don't think so."

John felt the weight of Billy's problems, and he hurt for the kid! Hell, nobody deserved this kind of stark, bitter reality! Every kid in the world deserved folks like Robert and Sarah Pope!

"Billy, here's what I think we better do. I'll go to the D.A. and try for a warrant. If I get it, I'll be right out. If not, then I'll wait for you to let me know what you find out there."

"Okay."

"Watch and search. We'll get him. You'll find something, or something will make a break for us."

Billy shuffled home, hands thrust deep in pockets.

John walked to the D.A.'s who thought it sounded like the imagination of a boy.

John said, "I'm sure something happened and is bad wrong."

But the D. A., because he had a little authority, would do nothing at that time.

Pope thought as he walked back to his office, "Someday I'll pass the bar and run, and be elected to that job myself! Then God help me to use good horse sense. No more of this nonsense."

A day went by. Billy came back. He told John he thought his dad had buried his ma in the potato hole at the end of the house because he had turned water in and filled it with water. He said his dad worked quite a while around the hole and ditching the little stream of water into the hole.

Sheriff Pope told Billy what the D.A. said. He told Billy to continue to watch and poke around. "We will find something." Sad Billy walked back home with a heavy load on drooping shoulders. The sight haunted Sheriff Pope, as did the whole stinking case!

The next day about ten in the morning, he came running to the jail. He said he'd been digging around the hole like John had told him. When his pa, Ean, saw him, he jumped on his horse and rode away. Pope sent a deputy to get his horse watered, grained, and saddled up and ready. He went to the D.A. for an arrest warrant for Ean Davis for murder. The D.

A. said John had no evidence, and he was a bit previous. "Too hasty," the D.A. snuffed.

John T. cut him off saying, "Too hasty, hell! I want it NOW!" The volume rattled the window panes and frightened a cat. The sound of John's voice seemed to also raise the hair on the D.A.'s head a bit, and blessedly opened his eyes. He wrote it out.

John beat it back to the jail where he picked up his horse, made sure he had handcuffs, plenty of ammo, a sack of grain, and filled his canteen and pockets full of jerky. He mounted and rode to the Ean Davis' place where Billy pointed the way his pa had taken. Pope went away fast. He found a set of tracks and got down and looked them over so he could follow Ean Davis wherever he went.

He rode fast and caught up after sundown. The campfire smelled and looked inviting. He watched a few minutes and made sure this fellow was alone. He rode closer and hollered, "Hello."

He was invited to come in and share if he wanted. Pope knew instinctively this was not a fugitive. He dismounted, watching his man closely. He introduced himself as Sheriff John T. Pope.

The fellow smiled and said, "I've heard a lot about you, Sheriff. I'm Dave Jones. I'm really glad to meet you."

"Do you have anything on you to identify you?"

"Like what?"

"Do you have a letter, or check, or something?"

"I have my belt. My name's on it."

He turned and pointed. Sure enough, *Jones* was engraved in the back of the wide belt.

"Hell, I've been tracking you from Vernal this morning. I have gone fifty miles on the wrong trail!"

"I am sorry Sheriff, but woefully happy to not be your man."

He unsaddled and led Shorty Two to water and poured out a bucket of oats for him, then came to the fire and got coffee. He said he was on the trail of a woman killer and didn't take time to get outfitted properly. Also, he noted he should have taken the trail from where it started instead of trying to cut it.

"I just cut your track instead of the right one. I'll go back and get it right day after tomorrow. Tonight I'll rest up and ride the fifty miles back tomorrow so I can be ready to get on the cold trail the next day. I'm not used to making such a dumb mistake."

Dave said he was going to a cow camp to bring herders home to help put up the hay. Both men fell asleep while visiting, having ridden a long ways.

Next morning John T. woke early, watered his horse and grained him again, and as he saddled up, Dave built up the fire and added water and more coffee.

He said, "I've got bacon, if you've got time for a bite of breakfast.

"It sounds good."

A pan went on the fire and bacon was soon sizzling. Dave dug out a couple of potatoes which was sliced thinly and put in the bacon grease to fry to a golden brown.

John ate a good breakfast before climbing on Shorty Two and starting back. He knew the destination without having to watch for tracks. It was mostly downhill, so John kissed to his horse a few times. He went into the ground-eating trot about every five or six miles. He slowed to a walk about a mile to rest a bit then kissed back out again. About three in the afternoon, he got back to the Ean Davis place.

Billy came right out and learned of the mistake. They went to the corrals and studied the tracks of Ean's horse, and John followed them carefully. They paralleled about thirty feet distant from the track left by Jones' horse. John T. followed it about a half mile where it turned north into Steinaker Draw, then in a few minutes another turn to the west. Pope followed on a short ways and decided to go get supper and make ready to roll about daylight.

He rode to the jail, tended his horse, and walked to Mona's for a thick juicy rib steak, all the coffee he could soak up, plus a couple of rolls.

Pope told Mona, "That's the best steak I've had in forever." Beef was really scarce, so when it was available it was a hit. There were plenty of cattle, but it was hard to use a whole beef before it spoiled.

Dick came in with supper for the prisoners. John walked back to the jail with him explaining everything. He said they would have to get in the potato hole and see if a body could be found. Also, he told Dick he'd feel better if someone would take Billy, or at least look in on him. Being twelve years old, he could use a little help. "Maybe the Relief Society might help his mental state a bit if the body is found."

"Consider it done—but the Relief Society will do more than just tend his mental state, brother. They'll see to his physical state as well! I'll bet that kid is fed, clothed, and loved before the sun goes down."

John rode out of Venal about daylight. He rode to the track and followed it west. It worked a bit south until it was going down the main road toward the Strip. He was about to Myton at ten thirty. He met two horsemen coming toward him. John pulled the telescope from his bag and stopped, looking at the fellows. He dismounted and sat down to hold still. He discovered the man in the lead had handcuffs on, so John put the telescope away, mounted up, and waited for them.

Heber Jones, policeman for the Indian Agency, had caught this fellow selling liquor to the Indians. He not only sold the spirits, but he traded whiskey for the use of a squaw who was not happy with the arrangement. She had scratched his face badly, so he beat her, badly. He took little but a few scratches. The police were notified, and Heber Jones was bringing him to the jail.

"I hope they don't just turn him loose again, because either I, or the Indians, will kill him if they find him out of jail."

John said, "You won't have to worry, because we've got a prior claim on Ean Davis for the murder of his wife."

John joined Heber in transporting Ean to the jail in Vernal, where he was charged with rape, selling whiskey to the Indians, and the murder of his wife. All papers were properly executed. At the hearing several days later, he was bound over to the District Court in Provo, Utah, where criminal cases were heard. Mrs. Davis's body was found buried in the muddy potato hole. Examination showed she was hit with a hammer, or pistol butt, caving her skull in while she slept.

"It takes a big man to do that to a sleeping woman," John said. A bad taste settled in his mouth, and he was eager for justice to settle on the black hearted villain. "It will be my pleasure to escort you to Provo, Ean. I'll soon testify against you, and you will face your maker and be unworthy to do so. Justice is coming for you."

Chapter Twenty-One

Tending Colorado

After the initial hearing for Davis, Pope strolled down the road toward Mona's when he saw three Mexicans ride up the street to the store, dismount, and go in. They led a pack horse. Being curious, he walked up and looked the horses and outfits over, then stepped in for some licorice and peppermints. He judged the three men as dangerous. Two were very greasy, swarthy, middle aged men, with rifles in hand, plus pistols. All three wore wide brimmed hats. The one younger man was taller and well set up. Pope thought he might be good looking if about three month's growth of whiskers were shaved off. He wore a pistol tucked in his waistband on the left side, handle to the right. He had a leather belt full of shells that was carried over one shoulder and under the other arm.

John leaned against the pot bellied stove and observed them buy six boxes of 45's, tobacco, coffee, and enough food to last at least a week. They spoke English with a heavy accent but chattered to each other in Spanish. One of the older Mexicans kept an eye on John. When they left the store John followed them out and leaned against the awning post, watching them as they rode away. Pope checked and memorized the tracks. He knew somehow he'd be tracking them before long.

The store keeper stepped out and said, "Thanks, John. I was so glad when I saw you step in. They looked like trouble."

"They are trouble. I'm glad I was here and saw them coming."

He walked to the jail and checked all his wanted and union posters. He could find nothing. The door opened and Lottie May stepped inside, grinning at her dad. A basket of tantalizing aromas hung over her arm. "Mother sent supper, and chocolate cake."

"Your mother is the best! Be careful going home, Lottie. You are getting a might too pretty to be dodging around this town."

Lottie's cheeks pinked and she said, "I will Dad, and thank you for noticing."

John ate his fill, then gave the prisoners their supper and walked thoughtfully home. The next morning while Dick and John studied law together, which they did as regular as possible, they were interrupted by a sheriff from Meeker, Colorado.

"Please, I need help! I am trailing some fine horses, stolen from Meeker." He said it was easy enough to trail them to a ways from Vernal. He knew he was in Utah, and he was over his head anyway. He didn't have a clue who had stolen the horses or how many. He wasn't that good of a tracker. "Please let me go with you so I can take the horses home, and return the prisoners."

John stood up and put his hat on. "I knew it," he muttered, "that's why my horses are still tied where I grained them a while ago."

Dick put the pack saddle on the tall bay. John saddled Shorty Two. They stopped at the store for supplies. John bought bacon, potatoes, salt, pepper, flour, jerky, and an extra box of 45's, a canteen for Colorado, fish hooks and line, a whole box of peppermint candy, and licorice, coffee, an extra tin cup, plates, forks, and a towel.

They left Vernal, following the three Mexicans tracks. Soon they were following a bunch of track as they came to the spot where the horses were left while the men had gone into town for supplies. They skirted around Vernal, finally winding up in Steinaker Draw, going east. Pope stood in the stirrups and kissed to Shorty Two, hitting his fast trot for about six miles. The sheriff from Colorado begged to slow down for a few minutes. He had a pain in his side, and his horse was lathered up. Pope knew if Colorado stayed with him, he'd have to walk.

They were soon starting a gradual climb up the mountain. It looked like these Mexicans were unfamiliar with the country because they stayed on the main trail, but they knew Colorado was behind them. They stayed at a fast pace as well, so John would be back in Brown's Hole sooner than expected.

That evening, riding through the timber on the mountain, John paused to shoot the heads off of two pine hens, taking a few seconds to throw the entrails out and hang them on the saddle strings. Colorado said he had never seen anyone do that with a pistol. It was full dark before they got to the Green River, but Pope saw they took the trail to the Jarvie Ferry, so the lawmen continued in the dark. Pope shot three quick shots which was the signal for the ferry. Sure enough, in a few minutes a lantern could be seen moving around to the ferry. Then it came slowly across.

John Jarvie said, "You better have a good reason for getting me out after dark."

"Chasing some horse stealers is why."

"Sheriff Pope? Good to see you! I might have known it would be you, chasing those buggers. They were a rough bunch of desperados, I'd wager."

"What time did you take them over?"

"About three this afternoon."

"Which way did they go?"

"Northeast."

"Damn," Pope said. "We will be going over the mountain again."

After they were safely over the river, John T. gave John Jarvie five dollars for taking them over in the dark. He then took Colorado to his cabin at Red Creek for the night. With the lantern lit, the fire started in his stove, the frying pan soon had bacon sizzling for the grease. The chickens were skinned and cut up, rolled in flour, salt, pepper, and dropped into the hot bacon grease. John clapped a lid on. By shortly after midnight, they had eaten an enormous amount of food.

"You got a hollow leg there, Colorado?"

"I never ate anything as good as pine hen before."

"We were hungry," John mumbled. "Take your pick of the bed or the floor. I'll take the other."

John slept in his own bed on Red Creek again. They were out and away before daylight and were following the horse thieves' trail by sunup. They never let up and that night about six o'clock, John spotted their horses. He pulled his telescope and studied the situation awhile, memorizing the lay of the land. He needed to decide how to approach to be able to brace these tough Mexicans. Then he handed the telescope to Colorado who also sat and looked for a long time. "We're about fifty miles into Wyoming from my ranch on Red Creek."

"That was *your* ranch we stayed at last night?"

"Yes."

"Hmm, no wonder you made yerself so at home. I thought you seemed mighty familiar."

John laughed, "Any time I build a place, I guess I'll be familiar with it if I want to be!"

"Absolutely," Colorado grinned.

"The best way to try to take those men will be to approach their camp in the dark, get in position, and arrest them as they crawl out in the morning."

Pope and Colorado rode into the hollow on the right, got down, and made coffee using dry sagebrush so as to make as little smoke as possible. Pope opened two cans of peaches, each man ate his share while soaking up a pot of coffee.

Colorado said, "I was so full last night, I didn't think I'd ever eat again. By this afternoon, I was so hungry I could have eaten old bloody afterbirth."

"Good hell," John gagged. "I guess I've never been that damn hungry."

Colorado laughed, his middle rising with rolling breaths.

"Loosen the cinch on the horse and roll in your blanket for a few minutes. I'll wake you in a couple of hours. Then you watch while I catch a bit, and we'll move up and get in position."

Colorado said, "It's still light. You sleep first, and I'll wake and trade you."

"Don't go to sleep yourself, or we'll be chasing Mexicans all day again tomorrow."

"Mexicans?"

Pope was rolling in his blanket. "They aint Pilgrims! Yes, they're Mexicans. They are dangerous, bad men."

"How do you know *all* this?"

"I just do."

"I mean—are those tracks you've been following shaped like little sombreros, or what the hell, Pope?"

John grinned vaguely, but nodded right off, snoring before Colorado could find out anything.

Colorado was suddenly scared. If they were that bad he sure hoped they would give up when they were confronted in the morning. He told himself that nobody would buck two sheriffs with cocked, loaded, guns, if they had the drop on them.

About two o'clock in the morning, the coffee had done its job, waking John for a bathroom break. He sat up looking around. The fire was out, but he could see Colorado setting up with his chin down on his chest, sound asleep. John rattled around a bit until Colorado came to, and stood up, looking all around.

John said, "Thanks for letting me sleep. The old man needs it the most anyway. Bring the coffeepot and coffee. We'll stow it, tighten the cinches, and bridle up. It's time to roll."

As they rode up the draw toward the camp, Colorado said, "I'm kinda scared, Sheriff."

"First time?"

"Yes."

Just do as I tell you, and you'll be alright."

"I will?"

"Quiet from here, Colorado, just shush."

After riding to about one-third of a mile from camp, John dismounted, tied the horses, and pulling his rifle, started on foot up a ridge. When they were nearing the top, suddenly Colorado remembered his rifle. He turned to go and John grabbed him and gave him his 25-35, along with a handful of shells.

"What about you?" Colorado whispered.

John grabbed a hand over his mouth and patted his pistol. The final approach was slow, and quiet as a snake. About twenty yards in front of the fire, he quit crawling, having found a rock which stuck up about four inches. By gesturing, he got the rifle in position over the rock and got Colorado lying behind it. Taking his knife, the spent about thirty minutes digging and scraping a depression, moving a mound of dirt to protect him as good as possible.

It was getting light by the time he was comfortable. It was light in the east where the sun would come up and still a bit dim around them as the men began stirring. The older men sat up about the same time, pulling on their boots, their hats already going on as they arose. John hoped Colorado would hold fire until he could locate the younger one.

But, as a man came to the fire, overzealous Colorado yelled, "Get your hands up!"

Damn it! The Mexicans both drew at the same time. Pope's pistol blasted about the same time. Two Mexican pistols blasted bits of rock and dirt off the rock which stung Colorado's face. Pope's pistol and another one blasted at the same time. Again, one more shot came from the Mexican side, then silence. Both men were crumpled down.

Pope put two shells back in his pistol, still trying to see where the third man went. Then a horse started running, John jumped up and ran forward, colt in hand. The horse was in sight for about fifty yards before dropping over the hill, far enough to be out of sight. The younger man had gotten to the horses, caught one, bridled him, vaulted on bareback, and was laying over the horses neck, going lickety-split over the hill about a hundred twenty-five yards away.

John stopped and took two well-aimed shots before he dropped from sight. The first shot John felt may have been a little high and behind. The second shot felt good to John, and he heard the shell hit flesh, but the man was still on as horse and rider went out of sight.

John then turned to see what had happened to Colorado. He was sitting up, trying to get stuff out of his eyes. John bent down and picked up the rifle, unfired. He un-cocked it and walked to the Mexicans. Both men were shot through their hearts. They had gotten off three shots, two of them hit the rock inches in front of Colorado's face. There were two blue scars about an inch and a half apart on the rock.

John thought of all the men he'd faced, these men were truly dangerous. Pope went through their pockets and left the things he recovered in front of the victims on the ground. Colorado asked if John could come try to see what he had in his eye and help get it out.

Pope had him stand up and look toward the east, but he couldn't open his eye. John said, "Just hold still. I won't hurt you . . . much, but I'm going to open your eye for you, then you look where I tell you to."

Pope took hold of a pinch of eyelid, opened it and said, "Turn your eyes to the right."

As he did, John revealed a small chip of rock. While he held this position, he pulled his bandana up and dabbed it in his eye. After a try or two, he removed the chip. He let loose of the eyelid, and Colorado groaned. "Did you get it?"

"I got that one."

After a minute, Colorado had gotten so he could see a bit, so John showed him the chip. Colorado said, "That little thing? I thought it was as big as my fingernail, at least. So did they get away?"

"One man did."

Suddenly Colorado saw the dead men and quit talking. He seemed to turn a bit pale and green.

"When it comes to sheriffing, Colorado, you seem like a virgin. Aren't there bad guys where you come from?"

Colorado sputtered, still looking incredibly pale.

"Look at the rock your face was partly hid behind, then thank God you're still alive."

As Colorado looked at the bullet scars, he became even quieter.

John said, "Hike back and bring our horses up, will you?"

Colorado gladly turned back to bring the horses. John looked through their pack saddle. No shovel, but an axe. He went through all their saddlebags. One had a roll of bills, so John stuck that in a vest pocket. He put the money from their pockets in one saddle bag. He put their belts and pistols in saddle bags, and looked for a place to bury the two bodies. He couldn't see a good place, so John started chopping the ground by one corpse. He'd chop up about two and a half by two and a half area and scrape the dirt out with his hands.

When Colorado got back with the horses, John had a trench scooped out long enough and wide enough, but only about ten inches deep. So he started chopping on one side. When he was about three feet down, Colorado started scraping it out, so John worked the length of the grave. It was about fourteen inches deep, so John rolled the guy in, and they covered him. They started on the other grave where the other outlaw fell. In thirty minutes, this guy was buried as well.

John asked Colorado if he could find his way to Meeker from there. Colorado pointed south with a question mark.

"Yes, and a little east. If you travel east, southeast, you'll be able to get around some mountains 'til you hit the road from Baggs to Craig, then south to Meeker. I'm going on after the other one. Turn those horses out. Drive them if they won't follow, and take 'em home. Saddle three of 'em so you've got their outfits. I put their money in one of the bags. You'll have to saddle their pack horse, also."

Colorado shook hands, thanking Pope profusely. "You are as great as they said you were."

Pope went on Old Shorty Two, and leading the bay, took after the last one. As he rode along the Mexican's track, John saw a drop of blood on some sagebrush. His bullet had hit flesh. About a half mile further along, he saw another drop on a rock. It was easy to follow the track. He wasn't trying to hide his trail. It looked like he was just going straight for Baggs. John stood in the stirrups for about five miles when he realized he'd lost the track, so he slowed, riding south about fifty yards. He was on it again. His man had about a two-hour start, but John was traveling fast and hoped to catch him and get on the way home before too long.

About ten o'clock, they crossed a small creek. His prey had stopped here, dismounted and drank from the creek. A lot of blood was on the ground here. One clot of blood, dark colored, nearly as much as a cupful, was seen in one spot. Pope figured he had pulled his shirttail out and let it fall to get rid of it or something. It was the man who was wounded, not the horse. But he had gotten back on his horse and gone straight on.

As soon as Pope's horses had finished drinking, he took off on the trail once again. He stuck his knife in a can of peaches as they traveled along the trail and sucked as much juice as possible so he wouldn't spill while he opened it. Then he held it on the top of the saddle horn while he cut the piece of lid and folded it down to make room to extract the peach slices with his knife.

The saddle horn was a constant rhythm back and forth as his horse hurried along the trail. He wondered if he would cut the wrong thing, but he prevailed. He threw the can away and pulled the cork out of the canteen and took a long drink. He then settled back in the saddle and thought about how tired he was.

He laughed out loud as he remembered the mistake last night which allowed him to sleep a few hours. Thank goodness! Two more times he passed water that day, and each time, his prey had stopped to drink and left a lot of blood each time. He, however, was still able to mount bareback and go on.

The day slowly wore away. That night at sunset John arrived on the crest of a hill. A river valley was in view. He stopped and pulled his telescope and studied the area about a mile ahead. Down on the bank of the little Snake River, a horse stood with head down.

John took off straight for the spot, going all out. As he approached, he could see a man down under, or by the horse. John remembered Kid Reader. He rode up with his pistol in his hand, but as he drew near, he put it back in its holster. The kid was lying on his stomach, face down in the sand. His whole back was covered with blood; his pants were blood soaked, stiff, and wrinkled, with horsehair covering the whole inside of both pants legs, as well as his backside.

Pope bent down to find his shot had hit him in the back, missing the backbone, but breaking a couple of ribs, then ranged up through his lung because he was bent over the horse's neck when it struck him. It never exited, so must be lodged in his shoulder someplace.

"How did you make it so far?" Pope asked out loud. "You're the toughest s.o.b. I've ever met," he said admiringly.

It was about nine now, so John had been riding for fourteen hours. This kid had ridden at least seventy miles, bareback, for sixteen hours, bleeding from this terrible wound. John turned to let the horse loose so he could go home. The horse was worn out, and had the worst sore back John had ever seen on any horse. This kid, riding too far bareback with bloody pants, had galled the hair off the horse's back and down his sides. It was swollen, so John led him to water and tried to wash the blood off. The cold water seemed to help, but John knew he probably couldn't be ridden again that year. He wondered if the hair would come in white after it healed. John talked soothingly to the horse while trying to help it.

John pulled a beautiful, silver, spotted, bridle off with a silver mounted bit. It was dark, so John pulled his own saddles off and gave his horses half the grain he had left, took the ground sheet and spread it on the sand. He got his blanket, rolled up, and lay listening to the frogs and crickets.

He was too tired to pull the boots off, besides the blanket went over his head to keep mosquitoes out. He woke up to daylight, and just as the sun came up, John answered a nature call where he could wash his backside in the river. A dry dead willow bush on the bank provided plenty of fuel for a fire, so John made coffee, fried bacon and potatoes, and had a feast to make up for some he'd missed.

He hollered and shook the grain sack, bringing his horses up. While they ate, he saddled up and made ready to go home. He buried this tough Mexican kid under a bank of the Little Snake River.

John borrowed his silver mounted spurs with large rowels. He found a roll of bills to match what he'd put in his vest pocket. John rinsed each bill to try to wash the blood off in the river before putting them in his bag, nearly two thousand dollars. He rinsed the end of the bridle reins and spur straps as well, and put them in the pack.

John would never forget this tough Mexican kid. The agony he endured with that wound! How he could go so far? He was an extra ordinary, tough, and determined man.

One thing livened up the party on the way to Red Creek. John saw three coyote pups peeking over the loose dirt of their den watching him. They were about seventy-five yards up a hill. John stopped and sat down, using his knee to help steady the 25-35. John popped one off. In a minute another head popped up. He wound up getting three out of three pups.

John loved to shoot and knew these predators were good only for target practice. They could always pick the fattest, best lamb to kill. No lamb that a coyote bit, even when not killed, ever survived long because, Pope guessed, they were so dirty. Their saliva naturally carried poison. The lamb would die of infection. Coyotes cleaned up sage chicken eggs, duck eggs, killed and ate anything smaller than they were. They ate grass, berries, and even sagebrush. You couldn't starve them. They carried diseases including hydrophobia.

John spent that night at his ranch on Red Creek. The next morning he put his saddle on the bay and packed Shorty Two. He ferried across the Green River at Jarvie's Ferry. John Jarvie asked if he had got his horses and men.

Sheriff Pope said, "Yes. The Meeker Sheriff has taken the horses home, and the Mexicans were too smelly to haul back to bury. We just buried them where they fell."

"Adios, amigos." Jarvie laughed heartily at that, but couldn't know for sure how true it was. On the way over the mountain, John killed five pine hens to take home for Charlotte and his family to share, which they did the next day.

John T. Pope loved to shoot because he was good at it. He took his boys shooting for an hour or so when he returned home. He only had a day at home, and then it was time to take the prisoners to Provo for trial. John took Ean Davis and three other prisoners. Rock Pope drove the wagon for this group.

While in Provo, John asked an attorney about the bar exam. He learned how to set up a date to take it, and where. He testified in Ean's trial, giving damning evidence of the murder. Ean Davis was found guilty, and the judge ordered him to be executed. John's words to Ean rang like a prophecy.

It took two days to Price, a few hours to Provo, five days of court, and then the time consuming process was reversed in going home. Hauling prisoners cut down a bit on the work and expense at the jail in Vernal until others were locked up to care for.

The next few days at home saw John T. Pope reading, studying, and memorizing law. One morning, he was visiting with his deputy, Tan Kempton. Tan had been one of John's deputy's along with Dick for years. Sheriff James Murdock of Wasatch County, Utah, came into the office in a hurry. He introduced himself and explained he was after a gang of bullies and hoodlums who had been causing trouble in Heber City for quite a while. Finally, the hoodlums had gone too far. He said he had a posse close on their trail. He asked for help. He said he felt he needed local law to at least be aware of what he was doing.

Within five minutes, John and Tan had saddled up and rode out of Vernal, north on a lope with Sheriff Murdock. John was riding his big bay horse today because Shorty Two had gone out in the pasture. Bay had still been in the corral where they had been grained a bit earlier.

John asked Sheriff Murdock where his posse was when he left them and what direction they were going. This discussion took place as they loped along side by side. James pointed northwest and noted, "They were about fifteen miles that way when I left them, but they were following the base of the mountains to the east."

John said, "Why not cut across to the northeast and see if we can get ahead of them or cut their tracks."

They changed direction but continued to lope, kicking up a lot of dust, but eating miles pretty fast. John noted a dust about a mile east of them and a small dust ahead as well. In a few minutes they came to the posse tracking along on a walk. As they pulled up, Sheriff James Murdock introduced John T. and Tan as sheriffs from Uintah County.

John said, "You boys are pretty close to your prey. The men you're after are going into and up Steinaker Draw. They are only about a mile and a half ahead of you."

"Should we try to go up and get closer by flanking them?"

"I might be able to shorten this campaign a bit for you."

"How do you know where they are?" Sheriff Murdock asked.

John T. pointed at the dust cloud hanging over the cedars. "See the dust cloud? Well, that's what they're stirring up. Steinaker Draw is a sun baked flat. It stretches out a lot farther than it looks. It's dry and dusty all the way to the hills."

John had noted their horses all looked like they had been over the mountain. He asked, "How long have you been out after these men?"

"This is the fourth day."

"Have they got any extra horses?"

"No."

Pope said. "Follow me. We will just walk because your horses are tiring."

About two hours later, they were almost out of Steinaker, and the hills were beginning to close. They had caught up even with the gang, but to one side of them, about six hundred yards.

John wondered if they charged down on them, if they might get in range before they were seen. They decided to try. They whipped up to a fast run, quartering down on the wanted men. They were discovered immediately though. The outlaws whipped into a run as well.

Pope's horse was fresh grained, and he could run quite fast. He was gaining until the outlaws changed direction, going straight away. When they were nearly to the brink of the hill, Pope hauled up and lobbed a shot into them with his colt. They were still some four hundred yards away, and Pope knew he'd be lucky to hit a man. However, they were bunched up and John knew he could drop a shot in the middle of them and hit something.

Pope rode on to the top of the hill where they crossed, and there was blood—a lot of blood. Pope waited for the posse who thought John was crazy to try a shot with his pistol. Now, however, they were glad to see he had slowed them by wounding a horse. Just a bit further on and a horse lay dead.

Once again Pope waited for them and explained, "They are going up Brush Creek. It's steep and rocky and brushy up ahead about a mile. There are some ledges and a bit of a knoll covered by cedars. The main canyon, though, is a lot wider. Because we've killed a horse, they will take a stand in the cedars and ledges and ambush us as we advance. So let's fool them. Let's leave our horses on grass and water and go up both sides, around them on foot.

Before James left with his posse, Pope said, "Try to stay out of sight until we are all ready."

John and Tan took the opposite side. About an hour later, John and Tan lay watching from their side of the canyon. John had his telescope and had been studying the place for a few minutes.

Tan whispered, "Sheriff Murdock is in position."

John nodded.

"I'll bet they're gone."

Sheriff Pope whispered back, "No, see that big cedar lowest down? Take this scope and look at the base of it. What do you see?"

"Oh! There's a man's leg."

"Do you think you could hit that?"

"No, but I'll bet you could."

John cocked the rifle and studied the wind and estimated the distance to be about a hundred and fifty yards. After getting a perfect sight, he finally shot. *Crack!* The shot echoed up the Canyon. A howl that came from down below was nearly as loud as the shot had been.

"Yeeoww! I'm hit—" someone screamed. A man came rolling from behind the tree holding his leg and yelling "Don't shoot! I've been shot. I give up!"

Sheriff Murdock ordered the others to throw their guns out, or they would all be shot. They followed the sheriff's advice. When mighty Texas, their leader, let out the scream and gave up, it unnerved the others.

Pope and Tan slid down to keep them covered while Sheriff Murdock's deputies searched and handcuffed them. They pulled the pants leg up to bandage Texas's leg to find a clean, little, blue hole shot through the calf of the leg. No bone had been hit, and there was very little blood.

The victim yelped and cried, "It should look worse than that!"

John T. Pope thought of a time he had been shot by a 44 caliber bullet in the same place. He hadn't yelled, but he'd left his ambushers all buried there. He also compared this bully to the Mexican who had ridden seventy miles with a bullet in his lung. "Hell, there is no comparison."

John looked at this big bully with a grimace on his face while Murdock wrapped the leg. He couldn't help but say, "Hell, Tex, that little wound is just enough to make a tough man want to fight."

One of the members of the posse walked up for their horses. They had to lift this big boob on his horse. They made the outlaws walk to their horses while the posse rode. John had hiked up as well. John invited them to use the jail if they wanted. He told them it was two days from Vernal to Price, where they could board a train to Provo, and then ride up the canyon to Heber City, or it was about three days home the way they had come.

Sheriff Murdock shook hands with John and Tan and said, "We'll just go back. One of those toughs can just walk or they can all take turns. We might have given up if it hadn't been for your help. I've never seen anybody shoot like that, Sheriff Pope, and wouldn't have believed it was possible."

John and Tan went back to Vernal, part way in the dark. They had received thanks for their labors.

Chapter Twenty-Two

Cleaning up

PERSONAL TRAGEDY STRUCK JOHN and Charlotte's happy home, claiming the lives of two children within two days, John's darling little sunshine girls, Francis Lavina, and her beloved sister, Hazel Sarah. Francis was only six, and died on the Twenty-second of December. Four year old Hazel followed two days later on Christmas Eve. John had never felt the white hot scorch of the refiner's fire as strongly as he did then, burying his tiny daughters in frozen soil while their beautiful mother's heart broke into pieces. No sacks of candy or gifts could succor the heartache of the Pope Family that Christmas.

The cycle of living and dying continues, no matter how hard to bear, and the Lord sent twin daughters, Merle and Mildred a short time later. John and Charlotte dug deep, clinging to faith and hard work, and bore the load the best way they knew how.

Because of the law coming to the Basin, it was quiet between one bunch of horse thieves or rustlers who were making the mistake of going that way. However, by 1905, the lawbreakers were learning it was unhealthy to venture there anymore. As a result, the comparison between Vernal and the Strip became so apparent to the people in Myton, Utah, that these full-time citizens began demanding law in the Strip.

The Strip was such a collection of undesirables! Back shooters, and bootleggers selling whiskey to Indians, bars, whore houses with madams and numerous painted ladies, along with a row of filthy cribs containing more prostitution than anybody ever wanted to claim. The Strip seemed hell-bent on mirroring the sinful Barbary Coast of San Francisco, so debasing was the immoral, unlawful behavior. No law had ever bothered there. Finally, a delegation of people came to Vernal to see if John T. Pope would go and clean things up for them.

John asked what they would pay. One fellow said they were prepared to pay three hundred dollars to shut everything down and run the riff raff out.

"I already make that a year as Sheriff. What if I do this in a couple of weeks?"

"We'll still pay. A couple of weeks you say? That would be first rate, Sheriff Pope!"

"What if I have to kill a half dozen of them?"

"Feel free to kill more of them if it is necessary!" These citizens indicated that was why they wanted John T. Pope to do the job! It had been agreed in Myton that Pope could do it. They couldn't think of anyone else. There were at least fifty graves out there. People had been robbed, killed, beaten, and buried in basements or whatever. The soldiers from Fort Duchesne said they would kill anyone trying to clean it up. In the last week, Jack Thomas had been killed in the saloon by soldiers from Fort Duchesne. The citizens had tried to find out what happened. Two of their men had checked Jack's body. He had been shot by a group of soldiers, all shooting from different angles. The bartender said Jack Thomas had started it, and the soldiers had finished it. Any poking around out there was dangerous. The Strip was out of Uintah County. No other county would claim it! It lay just off the reservation, and it was a place where the outlaw element gathered.

A day or two after Jack Thomas was shot to doll rags, George Hughes was murdered. George Hughes was a gunslinger and had ridden with the Wild Bunch. He was a dangerous man, and the world might be better off without him. At his killing, the citizens from the Strip once again investigated. Again, the bartender had a pat story. He said, "George was half drunk and quarreled with a man by the name of Miller. Miller knew he had no chance to survive a gunfight with him, so kept his mouth shut and took his abuse. Finally, George walked out to untie his horse. As he was preparing to leave, he saw Miller out of the corner of his eye, drawing on him. Hughes didn't get off a single shot before he was killed by Miller."

"However, the Strip men found out the firing pin on George Hughes' colt had been filed down till it wouldn't fire. By the time our men got there, George Hughes' worldly possessions were his horse and the colt that had been ruined. Who got his money and other property is impossible to tell."

John Pope listened and agreed they needed help. He said, "They have thrown the Indian Reservation open to be homesteaded, and we expect a large crowd to gather before August first. I'm gonna be real busy for about a week keeping the peace here. In a couple of weeks, I'll stop over and let you know what I decide. Okay?"

"Okay, but please decide in our favor. If this mess is cleaned out, it will benefit Vernal and the state. Everybody wins without that stinking riff raff."

John agreed with them. He told them his second four-year term as sheriff was nearly over. He wasn't sure just what he might be going to do, but he was thinking of changing his life some ways so if they wanted to wait a few weeks, he'd let them know.

The citizens from the Strip knew the reservation was going to be settled up and that was another reason why they would like to see things cleaned up. They thought the Strip would annex into Uintah County. They would be given a badge and deputies enough to take care of the area.

John had been in the bar at the Strip, and had been given double talk himself. He would like to brace the bartender. The bartender's bouncers and card sharpies were just the kinds of individuals that John could handle and would enjoy doing so. John felt in his heart he would probably go and do it. He'd known for years that if that infernal place got cleaned up, and God didn't send a whirlwind of fire to destroy it first, the duty would fall on his shoulders. Suddenly a still, inner voice whispered, *"You are the Lord's whirlwind, John T. Pope!"* The whisper was followed by a quivering chin and a few quiet tears. John walked to a secluded area behind the jail and knelt in prayer. He told the Lord about the Strip, the challenge of cleaning it up, and of the still voice he had heard speak to his heart. He asked the Lord to help him know if it was truth, or if his imagination was just working against a tired mind, when again he heard the words, *"You are the Lord's whirlwind, John T. Pope,"* followed by *"Clean it up!"*

John didn't have long to think about it before people began arriving from all over, hoping for a homestead. Vernal didn't have motels and accommodations for visitors then. A few old hotels put up all their beds. Tents were stretched in every direction. Vernal looked like a boom town. The city council passed a law forcing places of amusement to close at midnight. It was also a state law. In a meeting, the city fathers tried to find a way to handle the overflow of people.

John suggested they let the saloons stay open all night. Some opposed this suggestion, but John said it would keep a lot off the street which would keep order as long as he kept tabs on things all night. They tried it, and it worked. Men slept in chairs, on billiard tables, on the bar, and on the floor. John didn't have to make a single arrest. Several days later, after people were out on claims, order had returned.

A letter came from Governor Cutler, requesting John to come to Salt Lake City, to see him as soon as possible. Sheriff Pope rode out of Vernal immediately. On arriving in Salt Lake, he went to the governor's mansion and presented himself. Governor Cutler wasn't polite and didn't even introduce himself. He started to reprimand Sheriff Pope for defying state law and throwing all the bars in town open, especially at a critical time such as that. Governor Cutler was a man who prided himself on his fine oratory. The more he said, the more eloquent he got in his velvet tongue lashing.

John stood, hat in hand, and listened for a few minutes. Then he began to lose his control. His hat went on and was pulled down hard, his left fist balled, his right hand was always ready, subconsciously, for the draw.

Suddenly John's voice boomed, "One more word out of you, and I'll bust you just as damn hard as I can! I'll knock some sense into that empty shell of yours! The fact that you made me leave my work to travel two hundred miles to listen to this abuse is as crazy as you are. Every time the nation opened land to be homesteaded and crowds gathered, there was always trouble and arrests, except this time. Public places were left open to keep people *off* the street and give them a place to stay. I stayed up and walked a beat all night! We had absolutely no trouble—until now."

John's words came loud and fast. The Governor stepped back and knew he was on thin ice. John turned and walked out before he really lost his temper and kicked some sense into this high-ranking state official. He walked down the sidewalk and started up the street. As he walked, he kept remembering when Governor Wells had called him to Salt Lake City to present him with a plaque for bravery for bringing in Matt Warner, William Wall, and LeRoy Coleman; for keeping the peace among the townsmen and for his handling of the Wild Bunch against great odds and in peril of his own life.

John heard someone holler, "Sheriff Pope!" He looked around to see the governor hurrying up the walk to catch up.

The governor said, "I apologize. I had no idea that's what happened. If that's why you opened the bars all night, it's a different story. I was wrong and apologize."

John said, "Not everybody in Vernal agrees with me. I've made enemies, and I guess they are *not* all dead. Whoever stirred you up only told part of the truth!"

They wound up shaking hands, and John went to find a room in a hotel for the night. He wished he had time to review his law books. On the other hand, he told himself, he might as well do it and see what happened. If he didn't know it, he'd at least know where to study. If he passed, that was good. He would have a decision to make which could change his life. John was tired enough to sleep anyway, after riding two days to Price and taking the train to Salt Lake City just to be cussed out.

The next morning, after saying his prayers, he spent a couple of hours getting scheduled to take the bar exam for the next day. John walked around Salt Lake City, and marveled at all the things being built and of the foresight and genius of Brigham Young. Mostly he admired the many horses which were being driven in a busy city. Buggies, freight wagons, carts with shays, and saddle horses were everywhere. John T. Pope came by his love of horses from his dad, who also loved horses with a real passion. He very much enjoyed such a parade of vehicles and animals that were being driven by.

John leaned against a fence and marveled at the massive spires of the grand Salt Lake Temple. It was as breathtaking a monument as had ever been built in the west! It had taken forty years of sacrifice, blood, sweat, and devotion to erect. John's mind fell upon the simple task of building the little Fish Haven chapel, and his heart was filled with respect for the towering spires once again. A foolish and passing question shot through his head before John chased it away with a laugh. The thought was this, *what if someday a temple to the Most High could be erected in Vernal?* John shook his head. "Ludicrous thought," he said to himself. "Ludicrous for anyone to ever conceive of building a temple in a land that has reigned so hard and lawless. Of course I could not have believed that we would be busy constructing a tabernacle either, and we are." John's eyes swept the grey granite, from the foundation of the great temple to the golden angel on top. "Still a temple would be something," he whispered.

Time passed, and the exam was over. Sheriff John T. Pope was now John T. Pope, Attorney At Law, as well as ranch owner and operator! It was a high goal John had set for himself. Now he was proud and happy to have achieved it! He couldn't seem to get the smile off his face.

John's smile was still plastered on his face all the way back to Vernal, or Ashley Valley, as it had once been called. He would open an office and build a private law practice in Vernal! *Ha!* A law practice right in the heart of the old outlaw territory! John would do as he had vowed to, and run for County Attorney and bring as much justice and good common sense to that job as possible. It had been lacking before.

As he dreamed of possibilities this new direction to his life could bring, he made a vow to not get so busy that he didn't take time out to fish and ride and spend time with his family. He was still young and strong. Much of his bravery and courage in trouble came from his confidence in his ability with the colt 45, and from long and continuous practice. This confidence also came from his trust in Almighty God to help him on the side of right. If he resigned as sheriff now, before he became hard and bloodthirsty, as he had been told by many who lived by the gun eventually did, then, even though he had sent many to the Eternal Judgment, he still felt like he had won. Victory smiled on the Lord's whirlwind.

Carolyn W. Davidson

Prologue

The Rest of the Story

JOHN T. POPE RETIRED from the last month or two of his term as Uintah County Sheriff. He bought a nice home on Main Street, down town, and converted it into a comfortable law office, which turned into a good, private business. John T. Pope, Attorney at Law, was just as busy as he wanted to be, and his reputation for being sensible, wise, fair, tough, and honest was the best advertisement around.

John accepted the call to serve as Marshall of Myton. He went to the printers and ordered a stack of handbills saying that the Strip was on its way someplace else. John rode to Myton with them. Three men were curious about what he would do, and rode with him, acting as deputies.

John rode up to the big bar first. He walked in and handed the bartender the handbill.

"What's this, bum fodder?"

"No, I'd like you to tack it up." John's eyes were squinting and his look menacing and stern. The bartender complied, and by the time he finished tacking it up, he had actually read what it said. His face turned red.

"What does this mean?"

"It means you've got three days to get your personal belongings out of town. We're going to close it."

"You can't close the whole town!"

"Try me."

"What about the rest of the Strip?"

"It all goes."

"You've got no business doing this!"

John said, "It's my business to do this job! It's giving me great pleasure to do this."

"What if we just shoot you?" A surly soldier asked.

John angled toward him, keeping the others in his sight as well. "If you are going to try that, do it right now. It would give me pleasure to shoot you and about four of your gambler dummies at the same time!" The room went absolutely still. John could hear parched throats trying to swallow, that's how silent things fell. He continued, "When I come back in three days you'll be gone because I'll kill you on site if you're not. I'll bring enough men with shotguns to keep everyone off my back without your customary, yellow, back-shooting!"

The soldier wiped a trembling hand across his brow and gamblers exchanged wary glances around the tables, but nobody moved. Pope shifted his weight and said, "Go for it now while I can, and will, enjoy it!" His voice was like a roaring lion, and window panes shuddered slightly at the challenge.

The bartender finally squawked, "We are not going for it, now."

"Okay, get packed. I'll be back the day after tomorrow to get rid of any slow-learning stayers. There will be extra stages and wagons here tomorrow to help you all clear the hell out!"

John backed out of the bar and walked to his horse. He threw his weight on his horse as his companions covered him, making sure no movement followed him from the bar. When stillness was the only reaction, they mounted up and followed him to the big Red Light House.

John dismounted and took a handbill and spread it across the front door. He tacked it up with the butt of his pistol. A middle aged woman opened the door and said, "You just walk in here, you handsome hunk! You don't have to bother knocking." She reached out to grasp John's arm, but he swung it away from her, distancing himself from her groping clasp.

"I've just hammered up a handbill and you'll want to read it."

"You read it to me," she purred, nudging her weight against him. John stepped backward and the woman nearly fell.

"No, *you* do it."

The woman righted herself, glanced at John's companions, and then stepped forward, complying with the lawman's wishes. Her cheeks flushed scarlet as she read the words. "You are not telling us where to go?"

"No ma'am, for I don't care if you all go to hell, just as long as you are gone from here by day after tomorrow. There will be extra stages tomorrow and some wagons. Any men still sneaking around here will be killed, and madam, you shall be gone before night! Get packing, there's not much time."

"You haven't given us *any* time!"

"Day after tomorrow—I've given you enough time to get the hell out."

John retreated to his horse, leaving the woman shrieking in hysterics on the front steps of her washed-up gold mine.

John and his delegation rode through the Strip, tacking up handbills, delivering their startling message. They rode two hundred yards past the end of the Strip, to a big still. It was built in the open for everyone to see. Smoke came from the fire under the vat. Long pieces of copper tubing came from the vat, emptying into barrels. Alcohol rose from the vat, up the tubing, in the form of steam. It reached a point in its progress where it cooled enough to convert back into alcohol. It ran down the pipes to drip in the barrels.

John looked at all the barrels. There were sixteen full now. If John waited to destroy the whiskey until the day after tomorrow, it would all be gone so he told the men to borrow axes off of wood piles along the cribs and bust it to hell.

"I know of three Indians that have been blinded by bad whiskey."

One of the men with him said, "There have been others, white men blinded, too. This stuff is hard poison."

"Get chopping," the new Marshall of Myton ordered. The men broke the barrels open and cut up the copper tubing as well.

Next John and the men rode up and down the cribs, tacking up handbills, issuing warnings to prostitution dumps and houses of ill repute.

Many of the ragtag girls staggered out, truthfully relieved to be moving on, rid of the lowlife pimps who controlled them, thriving off their bad business.

When the "day after tomorrow" came, not a soul was left along the Strip for John T. Pope to shoot! The filthy lucre had ridden out of town on the wagons and stages provided by the keen marshal of Myton. The decent folks in the area rejoiced in the cleansing force of the whirlwind.

John T. Pope, colonizer, fearless sheriff, mighty marshal, common sense attorney at law, rancher, freighter, trapper, and family man, accomplished many goals in his quest for personal growth and the betterment of his community.

John was actively engaged in helping with the efforts on the new tabernacle, in any way possible. It was dedicated in 1907, and at that time John T. Pope heard the Mormon prophet, President Joseph F. Smith, prophesy that Vernal could well be the home to a temple of the Lord, in some future day. As the words fell from President Smith's lips, John remembered his fleeting thoughts as he gazed at the Salt Temple the day he had taken his bar examination. Mighty chills worked along his spine at the very thought of it! Here? Vernal! The former heart of the outlaw territory may one day house a temple to the Most High? The thoughts made John shake with laughter and joy.

(Ninety years later, church president, Gordon B. Hinkley, dedicated the old Uintah Stake Tabernacle as the tenth temple in Utah. The historic tabernacle had been gutted and remodeled to temple standards, the first pre-existing building to have ever been converted into a temple. The pioneering endurance of early settlers in the valley had truly laid the foundations for this great work to come about. Just as the tabernacle underwent a transformation, so did the moral climate and temper of the Uintah Basin.)

John kept his mind active and enjoyed the advances of technology, proudly owning the first motor car in Vernal. Citizens of the city were not surprised when the former sheriff drove down the street, grinning at his friends and neighbors. No doubt Sheriff Pope drew comparisons between the modern wonder and Old Shorty. The car probably came up short.

John was the first man to do experimenting with rock asphalt. (John perfected formulas for his asphalt in his laboratory and factory, which was located four and-a-half miles southwest of Vernal. He was successful in extracting the "gum" from the sand asphalt without the use of fire heat. He said often after his discovery, "This method is so simple, I don't know why I didn't find out about it years before.") He paved a section of sidewalk in front of his home with it, and then showed the mayor. The mayor asked him to pave in front of the city office. This amazed the people of the valley, and they realized they could have paved streets in their city. Industry boomed in the area, due to the realization. The asphalt began drawing wide interest. Miles of sidewalks and roads were then paved, using the materials from Pope's claim west of Vernal. John T. donated all the asphalt used by the city, county, schools, churches, and state institutions, proving his generosity to a fault.

John was interested in bringing lights to the streets of Vernal. He had spent plenty of his nights paroling the dark streets, and knew the benefit electricity could bring. John had fought too many outlaws under the cloak of darkness! He was interested in free energy and surveyed the fall of Brush and Ashley Creeks, and determined where there was enough of a fall to supply Vernal with all the lights and power that it would require.

John filed on the water for the purpose of lighting the town. He had a crew of men and a surveyor, surveying ditch lines, finding the best place to house the power site. John T. then said, "Vernal will be lighted, and with ample electric power for all."

The town's civic leaders went over the plans and reported it as feasible. After much discussion, John T. said, "Sign a contract to the effect that the plant will be put in and that all the citizens of the town who want lights and power shall have it, and all wanting stock in the new company may have it at actual cost, and then pay me what I have out, and you can have the project." This was agreed to, and Vernal became a modern, well-lit city.

Among his many other accomplishments, John drafted the first blueprint of the Flaming Gorge dam. He had often ridden for outlaws in the area, and had daydreamed about the possibility of building a reservoir that could move enough water to generate electric horsepower. Call him a visionary!

John T. Pope hired an engineer and a crew of men and set to work, needing estimates to know the cost of a three hundred foot dam. A survey was made for a canal on the east side of the river to irrigate the land between the Green and White rivers. The crew checked the land that would be irrigated and found it could cover about three hundred thousand acres, partly in Colorado, the rest in Utah. Pope's blueprint included the estimated costs, and the estimated horsepower, which were two hundred and eighty thousand units. John submitted this information to the state, and anyone familiar with the beauties and recreation of Flaming Gorge, anyone on the receiving end of the generated power and irrigation use, might thank John T. Pope for his vision and foresight.

John supported his community in all facets! He and his brother Richard even played musical instruments in the first organized band. After chasing bad men, and being chased in return, mastering a musical instrument seemed easy! John became involved with the band during his tenure as Uintah County sheriff, even though his time was tight, stretched between his law duties, young family, and his ranch at Red Creek.

John served two terms as District Attorney, proudly doing the job with common sense, as promised. He ran a successful private law practice for many years. He also served as deputy to his brother, Richard, upon Dick's election to serve two terms as county sheriff. He rode as back-up support to other sheriffs and elected officials as needed.

Despite living with an outlaw-issued reward on his head for many years, John T. Pope survived, finally dying of old age in 1943. He is buried near Charlotte, and his beloved parents, Robert and Sarah, in the Vernal Memorial Park Cemetery. He is surrounded by many of his children, brothers and sisters and other relatives. (As a note of interest, William Wall and Matt Warner are also interred there.)

The Whirlwind of the Lord well deserved his rest.

Author's Notes

The Wild Bunch, Marshal Joe LaFors, and Tom Horn:

Joe LaFors, who chased Butch and Sundance in the famous western movie, was deputy U.S. Marshal during that time when Butch, Sundance, and Ann were being chased by the Pope's from Ashley Valley and Brown's Park. They had just skedaddled out of there. LaFors was gathering evidence in a Nichol case on Tom Horn, eventually catching Horn. Tom hung on November 20, 1903. LaFors probably manufactured some of this evidence for his part in the killing of young Willie Nichol, but Tom Horn worked with Al Seiber, Chief of Scouts for the U.S. Army in Arizona at the San Carlos Apache Agency where he murdered Indian men, women, and children for their scalps which brought a good price. Hundreds of Indians were killed. So, in this author's opinion, manufactured evidence or not, justice was served.

Queen Ann Basset:

Ann grew up in Brown's Park, the first white child born in the wild and rugged area. Both she and her sister Josie were sent to finishing school in the east, where she learned manners and etiquette, despite her wild and wooly upbringing. She was called Queen Ann Basset by ranchers. She was arrested and tried for rustling in Colorado, but as the trial approached she made bail, and while in town, she bought the best and prettiest dresses. She had her hair fixed and applied make up. She was on good behavior and considered very beautiful by everyone, as a result, the jury wouldn't convict her of rustling. She was just too ladylike.

She was pardoned and released. When John T. Pope got too close and was pushing to arrest Butch and Sundance, Ann rode out with them, taking the alias, Etta Place.

Coffee and the early saints:

Coffee and tea were staples for the early settlers of these vast regions of the west. Brigham Young commanded every family to take so many pounds of it in their wagons as they journeyed west. As the settlers built and established reliable water systems, and easier methods of transportation, and as heating, electricity, and more comfortable living was developed, the need for blood-warming coffee and tea diminished. The habit of it has softened by the generations, but many good, good saints were used to the necessity of it in their youth, and preferred to keep with their pioneering traditions. It took a while for the church membership as a whole to take hold of that part of The Word of Wisdom.

A bit of interesting family history:

John T. Pope's brother, Robert Alexander Pope, was my great grandfather. He married Amanda Calder, (always called Polly) and they stayed in Bear Lake. Their son, Royal Robert Pope was my grandpa. Royal was most often called Rile or Riley.

The last few times that John T. Pope's family visited in Garden City, they stayed with Riley and Alice, because Robert Alexander had died. My uncle, Arden Pope, was a young boy during one of these last visits. It seems his folks sent him up to bed, but because he wanted to hear the stories so badly, he snuck back to the bottom of the stairs, to sit out of sight and listen. He told me that he wished he could have remembered all the stories better, but he shared some with me, and now I've shared what I heard, and what I've studied and learned with you.

About the Author

Dale B. Weston

Dale Benjamin Weston was raised in Pickleville, Utah, near the shores of Bear Lake. His parents were Ben E. and Marie Pope Weston. He attended elementary school three miles north, in Garden City, and spent a lot of time with his grandpa, Rile Pope. His other grandpa and grandma, Ben and Lauretta Pearl E. Weston, lived a few miles south, in Laketown. Dale enjoyed working with his uncles and cousins on both sides of the family, and learned to love hearing stories of days gone by, sharing good humor, and lots of laughter.

Dale liked fishing, hunting, and horses, and he liked those three things better than school, but he stayed in school to play basketball. He was a tough competitor, with no give in him at all. During his senior year, he served as student body president. He graduated from Laketown, and spent time at Utah State University before serving a mission to the Southern States Mission, which included Texas, Louisiana, and Mississippi.

Weston enlisted in the Army Reserves after his mission release, and earned Top Marksman honors, a high accolade. He figured his ability to bow his head and say a prayer had helped him with that. He also credited all the shooting he'd done as a kid.

He married Pam Porter from Morgan, Utah, and they are the parents of three children, Kevin, Lyn, and June Marie. Dale loved his family, and spent a lot of time taking them fishing and on picnics.

Dale served as the last bishop of the Garden City Ward, and the first bishop of the newly consolidated Bear Lake Ward. He got the ball rolling for the new chapel in Garden City, and felt like it was one of the great accomplishments of his life.

Dale and his dad bought the B.Q. ranch from his Uncle Arden Pope, and moved eighteen miles south of Cokeville, Wyoming. He spent a lot of time trapping, cleaning up beaver and muskrats along the canals and river. Dale was always interested in the history of the ranch, and how it connected to his Bear Lake roots. He enjoyed hunting for Indian artifacts, and accumulated quite a collection. Dale was a scholar, always learning. He loved history and shared what he knew with his family. He read to them in the evenings and in the car as they traveled to church, or wherever.

Dale raised Hereford cattle, and lots of hay. Dale's three kids and five Davidson nephews were recruited to the hayfields as well. Dale was a ranching partner with his dad, and actually partners in everything, being best friends. The two men enjoyed every new venture together. Dale made improvements on the land, transforming a sagebrush covered hill into hundreds of acres of grain. He loved his horses and stock, and always took pride in his ranch.

After a forced retirement from the ranching industry, Dale and Pam moved to Cokeville. He spent a lot of time trucking with his boys, and drove the school bus some. Dale continued to fish, converting his twelve grandchildren to the sport of it. He was fiercely proud of them and their accomplishments, trailing to watch them in various activities, far and wide. He was talented in many areas; he could whittle, and carved many items. He could do rope tricks, and could make a bull whip snap like thunder. He made the best willow whistles for his kids and grandkids, and was never too busy to whittle sticks for a weenie roast. Dale had a good singing voice. He was gifted with art, and could sketch or draw anything. Dale was a carpenter, and enjoyed building things, always being busy with his hands. He was a scholar of the gospel, quite a scriptorian, and a fantastic teacher. Perhaps Dale's greatest talent was that of a storyteller and loyal friend.